The Nexus:
Samhain

By Ian Cadena

For my dog Sausage who spent many mornings by my side on the balcony during the creation of this book before he passed, for my dog Nacho who shared the same balcony by my side during its completion, and for my husband James who is still by my side. James' unwavering support allowed me to complete this work.

TABLE OF CONTENTS

EPILOGUE
SAMHAIN • 447

PROLOGUE

The boy's body bobbed in the lake.

Max Dane was barely able to see him. The fog clung to the top of the water like wet cotton balls. Max's pale eleven-year-old frame shook as he stood at the end of the wooden pier. He stood there in only his swim trunks, the cold air swirling around him nipping at his skin. He couldn't believe he was out here but the fog came suddenly bringing the cold and torrent water. He couldn't see him anymore. He shouted to the boy.

No answer.

I have to find him! His thoughts screamed. He shouted again and again. Only his teeth chattering in his skull answered. The cool air crawled through his pores making him colder and colder. He clasped his arms together. Max shouted desperately, his tears mixing with the mist. He had to do something. He should have done something sooner. Suddenly, Max was in the freezing water. The water was much colder than it was earlier, but he didn't care much now. He needed to find the boy. Max's limbs tightened in the liquid freeze. He huffed small frozen clouds as he paddled to where he saw the boy last. He tried to yell to the boy again but only gargled the sloshing water. The liquid freeze was determined to bring him down. He couldn't feel his arms or legs now and realized he was sinking. He gulped freezing water as he struggled to the surface and managed to cling his way up for another breath before the fog and water pushed him back down defiantly.

As cold and cloudy as the surface had been the cold underwater was clear. Max desperately tried to revive his limbs and thrash through the freezing water. He couldn't give up. He needed to find him! He needed to save him! But he felt his body becoming heavier as the cold pressed into his chest, and Max glided down through the liquid freeze. That's when he saw him. The boy was drifting through the lake effortlessly, peaceful like a snowflake.

Still.

Max was close enough to touch him, but he couldn't bring himself to do it. The boy's blonde hair swayed eerily in the icy fluid. Max stared into his dim blue eyes, but the boy didn't blink. He looked almost like an angel suspended in the liquid tomb. He looked tranquil. That wasn't much consolation to Max. Max wondered if the boy recognized him, or if it was too late for that. He wanted to reach out to the angel and touch him. Max could feel some sensation in his fingertips now and that's when he felt alive again, if even for a moment.

He was out of air. His heart flipped. His limbs jolted involuntarily as the cold tore into his skin. His body seemed on fire. How could it? He was in the cold.

He thrashed about crazily searching for a way to

propel to the surface. He felt like he was being stabbed by ice picks all over his body. The liquid freeze hammered at his chest demanding entrance. He could feel the water pressing harder on his chest. His heart somersaulted. He'd be with the angel any moment now. It was better this way. He could feel his eyes bulging from their sockets. It's better than coming back empty-handed.

The liquid freeze forced its way into his nostrils and mouth and jammed down his throat. His body twisted and jerked like some bull ride. His brain seared worse than when he ate ice cream too fast.

Can't I just die already?

The angel flickered in and out of view.

Can't the angel take me?

He tried to call to it for help, but only gurgled as his sight frosted over to darkness.

Max sat upright in his bed. His eyes popped open. He was drenched in water. *No. Sweat?* Max clasped at his bare chest and examined his trembling hand in the fading moonlight. Definitely, sweat. He flopped back on the bed and stared at the ceiling as his chest flew up and down. He rolled over on his side and could see the moving boxes as he wiped the tears from his eyes and cheeks.

CHAPTER 1

The severed head hit the stone floor with a thud and rolled.

It flipped along the floor—ear, nose, ear, ear, nose—and stopped on the back of the head staring up. The man's mouth was agape: frozen in horror at the sight of his executioner. A green gauntlet snatched the head from the floor and deposited it in a saddlebag.

The emerald knight glowed in a ghostly hue. Its armor was a bold design with a skull motif. A large skull comprised the entire chest piece with cavernous green tinted eyes. The shoulder pieces were skulls with a single spike shooting out of the forehead as if emblazoned by the dead head of a unicorn. Another spike protruded from the mouth of an upside down skull on its elbow pieces. The knee and greave were one piece with a horned skull covering the knee and the teeth of the skull extending down the shin. Underlying the skull motif were swirls and straight edges etched into the armor. The patterns seemed purposeful. The intricate design was a mixture of esoteric patterns and runic symbols. The helmet of the emerald knight was the only part absent of design and adornment. It was sleek and visored with a lip at the back that extended to the top of the shoulders. No eyes hid inside the helmet. Gloom was the only thing visible into the visor. This was no man in a suit of armor. This was no earthly knight.

The other green gauntlet held a silver double-headed battle axe with a fanged skull that ran along the hilt and up the haft of the axe. Skulls and intricate lines were etched into the blades of the axe. The blades were razor sharp and stretched out looking like wings with hooks. The knight hung the Death Axe on its belt as it passed over the castle floor effortlessly. For all its armor it moved completely silent. Its sollerets touched the ground with a hush. The knight whisked along the stone floor making its way to the entrance of the castle.

The Knightmare was forged from the fires of Hell, but not the Hell you have been told of in fairy tales. Not a make-believe place where people are damned for forgetting to say their prayers, cheating on their spouses, or not going to church. Rather, this is a true Hell: a state of misery and torment, void of freedom, contentment, or satisfaction. For the Knightmare it began with a spark at the ending of its mortal life. Restrained from its afterlife the spark flashed. Anguish fanned the spark inciting a flame. The flame flickered, agonizing in the lonely darkness. Contempt and fury fueled the flame, igniting a blaze. The blaze spawned a Hellfire. And in that Hellfire the Knightmare was wrought. This Hell for the Knightmare began when its soul was snuffed by a great injustice—an injustice it burned to rectify!

CHAPTER 2

Lindsey Dane froze in the shadow of the scarecrow.

Max was recording his sister with his digital camcorder from a distance. They stood on a gentle green grassy plain just on the outskirts of their new town. His mom suggested Max document the beginning of their "fresh start," as she kept putting it. Why couldn't she just say divorce? He already heard the word plenty of times. Why did grownups try and give good names to bad things? It made him wonder if there really were such things as monsters, and grownups just decided to call them something else so kids wouldn't find out.

It was autumn in Northwest Vermont, Max's favorite time of the year. He panned the camera so he could get the surrounding scenery. Leaves of varied bright hues drifted off lush trees of different sizes. Rolling green hills and dairy farmland blotted the landscape mixing and stretching in every direction. An easy crisp breeze piggybacked the morning sun. With every breath, calm filled his lungs. The air seemed cleaner and crisp on mornings like this. What was it about this time of year that made everything seem…right? He loved it. He wished he could capture that sensation and the smell of the October cool air on camera. He closed his eyes and felt the cool breeze flow over and through him. It made him feel good. He didn't get this sensation often so he was going to take advantage of it. Why couldn't he feel this way all the time? The air soaked his lungs with calm. It was amazing. It was like his body was vibrating calmness.

Max watched the grass sway back and forth for a little bit before noticing he was feeling a little cold now. Maybe he shouldn't have worn shorts and a muscle shirt. He didn't have any muscles to show off but he hoped someday soon. His dad had promised to start taking him to the gym in a few years, but he wanted to start now. His dad said he was too young. Was that a stock answer all grown-ups used? *You're too young!* Maybe they were just bitter because they weren't. Now, Max wasn't even sure if his dad would get to take him to the gym at all. Max looked over his shoulder toward the road. He recorded his mother half-cocked in their silver frost SUV parked by the road. She sat poised with her cell phone up to her ear in one hand and an electronic tablet on her lap and poking at the screen with her other hand. Today she was dressed a little more casual than usual. "Business casual," he was pretty sure was what she would call it. Like one of those moms you'd see on a magazine cover for business women or high-powered home moms or self-made accomplished women. Max shrugged his shoulders at the thought. It only made sense she dress the part since she was the editor of one of those magazines. Or was it all of them? He couldn't remember. He just knew she was always glued to her cell phone and computer. Her hand would come up from the tablet from time to time and punctuate the air. Then she would roll her eyes and tug at her shoulder-length auburn hair. Max thought her hair looked brown. But she told him her hair was distinctly auburn.

"Only people who lack imagination have brown hair, dear."

As she jabbered on the phone, she tugged on her hair even more. Max figured that's why it was so straight. Max could now see that his mom was making a face like she just ate a super sour candy. *She's talking to dad!* He wanted to talk to dad but he could tell they were fighting right now. That's all they ever seem to do anymore. Anyway, he knew she wouldn't let him talk to him while they were fighting. Of course, she wouldn't call it fighting.

"Your father and I are just having 'differences'," she'd say.

Differences? Divorce! That's what it was. Why couldn't they just say it? Grown-ups never say what they mean. They always tried to sugar-coat bad things or situations by giving them cutesy names. They weren't fooling anyone but themselves. Do they really think that giving something a cute name is going to make things better? Or seem less bad? *They honestly must think I am so stupid!* His hand tightened on his camera. It made him so angry. He could feel the calm evaporating from his skin so fast he swore there were vapors. Max tried to think of something else. He didn't want to lose the soothing sensations of this Fall morning, but he found his mind drifting back to his parents. Maybe he was a monster.

"Your father and I just have our differences," his mom kept telling him. "It has nothing to do with you. It's not your fault."

He knew it wasn't true. It *was* his fault: the divorce, the move; everything. Every time he thought about it his stomach twisted inside. And if it wasn't his fault why was he the one going to therapy?

"Hi, Max. My name is Dr. Kern." She sat in a micro-fiber chair that was positioned next to the leather couch that Max was sitting in. "Do you know what kind of doctor I am? Sometimes people get confused since I don't wear a white coat," she gave a self-congratulatory laugh.

"You're a psycho-babble," Max said flatly eyeing a piece of glass artwork that sat on a glass coffee table in front of him.

She let out a forced laugh, "that's cute."

"Well, if you grown-ups can do it, why not me."

"I don't think I follow you."

He shrugged his shoulders dismissively still looking at the artwork. It screamed *I'm a refined and cultured individual. Take me seriously or else!*

"I'm a psychologist," she said slowly enunciating.

"Yeah, I know."

"Then you know I'm here to help you with your feelings."

"You're here," Max said slowly, "to make my parents feel better."

"Now, why would you say that?" she leaned in toward Max.

"Because it's true," he said matter-of-fact. He looked across the coffee table to the wall opposite him. Her diplomas and certificates were positioned at eye level in a uniform manner. They were housed in expensive eye-catching frames. She obviously didn't want anyone to miss that she was educated and important. Or at least that she should be thought of as important.

"Max, the truth is that your parents want to help you. They understand that you're going through a difficult time."

Max knew that was partially true...But...*He was going through a difficult time? What about them?* They

9

weren't having an easy time with this. He could see it in his mother's face and the sideways stares she'd give him. She blamed him for everything but wouldn't even confront him. She was taking it out on dad and that's why they were getting divorced. They needed counseling too just like dad suggested but she wouldn't dream of that. This was just like her to make him have to see a psycho-babble but not her. It was always somebody else that needed to be fixed. She couldn't dare admit that she was wrong or had some flaw. He hated that about her.

The glass artwork cracked. "Oh," Dr. Kern jumped up examining it trying to patch the piece that clinked out on the table. "Are you alright," she added to Max as an afterthought.

"You can't help me," he said softly. His eyes moved from the decorated wall in front of him and grazed past her over his right shoulder. The doctor's desk sat broadside to the corner of the room. Her desk was black, simple, straight edged, and elegant. She could see over her posh office from that desk. From there she could lord over her empire…and her subjects.

"There are a lot of changes going on in your life, Max," she said sitting back down. "Why don't you tell me about that?"

"I don't want to talk to you."

"I know it's not easy opening up to somebody that you don't know. But I'm not asking you to do that. Just tell me about what's going on in your life. You can talk about anything, Max. It's okay to be nervous."

"It's not that."

"Then what is it, Max? What's making you uncomfortable?"

His eyes were still bouncing around the room, "Your office is very contemporary. I see why my mom picked you." His eyes had moved back toward her. He didn't like what he saw when he looked into her eyes. So he told her. "You're not concerned about me," he said without emotion. "You're concerned about the rent on this office."

She pulled back.

Max continued, "You're concerned about the rent on your lake view condo." His eyes joined hers, "You're concerned about Brad leaving you."

Her mouth dropped open and for the first time she seemed at a loss.

"You have a problem with male figures in your life. You had a chance to join a large practice but all the other partners were men. You convinced yourself they were chauvinistic, but the truth is you had to start as an employee first before you could be made a partner just like everybody else did before you. But you thought you deserved better than that. You were better than them you told yourself and so you became convinced they were sexist. That's why you opened your own practice." Max continued without emotion, and without raising his voice.

"And you chose this profession because you revel in seeing broken-down people come in here at their most desperate crawling to you for help, especially, the male clients. It makes you feel better about yourself. It makes you feel superior. You get to dangle hopes of sanity and reason in front of people if they play your game right. You get a twisted satisfaction out of knowing that you can hold the key to people's tranquility. And you take your superiority and male issues home every night to Brad. He wanted a more serious relationship with you but you want it on your terms; when you're ready. After all, he's just a guy. He's not even as educated as you. So finally Brad got to see your true face. He saw inside you." Max began to whisper now, "And what did he see? He saw that you are just as empty and imperfect as this perfect office. It's filled with emptiness. It's a great presentation but there's no substance. That's why you can't help me."

Max stood up, "That's why Brad left you. And that's why I'm leaving you." And Max walked out of the office.

The high grass gently tickled Max's legs, bringing him back to his recording project. With a blink of his glassy green eyes he was refocused on his camera's monitor. His mother finished up her phone conversation, stuffed her phone and tablet into her purse, tossed it into the SUV, and headed toward him and Lindsey with a wave.

Lindsey Dane hadn't moved. The scarecrow loomed over her four-year-old body with its arms and legs outstretched, ready to pounce. Its towering frame eclipsed the morning sun. Lindsey shifted slowly out of its shadow to get a better look at it never taking her eyes away from the scarecrow. She could see it better now in the orange rays of the morning light. It was frozen in mid-jump like it was trying to perform a jumping-jack. Lindsey hated doing jumping-jacks, well, except that time she got to do them on a trampoline. That was a lot of fun.

It wore a black weather-worn hat with a broad brim that was almost pointed at the top. It made her think of a shortened witch's hat. Beneath the hat was bark. It was an oak tree that looked like it had holes for eyes. Lindsey wasn't sure if it was natural or if someone dug them out. The bark twisted into some form of a head. It couldn't have meant to look like a human head because Lindsey couldn't think of any person she'd seen with a head like that. Maybe it was supposed to be an alien head. There was a knot in the bark that looked like it could have been a mouth sewn shut. Lindsey didn't see any straw poking out anywhere like a real scarecrow.

There were no boots or shoes on the scarecrow. Its feet grew right out of the ground. They were roots of what must have been two different oak trees that twisted around each other and then shot out in separate directions to form the arms. The hands were either the top of the trees or branches. There were no leaves; just twisted bark that came to several points and looked like gnarled skeletal fingers. Lindsey couldn't see the torso to really know if it was two twisted trees because it was covered in a cloak. *How did somebody get a cloak on this thing?*

The cloak was a strange color. It was a kind of black. Like the night sky. But it seemed to have different hues depending on how the morning sun struck it. At times it almost seemed a midnight blue. Her brother told her that once when he took her outside one night to look at stars. He said the sky wasn't completely black when you really observed it. That was a great night. Lindsey thought of that night with her brother often. The cloak had markings on it. The entire cloak seemed to be embroidered with patterns. She didn't notice it from a distance but now that she was closer to the scarecrow she could see the designs. It looked like some of those crop circle formations she had seen in a UFO program on TV. It gave the cloak texture. It was very pretty. How odd that something so creepy and grotesque was also kind of pretty.

She wondered how soft the cloak was. Lindsey wanted to touch it. It skipped gently in the cool breeze making a small flapping noise. She stretched out her hand slowly then stopped. The cloak fluttered every so often.

"Lindsey," her mom shouted.

Lindsey jumped with a yelp of fright.

"Go stand by the scarecrow. I want Max to get your picture."

Lindsey shook her head fiercely in reply.

"Oh, c'mon, it'll be fun."

"No," Lindsey insisted, not taking her eyes from the scarecrow. She just knew he would move. She squeezed her hands into tiny fists. "He's scary."

Her mom looked at the scarecrow, "Well he's supposed to be." She shrugged her shoulders. "Max, you go stand by the scarecrow."

"But I have the camera."

"I'll take it."

"No, mom, you'll just break it. Besides, I already have a shot of the scarecrow...and Lindsey."

"But she's not in front of it," she grabbed Lindsey's arm and tugged her over to the scarecrow. "C'mon, honey, we'll both be in the picture."

"No," Lindsey protested. But it didn't do any good. Her mother propped the two of them in front of the scarecrow.

"Now, be sure to get all of us, including Mr. Scarecrow."

"I know mom," blurted Max. "I'm a director, remember?"

"Oh, yes, of course. I forgot. Well, isn't there a way you can be in the picture with us? Didn't I buy you a tripod for that thing?"

"Mom," Max said impatiently, "I just told you I'm the director. I'm not supposed to be in the picture."

"Right, well, even directors make appearances in their own movies. Hitchcock did."

Max took his eyes from his monitor and stabbed them at his mother.

"Okay, fine," she gave up with a wave of her hands. "Just get me and Lindsey then." She noticed Lindsey with her head turned back to the scarecrow. "No, dear, look at the camera. Look at Max, wave to your brother."

Max got a perfectly framed shot of the three of them: his mom, sister, and scarecrow. His mother was still unable to pry his sister's attention from the scarecrow. Lindsey wasn't about to let her guard down. Max started to tell his mother that he got the shot, when he looked up from the monitor and into the pitch black eyes of the scarecrow. The words shrank from his voice as a chill crawled over his skin. The sunlight leaked from the sky into night. He could feel his pupils widening. Max suddenly found himself standing in the middle of a pumpkin patch.

A pool of moonlight splashed from the night sky offering some visibility for Max to try and figure out where he was. The cold night air swirled around him. His breath puffed from his mouth and nose. He turned around slowly in a complete circle still holding his camera. Max was wide-eyed in apprehension. The road and SUV were gone. His mom and sister were nowhere to be seen. The scarecrow wasn't there. He obviously wasn't standing in the same spot as just a few moments ago. Dozens of pumpkins from knee to ankle-high were strewn over the soil. They were tethered by twisting snakelike vines that jutted above a light layer of fog that crept along the ground. Beyond the pumpkins, to either side and behind, was a flat plain of farmland. In front of him, past the pumpkins, was a patch of gnarly trees that wrestled each other in the soft wind.

He thought his mom and sister might be beyond the wrestling trees, but he had a doubtful uneasy feeling in his stomach. His stomach started to twist again. But he didn't have many choices so Max started slowly through the rows of pumpkins toward the trees, sliding a little with every other step on the moist ground. Max wrinkled his nose. The air smelled of mist and mud. He tweaked his ears trying to get some feeling back as they were going numb in the cold. He stopped with a squish on the ground and his fingers pinched on his ears.

He thought he heard someone yell his name. It sounded like his father. Did he really hear someone? He didn't move his body. His eyes poked around at the trees. The wind picked up drastically. The trees were fighting each other now. The air whisked about his ears. His heart flipped with a distinct yell. It bellowed from the trees. He distinctly heard his name. It had to be his father.

Urgency jolted through Max's legs as they began to move again closer and faster to the trees. He forced his legs to stop again just at the edge of the forest, his heart hammering his chest. Something else was moving closer pushing through the branches, but the trees were thrashing about in the strong wind and flying debris was obscuring his view. Then Max heard a whoosh and a crack. A whitish pumpkin flew from the mangled branches and whomped Max square in the chest with such a force his legs flew out below him and he fell back on his backside in the foggy earth. The wind stopped.

Max looked to the forest.

Nothing.

He closed the monitor on the camera and left it on the ground. He stood up, his heart still flapping in his chest. He could barely make out the luminous pumpkin just below the creeping fog. He reached down into the fog amongst the struggling vines and picked up the pumpkin.

Max's eyes swelled. As he picked up the whitish pumpkin he found himself staring not at a pumpkin at all, but into the dead eyes of a balding man's severed head with a hooked nose. His mouth fell open and a scream wedged in his throat. He dropped the head just before his muscles began to cramp and tighten in his arms and legs. Max couldn't blink. He couldn't scream. He felt his entire body begin to frantically shake.

Max's mother grabbed his arms. "Max, can you hear me? Oh, dear me, you forgot your medication." She called over her shoulder, "Lindsey, help me with your brother."

"Mommy, mommy," Lindsey screamed running toward her mother. "It moved, it moved. The scarecrow moved."

Her mom looked back at her, "Not now, Lindsey, I need your help. Max is having a seizure. Grab your brother's camera."

She looked back at Max and paused for a moment when she thought she saw cold air huff from his mouth. She was clenched onto Max's shaking body. Then his skin began to turn purplish as she saw his eyes roll back into his head like some attacking shark.

"Oh no, sweetie, don't do that," she pleaded as she began to cry. She whipped off her belt and wedged it into his mouth so he wouldn't bite his tongue. She swooped Max up into her arms and ran to the SUV. "Grab his camera Lindsey," she yelled again. "It's okay, sweetie, mommy's got you. Everything's going to be okay," she sobbed to Max as she reached the SUV.

The doors to the SUV slammed as it sped away down the road passing a sign reading: WELCOME TO RAVENCREST.

CHAPTER 3

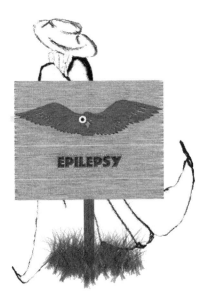

Evelyn Dane shambled around the emergency room waiting area of the Ravencrest hospital.

The building was larger than she had thought it would be for such a small community. It looked clean, with updated computers and flat screen televisions, and the décor seemed nice, and that somehow made her feel the medical care would be very capable. Lindsey was marking in the waiting room magazines completely ignoring her coloring books.

"Look, mommy, an alien," she said displaying a scribbling on one of the pages from a magazine.

"That's nice, dear," Evelyn replied, biting on her thumbnail without looking up. She was watching her own feet shuffle back and forth on the cobalt blue-tiled floors.

She considered the color for a moment when a voice grabbed her attention.

"Mrs. Dane?"

She spun around looking up from the tile, "For now," she saw a not too bad looking man in his late thirties, maybe forty, wearing aqua scrubs under a wrinkled white lab coat. He was tall and lanky with brown hair and some flattering gray here and there. She noticed he was cleaning his oval shaped designer glasses with the edge of his coat. "Yes, are you the doctor?"

"I am," he replaced his glasses on his face in front of his green eyes with one hand and flipped out his other for a handshake. "Doctor Evans."

"Please, call me Evelyn," she said with a suggestive smile.

"Max is fine. I need to ask you a few questions though," he grabbed for an electronic tablet that was under his arm and flipped through it with an electronic pen unaffected by her charms. "You say that he's been taking Depakote for his epilepsy?"

"Yes…well, when he remembers to take it," her smile was more forced.

"And when he doesn't?" He peered up at her from the chart.

"When he doesn't, what?" Her smile retreated.

"When Max doesn't remember to take his medication, does he still get his medication?"

"If he doesn't remember to take his medication I suppose he wouldn't get it," she quipped.

"You are his mother," Doctor Evans said irritably. "You should make sure he gets his medication."

Evelyn's mouth dropped open, "I don't like the implication—"

He smacked his hand up in the air, shushing her, "How long has it been since he's taken his medication?"

Evelyn folded her arms. "Only about a day things

have been busy with the move. I guess we *both* forgot."

"'*About* a day'? So has it been *a* day or more than a day?"

Evelyn bit her lip slowly contemplating knocking those designer glasses right off his face, "It's been...*a*...day."

"And when did he last eat?"

Evelyn responded condescendingly, "If you're talking about a ketogenic diet save your breath. We're already doing that."

"How's that working?"

She flipped her hands out as if to say *duh*, "We're here aren't we?"

"He did forget to take his medication though," he gave a coy smile.

"The diet was supposed to take place of the medication, which means it's okay if Max or I forget. But obviously the diet isn't working. So Max will be glad he can eat more."

"I'm not suggesting you stop it—"

"I wasn't asking you," Evelyn crossed her arms defiantly.

"I see," Doctor Evans considered her for a moment. He scratched his chin with the end of his pen. "When I was talking with Max he didn't describe seeing any flashing or blinking lights. At first it sounds like he had an absence seizure, but everything else—collapsing, the jerking, and urination—that's more characteristic of a tonic-clonic seizure. How was he acting before the seizure? Was he communicating? Walking in circles? What was he doing just before the seizure?"

"He was filming. He wasn't really interacting with us much," she sounded less guarded now. "When Max is focused on his filming, he's pretty much focused."

"I see. So he may have been staring into space really. His plasma prolactin levels came back normal. You would expect them to be five to thirty times the normal levels in a tonic-clonic seizure," he tapped his chin with his pen. "In any case, it's hard to say whether this happened from missing his dosage of Depakote or whether we just need to change it all together. We might have to consider something else like Phenytoin."

"I'm sorry," Evelyn threw her hand up this time. "Aren't you just an ER doctor?"

"No, I'm on call. I'm a neurologist. Actually, I'm the only neurologist in town," a smug look came over his face. "And I'm a psychologist. In fact, I'm Max's psychologist." He read the confused look on Evelyn's face. "You recall that the judge back in Burlington is ordering Max to report to a psychologist within the first week of your move to Ravencrest. The court appointed me. I remembered Max's name from the order," he leaned in close to her and whispered mockingly, "After all I am smarter than *just* an ER doctor. And he's my only case like this."

Evelyn stood up straight recovering quickly and blinked her eyes willfully, "Well, then we're ahead of schedule. Consider Max reported to you. But I'm going to be late to meet the movers. They should be at the house anytime now. I would like to get my son. Max is alright now isn't he? He can go?"

"Well..." he said slowly scratching his chin again with the end of his pen. "I would like to get an EEG and an MRI."

"Is that really necessary?" Evelyn shook her head.

"No, but I have a trip to the Bahamas coming up and a Ferrari to pay off."

Evelyn's mouth dropped open. She realized he was being sassy. She could have slugged him if he weren't so damned cute. "Seriously...you have a Ferrari? Never mind..." she stopped herself. "Look, we've been through all this before. I don't see any reason to do it now."

"Well, you are the doctor," he said condescendingly.

"That's right. Doctor Mom." She cocked her head a little.

"And how many years of school did you go for that?" His eyebrows furrowed.

"Pompous ass," she blurted.

"Soccer mom," he retorted.

"Where's my son?" she started to walk away.

"Fine, I'll get one of the nurses to take you to him. He can go for now." He grabbed her by the elbow and turned her around. "Just remember, Mrs. Dane. I have to send a report to the judge. You don't want to lose Max do you?"

"Of course I don't," she raised her voice. She paused a moment and regained her composure. "Look, I'll bring Max in to your office. You can do whatever testing you need. I just need to get this move over with, okay?"

He looked at her for a long time seeing the sincerity in her eyes. "Okay." He ventured a genuine smile, "I look forward to it."

Lindsey jumped up from her chair scattering crayons all over the tiled floor. "Where's Max going? Is he leaving us too?"

"No sweetie," Evelyn bent down to pick up the crayons. "Max isn't going anywhere. He's staying with us."

Lindsey looked up to the doctor, "I saw a scarecrow move."

"Oh," he chuckled. "You must mean Mr. Creeps. We get that a lot around here." He looked down to Evelyn. "I do have one more question."

Evelyn looked up as if to say okay.

"Does Max sleep well?"

"No, not at all," she answered slowly thinking it an odd question. "He has nightmares."

Max sat on the edge of the exam table fumbling his shirt on. His bones felt as though they were rocking about in his skin but to look at him he seemed fine. He looked over to the mirror and fussed with his hair a bit thinking it was time for a haircut, his bangs were growing out. Sometimes he liked to spike his hair up a bit. It was harder when it got longer like it was doing. He let out a deep sigh trying to calm his bones. He felt like he just got off a roller coaster. He put his hands out in front of him, they were shaking a little. He then got disgusted at the thought of what he was holding in them what seemed like just moments ago. He barely remembered waking up in the hospital and vaguely recalled the doctor asking him some questions, but didn't remember at all what he answered. It was all a foggy dream. The only thing he did remember distinctly was...*the head.*

His mom walked into the room holding a folded up pair of jeans.

"Where's Lindsey?" Max asked looking up from his hands.

"One of the nurses took her to find a treat."

"She's not a dog, mom."

"I see you're feeling better," she mussed his hair. She was examining it now. "I think it's time for a haircut."

"I was thinking of growing it out." He pawed her hand away, "Maybe something more emo or punk."

"I see," she said not impressed in the least. "You gave me quite a scare today young man," she wanted to change the subject.

"I pissed myself, mom," he said annoyed.

"Well, it's perfectly natural, dear." She attempted to make light of it.

"Really," Max flapped his green eyes up at her doubtfully. "How many people do you know that black out and piss themselves?"

"They're called college students, sweetie. You're

getting an early start."

Max almost smiled.

She handed him the jeans, "Oh, and there's a clean pair of underwear in there too."

Max prodded his mom with his eyes to turn around.

"Oh, please. You don't have anything I haven't seen before." She thought she'd give him a hard time.

"Mom!" Max protested.

"Okay, fine," she turned around with a smug.

Max agilely got out of his soiled shorts and underwear and into the clean ones. Once he finished his mind drifted back to what he had seen. What *had* he seen? Was it a vision, a hallucination?

For as long as he could remember he knew things about people. Things he should have no idea or clue about; like faces and names and details about their lives and the lives of the people they knew. It just came to him like a text message (of course, not a text message to his *own* phone). Other times it was more like a picture in his head. And then there were the nightmares. Those only started a year ago. But nothing had ever been that vivid as what he had seen in the pumpkin patch.

Max talked to his parents about the nightmares and images a little but they always blamed the epilepsy. Max had a hard time believing that. How should he know things about people? He didn't talk to them about that because they were going through the divorce and he was to blame for that. He knew they thought him a monster already. He didn't want to give them any more reason to be scared of him. But Max was scared now. He didn't know what was happening to him.

He looked at his mom with her back turned. Even though he knew what response he was going to get he didn't know what else to do. He bit at the inner cheek in his mouth and coyly said, "I saw a head."

"What dear?" Evelyn turned around and faced

Max.

"Before the seizure," he put his thumbs in his jean pockets and looked sideways not making eye contact anymore. "I think that's what caused it." His breathing became more rapid. "I picked up a man's head. It was chopped off."

Evelyn stared at Max for a long moment in disbelief. She knelt down in front of him and grasped his arms reassuringly. "Max, sweetie, you know the seizures cause hallucinations. We've been through this before."

He yanked his arms away, "You don't believe that. I can see it in your eyes." He was right. But she wasn't going to tell him that.

"Max, you're wrong. It's the only explanation, dear. What else could it be?"

Max looked at his mother and got a frustrated look. "I don't know?" He paused for a long moment. "But I'm not going to hurt Lindsey." He raised his voice, "I wouldn't ever do anything to hurt her. I don't care what you think. That's why you didn't bring her in here to see me. You're wrong! You're all wrong!" and Max stomped past her and out of the exam room.

Max almost stomped into the chief deputy sheriff. The chief had his back to Max and was standing at the edge of a hallway talking to someone around the corner. Max couldn't see who it was. He was about to excuse himself for almost stomping into him but stopped at the deputy sheriff's words.

"Is your examination done on the body, Seenu?"

"Well everything's preliminary right now." Max could tell the doctor was speaking with an Indian accent. "We still have to wait on some more tests. But I can tell you he's been decapitated."

"Wow…really? Is that what I get from your expert forensic pathology?" The chief spoke with a strong Vermont accent. Max didn't speak with one even though he was born in Vermont. But his parents weren't from there originally. "Can you confirm it's Watu Warakin?"

"The clothes, jewelry and tattoos match. Oh, and his wallet was on him, so yes."

Roy sighed, "I have to get his son up here to identify a headless body. Am I dealing with a homicide?"

"No, I found puncture wounds and stretch lacerations with ragged edges at the neckline."

"Meaning?"

"Bear attack."

"You have got to be kidding me. Jesus, I don't need this."

"Better than a homicide, right?" Seenu reasoned.

"For sure," Roy agreed.

"I took a hair sample to have the DNA run. I'm only guessing a bear. But nothing else is that big around here to do that. I'll put my money on Black Bear. But I should know for certain in a couple of weeks."

"A couple of weeks?" The deputy sheriff was annoyed.

"Roy, you know how it is. I have to send this off to Burlington and hope they'll give me priority. So yeah, a couple of weeks at best. Don't be surprised if it takes six weeks."

"Yeah, I know," the chief sighed. "I'm just dreading having to tell Joe. We're not best of friends to begin with."

A decapitated body; after his "hallucination." Max thought this was too coincidental.

"Who died?"

Max's heart just about leapt out of his chest and through his skin. He reacted by putting his fists up about to punch the source of the exclamation.

"Whoa, hey…" the blonde boy put his hands up as if to surrender. He was standing right next to Max. "You wouldn't hit a guy with glasses would you?" He chuckled at his own joke.

Where did he come from? "Who the fuck are you?" Max was pissed as his heart raced.

"Jonas!" The deputy sheriff answered. Both the boys looked at the deputy sheriff shocked as if they had been caught doing no-good. His uniform had black pants and shoes. His shirt was khaki with contrasting fern green shoulder passants, cuffs and pocket lapels. He wore a fern green necktie and round campaign hat that reminded Max of something a drill sergeant would wear. "What are you doing here?"

"Oh," Jonas pushed his glasses up on his nose. "Asthma attack. Turns out I'm highly allergic to Mountain Ash."

"Yeah, well you and your friend shouldn't be here." The deputy sheriff didn't sound interested in Jonas' allergies or well-being. "You're gonna trip a patient running around these hallways, now git."

Max headed down the hallway and around another corner away from where he was earlier. Jonas, the blond boy with glasses, was in tow.

"Where are you going?" Jonas asked.

"I have to find something out."

"Do you know where you're going?"

"Sort of...not exactly. The morgue...or pathology."

"Oh, pathology is this way." Jonas jumped in the lead taking Max down another hallway.

"Why are you following me?" Max asked.

"We're friends. You heard the chief." Jonas chuckled again. "Wait..." Jonas stopped. "Did you say morgue? Why are you looking for the morgue?" Jonas' voice trembled.

"I told you I have to find something out." Max looked the boy up and down for the first time. He had blue eyes. His glasses had a thin frame, with small oval lenses—very fashionable. His mother would approve. He rolled his eyes at the thought. Max was taller than him. He liked that. Max was the smallest in his class and neighborhood back in Burlington.

The blonde hair boy was thumbing his backpack and then shot out his hand for a shake.

"Hi, my name's Jonas Lee. What's your name?"

He shook it cautiously, "I'm Max. Max Dane. Why are you wearing a backpack? It's Saturday. You're not carrying your homework with you are you?" This guy had bookworm written all over him.

"Oh…no," the boy blushed.

Max knew he was lying but didn't say anything.

"I used to carry my laptop in this but then my dad bought me the *mi*Tablet. I also have the *mi*Phone. Do you have one of those? My parents say I should keep my phone on me at all times so they can keep track of me. You know, in case I get in trouble. Or somebody tries to abduct me. What kind of cell phone do you have?"

It was Max's turn to blush. "Uh…I don't."

"Oh my Universe!" Jonas' face turned white. "Of course," his breathing got rapid, "you're dead. I can't believe it. This is my first paranormal case. It's just like the movie. That's why you want to get to the morgue. Back to your body right?"

Max stared at Jonas for the longest time in disbelief. "Are you for real?"

"Are you?" Jonas put his finger out cautiously and poked Max's shoulder. Jonas sighed in relief as he decided Max wasn't a ghost.

"C'mon," Max said walking up to the door marked PATHOLOGY and entered.

"What are you doing?" Jonas followed protesting. "We can't be in here."

"The doctor is out there talking to the sheriff. We don't have long."

"Deputy sheriff," Jonas correct. "Yeah, well what if somebody else is in here?" Jonas followed Max to the back of the department as it seemed he knew where he was going.

"I figure since it's a Saturday and a small town there's probably not anybody else in here today."

"Except the bodies!"

"Exactly!" Max gave Jonas a pointed look.

"Oh…I think I'm gonna be sick."

"Well, at least wait until you see something to be sick about." Max came to a halt. There was a steel door. "That's the freezer," he said gloomy staring at it. He turned to Jonas. "You don't have to go in. I just have to see if I'm right or crazy."

"I think you're crazy if you go in."

Max reached for the door handle as it opened— Max moved fast—he clapped his hand over Jonas' mouth stopping him from yelling and yanked him down in the same motion under a nearby table. Both boys watched a pair of black slacks and shoes walk out from the freezer and out of the PATHOLOGY room.

"You see," Jonas wrestled free from Max. "We need to leave, now."

"No," Max insisted. "I need to know." Max unlatched the door and edged it open. He was about to step in when Jonas grabbed his arm.

"I can't go in with you, Max." His breathing was rasp.

"It's okay," Max grasped Jonas' arm in reassurance. "Stay here and keep an eye out. Warn me if someone comes."

Jonas nodded silently in agreement and relief. Max inched into the walk-in freezer leaving the door open just a little. There was a strong odor in the air. The words Cypress and Calamus popped into his mind. He knew he didn't have much time. His breathing was becoming rapid as cold and fear set in. He didn't have time to be scared. And he wasn't about to wet himself again so he had to suck it up. The body was easy to find. It was the only one. But there was no sign of a head. Max glanced around at other stands and trays. He had to know if it was the head he saw in his hallucination. *Duh, they were just talking about how they didn't have a head. What was he thinking?* He suddenly had another thought. Maybe he was crazy like Jonas said. Max took a deep breath and held it and put his hand on the skin by the neckline.

A fur covered face charged at Max. Max heard screams and bellows as large incisors tore at him. Max's hand came off the body and clasped his throat as he struggled for air. His breath huffed in the freezer. He rushed out slamming the door. "Let's go!" He yanked Jonas out of the morgue and lab.

"What? What happened?" Jonas asked with a morbid apprehension. "Did you find out what you needed?"

"Yes…no," Max put his arm against the wall in the hallway to keep himself standing. He was queasy and trying to regain his breathing. "It's not who I thought it was…but…I was attacked."

"What?" Jonas looked around nervously. "There was someone else in there?"

"No," Max waved his hand. He felt like he was gonna hurl. "I felt him get attacked…by the bear."

Jonas looked up and down the hallway to see if anyone else was around. He waited until Max regained his composure. "Did you touch the body?"

Max stood up straight, now that the sick feeling was passing. "Yeah," he admitted looking at Jonas solemnly, thinking he would surely find him weird and gross.

Jonas sounded excited again. "I think you might be clairvoyant."

Max's mouth dropped open. "Fuck you, I'm not queer! I'm almost twelve and I haven't had sex with anybody. Yeah, I'm still a virgin. Screw you!" Max tried to head back up the hallway but Jonas grabbed his arm.

"Uh, okay, I don't even know what that damage is about, but I said 'clairvoyant'…not *queer*-voyant," he laughed. "But that's kinda funny. I have to remember that."

Max's face flushed. He was always misunderstanding people. *How could he know so much about stuff he's not supposed to but get everything else wrong?* He felt stupid a lot.

"Clairvoyant means like 'psychic'."

"Oh," Max didn't sound so mad now. "Well, I'm not psychic. I'm epileptic." And he continued up the hallway and back around the corner where they started.

"There you are!" Max's mother was standing holding Lindsey's hand. She was with an Asian man and woman that were smiling broadly. "These are the Lees. They're our next door neighbors. Can you believe that?" His mother sounded delighted.

"There's my boy," Mr. Lee said spotting Jonas coming around the corner.

Max looked at Jonas and then the Lees. He was feeling stupid again.

"Oh, I knew they would find each other. I told you so," Mrs. Lee grinned. "Did you find the snack machine?"

"No," Jonas looked sheepishly.

"That's okay, honey," said Mrs. Lee. "We'll get some lunch on the way home."

"Actually," Jonas blurted as a thought came to him. "I was wondering if I could take Max to the comic and coffee shop and get something there."

"The kids love that place," Mr. Lee explained still smiling.

"That should be fine, honey. You have your

inhaler?"

Jonas nodded.

"You have your phone?"

Jonas nodded.

"It's close to the house," Mr. Lee explained to Evelyn. "I'll give you boys a ride."

"That's okay, dad. We'll walk. It'll give me a chance to show Max the area."

"Good idea. Max, maybe I should get your cell number, just in case."

"I don't have one."

Mr. Lee's smile disappeared. He looked at Evelyn as though she just punched Max.

"Uh," Evelyn began to squirm. "I don't believe in them," she tried to explain as she thumbed her own cell phone in her palm. "Well, not for kids," she let go of Lindsey's hand and flipped her hair. "Okay, Jonas maybe I should get your number."

Jonas bumped her hand quickly with his phone. "There."

"What?" She was caught off guard and heard a beep and then looked at her phone. "Oh, would you look at that."

"Okay," Mr. Lee turned back to Jonas and Max finding his smile again. "You boys stick together and call if you need anything. Have fun!"

"I wanna go," Lindsey protested.

"Oh no, dear," Evelyn grabbed her hand again. "We're going to let Max and his new friend have fun."

"I wanna have fun," Lindsey scowled.

"Lindsey," Max stepped up, "you need to check out the new house for me and see if there are any aliens."

"With pie-wedge heads?"

"Especially those."

"Okay," Lindsey seemed satisfied.

Max and Jonas left the hospital for the comic and

coffee shop.

CHAPTER 4

"Watch it asshole!"

Max and Jonas had just entered the CONONUNDRUM CAFÉ when an athletic red-headed teenager slammed past Max knocking his shoulder and sending Max off-balance.

"Hey!" Max yelled at the teen.

The teen just cocked his head to the side with a sneer and continued over to a table with more boys his age.

"Don't mind Derek, he's one of the swim team douche-bags," Jonas whispered to Max.

But Max was gone. He was following the teen briskly.

"Hey, Jonas! Good to see you. What'll you have today?" The middle-aged man behind the counter had the sides and back of his head shaved. The hair on the top of his head extended into a braided ponytail in the back. He was obviously Native American. He wore blue jeans with a blue and white checkered shirt and a bolo tie. The bolo tie had a round piece of silver with the design of a paw etched into it. The pad of the paw was a piece of turquoise.

"Uh," Jonas was distracted and following Max with his eyes.

"Hey, douche-bag I was talking to you!" Max came up behind Derek.

Jonas whispered, "Oh shit," to himself worried he was going to be blamed for that comment.

Derek spun around looking down at Max with his dark eyes. "What'd you say you little—?"

He didn't finish his sentence. Max took a swift kick square into Derek's groin.

Jonas' tongue could've fallen out of his mouth it was agape so far.

Derek fell instantly and didn't even have enough air left in him to scream in pain. All the boys at the table stood up. Some laughed. One with dark short messy hair and dark eyes put his hand on Max's shoulder to stop him from doing anything else. Max noticed the boy was about the same size as Derek but a lot more muscular. He looked at Max softly which caught him off-guard. He figured he'd be pissed about his friend.

"None of that in here," the Native American man yanked Max back over to Jonas. "Derek, you had that coming," He yelled over his shoulder. "You sit down and behave or I'll let him finish you off. Everyone behave or I'll get the sheriff out here." He moved Max next to Jonas and then walked back around the counter. "You have a temper. I won't put up with that here in my store. You're Jonas' friend so I'm gonna cut you a break," he said sternly. "And I see you're new to Ravencrest. I'm all about giving people a fair chance. I don't care what differences you have with each other at school or home. You leave that outside when you come in here. Here at my place—the CONUNDRUM CAFÉ—everyone is equal. Got it?"

Max nodded.

"Okay, great." He smacked his hands together and rubbed them fiercely. "My name is Joe Warakin. This is my café. My wife, Meredith, runs the comic shop that's connected. You're always welcome here." He stuck his hand out at Max to shake. "What's your name?"

"Max Dane," he shook Joe's hand. Then a glossy look came over Max's eyes. *"One day when my wheel is complete I will watch the four winds from atop a mountain. Do not morn my passing for I will have not gone. I will have merely begun a new journey with the Great Spirit."*

Jonas' mouth was wide open. "What did you just say? Was that English?

"No," Joe replied. "That was Abenaki. I'm Abenaki. My father has been telling me that since I was a kid. How do you speak Abenaki?" Joe looked at Max extremely confused and in awe.

"Uh," Max looked at Joe and Jonas dumbfounded. "I just introduced myself. I was deciding what to order."

"Oh," Jonas waved his arms in front of Max's face. "Was that a seizure? He's epileptic," he explained to Joe.

Joe looked at Jonas and then Max curiously. "Okay," he said slowly. Then he decided to continue with introductions to his café. "We have several signature drinks and sandwiches and we're open for breakfast." He aimed his finger at the boys like he was firing a gun. "Jonas, what'll it be?"

"I'll have a Chupacabra Chai." Jonas answered him.

"Bigfoot size?"

"For sure."

"Coming up! Max, we don't say small, medium, or large here. It's Gnome, Minotaur, or Bigfoot."

"What's a Phoenix?" He searched the list of drinks.

"That's our signature pick-me-up Latte drink: guaranteed to raise even the dead."

"Oh," Max didn't sound impressed. He eyed the menu on the wall behind the counter. "I'll have the Monster Macchiato."

"Size?"

"Bigfoot," Max decided to follow Jonas' lead. He could tell Jonas was delighted.

"Great. You boys eating anything?"

"I'll have the Champ Club," Jonas answered.

"I'll take the Chomp," Max said.

"Excellent choices! You boys go grab a table. I'll bring your orders out to ya."

Jonas slinked by the swim team and over to a table next to the entrance to the comic shop. Max followed and noticed some of the teens glaring at him. Derek was on a chair now with his head on the table moaning. Joe came over to check on him. The muscular teen that stopped Max was eyeballing him as he walked by. Max couldn't tell if it was anger or curiosity in his eye. That made Max pause in his head for a moment. He was usually good at reading people. *Why not now?*

"You're crazy! I can't believe you did that!" Jonas stuttered unable to get any more words out...he didn't know what else to say his brain was so mesmerized by Max's actions.

"So who's that?" Max sat down across from Jonas and pointed over his shoulder to the muscular teen.

"That's Chance Drake: the captain and star of the swim team. He's also the chief deputy's son—the cop from the hospital."

"Oh," Max sounded depressed. "Chance? Is he a stripper? Really, that's his name?"

"Yeah," Jonas rolled his eyes. "All the girls in school are like '*I'll take a Chance*,'" he cooed in a girly imitation. Suddenly, his face went white as he looked up over Max's head.

Max turned around seeing Jonas' expression. Chance was standing there next to Max. "You could've killed him."

Max looked him in the eye still unable to get a read on him. "I know." Max sounded unconcerned.

Jonas' mouth popped open again. Chance stared for an extended time at Max considering him. Then he shook his head slightly in disgust. "Maybe Derek was right, you are an asshole." He turned to walk away.

Max wanted to say something but no words came out. For some reason Chance's comment really bothered him. He didn't know why.

Chance turned back around abruptly. "Next time just beat the drums," he pointed to the side and then went back over to the table with his swim team.

Max followed where he pointed and saw toward the back of the coffee shop was an area like a stage where there were different kinds of drums set up. They were elaborately decorated but Max couldn't make out exactly what was on them from where he was sitting. Some drums were large and hand-held. Some looked like they were carved from tree trunks. Max even saw various decorated Maracas. "What's that?"

"Drums," Joe answered handing them their drinks. "Sandwiches will be out in a moment. We hold drum circles here. Also, anytime you just wanna jump up there and drum you're welcome to. Drumming helps let off steam and sort your troubles out. Hence, the name of my café," he winked. "I got all kinds of drums: Bongos, talking drums, Taido drums, Junjun drums, water drums, trunk drums and frame drums which are perfect for spirit journeys. Go on, go jump up there," Joe encouraged him.

"Uh, thanks, but maybe later," Max was too embarrassed.

"Okay, later then, sandwiches are coming up," Joe smiled and headed back behind the counter.

"He seems nice," Max said ashamed he didn't make a better first impression.

"Oh yeah," Jonas agreed. "Joe is the best. Everybody calls him Genuine Joe."

Max smiled at that.

"You're hot," a girl with braces plopped down next to Max on the bench seat. "I can't believe you just kicked Derek Reid's ass!"

"Balls!" Jonas corrected.

"Right, balls! Oh my god, were they huge? Could you tell? I heard that about red-heads."

The girl looked to be a few years older than Max and Jonas. She had frizzy auburn hair. She was wearing a plaid sweater with a plain black skirt and striped knee high socks with ruby red heels. It made Max think this could be the wicked witch's sister...except...well...her face was kinda pretty.

"This is Cassandra. She's constantly horny."

"Shut up, dweeb!" She threw a crumpled napkin at Jonas. "Why do you hang out with this loser anyway? You're obviously way too cool to be around him."

"She has the total hots for Derek."

"Shut up!" She turned back to Max. "It's true! Who can blame me? His ass...oh my god...it's the only reason I go to the swim meets...to see him in those Speedos." She looked longingly at the swim table. "He's so hot his dad probably wants to have sex with him."

"Ew," Jonas made a sour face.

"I'm Cassandra Creevy," she smiled at Max offering a handshake.

"Cassandra *Creepy*!" Jonas sniggered.

She shot Jonas the finger. "Aren't you past due to be stuffed in a locker?"

"Max Dane," he shook her hand interrupting their

bout.

"So you're new here. Where are you from?" Cassandra asked.

"Burlington," Jonas answered enthusiastic.

"Do you piss for him too? I was asking the cutey."

"Here are your sandwiches," Joe dropped off plates to Max and Jonas. "Cassandra did you need something else?"

"Oh no, I'm fine, thanks, Joe."

"You just had a salad are you sure?"

"I'm on that no-carb diet."

"You mean no-food diet," Jonas took a bite out of his sandwich.

"You're much too young for that," Joe said concerned. "You look great. Hey, if I can get married anyone can." He smiled and left the table.

"I want to go to college in Burlington," Cassandra continued her conversation with Max.

"Where do you go to school now?"

"Awwww…you're so pretty." She held back a hard laugh.

Jonas laughed. "This is Ravencrest. There's only one school here…Ravencrest Academy." He darted his eyes at Cassandra. "Is it okay if I explain that?"

"As if I could stop you," she shot her eyes into to the top of her head.

Max was feeling stupid again. "So even my little sister is going to the same school as me?"

"Yeah," Jonas confirmed with a mouthful. "All grades up to senior in high school." He took a big swallow. "Then most kids head to Burlington after that. The great thing about Ravencrest Academy though is the facilities are huge…lots of stuff to do."

"The comic-book reading room is phenomenal!" Cassandra was making fun of Jonas again.

"It's called a library!"

"So what grade are you in?" Cassandra asked Max ignoring Jonas' comment.

"Sixth."

"Me too," Jonas exclaimed.

"Well, I'm a little ahead of you guys. I'm in ninth, but that's okay. Give me your cell phone number," Cassandra said to Max pulling out her phone.

"Uh," Max looked at Jonas embarrassed. "I don't have one."

"Lost it? I do that all the time. That's okay, just tell me your number."

"No," Max said bashful, "I don't have one at all."

Cassandra was dead silent for the first time since she sat at the table. Finally she spoke. "Max, I am going to have to seriously reconsider this relationship." She turned on Jonas. "You...here...take my number, but don't you dare call me you little troll unless Max needs to get hold of me." She put her phone out.

Jonas surrendered and bumped her phone with a spin of his eyes.

"I have to go!" Cassandra said suddenly, watching the swim team get up from their table and leave.

"Where are you going?" Jonas asked.

"They practice on Saturday. I have to cheer them on."

"You mean stalk them."

"Semantics."

"Maybe Derek will let you massage his balls."

"With my mouth," Cassandra said hopefully. She gathered her belongings. "Call me," she pinched Max's cheek and left the café.

"She's so inappropriate," Jonas shook his head.

"I think she's kinda fun," Max smirked biting into his sandwich finally.

"You would...she thought you were cute."

Max finished his sandwich when he saw the deputy

sheriff walk in.

"Oh no, do you think Joe called the sheriff about you?" Jonas was panicked.

"I don't think so," Max said softly.

The deputy sheriff walked outside with Joe.

"I think that was Joe's dad in the morgue." Max looked at Jonas morosely.

"Oh no," Jonas clamped his hand over his mouth.

"I should've put two and two together."

"Poor Joe." Jonas sipped the last of his Chupacabra Chai.

Joe came back in and walked past them into the comic shop. Then he came back out and walked behind the counter. A tall dark-haired woman with pale skin and light brown eyes followed him. She walked with confidence. She looked about a decade younger than Joe.

"That's Meredith," Jonas saw Max's questioning face.

Joe crossed back over to Max and Jonas. "Boys, I'm gonna have to leave. I just got word that my father passed." He looked at Max. "But I suspect you already knew that."

Max wasn't sure if the look was recognition or resentment. From his experience most people felt intruded on when he told them things that he shouldn't know. And most people got angry with him. So he learned to just keep it to himself. It was aggravating when it just spilled out without him really knowing. He needed to work on controlling that.

Joe studied Max for a moment. "Boys, tonight is the new moon. I usually do a ceremony with the swim team. The passing of my father makes tonight even more special. Why don't you two come?"

Jonas' mouth dropped open in shock and excitement. Max looked at Jonas and saw that he was speechless with delight. So he answered, "Sure."

"We'd be honored," Jonas finally blurted.

"Great," Joe smiled. "9:30 you know where right, Jonas?"

Jonas nodded eagerly.

"See you then," and Joe left.

"This is amazing! It's because of you," Jonas slugged Max's arm. "I bet it's because you spoke Abenaki." Jonas was all smiles. "You know how long I've wanted to go to one of those ceremonies?"

"What do they do?"

"I don't know! I've never been! Guess, we'll find out tonight," Jonas grinned. "I better ask my parents if it's okay. Maybe we should go home now and ask?"

"Sure," Max agreed, "but first, do you know where a pumpkin patch is?"

"Yeah, you wanna bring a pumpkin home to carve?"

"Actually…a head."

CHAPTER 5

Pools of black coagulate dotted the floor and stone walls.

Suits of armor were strewn along the ground. They were splashed with carnage and blood leaked out of the suits.

A horse edged across the drawbridge and into the barbican. A few torches and the moonlight made the bodies visible in the night. However, most of the castle grounds were in darkness as the majority of the torches were extinguished and the full moon was fading behind approaching clouds. Sir Percy had just returned from an errand to the abbey. A messenger was usually sent, however, he was told the package was far too important for just anyone to deliver. He also had to make a trip to the Isle of the Dead. Percy felt the blood chase through his veins and rush into his heart. His sword was still sheathed. He grabbed the hilt and hesitated. His eyes froze at the sight of the bodies. He was in shock. *Who could have done this?* It would have taken an army to overtake the castle. *How could he miss an army? And how come the drawbridge wasn't raised? A sneak attack? It was night. But where was the army now?* It didn't make sense to the knight.

His horse shuffled through the barbican and into the bailey when it came to a halt. The wind whistled through the buildings in the chilling night. Percy was not accustomed to seeing the castle look deserted; the clouds strobed in the distance. He glanced by the gatehouse and in the vanishing moonlight he discerned a tall dark figure. Suddenly, the horse reared and neighed tossing the lone knight to the ground and galloped past the gatehouse. Warhorses were trained not to get frightened. This panicked Percy even more than he already was. He was able to scramble to his feet quickly as he was only in leather armor this evening. And that's when he saw what must have spooked his horse.

It was an impossible sight. A green light came from the gatehouse. The light was getting brighter. A shimmering emerald knight came out of the gatehouse dragging a saddlebag along the ground. The skulls on the armor did not seem a familiar rival. Its armor glowed in the night. Percy was overcome with a sense of dread. *Was this knight what was left of the attacking army?* He knew there was something more sinister at work; something unearthly. His hand froze on the hilt of his sword as the shimmering knight came closer. Percy noticed the glowing knight was not handling a weapon but dragging a saddlebag; perhaps he could outmaneuver it. Rage and fear swelled in his chest constricting his throat and breathing. His hand squeezed the hilt of his sword. His heart hammered. The emerald knight advanced with no hesitation. It was as if he had not seen the king's knight or didn't care. As the Knightmare stepped closer the last of the torches extinguished. Percy thought of the bodies again. Something in his head said the ghostly knight couldn't be killed. That it was dead already. Percy shook his head slightly. That was fear talking. He must avenge his brothers.

As the Knightmare stepped up to him Percy was about to draw his sword when he heard a desperate voice next to him say, "move!" He instinctively stepped aside. The voice was not threatening in any way. It was almost like a child's desperate voice but there was no one to be seen except the glowing knight. The voice seemed as if it could have been in his head. The Knightmare stopped next to Percy. The man swallowed. He was within arm's length of the emerald knight and definitely within sword's reach. Percy held his breath ready to defend himself. He looked into the visor to see what the ghostly knight was looking at, but Percy could not see its eyes. There was only pitch black. He watched the knight intently, studying it, waiting for the slightest gesture it might turn on him. The Knightmare did not turn to the man, but raised its arm in the air and clenched a fist. The wind howled and picked up. Leaves and twigs moved violently through the air and a piercing scream penetrated the night forcing Percy to cover his ears. That's when Percy saw the second impossible thing this evening. As if it had formed out of the darkness itself a horse arrived. One like no other the man had seen before.

CHAPTER 6

"These woods are haunted."

"Where are we?" Max asked as they walked along the dirt path.

"Shadow Lake Forest. This borders Lake Champlain which we actually have a good view of from our backyards. You'll see later. Before it was named Champlain—after the French discovered it—it used to be called Shadow Lake by the Indians in this region. They noted a lot of strange happenings around here. And people still report supernatural phenomena today."

Max glanced around. "When does the next tour group start?"

"Shut up!"

"Dude, you so sound like a tour guide. You might

want to check into that, you'd be great."

Jonas was looking around nervously. The afternoon sun dove through pockets of trees.

"If you're so scared, why did you take us this way?"

"It's the quickest way to Yorick's farm, you'll love George Yorick's farm, its lots of fun. He has a corn maze that he does every Halloween and a pumpkin patch. At Christmas, you can get trees there, and he decorates the ones that are left over. He also has a dairy farm, an orchard, and makes maple and honey. Besides…I'm not scared." Jonas didn't sound convincing at all. "It's daylight, nothing paranormal happens in the day…I don't think."

"So you're really into this paranormal stuff aren't ya?"

"Oh yes, I want to be a parapsychologist."

"I don't like psychologists."

"No, they're not shrinks. A parapsychologist investigates supernatural phenomena like ghosts and psychic abilities. They can also do research into extinct species or creatures, but those are technically called Cryptozoologists. I want to get my doctorate in parapsychology and prove my hypothesis that not only do ghosts exist but so does an Otherworld that borders and sometimes intersects our third dimension, which explains not only ghostly phenomena, but other paranormal activity and psychic abilities as well."

Max looked at Jonas with a blank face. "So you're a virgin too."

"C'mon," Jonas waved for Max to continue following him. Annoyance overtook his fear. "The Abenaki also believe this forest is magickal."

"Why is that?"

"Something about how trees are potent energy conduits, since they're rooted in the ground and have a direct connection to the earth. Also since they're natural and living and have been around for so long. It's said that the trees—this forest in particular—can be a gate to the Faerie world, which I happen to believe is just another name for the Otherworld. Some even believe trees can extend into the Otherworld. The Abenaki tell stories of people coming into these woods and disappearing for hours or days."

"I bet they just got lost."

"Well these same people report being abducted by Faeries; or accidentally finding themselves in the land of the Faerie—only to be attacked. Anyway, none of these people had a pleasant experience."

"I thought faeries were supposed to be nice."

"Yeah, you're probably thinking of those cute little ones you see in movies with wings that sprinkle dust everywhere."

"Yeah," Max nodded.

"That's not what they really are. Actually, pretty much most paranormal entities you've ever heard of could be considered faeries: Demons, elementals, goblins, and even ghosts. The list goes on. It's said that faeries are mischievous and untrusting. Generally speaking they aren't fond of humans and protect the Otherworld from us and any that would invade it."

"How do you know all this?" Max was astounded by Jonas' wealth of useless knowledge.

"I read a lot. And Genuine Joe tells me lots of stories."

"What kind of weird stuff have you seen here? You said these woods are haunted."

"Oh, all kinds of things," Jonas sounded less scared than a moment ago. "Well, there seems to be a lot of ghostly fog around here. And there's been lots of howling at night."

"Fog and howling?" Max didn't seem that impressed although he had his own creepy experiences in the fog.

"A *ghostly* fog," Jonas corrected. "And the howling could be from a werewolf!"

"Werewolf? You're kidding right? Maybe it's just a regular wolf."

"No," Jonas snapped. "Everybody says that. It's annoying. There aren't wolves in Vermont. They were wiped out in the nineteenth century." He sucked in some air, "Then there are the sightings of a headless horseman." He continued to validate his theories of what he thought was great paranormal activity in Ravencrest.

"*THE* headless horseman? Like from the book?" Max was overwhelmed with doubt.

"Maybe not *THE* headless horseman but *A* headless horseman. There are regular sightings of him riding through this forest every Halloween. But I can understand your doubt. It seems every New England town has a headless horseman tale."

"Does it?" Max asked not ever hearing one.

"Oh yeah," Jonas responded like it was common knowledge. "Usually the tale goes that it's some soldier who had his head blown off by a cannon during the Revolution. And of course, he's in search of it."

"And what happens if he finds it?"

"I don't know. Nobody ever talks about him finding it. I guess the haunting would stop. Anyway, there was only one battle that was fought in this area that could give credence to the story. But...and it's a big but...The Abenaki in this area have been talking about this headless horseman long before that battle; even long before the French colonists came over."

"So you don't believe the story."

"I don't believe the headless horseman was a soldier in the Revolution. I think he or it was something else. Oh the spirits," Jonas stopped walking. "I just had a thought. Joe's father was decapitated. What if the headless horseman got him? Did they say where they found his body?"

"I don't think so. Or maybe I wasn't paying attention. I don't know. But it couldn't be the headless horseman. I saw him attacked by the bear, remember? Unless, you don't believe me," which Max could understand completely, "It could've been another hallucination from my epilepsy."

"No, you're right," Jonas sounded relieved. "I believe you. By the spirits!"

"What?" Max got a little worried at the urgency in Jonas' voice.

Jonas fumbled his inhaler out from a side pocket of his backpack. "I think I saw something large and hairy." He pointed to an area of trees and took a puff from the inhaler.

Max suddenly got annoyed. "Jesus, don't tell me it's Bigfoot."

"No," Jonas exclaimed in a hush. "The bear! Remember?"

"Oh shit!" Max was worried again. "What are you supposed to do if you see a bear?"

"Yell I think," Jonas shrugged.

"Don't worry, if I see it I'm gonna yell alright. Shit, I'll probably wet my pants again."

"You wet your pants?" Jonas looked at Max's jeans.

"Wait, I think I see something." Max started to walk to a large Mountain Ash tree.

"What are you doing?" Jonas hissed through his teeth softly trying not to yell. He grabbed for Max's arm to stop him but he was already approaching the tree. Jonas was too scared to move from his spot.

Max could feel his heart thumping loudly. His skin became moist and cold. He slinked around the large trunk of the tree and saw a teenage boy. He was handsome. He was dressed strange like right out of some medieval movie. He wore a short light brown tunic with white braies. He was barefoot and holding a small spear. Max supposed he was trying out his Halloween costume early. "Hi, we thought you were a bear."

The teen jumped, obviously startled by Max. He looked at Max horrified. He was struggling for words. "Are you a fairy?"

"Ha, ha…I've had enough queer jokes for the day."

The teen looked confused and terrified, but could tell Max was annoyed. "A tree spirit?"

Max noticed the boy spoke with a British sounding accent. He was about to introduce himself when knights on horses approached. They were flying a red flag with two golden dragons on it. Max smiled broadly. *Wow this town really gets into Halloween.* He went around the trunk of the tree to see Jonas' reaction. Jonas wasn't there. In fact, the terrain was completely different. "What forest is this?"

"The Wild Forest," the teen answered.

They both turned as they heard a woman yelling. She stopped the small caravan of knights. She too was in medieval garb. Max could hear her pleading with the knights to take her son. Did he hear the word "King?" It seemed the king wasn't interested in taking in strays. She continued to plead and boasted what a great hunter her son was.

"Which son is the skilled hunter?" He looked at the teen and Max.

The woman looked back at her son confused. She only saw her son.

"Max!" Jonas was shaking him.

"What?" Max was looking around confused at his surroundings. He huffed cold breath.

"What was that? It's not that cold." Jonas was shocked.

"You saw it?"

"We need to get out of here," Jonas was talking very low. "The bear, remember?"

"Jonas, I don't think there's a bear," Max stepped around the trunk of the tree and bumped into a large man. He fell back screaming and then Jonas screamed reacting to Max's scream. Max stopped screaming as he saw the large rotund man was wearing a uniform like the deputy sheriff except with a cowboy looking hat. This man was definitely Native American and looked to be the same age as Joe.

"Sheriff Alahmoot Tahamont," Jonas yelled relieved. "We thought you were the bear."

He put his hand out to lift Max up. "I don't know you."

"I'm Max Dane," he said embarrassed he screamed like he did.

"Oh yes," he said slyly. "You have an appointment with Dr. Evans Monday."

"Do I?" Max was confused.

Jonas was confused too. He looked back and forth between Max and the sheriff wondering why the sheriff would know something like that.

"I'm sure your mom knows about it," the sheriff said. "If you boys know about the bear then you know you shouldn't be out here. It's dangerous."

"Max saw Watu's head. It's at Yorick's farm," Jonas blurted.

Oh shit, Jonas! Max thought. *The sheriff can't hear it came from me!*

"Wait, how do you boys even know about this? You saw the head?" He pointed at Max.

"He saw it in a vision," Jonas answered.

"A vision?"

"Yeah at the morgue...or hospital...whatever."

"Okay, backup and explain."

"It's not what you think," Max started to talk.

"No," he put his hand up shushing Max. "Let him talk. Jonas, tell me everything," he looked sternly at him.

Jonas felt like he was about to be arrested and spoke nervously. "We were at the hospital because I had an asthma attack and Max had a seizure because he's epileptic and we heard Roy Drake talking about Watu's death and that they thought it was a bear attack and then Max wanted to see the body so went to the pathology room…"

The sheriff looked at Max appalled.

Jonas pushed his glasses back up on his nose, "…And Max touched the body and had a vision because I think he's clairvoyant and not a queer, because he's not, and he knew that his head was out here in Yorick's farm so we came out here to find it."

The sheriff took a moment to take in Jonas' explanation. He addressed Max. "What did you see?"

Something told Max now was not the time to make something up or try to discount what Jonas said. "I saw a large furry face and teeth lashing at him."

"That's it."

"Yeah."

"And it looked like a bear?"

"I guess. What else could it be?"

"Okay, you boys get going it's dangerous out here. Yorick's isn't too far. And don't go looking for a head. Go over there and find a pumpkin for Halloween."

"Yeah, yeah, that sounds great," Jonas stammered. He grabbed Max's arm. "C'mon," and yanked him through the trees.

"What's he doing out here hunting a bear by himself?" Max asked leerily.

"Who cares? Let's get the hell out of here," Jonas demanded and tugged Max around a patch of trees.

Max was suddenly clawed across his right shoulder by a huge hairy paw.

Jonas screamed so loud Max couldn't tell if the ringing in his ear was from that or shock. He could feel blood pumping out of his shoulder. Jonas grabbed Max's left arm and yanked him through the forest at full speed. Both boys were running hard, but Jonas never left Max's side. Max could hear something behind them tromping through the foliage. It was fast on their heels. Jonas lead him through the trees and finally into a grassy plain. Jonas was wheezing and struggling to breathe. Max felt himself go cold. Not like his seizures. He felt this once before. *Perhaps now he could rest.* Max couldn't run anymore. His body gave out and he collapsed. Jonas was yanked down with him.

Max looked up at Jonas as he saw him battling his asthma attack. Jonas put pressure on Max's shoulder. Jonas' arms were covered in his blood. Jonas went pale and passed out. As Max stared up from the grass—his ears ringing—he saw the blue sky and clouds floating by. He also saw an interesting cloak with designs; flapping in the wind. It was the scarecrow he saw earlier. A peculiar raven landed on its shoulder. Something was weird about the eyes. The wind was picking up. The grass was kicking. Max thought it looked like when a helicopter was about to land. He looked at the scarecrow again and tried to study the symbols on its cloak when a dark tunnel closed all around him. And everything went black.

CHAPTER 7

A brilliant flame snorted from the horse's nostrils.

Even though the Knightmare's soul was trapped in a Shadow Realm it possessed its own power. And it could command many of the elements of that Realm and do remarkable things; at least they looked remarkable on our Earthly Plane. This Realm is different than the known Planes of Earth, Air, Fire and Water. This Realm is in-between the other Planes yet intersects them and exists outside time and space. The element that comprises this Realm is Ethereal Energy. Ethereal Energy runs through all living things throughout all the Planes. Some also call it Universal Energy or Chi and like Ethereal Energy the Shadow Realm was known by other names. To numerous it is the Land of In-Between, to some the Spirit Realm, and to the exceptional it is known as the Nexus. The

Knightmare chose to mix its fury and elements of the Nexus to create a menacing steed.

Percy was awestruck. The nightmarish horse literally formed out of thin air. It had the shape of a horse and its coat was charcoal but that was where the similarity ended. The fierce steed was larger than any draft horse he had seen. Its eyes were embers; radiant in the darkness. Flames jumped from its hooves scorching the ground it stood upon. Its mane was rolling molten magma and its tail whipped about in a blaze.

The Knightmare ignored the last of the king's knights and threw the saddlebag over its steed. It mounted the fiery beast with no effort. The horse reared ominously; letting out another piercing scream and snorting a jet of flames. The symbols on the green knight's armor glowed. The Knightmare was not done this evening. It turned its steed toward the barbican and charged across the drawbridge. The Knightmare was headed to the town below; leaving a trail of burning hoof prints in its wake.

CHAPTER 8

"Thou art dead."

Max was lying face-up in the grass staring at a huge dead tree. It was night. There was a blond-haired young boy sitting on his knees to his side staring at him. He looked to be about seven or eight-years-old. He was wearing a green tunic. He had tranquil green eyes. Max sat up and looked at his shoulder. There was no sign of an injury. Not even a rip in his shirt. Max realized his surroundings were gray and dark. It seemed like grass but not. It wasn't simply that it was night. It was as if there was no color to begin with. And it wasn't night. It was dark but there was no moon or any light source. *How could he see the boy perfectly?* The air was cold. Max rubbed his arms briskly. "It's cold. Aren't you cold?"

"Nay, I can't feel anything. I'm dead."

"I've been dead before," Max said impassively. Max noticed that like the teen he saw in the forest he spoke with a British accent. The view was odd because just beyond the grass patch he was standing in with the boy was a cold wasteland: a white, snowy vista with mountains perforating the horizon.

"The Desert of the Dead," the boy explained seeing perplexity in Max's face. "A cold desert wasteland: It is why when this world sometimes intersects with the living world that people perceive a drop in temperature."

"How does that happen—the two worlds intersecting each other?"

"Some can open portals and pass through. Some areas are thinner than others; like walking through a waterfall to the mountain behind it. Mainly, it's an occurrence of time and place. With the right combination of things the living can pass through here and vice versa. Like turning a key in a door so the key aligns properly to unlock it. And tonight is one of those most magickal nights—when the veil between the land of the living and the land of the dead is lifted—it is the beginning of winter and the New Year. Tonight is Samhain: The night I was murdered."

He was just a small boy. "Why would anyone want to kill you?" Then Max felt the color seep from his face as he had a horrible thought. *Maybe the boy was murdered because somebody just felt like it.*

"I do not know. I must think our castle came under attack. I saw Llamrai, my horse," he choked on tears. "She was mutilated!" He paused for a moment. "I rushed up to my mentor's room to see if he could save her. And then I saw it." He had horror in his eyes.

"What did you see?" Max couldn't help but insist.

"My body, you don't die right away when your head is severed. I felt the blade pierce my skin and saw inside my neck cutting the bone. I choked on my own blood as I saw my body drop to the floor."

Max almost hurled; that sounded like a painful and horrible way to die. Max instinctively reached out to the boy to comfort him. He put his arms out to grasp his shoulders when the boy took Max's palms and placed them on his face. The boy closed his eyes savoring Max's touch.

The boy then reached out and held Max's face in his hands. He caressed his cheeks with his thumbs. "Thou art beauteous."

Max was flattered but somewhat embarrassed. He didn't know what to say but an introduction seemed appropriate. He didn't know who the boy was. "My name is Max."

"To many my name is Jack." The boy let go of Max and sat back on his heels. "Thy energy is vibrant. Yea, thou art not dead." He looked at Max from side to side inspecting him. "Where are thy glyphs?"

"My what?"

"Thy glyphs: Magickal writings—for protection. It is dangerous for the living to occupy the same area as the dead for a long period. The Fae and the dead are attracted to thy vibrant energy. Thou would have to have the protection of magickal glyphs to keep them at bay or a guardian spirit to protect thou."

"Oh, like a guardian angel?"

"I do not know this word 'angel'," Jack was confused. Then he remembered something. "Or a protective circle. Did thou cast one before thou entered here?"

"No," Max didn't know what a protective circle was but he knew he didn't cast one. "I was attacked by a bear or something and wounded."

"Ah, then thou must be near death. That would explain why thou art here."

"I don't even know where *here* is."

"This place is the Otherworld. Some call it the land of In-Between. It depends on thy belief or culture. There are many names for often the same thing I have found. The dead come here and since thou don't possess any glyphs or protection we should do something so the Fae don't come for thou," his voice was urgent.

Thanks to Jonas, Max somewhat knew what Fae are. "Maybe you're my guardian spirit," Max offered.

Jack smiled immensely liking the sound of that. He reached out and touched Max's face again. "It feels like I haven't touched a living being in a long time."

"How long have you been here?"

The boy had a confused look. "That is a precise question. I do not know the answer for certain." Tears formed in his eyes. "At times it seems like I was just beheaded a moment ago. At other times it seems an eternity that I have been wandering the desert and coming to this tree."

"I've been here before, but I've never seen this tree." Max marveled at its massive size.

"It's an Ash tree. It's called Yggdrasil. It's dead."

The tree did look barren Max thought; like it was the dead of winter. The tree was humongous. It was as tall as a skyscraper. Max had seen pictures of Redwood trees on the internet with a passage for cars to drive through the trunks. This tree looked larger than any of those. Since this was the land of the dead it only made sense to Max that the tree should be dead too. But Jack made it sound otherwise. "And that's not supposed to be the case?"

"Nay," Jack replied. "The dead are supposed to eat an apple from its branches and enter enjoying a youthful immortal afterlife," he pointed to an arch in the trunk. "Just beyond is the River Styx where there is the Rainbow Bridge that leads to Tír na nÓg—the Land of the Young— the afterlife," Jack said in a starved wonderment. The arch was huge as if it was meant to be a throughway, however, a door blocked the passage. The door was slick and a gunmetal color. There was no handle. The door itself had a single design that looked like it could be the shape of a key with a cross at the end of it. The archway contained several designs along it.

"Is there another door on the other side of the trunk?" Max was wondering if it just went all the way through. He would have looked except the trunk of the tree was so massive it would be quite a hike.

"I do not know," Jack seemed to know what Max was thinking. "You can't walk around. It's an illusion. Just before you make it halfway by the trunk you will hit a wall. It's a mirrored wall. We are only seeing a reflection of the desert behind us."

"Really?" Max was fascinated. He looked behind him and then started to walk by the trunk of Yggdrasil. Jack accompanied him. Max did hit a wall like soft cushion. When he thumped the wall it rippled like a rock being thrown into a still pond. Max looked at Jack confused and back to the wall and back at Jack. "If it's reflecting the desert how come I can't see us? We don't have reflections."

"Samhain is an ideal time to scry. People attempt to see the future. Samhain is when the veil is dropped between the two worlds and so I believe that what is actually happening is people are seeing through this mirrored wall into this land of In-Between where you are able to see other realities and possibilities, and communicate with the dead and the Fae."

"But...how come we can't see ourselves?"

"My mentor told me that mirrors reflect here onto the Shadow Realm: and so it reflects thy shadow soul; thy true self. He told me some cultures will cover the mirrors where a person has died so they won't become trapped here. I believe I have become trapped here. I believe my soul is trapped so that is why I don't have a reflection.

That's why I wander this desert." Jack looked remorse. Then he had a thought. "But that wouldn't explain why thou can't see thy reflection! Thou art not dead. Thy soul should be intact."

"No, it explains it just perfect," Max looked dismal. He walked back to the arch in the trunk of Yggdrasil. He looked at Jack. "So we need to find or free your soul or figure out how to open this door so you can get to Tijuana."

"Tír na nÓg," Jack corrected.

"Yeah," Max said dismissively focusing on the door. "And what are those symbols?" Max pointed at the designs on the arch.

"I recognize some of them as runes and sigils. The others I do not know."

"Some of them are Egyptian," Max recognized symbols from his History textbooks and shows he had seen on TV. "And I also notice something that looks Arabic, maybe oriental of some sort." Some even looked like astrological signs but he couldn't be certain.

"It would seem there is a mixture of cultures on the door; perchance it is a riddle," Jack sounded hopeful.

"I've seen stuff like this before. It was on Mr. Creeps." Max wished he had a camera phone to capture the image.

"Mr. Creeps?"

"A scarecrow back home."

"Aye," Jack understood. "I was a scarecrow for a time."

"What?" Max laughed sure that Jack didn't understand him.

"My charge Percy thought it would be good for me. I think he wanted me to get away from the castle and outside. I would work at times in the fields of the monastery of Abbot Conleth. I would chase the birds away as they landed in the crops," he said with a smile like it was the most fun possible.

Max was dumbfounded. "I guess you were a scarecrow." He never thought there were live scarecrows.

There was a piercing howl that shot across the desert at them that sent ripples through the mirrored wall.

Jack looked over his shoulder in panic.

Max saw a galloping glowing green knight with skulls and symbols etched into its armor on a fiery horse coming at them. Max's mouth dropped open. *Where did it come from?*

"It's a Fae," Jack looked back at Max with fear. "It's a Knightmare!"

"I'll say," Max understood it as nightmare. "He looks scary."

"You must go," desperation was in Jack's voice.

Jack's frenzy was contagious. Max felt himself getting more agitated. "Go? I don't even know how I got here."

Jack looked at the arch. He pointed to the symbols. "Thou said thou saw some of those back home. Concentrate on those," his words were fast. "Sometimes I find that when I concentrate hard enough I am able to visit and communicate for a just a bit with the living. Maybe it will bring thou back."

The Knightmare was approaching fast as the Hellsteed snorted flames.

"I can't leave you with that thing!"

"I'm already dead."

Max could tell from his voice that Jack wasn't actually convinced he was out of danger.

"Thou have to go, Max. Please, for me!"

Max grasped Jack's face. Tears pooled in Max's eyes. "I'll do whatever I can to free you. I will free you!"

Jack kissed Max on the cheek then turned Max's face to the arch and pointed at it. "Which symbols do thou recognize? Where were thou when thou saw them?

Concentrate."

Max turned to see a frightening horse breathe a swirl of flame on him.

CHAPTER 9

Deadly nightshade hissed from the cauldron as it was added to the mixture turning the gray smoke to black.

Two hooded figures stepped from a warmly lit cave and walked to a lone hunched figure at the cauldron outside.

The wind kicked along the night sky as the huge cauldron gurgled under the sanguine moon. This triad preferred to cast in the secrecy of dark—in the open of nature—adding strength to their spell. However, the round moon offered little protection this night from persecuting eyes, but it was worth the risk since this was the most magickal night of all year. It was Samhain.

As the two approached the cauldron they saw a smoky figure reach for their sister. With a wave of her hand she dissipated the entity. "Sister," the tallest asked, "was that the Guardian of the Nexus?"

"Aye," the smallest replied. "Interesting...I expected the Guardian to be...bigger," she pulled her hood back on.

"Is it ready?"

"Aye," the smallest answered clenching a bottle with a dragon etched on it. "I have the last ingredient— Breath of the Guardian."

"Is everything in order?" The eldest detected there might be a problem.

"Jack is dead," she revealed. "Murdered."

"Ambrosius' pupil?" The eldest said concerned.

"Aye, and there's more. I saw a green knight; a green knight of death. It will come for us. It will never stop until we are dead."

"All the more reason for us to complete our task," the tallest rationalized.

"Do you know who murdered his pupil?" The eldest asked.

"Ambrosius."

There was silence among the hoods as they understood that horrific significance.

"And Ambrosius didn't bring us the Elixir himself."

"Whom then?"

"I didn't see anyone."

"He must have made haste to the Giant's Ring. Where is he now?" The tallest asked.

The hunched hood seemed to scour the night sky for the answer. "He was at the castle. Now, he makes way to the monastery."

"With Abbot Conleth?" The tallest sounded infuriated. "He is supposed to be at the Giant's Ring!"

"I knew it!" The smallest growled. "He's been talking too much to those humdrums. They've turned him," she insisted. "He's betrayed the Council! Forming the Table was a bad union I said all along!"

"I can't believe Ambrosius would do such a thing," the tallest motioned for the hunched hood to hand her the bottle. "You are sure the elixir came from Ambrosius?"

"This was left by it," she pulled out a ring with a runic "R."

"And you are sure the spirit you communed with was the Guardian?"

"Aye, he knew my name. And he knew of Ravencrest."

"Very well then," she seemed satisfied with that answer. "Then before we go any further with the ritual let's abate the suspicion that we all have; that Ambrosius gave us a false elixir." The tallest held the bottle up to the dim sky. "With the Guardian's breath upon the liquid the moon shall reveal the concoction."

The harvest moon hung above the tree line bathing the horizon in blood-orange moonlight. The waters from the Isle of the Dead were hardly still this night. They crashed upon the shore not far from the witches.

The three hoods watched the bottle keenly. A bony finger protruded from the sleeve of the hunched hood. "It should be swirling red." The liquid looked a stagnant black.

"HEX!" The tallest screamed smashing the bottle upon the earth. "We've been duped."

"Betrayed!" The eldest screamed.

A bolt shot into the hood of the smallest witch penetrating her skull. She fell to the earth shrieking. The other two witches instinctively ducked behind the large cauldron inadvertently dodging the bolts aimed at them.

"They're using Rowan wood," the first was vexed.

"Hex," the tallest cursed understanding now why their protective circle hadn't deflected the attack. Their backs were to the Isle of the Dead and to their sides were open fields. Dead ahead was a small clearing, then the forest. That's where their attackers were and they would have to come into the open to get a better shot. She grabbed the leg of her fallen sister behind the cauldron where they all were now. "Are you still with us?"

The smallest witch grumbled in pain twisting the bolt out of her skull with one hand. She grabbed the knee of the tallest letting her know she was still with them.

"They're coming," the oldest nudged the tallest. They peered over the cauldron and saw three mercenaries charging out of the forest, arbalests at their sides, and now carrying pikes.

"A little cover sister," the tallest suggested.

"Of course," she quickly threw Fern and Heather into the cauldron and reached for the sky squeezing her fists. Rain began. "I'll deal with this," the oldest said standing up from behind the cauldron and grasping the hand of the tallest. The three were linked now.

"Die witches!" The three mercenaries yelled as they advanced through the downpour. Bertrand stopped, dropped his pike and began to load his arbalest. He cranked the ratchet drawing the string back. He fumbled with the bolt in the rain as the other two mercenaries continued ahead. He locked the bolt in place and took aim when suddenly he was yanked by his feet. He yelped, firing the crossbow. It struck Jean-Luc in the back sending him down to one knee. Auguste stopped, hearing his comrade's yell. He looked to his side seeing Jean-Luc struck down and turned quickly around to see Bertrand pulled high into the air by the vines of several trees. More vines wrapped around Bertrand's neck and upper torso stifling the man's screams that he undoubtedly would have let out as he was torn in half; his organs spilling out of the two sections.

Auguste ran to Jean-Luc. The bolt had penetrated his armor and he was still down on one knee letting out slow and rasping breaths. Jean-Luc looked up; the rain pelting his face. "You can't help me. You must stop the witches!" He spoke in Swiss.

Auguste pointed back toward the trees; his hand was shaking. "Did you see? Did you see what they did to Bertrand? We can't stop them."

Jean-Luc could see that Auguste was overtaken by fear and horror. "They are powerless against your weapon," he looked at the pike. "Be strong! We are making this world a safe place for our families. You have to stop them."

Auguste swallowed hard and paused for a long moment as he regained enough courage to turn toward the witches and approach. This time he didn't dash at them, instead he advanced cautiously. The witch's circle was resistant to the drenching rain. He stopped. He wasn't close enough to attack but he could see the one witch standing behind the cauldron. He knew the other two witches were down out of sight. One had to be dead and the other crouching in fear. This increased his confidence.

"Who are you?" The oldest called out.

"Servants of God," he spoke slowly in English.

"Which one?"

Auguste was confused by the question and hesitated, "The one true God."

"You speak with an interesting tongue."

"I am Swiss."

"You are quite some distance from home then."

His grip was tightening around the pike as he was working up more courage to attack. "The distance is trivial to stamp out evil and put an end to the Devil worshiping of you and your kind."

"Devil worshiping?" She asked softly looking down to her side at the tallest for clarification. The tallest didn't have an answer and was busy mixing herbs with one hand. "I don't know this Devil," the first replied to the mercenary.

"Lies! That is the way of your kind. The truth is you and all your kind will die this night. We have already killed one of you and you two shall die at the hand of God with me as the instrument of his judgment!"

The first had been examining his pike all this time. She had struck up the conversation just for that reason. She recognized the blade was silver and the shaft made of Rowan wood. It would penetrate their protective circle easily and the Rowan wood would protect him from a lightning strike and he was out of reach of the trees. She could see he was about to attack. She cast her arm out toward the mercenary and the fire from the cauldron shot at Auguste in a flaming arc. Auguste leapt to the side to dodge the arc but it had ignited the pike. Auguste rolled quickly back up to his feet and instantly picked up his arbalest. But his bolts were sprayed around in the grass. The pike was disintegrated except for the silver blade lying in the wet grass. "There's always a work-around," she said to herself.

The witch called out to Auguste, seeing that he was now without the protection of Rowan wood. "Yes, you have struck down my sister with a bolt. We possess deadly bolts as well," and she cast her arm up to the clouds. The night sky lit up brilliantly as a bolt of lightning smacked the mercenary. His eardrums burst. His eyes popped like egg yolks. The parts of his skin that were shielded by metal melted. The rest of him cooked from the inside out as his scorched body fell over in a smoldering heap in the rain.

"Sisters!" The smallest called from the ground writhing in pain and holding the dressing in place that the tallest had prepared. "They are going to slaughter our brothers. We must go to the Giant's Ring."

"We should consider transferring our power," the eldest advised.

"That will leave us weak," the tallest doubted that

suggestion.

"Aye, she is right," the smallest agreed. "Our end is inevitable."

"Very well," the tallest conceded and the three witches put their hands on the cauldron. A crack of thunder erupted. "We must go. Can you make it?" The tallest asked with concern.

"Aye, I can make it." The smallest insisted and got to her feet. "We will need broom."

The eldest reached into her cloak and pulled out a handful of the herb. "I have enough for us all," she distributed the herb to each.

"Join hands," the tallest instructed as they made a circle around the cauldron and began a chant:

INTO THE AIR WE LAUNCH OUR BROOM;
RAISE THE WINDS WITH THIS POWERFUL BLOOM.
MAKE US LIGHT AND LIFT US HIGH;
TO THE GIANT'S RING WE SHALL FLY.

They tossed the broom herb into the air and the winds grew in strength. The air howled as the witches were lifted into the sky.

Jean-Luc was down in the grass breathing slow and painfully as he watched the witches fly through the shrieking air.

CHAPTER 10

Max was on fire!

"Jack!" Max screamed with a puff and sat upright. His right shoulder felt on fire.

"Don't sit up right away." It was a tall elderly lady that spoke with a British accent and with a severe demeanor. She made a mental note that Max's scream was vaporous. She had small square glasses and a square jaw to match. She seemed quite nonsensical. She eased him back into the comfy window seat.

His shirt was off and there was gauze on his right shoulder. It felt sticky and wet underneath. "I think I'm still bleeding."

"That's just the paste Martha made," said another elderly lady with a British accent and eye patch. She was small and hunched. Her voice was rough like she gargled glass. "Better than a hospital. Believe me, her concoctions are the best at patching people up," she tapped her eye patch.

That didn't instill much confidence in Max.

"I know those plants you used in that paste," Jonas said to Martha as he was hunched over a round mahogany table with matching chairs. "You mixed *Capsella bursa-pastoris* and *Calendula officinalis*," he wheezed.

"Very good," Martha congratulated him. "You recognized Shepherd's Purse and Pot Marigold. I also mixed in a little Tea Tree Oil."

"Oh, he's a smart one," another elderly lady with the same accent said from the counter decorating cookies.

"Maybe too smart," the patched lady said severely.

Max looked at his wrap questionably. Somehow all those ingredients whatever they were didn't sound very clean even though his shoulder felt better.

Jonas got up unsteadily and stood by Max where he could see into the backyard. "You have lilies surrounding the house." He had always seen them in the front yard but didn't know they were in the back as well. "Is that to keep ghosts out?"

The sisters were silent. Max was studying them.

Jonas ignored the silence and persisted. "I also see Mountain Ash—"

"Also known as...?" Martha was testing him.

"Rowan wood," Jonas answered easily.

"Very good," belted the old lady baking and clapped her hands impressed.

Jonas didn't seem impeded by the small interruption. "Mountain Ash is good for deflecting the Evil Eye." The words came out sounding doubtful. Jonas didn't believe that was why they were planted. Then he decided the more likely reason the sister's had it. "...Preventing the entrance of evil spirits!"

Martha nodded with a congratulatory smile.

Jonas also noticed Mullein and other plants that could serve the same purpose. He felt groggy and sat back down next to the one-eyed lady as she chose ingredients from various piles that were spread across the table and placed them carefully in the middle of a beige cloth that was cut into a square. Jonas tried to catch his breath. The kitchen was brilliant, neat, and smelled of baked goods.

"Snake's tongue!?" A hand shoved a plate under Max's nose. It was a cookie in the shape of a snake's tongue. The elderly lady holding the plate wore a Cheshire smile on her face and an apron reading: LIFE'S A WITCH AND THEN YOU FLY! She was holding the plate with an oven mitt that looked like a bat: Complete with wings on the sides.

"Not now, Dorothy," Martha peered over her square-glasses shooing her. "He needs to rest."

Max examined the kitchen. Light shone in from several brightly decorated windows that honeycombed the room. Looking outside from the window seat Max could see what was obviously the backyard. Max thought backyard was putting it mildly. This was a lavish garden. A small stone waterfall ran a slow stream of water through the center of the garden. Parts of the stream were narrow and could easily be stepped over but other areas widened. Across those areas were stepping stones shaped like bare feet. *Bigfoot casts?* Jonas would probably think so. From what Max could see there was an extensive range of colored flowers and vegetables as well as herbs. There were various botanicals from lilies to pumpkins. There was a greenhouse in one far corner of the yard. The grass was low, lush, and trimmed. The garden looked like it could be featured in one of the magazines that his mom was an editor for. He could see the article now: *RAVISH RAVENCREST NURSERY.*

In the center of the garden were a birdbath and

fountain in the cement shape of a lion's head. The water spit out at an arc from its mouth. He spotted a stone bench by some foliage. The yard was tranquil. Max ventured sitting up a bit so he could peer back toward the corner of the window looking to the front of the house. He could see that the house had a wraparound porch. There was a swing and a couple of rocking chairs.

Dorothy turned to Max quizzically, "Surprisingly, you didn't lose a lot of blood. You heal fast."

"Where am I?" Max asked woozily.

"Our kitchen," Martha answered simply. "Perhaps proper introductions are in order," she said with a thin smile and standing up. She was the tallest in the room. "I am Martha Grimm." She pointed with an open hand to the gruff hunched lady as she hummed and chanted tying up the square cloths and making a little bag, "This is my sister, Glenda Grimm." And she pointed back into the kitchen to the cheerful lady decorating cookies, "And this is our eldest sister, Dorothy Grimm."

Max actually thought the gruff lady looked the eldest.

"And you are?" Martha offered for Max to reciprocate.

"Max Dane."

"He just moved to Ravencrest," Jonas chimed in sounding sluggish.

"Yes," Martha agreed. "I saw the moving truck across the street. Would you like for me to fetch your mother?"

"No," Max blurted with a sudden burst of energy. He didn't realize he was this close to home. All he needed was a second trip to the hospital in one day. He was sure his mother would kill him. It didn't matter that a bear attacked him. He was sure his mother would find a way to make it his fault.

"And you're the Lee boy," Glenda said to Jonas.

Jonas gave a smile. He was excited the sisters knew him.

"You get stuffed in lockers don't you?" Glenda snarled.

Jonas' smile disappeared.

"How are you feeling?" Martha asked Max.

"Uh, fine," he thought impressed. He was just attacked by a bear and he felt fine. "The sheriff," Max said concerned. "I almost forgot. He was close by when we were attacked. We need to warn him. How long have I been out?"

"Twenty minutes. Sheriff Tahamont was with you?" The hunched lady asked carefully.

"Yes," Jonas confirmed. "We ran into him in the woods."

"Does he know you?" The one-eyed lady didn't take her eye off Max.

Max wasn't sure how or if he should answer that. "Sort of…"

"Good or bad?" She seemed to realize Max's apprehension.

"Bad," Max admitted. "Why?"

Jonas was starting to wonder what all the undertones were about.

"And you were attacked soon afterward?"

"Yeah…"

"By a bear?"

"Right, so he might have gotten attacked too." Max was worried about the sheriff.

"You saw the bear?"

"Well, I saw a huge furry paw claw me!" Max was starting to think these ladies doubted his story. "I didn't imagine it!" He screamed in frustration.

Dorothy let out a little scream. There was a quick burst of flame from the oven. Everyone in the room jumped. "It's okay," Dorothy smiled. "It was just a flash fire; happens all the time."

"Really?" Jonas asked seriously doubting it.

"You betcha," Dorothy pointed her oven mitt at Jonas never losing her smile. She pulled her cookies from the oven fanning them; the bat wings fluttering.

"Glenda," the tall lady addressed her sister. "Where is the sheriff now?"

Max and Jonas both thought that odd. *How should she know?*

Glenda's eye hobbled around in her head. "He's at Yorick's farm. He's fine. He's with others. They have dogs. They're looking for something."

"The bear," Jonas figured that was obvious.

"How could you know that?" Max said to Glenda. He didn't see how it was possible for her to know that for sure.

"I see everything," she started to thread a needle.

"Yeah, I bet." Max said doubtfully studying her eye patch.

"Or Watu's head," Jonas was still in thought. "I almost forgot. That's probably it."

The sisters exchanged silent glances. "His head is missing?" Martha looked at Jonas inquisitively.

"You didn't see that?" Max quipped to Glenda.

"I knew he was dead," Glenda frowned. "Mind your manners young man!" She boomed at Max.

Jonas nodded queasily not fully recovered yet. Glenda whipped her hand out and cracked an herb under Jonas' nose. Max hadn't seen a crone move so fast. Jonas jerked his head at the pungent scent.

"But how could his head be missing?" Martha looked concerned for the first time since talking to Max and Jonas. "It's not Samhain, yet," she said to her sisters with a loss of some of her composure.

"What's Samhain?" Max asked.

"Halloween," Dorothy grinned throwing her arm

up jostling the bat-wings on her mitt.

"Oh," Max replied. "And what does Halloween have to do with people missing a head?"

"Poor Watu," Dorothy tutted putting a tray of cookies in the oven and ignoring Max's question. "He was such a nice man."

"Is his head at Yorick's?" Martha asked Glenda putting ingredients away she used to make Max's shoulder paste and sounding more secure.

Glenda shook her head.

"It has to be," Jonas rubbed his nose and put on his glasses. "Max saw it."

Max gave Jonas a look to shush but he didn't notice.

"A vision," Glenda declared. "You have the sight," Glenda squinted her one blue eye at Max suspiciously. "I can tell. You see things that other people don't," Glenda explained sifting through purple, blue, and orange cloth squares.

Max was surprised the one-eyed lady didn't assume he saw the head in person. "They're called hallucinations," Max said thinking of how his parents and doctors discounted everything he saw, which made him hesitant to reveal his *visions*.

"He's epileptic," Jonas blabbed without even thinking if Max wanted everyone to know this. "He hallucinates," Jonas explained more.

"How do you know they're hallucinations?" Glenda scolded Jonas.

Jonas could only stammer in response. Max was almost starting to like the gruff old lady.

"Where were you?" the patched-eyed lady barked at Max.

"At Yorick's farm—I was looking at Mr. Creeps when I had the vision."

Jonas had a scared look on his face compelled to

listen to Max's words.

"It was suddenly night and my mom and sister where nowhere to be seen. I found the head in the pumpkin patch."

Jonas hadn't heard this story. He looked among the sisters studying their reaction. Dorothy took a bite out of a bat cookie looking at Max baffled.

Glenda merely looked at Max and gave a grunt. "No," she pointed her finger at Max after tying up a pouch of ingredients. "I meant while you were unconscious. Where were you?"

"Oh, that. The Desert of the Dead," he answered freely. He didn't think much should come as a surprise at this point.

"The Desert of the Dead? What's that?" Jonas' mouth was open in anticipation.

"The land of In-Between," Dorothy answered.

"The Otherworld?" Jonas stood with elation suddenly feeling more himself.

"We call it the Nexus," Martha said coolly and stood over Max. "If you were there then your injuries must have been more severe than they looked. You must have been near death."

"Or dead," Glenda blustered.

"Oh pooh," Dorothy took another bite out of the bat cookie. "Oh," she grimaced at it, "needs more salt." She grabbed a stone bowl and poured more salt into the mix. "Just look at him. He wasn't dead or near dead. He's obviously gifted. You said so yourself, Glenda, he has the sight," she beat the mix. "He was just communing with the dead. That's why you screamed, '*Jack*', when you woke up. You met someone named Jack that's dead?" She looked over her shoulder at Max with a smile, stirring the cookie batter.

"Uh, yeah," Max confirmed astonished. He didn't know if it was more inconceivable that Dorothy figured out what happened to him or that she was so blasé about it.

"Who's Jack?" Jonas asked with salivating eyes.

The sisters turned interested eyes on Max as well.

"He's a boy about seven or eight I'd say. I think he lived in the Middle-Ages. He wore a tunic or whatever you call it. Anyway, he said he was murdered. He was beheaded."

Jonas flinched.

Max continued. "I think he's trapped there in the Desert or Nexus or whatever. He can't get past this door in a tree."

"Oh, a Keebler elf!" Jonas sniggered until everyone else's silence quieted him.

Max ignored Jonas. "He mentioned he was a scarecrow too."

A dish shattered. Dorothy had dropped it and responded with a large smile. "Oh, silly me," she beamed. "I do that all the time," she waved her oven mitt in the air as the bat wings flapped about.

"Hey," Jonas wagged his finger at Max. "You saw Watu's head when you were looking at a scarecrow. Do you think that's connected?" He looked for theories among everyone.

"Perhaps," Martha interjected, "you boys have more important things to worry about," she said with a stern look, "such as your shoulder."

Max's shoulder felt fine he wasn't concerned about himself. "I have to help Jack. He's trapped in-between; he can't get to the afterlife."

"Sounds like a classic unsettled spirit scenario." Jonas explained. "Jack can't rest because he doesn't feel justice has been done regarding his murder. Either he feels punishment for his murder wasn't adequate or his murder was never solved."

"You think that's why he's trapped?"

Jonas nodded eagerly.

"Well that's bleak! Like I said I think it happened in the Middle-Ages, and not even in this country. There's no chance of us bringing his murderer to justice."

"Then we'll just have to help him come to terms with his death." Jonas looked at the sisters for help. "Don't you agree? I mean you guys know about all this stuff right? You call the Otherworld the Nexus, so you have to know about it. I'm right, right?" Jonas pushed his glasses up on his nose anxiously.

"That's not entirely true!" Dorothy radiated. "Just because he was murdered a long time ago doesn't mean you can't still help him. Time is a wicked web!" She finished cleaning up the broken plate.

Glenda and Martha looked at her sternly forcing her from elaborating.

"Oh, poor dearie," Dorothy crooned and finished icing some cookies. "Alas, life…and death…aren't as simple as baking cookies," she took a bite out of another cookie. "Oh, charm! Much better!" She grinned.

"But…but…" Jonas stammered. "You have to have some kind of advice for Max to help Jack. You're witches right?"

Max looked from Jonas to the sisters anxious to hear their response.

"Of course we are!" Glenda had a wry look in her blue eye. "Everybody knows that! Besides, three old crones aren't gonna be much of anything else," she screeched.

"Or lesbians," Dorothy interjected, "We could be lesbians too. Although," she paused with her piping bag, "technically we could be both I guess." She started icing cookies again. "Because," Dorothy continued her thought, "even though we're sisters and witches we could still like other women, even though we don't have to like each other. Well, not that we wouldn't like each other. I mean, why would we live with each other if we didn't like each other? But *like* in the sense of romantic *like*."

"Heck, you're safer a witch than a lesbian these days," Glenda grunted as she put together another pouch.

"Maybe, we are lesbians," Dorothy furrowed her eyebrows thoughtfully.

"Well that wasn't always the case," Martha said.

"That we were lesbians?" Dorothy said shocked.

"Dorothy!" Martha whipped her head toward her. "Are you off your herbal extract?"

Dorothy hung her head shamefully and went back to her cookies.

"I was talking about the persecution of witches," Martha clarified. "It wasn't always an easy time for us."

"So you admit you're witches!" Max was astonished. "Like the fly on broom kind of witches?"

Glenda's good eye whirled up in her head. "Damn, Swiss!"

"We don't fly on brooms," Martha said stiffly. "We use the herb *broom* to fly."

"How do you think we got you here?" Glenda's voice bounded as her face contorted to one side that told Max that was probably a smile for her.

Max and Jonas looked at each other in a dumb silence.

"You mean…" Jonas finally spoke. "You mean we *flew* here!"

"Oh yes!" Dorothy flapped the wings on her oven mitt with a wide smile.

"But…" Jonas sputtered unable to believe it.

"Believe me, we were just as surprised!" Glenda roared. "There hasn't been enough ethereal energy in the world to pull that off in ages!"

"Well, they were near Mr. Creeps," Dorothy cheered. "That would probably explain it."

Martha frowned at Dorothy and Glenda. "Nevertheless, everybody's a witch these days," Martha said cynically. "Homeopathic shops are making a killing, Wiccans are running rampant, and psychics are on every street corner. Being a witch is the new fad. Everybody's doing it."

"Besides, it's not like people go around burning witches anymore," Dorothy glanced up from her cookie making.

"Oh no, laddie," Glenda barged in. "No *real* witch ever burned at the stake. Any witch or warlock worth her or his mettle could escape a burning."

"Except for Helen Driver," Dorothy said thoughtfully. She leaned indiscreetly toward Max and Jonas. She gave a small swigging gesture, "She was drunk."

"Damned fool was always drunk," barked Glenda.

"Remember that time she married her familiar," Dorothy picked at her apron.

"Oh, how could I forget," murmured Glenda.

"She married her cat?" Jonas was shocked.

"No, silly," Martha gave a chuckle, "cats aren't familiars."

"We turn into cats," Dorothy gave an eager smile and head nod. "Witches can have all kinds of familiars: lizards, goats, that sort of thing. Sometimes they can even take the shape of a young handsome man. Oh, but she looked so pretty and he so handsome," Dorothy reminisced.

"Except for his cloven feet," Glenda scowled.

The sisters shook their head.

"Whatever happened to their child?" Glenda asked.

"Moved to New Jersey," Dorothy answered. "Somewhere in the Pine Barrens, I believe."

"So what are you working on over there?" Max asked Glenda. He had been watching her make these pouches filled with herbs and was dying to know.

"I'm making charm bags and sachets," Glenda

answered.

"Charm...as in magic?" Max sat up from the window seat curious.

"Magick, with a 'K'," Martha was explicit.

"Uh, it's still pronounced magic, right? What's the difference?"

"Magic without the 'K' refers to the illusion type that you see in Vegas or other theatrical acts." Martha explained with a berating tone. "Magic with the 'K'," her voice became loftier, "refers to transforming the universal energy—that surrounds us—to your will. It refers to practices that bring you into harmony with the universe and nature. It refers to the mystical, esoteric, and occult arts."

"Oh," Max thought he understood, "Devil worshipping."

"Oh hex," Martha rolled her eyes. "Every time someone hears *occult* they think *the Devil*. Occult means 'secret'."

"And there is no Devil sonny," Glenda had finished making a small decorative pillow that could fit in your palm.

"The Devil only exists in fairy tales and the bible," Dorothy echoed in the kitchen finishing a batch of cookies.

"Same damn thing," Glenda snarled.

"And what are you gonna do with all this stuff?" Max couldn't help but notice they were in a frenzy making and baking. And there were a lot of sachets, charm bags and cookies.

"We're getting ready for the annual Ravencrest Halloween Bazaar," Dorothy said excited.

Jonas answered Max's questionable look. "Every year Ravencrest has a Halloween festival. You can buy all kinds of things and there's food and games," he blinked several times.

"Haven't you bought something from us before?"

Glenda asked as Martha walked back over toward Dorothy and opened some cabinets. There were many jars of different sizes, shapes and colors. She scanned them with her hand swiftly as though she knew exactly what she was looking for and began to take things out of several of them and brought them back to Glenda at the table.

"Uh, yeah," Jonas was embarrassed to admit in front of Max. He was afraid of looking like a complete dork. As if this little bit of information was going to alter Max's perception of him. "I've bought some incense."

"Oh, that reminds me...I have to make some up. Thank you, Jonas," Martha smiled warmly.

"So you're making Halloween cookies," Max wasn't really asking a question but was interested in this Halloween Bazaar.

"Oh yes," Dorothy whirled around with a bright smile again. "We love Halloween." Dorothy popped over to the table with a cookie tray offering one to Jonas. He grabbed a ghost shaped cookie with delight. She then handed a powdered cinnamon one to Max.

Jonas took a bite out of the cookie. "Isn't it a bit early to start getting ready?" He said drably. "It's still early October."

"Well, if the stores can start decorating in summer, we can certainly start a few weeks early," Glenda growled. "Besides we have a lot to do."

"How much are they?" Max wanted a charm bag. "Do you have one to ward off evil spirits or Fae?"

Max could almost hear Glenda's good eye swivel at him.

"Why would you need something like that?" Martha wasn't curious about his desire to make a purchase but that he used the word Fae.

"It's for Jack," he took a bite out of the powdered cookie. "I have no idea how'd I get it to him, but I just remembered that he was attacked by some Fae and I barely escaped."

Jonas froze in mid-chew with the cookie in his mouth.

"What kind of Fae?" Martha asked precisely.

"A knight," Max choked for a second spitting out the cookie.

Martha looked concerned. But it wasn't about Max's wheezing. He just seemed to inhale wrong.

"A glowing green knight with skulls," Max looked at Dorothy with a sick look. "Your powdered cinnamon is stale or something."

"Oh, that wasn't powdered cinnamon, dearie," Dorothy smiled brightly. "That was powdered Skull—"

Max sprang from the window seat pawing at his tongue. "You put someone's *SKULL* on my cookie!"

"Oh, don't worry, dearie," Dorothy was still smiles. "It's not anyone you know," she cackled.

Jonas dropped the remainder of his cookie in horror and vaulted from his chair spitting out what was left in his mouth.

"What do you know of the Knightmare?" Glenda snapped. She grabbed for Max. "What have you seen?" She flipped up her eye-patch revealing a large obsidian *raven eye*. "Look into my eye and show me!"

The eye fixed on Max. He could see his reflection in the glossy orb. Max and Jonas looked at each other screaming in terror and then bolted out the front door of the house.

Dorothy picked up the cookies. "Well they seem nice," she beamed.

"I wonder if they'll come back," Glenda flipped her patch down.

CHAPTER 11

The crown laid by the decapitated body.

Percy, the last of the king's knights, rolled the corpse over to examine. It was true then, the ghostly knight had indeed killed the king. And not only had it murdered the king it took his head. As his eyes scrutinized the body they were drawn to the king's hands. He had three rings on his hands. Two rings were very ornate and bejeweled, but a third was simple, round and silver. It had a runic "R" in the center surrounded by other runic symbols around the rim. Percy bit his lip. He recently became familiar with this ring. He noticed the bed was ripped to shreds and everything in the bedroom was tossed about. The king did not go down without a fight.

He heard the door being unbolted to the king's

chamber as it creaked open. He spun around drawing his sword and found himself jabbing his sword at the neck of a tall thin middle-aged man wearing black robes. The top of his head was bald and surrounded by a black fringe of hair. His nose was aquiline and he had thick red lips. His hands were fair and his fingers long that tapered at the end.

"Father Gregory," Percy recognized the castle priest instantly and sheathed his sword with relief.

"What...what have you done?" The priest's face was aghast at the sight of the decapitated king.

"What?" Percy turned back to the body. "Nay...nay I didn't do this. I just returned from town; from the monastery."

"Of course, yea...Please forgive me," he touched Sir Percy's arm gently. The priest was trying to regain his composure from the sight of the corpse. "Who would do such a thing? Why take his head?"

"Our people believe the head houses the soul. It is venerated above all else. To own and retain it is to have control over the power of that dead person. Father Gregory, what befell here?"

A look of horror and disbelief came over the priest's face. "I...I heard fighting and yelling," the priest stammered. "I...I thought we were under attack, so I ran out of the chapel. And that's when I heard it." Father Gregory stopped talking as his eyes looked off in bewilderment.

Percy grasped his forearm gently, "What did you hear?"

The priest looked at Percy. "It was the most terrible and terrifying sound I have ever heard." His hands trembled, "It was as if the gates of Hell had opened. And then the men started to scream." He eyes looked tearful. "They were terrible screams. I could see fire. I didn't know what do. I locked myself in the chapel." He grasped Percy's hand, "You must think me some coward. But you must know there was nothing I could do."

Percy looked back into the priest's eyes consolingly, "Believe me Father Gregory; you could do no more than myself. And you were no less brave than I."

"Who attacked us?" asked the priest. "Was it a dragon?"

Percy thought it odd to hear the priest mention a dragon. Father Gregory did not conform to their beliefs. In fact, he was trying very hard to convert the king and many others over to Catholicism. Perhaps, they instead were converting the priest. "A dragon has not been seen since the Valhalla War."

"I have heard of this war. The king spoke of it often. But certainly you could not have taken part in it. You are very young even now."

"Aye, it was many years ago, but I would have gladly fought with the king if I was not a babe. The king fought in the war with Ambrosius. Ambrosius..." that reminded him, "have you seen him? Was he here at the castle?"

"I am not certain," the priest was trying to recall. "I believe I heard him speaking of meeting with someone called Samhain."

"I have heard Ambrosius speak of this. But I believe it is a festival or some ceremony."

"Ceremony," he had a horrible thought, "a ceremony in which a head may be required?" The priest said more accusingly than inquisitive.

Percy didn't blame Father Gregory for making the remark. He was starting to think the same thing. He just didn't want to believe it. Ambrosius was the king's most trusted adviser. "We should check his room," Percy motioned the priest to follow him as they headed out of the king's chambers.

"You still have not told me who performed this heinous task," the priest said nervously as they passed bodies in the corridors.

They stopped at Ambrosius' quarters. "I am not certain I believe it myself, Father Gregory. I saw a ghostly knight. It glowed green. It illuminated the darkness."

The priest looked at Percy oddly. Percy was uncertain if this look was of disbelief or recognition. "It would seem to be a demon."

"Demon?" he asked confused. "I do not know this word. Or these gates of Hell you spoke of earlier. Is that an entrance to the Otherworld?"

"You haven't been to any of my services I hold in the chapel," the priest said critically. "Demons are servants of the Devil." Percy gave a curious look that told Father Gregory he did not know about the Devil either. "The Devil is a supernatural being that is the personification of evil. He rules over his fiery realm called Hell. He is constantly at work to torment, mislead, and cause harm to humans because humans are the children of the one true God. The Devil is the one true God's sworn enemy and he will sometimes use unearthly servants called demons to carry-out his evil deeds and plans against mankind."

Percy looked into the priest's eyes for a moment considering his words. Then he drew his sword. The priest stepped back startled. Percy unlatched the door to Ambrosius' quarters and pushed the door open and entered.

Percy dropped his sword at the sight.

CHAPTER 12

Max was knocked to the ground as he left the Grimm's yard.

What the hell did I slam into? It felt like steel. He was still shirtless. *Oh shit*, he thought. *The sisters have my shirt.* He looked over his shoulder to the house. *It was probably torn to shreds anyway.*

"You missed my balls," a helping hand was in Max's face offering to lift him up.

It was Chance. He slammed into Chance? *His body must be made of steel.* Chance's hair was wet and floppy. He was wearing a tight t-shirt or maybe it was just his protruding muscles that made the shirt tight. His jeans were tight too. He could see a bulge.

"I don't think so," Max responded sarcastically.

Then Max thought maybe he was staring too long.

"What's the hurry?" Chance was gripping a gym bag in his other hand. He pulled Max up easily. "And where's your shirt?" He looked Max up and down. "What happened to your shoulder?" He was eyeing the gauze patch and Max's flush torso.

"A bear attacked us," Jonas charged over.

"At the Sisters Grimm's house?" Chance looked at Jonas skeptically.

"No, at Yorick's farm."

"And why are you here at the Grimm house?"

"Because Max was getting his shoulder patched."

"You know Ravencrest has a hospital for that right?"

"Duh, I was just there for an asthma attack today."

"Of course you were wimp."

"And I bet Derek had to go there to get his nuts checked out."

Chance turned to Max, "Yeah, I'm still not happy with you about that whole thing."

Max gave Jonas a *thanks-a-lot* look. "Anyway, I cut my shoulder running through some trees. Jonas brought me over here because I didn't want another trip to the hospital today. My mom would've freaked out."

Jonas looked at Max amazed that he just lied.

"You've already been to the hospital today?" Chance was stunned.

"He's epileptic!" Jonas blurted again.

Max looked at Jonas as if to say *why don't you tell the whole city!*

"Is that why you act like an asshole sometimes?"

"What's Derek's excuse then?" Max retorted.

Jonas was enjoying the bout but was worried Max was going to get punched.

Chance looked at Max admirably and cracked a little smile. He looked Max up and down again, then focused on Max's nipples. "You could cut glass with those."

"Oh," Max looked at his naked torso suddenly feeling embarrassed about being half-dressed.

"Hey...child molester," Jonas barged in. "His mother is right across the street."

Max and Chance whipped their eyes to the moving van in front of the two-story pueblo style house. Max's mother was coming down the driveway directing the movers with her finger and enunciating exaggeratedly as if that would make it easier for them to understand her.

"So why are you here? You live in the neighborhood?" Max hoped so.

"No, Derek does..."

Of course he does! Max's face went south.

"...I just dropped him off."

"I thought Derek was with you," Cassandra yelled stepping out from behind a bush at the corner next door to the Grimm house.

Max, Chance, and Jonas jumped and spun their heads.

"Uh, he's at home," Chance yelled in disbelief.

"Damn," she said under her breath. Then she smiled broadly and waved good-bye. She was about to turn away then stopped. "Nice nipples," she hollered at Max. Then she put her pinky and thumb up to her face to mimic a phone. *CALL ME* she mouthed. And then she tore off. The boys had no doubt she was on her way to Derek's house.

"Well, I better get going," he pointed to a lava red Jeep parked on the street.

"You drive?" Max looked at the Jeep.

"Yeah."

"I just don't know anyone that's not an adult that can drive. How old are you?"

"Seventeen."

"Wow, you're that old."

"There's that asshole thing again," Chance smirked.

"C'mon, Max," Jonas yanked Max across the street toward their houses. "We need to get the hell away from those witches," he whispered. "Who knows what they did to your arm."

"Hey," Chance called after them. "Here," he grabbed a t-shirt out of his gym bag and tossed it to Max. "So your mom won't freak out." And he got in his Jeep.

"I'm gonna carve your guts out!"

Max and Jonas jumped about three feet in the air spinning around to face the source of the voice. It sounded like a mad man. There was a man standing there with a maniacal grin and brandishing a large carving knife! He slammed the knife down into a pumpkin the size of a riding lawn mower. It was Mr. Lee!

"Hey boys, look what we got while you were out: Pumpkins!" He said proudly.

"Holy Shit! Where did you get that, dad?" Jonas could barely contain himself. Mr. Lee gave him a quick look of dissatisfaction for cussing but forgave him quickly. The pumpkin was awe inspiring.

"We went to Yorick's farm to get them...Well, he delivered this one," he indicated the massive pumpkin. "Max, we're having you and your family over tonight for dinner and we're carving pumpkins too." He yanked the knife out and jabbed toward the back of the minivan. There were numerous normal size pumpkins piled in the back. "It's going to be a pumpkin carving party. Isn't that great? I'm gonna get those witches this year," he sneered toward the Sisters Grimm's house.

"A few years back," Jonas explained to Max, "we started an *unofficial* neighborhood pumpkin carving contest. The sisters have always won. They're pretty wicked at carving."

"Oh no, not this year," Mr. Lee shouted across the street as if they were listening. He leaned into the boys. "Look at the size of these. Besides, this year, I'm going to employ my bonsai tree technique. I won't fail," he shook his knife at their house victoriously and laughed maniacally again.

"Your dad is cool," Max was laughing.

"Max!" Another voice shouted behind them.

Max and Jonas spun around again startled. It was Max's mother with a smile this time. "So you hear we're going over to the Lees tonight? That was nice of them wasn't it? Especially since there's no way I'm going to have the kitchen unpacked in time to get to the grocery store to stock it. Much less actually cook dinner. Huh, I'm going to have figure out where the grocery store is. Oh well, I'm sure the Lees know. Are you losing weight?" She looked at Max in Chance's t-shirt that was obviously too big for him. "It's that medication I know it. It's making you lose your appetite," she sighed. She mussed his hair again. "Maybe we'll get you a haircut tomorrow. It might be a good idea before you start school."

"I was kinda thinking of growing it out," he glanced over his shoulder where Chance had drove off.

"I don't know," she said critically.

"Uh, Mrs. Dane," Jonas stepped in.

"Miss Dane," she corrected. "Well, actually, I guess you're right. I'll have to go back to my maiden name."

"Is it okay if Max comes over and checks out my room?"

"Oh, sure! You boys go have fun. Oh, I need to find Lindsey. She was in the backyard looking for crop circles." Evelyn sprinted around the side of the house.

"C'mon," Jonas waved for Max to follow him. They walked up the pebble driveway toward a large expensive looking two-story log home. It was constructed of natural wood and stone. The driveway made a complete circle in front of the house. It branched off to the side of the house where the garage was. In the center of the circle was Mr. Lee's bonsai tree garden. They continued up a swirling pebble walkway to the front door passing the front yard full of vibrant green grass and with mosaic pebble squares throughout. The front door was inlayed with stained glass. The boys walked into the house.

Max felt like he was on a mountain retreat. The floors were light hardwood with warm throw rugs splotching hallways and the main rooms. The walls were large logs cut at different lengths. The foyer had large windows above the main door stretching to the ceiling that peered out into the front yard. A room to Max's immediate right had a large window with a view of the front of the house. It seemed it was meant to be a formal dining room, however, it was made into a TV and game room with a pool table and mahogany chess table. Max was certain those were *STAR TREK* figurines on the chess board. To Max's left was a similar sized room that was a sitting room with large cozy leather chairs around a coffee table. There were side tables next to some of the chairs. All of the chairs were positioned with a view outside the large window. The foyer opened into the great room of the house. It was so large and open Max thought it was a *grand* room.

Huge wood beams ran through and along the steepled ceiling. A shiny wood staircase crawled up one side of the room to the upper level. Max could see the upper level of the log home as it was exposed and sat over three sides of the great room. Max could see that there were hallways beyond and assumed that's where the bedrooms were situated. The fourth wall of the great room was mainly large glass doors and windows that scaled up to the ceiling. The doors and windows looked out onto a large deck with a view of the sun setting over Shadow Lake.

Along the wall opposite the staircase was a large stone fireplace. Max thought it made the whole space inviting. The fireplace ran up the wall through the exposed upper level all the way to the ceiling. And to one side of the room was the kitchen. There was a large granite top island with four leather back bar chairs positioned in front of it. The cabinets were dark and Mrs. Lee had groceries spread out over the island. "You boys wanna help me put some of this stuff away?"

"Not now, Mom," Jonas stopped Max from walking over to help. "*TOYS IN THE ATTIC* are having a live webcast."

"Okay," Mrs. Lee smiled and waved for the boys to go on upstairs. "Don't forget we're having dinner soon."

"Okay, Mom," Jonas grabbed Max's arm rushing him upstairs and down one of the hallways around a corner and through a door to his bedroom. Jonas slammed the door.

"You like *TOYS IN THE ATTIC* too," Max was surprised. He thought the band wasn't nerdy enough for Jonas to appreciate.

"Yeah," Jonas said dismissively. "I lied about the webcast."

Max thought he must be rubbing off on Jonas.

"We need to get that bandage off your shoulder. Who knows what those witches poisoned you with?"

"You really think they poisoned me?" Max wasn't sure if he believed that or not.

"They fed you someone's skull! Who the hell knows what they did to your arm."

Max pulled his shirt off (Chance's actually), looking around Jonas' room. He had *TOYS IN THE ATTIC* posters as well as posters of quasars, crab nebulas or some astronomical phenomena that Max wasn't certain of. He had the typical stuff that he would expect: full size bed and a desk with a computer and large monitor. Jonas had loads of books—that didn't surprise Max one bit—and a telescope so large it looked like it doubled to cast the *BAT SIGNAL*. There was also an aquarium with bright corals.

Jonas put his hand on the bandage about to pull it off. He looked at Max cautiously as though he were about to disarm a bomb. Then he yanked.

There was a sting across Max's shoulder from the bandage being ripped off. He didn't want to seem like a wimp though. He looked at Jonas and responded simply. "Ow."

Jonas wiped the paste away with a look of horror on his face.

Now, Max panicked. "What? What is it?" He pulled his head back trying to get a good look at his own shoulder. Jonas shut his closet door revealing a full-length mirror on the other side and pulled Max in front of it. Max couldn't believe his eyes. He quickly checked his other shoulder. Max and Jonas looked at each other in shock. "How is that possible?" Max asked.

"I don't believe it," Jonas poked and prodded at Max's shoulder. It was completely healed. There was no sign of any claw mark or any injury at all. "There should at least be a scar or something." Jonas continued to push and pull at Max's skin.

Then Mrs. Lee walked into the room seeing Max shirtless and Jonas touching him. "Oh," she blurted more excited than shocked. "I just wanted to tell you the news said they killed the bear that attacked Joe's father," she said quickly and scurried from the room with a proud grin.

"Dammit," Jonas hung his head, "Mom!" He screamed after her.

"What's wrong?"

"Ugh, my parents think I'm gay."

"What?" Max chuckled.

"They've always wanted a gay boy," He rolled his eyes. "And they think because I'm nerdy and don't have a girlfriend that I'm gay. Never mind, that I'm only twelve. And besides, I've told them most gay guys aren't nerds anyway. But no, they don't listen. And now…" he indicated Max having his shirt off and Jonas' hands on him. "She's obviously ecstatic. Hold on. Mom," Jonas went running out of the room, "I'm not gay!" Max could hear him screaming after his mom.

Max waited for a moment to make sure Jonas wasn't coming back right away, then walked up to the full-length mirror and rubbed his nipple across it. "Nope, can't cut glass." He stepped back. He felt his shoulder where he was attacked. It wasn't sore at all and he couldn't make out so much as a scratch on him. He gave up and put Chance's shirt on and examined the corals in Jonas' aquarium. He jumped when he saw something move in the tank. It was blending in to the gravel on the bottom. It was hard to make out so he opened the lid and reached in to get it to move some more.

"You don't wanna do that," Jonas stopped Max from reaching into the tank. He closed the lid. "It's an octopus. It's a blue-ringed octopus. It can kill ya. Their venom is deadly to humans. If it bites you paralysis sets in and eventually your breathing shuts down. And there's no antitoxin for it."

"So naturally, you have it as a pet," Max said sarcastically and in shock. "Are you kiddin' me?"

"No," Jonas shook his head. "They're common in Australia and Japan. My dad got it for me. He thought it would help teach me responsibility."

"Yeah, or you die!" Max couldn't believe it. He couldn't imagine his dad letting him have something like that. "So do you have guns around here too?"

"Under my pillow."

"What?" Max looked at Jonas' bed. Then he looked back at Jonas and realized he was joking. "Got me," Max chuckled. "So why is it called a blue-ringed octopus?

It's not even blue. It's not very colorful at all." Max was noticing it looked more gray and brown.

"Oh, it's camouflaging right now. Yeah, it's kinda boring because it only turns blue and orange when it's about to inject poison in its victim. So feeding time is the only time it's interesting. One of the problems for people is that you can't feel it bite ya. So you only know you've been bit when paralysis and all the other bad stuff set in."

Max nodded his head walking over to Jonas' desk, computer and books. "So do you think the witches poisoned me?" He was worried after hearing what a tiny octopus could do.

"It's hard to tell. I don't think we'll know for sure until you," Jonas looked sheepishly at Max, "start to act sick or something."

"Start to die, you mean?"

"Well…yeah…kinda."

Maybe it was for the best Max started to think. This was probably a fitting punishment. He should die a slow and horrible death. After he died his parents wouldn't have to worry about him and would get back together and could focus on raising Lindsey.

"Actually," Jonas said suddenly, looking through his books. "There might be another way to find out if you've been poisoned. We might be able to use the new moon ceremony."

"So how does that help us?"

"Well, since we're suspecting witchcraft—and I mean black magick; not all witchcraft is bad—the new moon ceremony is full of Native American mysticism and magick; that I so happen to believe in." Jonas was tearing through his books looking for something. "With the correct spell and ingredients we should be able to determine if the sisters poisoned you. And if they did, how we can counteract it."

"So you believe in this magick stuff?" Max asked.

"Absolutely," Jonas put down *Voodoo for Dodos*.

"Isn't that kinda fairy-talish?"

"I've talked a lot of stuff over with Joe, Miss Ursa from the apothecary, and the Sisters Grimm at the Halloween Bazaar—but they kinda scare me—anyway, magick isn't any different than praying. You're just focusing your positive energy trying to make your will manifest."

"What about spells?"

"It's like adding a ritual to help focus your mind. Like going to Church or praying a rosary."

Max wasn't sure what he believed in. He knew his mom wasn't big into religion. His dad wanted him to go to church; however, his mother was adamantly against it. Max thought what Jonas said about magick seemed to make sense.

After a few books Jonas sighed, "I can't find anything on poison detection," but he didn't stop his search.

"Is it possible they didn't poison me?"

Jonas didn't look up from his books. "They used powdered skull. Who uses people's skulls in spells except dark witches and wizards?"

"So, there isn't some magick Cure All spell or a Master book of spells?"

"The occult means secret. That's why there's no definitive guide to witchcraft. Witches, gypsies and any magickal practitioner were hunted down and executed. So for protection of themselves and their ways, mystical knowledge and rituals were passed down secretly. And the way they would keep it secret was by not writing things down and just passing things along in stories. But those that did feel they needed to write things down did so through esoteric symbols and codes. Some think tarot cards and runes are an example of that, such as me, but don't get me started on that. So most of the books you find today—like mine here—have been interpreted by who knows how many people. Are they totally reliable? Who knows because perhaps it was translated wrong or purposely wrong? You never know a person's real agenda."

Max studied Jonas as he was searching furiously for an answer. "So why are you helping me?"

Jonas closed the book and looked at Max. "Because you're my friend."

Max noticed Jonas blush. Jonas probably didn't have many or any friends. Come to think of it. Max didn't really have any close friends either.

"Besides," Jonas added, "I've been trying to get into one of those ceremonies forever." Jonas' eyes popped with a revelation. "Fire, of course," he grabbed another book and flipped through it frantically. "They're bound to have a fire lit tonight. Here it is. Fire gazing."

"What's that?"

"It's a form of scrying."

"Jack mentioned something about that. What's scrying?"

"Scrying is the art of peering into objects to determine the future. Most people are familiar with crystal balls. You know, the old gypsy lady peering into the crystal ball telling the future."

"Oh, right," Max smirked.

"But people can do it with water, mirrors, smoke and fire."

"But I'm not trying to predict the future."

"Well, you can do other stuff. Such as ask a question. Like *did I get poisoned?*"

"You said it's an art form? Uh, does that mean you need to be skilled?"

"Yeah, you do and I'm sure you can't learn it in a few hours. But there's ways around it. You don't necessarily have to do a true fire gazing. You can do another form of divination. We have choices. You can throw bay leaves on the fire and if they crackle and sputter then it means you're poisoned."

"Isn't the fire going to crackle and sputter anyway?" Max wasn't thrilled by this option.

"Or, if you write down your question on something that burns easily, like paper, and throw it in the fire and it burns slowly the answer is yes."

"Okay, that sounds better. And then if I am poisoned...what do we do?"

"Oh, good question," Jonas studied his book again. "Okay, here we go. Bay leaves again. If we mix sandalwood with bay leaves it should lift the curse."

"Do you have bay leaves and sandalwood?"

"Yeah, my mom cooks with bay leaves a lot. I have sandalwood in my magick kit."

"Magick kit?"

"Yeah, I keep a stock of herbs and incenses."

"Okay," Max shrugged. At this point he wasn't really surprised by much that Jonas would divulge. "Oh wait, what if I write down my question on the bay leaf and then throw that into the fire? That way if it turns out I am poisoned we just need to add the sandalwood."

"Perfect," Jonas exclaimed. "That sounds smart— great idea! So tell me all about the Nexus...what you saw...what happened. Tell me about Jack."

Max explained everything and stressed to Jonas that he had to help Jack. "Maybe we can use this ceremony to help him somehow."

"Maybe," Jonas didn't sound confident. "I'm not sure how."

"Boys, come down for dinner!" Asuka Lee's voice carried up the stairs.

Max was having his second helping of Kobe steak and fire roasted red peppers while his mother was having a second helping of red wine. Lindsey used her garlic mashed potatoes as a canvas; carving a circular maze in them with her fork.

"Crop circle?" Max asked Lindsey admiring her detail.

"It's a Mandala," Mr. Lee commented. He seemed to admire Lindsey's work as well.

"What's a Mandala?" Max asked.

"Literally, it translates to 'circle,'" Mr. Lee explained. "In Buddhism and Hinduism they are used to aid in meditation and also used to induce trances. Some even believe Mandalas help access deeper levels of the unconscious because they represent the higher-self."

"The higher-self?" Max was confused.

"Also called your unconscious-self," Mr. Lee said. "Your higher-self knows all the right answers and things to do. Most people notice it as their first reaction. The trouble is most people second-guess themselves and then make the wrong choice. Then they think 'oh, I should've gone with my gut reaction,' that's your higher-self at work."

"So where did you see that?" Jonas asked Lindsey pointing at her mashed potatoes.

"On, TV I bet," Max guessed.

"No," said Lindsey, "I saw it on Mr. Creeps."

"Mr. Creeps?" Mr. Lee was perplexed.

"It was on his cloak. His cloak is full of designs."

"Huh," Mr. Lee sounded interested. "I never knew that. Did you know that, honey?" He looked at his wife.

"No, I never go out there." Asuka sounded like she wouldn't be caught dead out there.

"So what's the story with that Mr. Creeps setup anyway?" Max asked. "He's kinda…creepy."

"That's probably why they call him that, Max." His mom took a sip of wine. "After all, he is a scarecrow," she waved her glass in a matter-of-fact manner.

"Well, that, and he's got creeper vines on him."

Jonas weaved in his chair to avoid Evelyn's glass in case she splashed wine.

"How did you know that, son?"

"Oh, one of the Grimm sisters told me at last year's Halloween Bazaar."

"Oh, those sisters," Mr. Lee waved his fist in a sarcastic anger. "I'm winning that pumpkin competition this year. You boys need to see what I've done so far."

"That'll be perfect, dad, we can look at in on the way out because we..." Jonas looked at Max abashed, "we were invited to Joe's new moon ceremony tonight," Jonas spit it out quickly as if it were no big deal.

"Oh," Mrs. Lee shook her head, "I don't know."

"It's for Joe's dad."

The adult's faces turned sad.

"Well," Asuka sounded like she was embarrassed now and looked at her husband and Evelyn for any disapproval. She didn't see any. "I think that's okay then."

"But first," Haruto rubbed his hands fiercely together with glee, "we're carving pumpkins."

Everybody got up from the table with enthusiasm except Evelyn. She watched from the kitchen table enjoying her wine. Jonas and his parents worked on a couple of pumpkins turning them into traditional Jack-O-Lanterns. Lindsey was super excited and drew an alien head onto one of the pumpkins and Max carved it out for her. Everyone was smiles. Max couldn't remember the last time he had this much fun, especially with his little sister. He felt like he was part of a family again.

CHAPTER 13

The body was in the middle of a circle poured out in salt.

It lay upon a design inside the circle. Even with the body on top of it the men could see the design was a five-pointed star.

It was the body of a male child. It had been decapitated. Blood spilled out over the circle and above it on the floor was a triangle drawn out in salt. Inside the triangle were letters written in blood: At the top of the triangle the letters 'UR, CK, GON,' were stacked from top to bottom; the left side 'TH, A, DRA,' again on top of each other; and the right of the triangle had 'AR, J, PEN.' Percy looked to the monk with appalled eyes.

"Do you know who this is?" Father Gregory charged over to the body kneeling and making gestures in the air performing a blessing.

"Nay," Percy hesitated. "I cannot be certain with his head missing; however, I am not familiar with any children from the village," he lied. "Why take his head? There can be no revelry in displaying a child's head. This is most harrowing."

"Do you know what these symbols are?" The priest stood indicating the circle with the five-pointed star inside.

"It is a circle of protection," Percy was attempting to piece together what happened.

"I don't think it was effective," the priest replied.

"Have you seen this symbol before?" Percy pulled out the king's ring with the "R" on it showing it to the priest.

Father Gregory smacked it out of Percy's hand immediately. "What are you doing? Are you trying to summon more demons?"

"I do not understand. It is merely a ring with the symbol of Raido on it meaning '*journey*'."

"Do you not see what is going on this evening; this wicked night? These symbols," he indicated the ring and the circle on the floor, "these horrific deaths. Your people have long delved in symbols and rituals without knowing it has invited the Devil into your lives. Now, look." He pointed to the boy's body. "The Devil has manifested. He has sent his demon—his legionnaire—on this devil night. No good can come from dabbling in these symbols. Your people must bury and seal these practices away, Percy."

Percy found himself again considering the priest's words when his eyes widened as he recalled where he had seen a ring like the king's. "Brother Conleth," the abbot of the monastery, "I believe I saw Abbot Conleth wearing a ring similar to the king's."

"What…why would he wear such a thing?" the priest looked confused.

"I do not know Father Gregory. He had it on earlier

this evening when I saw him. I am certain of it." Percy picked up his sword and sheathed it. "This ghostly knight...this demon as you call it, I feel its tasks are not quite complete this night. If that symbol on the ring invites evil then Abbot Conleth might be in danger." He hung his head in shame. "I was not able to save my King, my fellow knights, or this boy. But, perhaps, I can save another life."

The priest outstretched his arm lifting Percy's chin, "Percy, you are indeed a brave young man...a good man. You have a pure heart and it will serve you well in the crusade that lies ahead of us. I am going with you," he insisted.

"Thou art not a fighter," Percy replied.

"We will need more than swords this evening. We are facing the Devil tonight and I will bring the power of God to our battle."

CHAPTER 14

The bright fire reached for the dark moon.

Max had noticed the teens that were gathered around the fire were the same teens he had seen at the CONONUNDRUM CAFÉ earlier. The only exception was another man, besides Joe. He looked to be in his thirties and physically fit. His hair was dark brown and buzzed tight on the sides with a little growth on top: Military style. His eyes looked shrewd. His t-shirt was tight so you could see all his muscles. Very much like Chance. And no sooner that Max had finished this thought Chance spoke up as if on cue.

"Coach, what are you doing here? You never come to the rituals." Derek was standing next to him.

The military guy—coach—answered Chance. "It's

no secret that Joe and I have our...'differences'—"

Max's eyebrows shrugged at this. That meant they argued a lot and didn't agree on much.

"But the one thing we *can* agree on is that Chief Watu was a great and honorable man and leader."

"Joe's dad was the Chief of Police?" Max bent into Jonas whispering.

Jonas looked at Max like he was the dumbest person on Earth. "No! Chief of the Abenaki tribe in Ravencrest."

"Boys," Joe interrupted coach looking at Max and Jonas, "you are guests here and this new moon ceremony is dedicated to my father. Show some respect please," he put his finger to his mouth indicating to be quiet.

"I'll let you continue with your ceremony," coach continued. "I just wanted to pay my respects."

"Thanks for coming, Brent," Joe called after coach as he headed out through the trees. Joe then continued. "Old passes away...making way for the new. As it is with the moon phases so it is with life." Joe stared at the roaring fire. He addressed the teenage boys circled around it. "However, the moon is never truly gone is it? The phases—moving from full to dark—are part of a necessary cycle of death and rebirth; destruction and rebuilding; cleansing and empowerment. It is no different with the circle of life. The lives we encounter in this life journey, whether it is human or animal, are always a part of us. They are never truly gone. And like a circle there is no true beginning or ending. So I now cast a Great Circle surrounding us and the bonfire to create a sacred and safe space for our new moon ceremony."

"Is he talking about a protective circle?" Max leaned in to Jonas asking quietly.

"Yes," he answered impressed. "You know more about this stuff than I thought."

"Jack mentioned it to me," Max admitted.

One of the teen boys started beating rhythmically on a drum that looked to Max as though it came from Joe's café.

"Billy," Joe summoned one of the teen boys to assist him, "we are going to cast the wheel now. Or the Great Circle." Billy picked up several stones that Joe had set aside. Joe walked to the bonfire with some kind of stick and lit the end of it. He allowed it to burn for a moment before blowing it out as its smoke billowed. Joe looked at Jonas and Max. "This is a smudge stick; it's made of Sage."

"It's like incense," Jonas whispered to Max because he could tell Max wasn't making sense of it. Max nodded thankfully to Jonas for his explanation.

Joe slowly began to walk in a circle surrounding the boys and bonfire. " 'One day when my wheel is complete I will watch the four winds from atop a mountain.' My father used to tell me that," Joe looked at Max. "I cast this wheel to protect all of us inside it," Joe was waving the smudge stick through the air. Billy followed him placing stones down on the earth as Joe spoke. "And now I call in the four directions and their respective spirit keepers to give us protection and wisdom." Joe went into a sort of dance wafting the smudge stick through the air like some baton.

"I call forth the cold purifying North winds and its herald the white buffalo to lend us its knowledge. I call forth the hot spirit of the South winds and its keeper the mouse to lend us feeling and emotion. I call forth the tempered East winds brought on the Eagle's wings to lend us vision and illumination. I call forth the strong cool West winds carried on the grizzly bear's back to allow us strength." The beating on the drums came to a crescendo then stopped. "If anyone has any spirit guides they would like to invite into this space; now is the time. I invite the spirit of my Father. He was my guide in life and I know he will continue in his new journey."

Suddenly, there was a cold hand on Max's shoulder. He felt it through the fabric of his shirt. He looked up and there was an older Native American man with dark and gray hair on top with braids down the sides looking at Max. He opened his mouth as if to talk but no sound came out. It looked like it was painful for him to try and speak. His skin was purple and his eyes were sunk in. He grabbed at this throat and then he flickered out like an image on a computer screen. Max had the icky gutter ball feeling in his stomach.

Max tapped Jonas' shoulder still looking where the man just was. "Do you have a pic of Joe's father?"

"Sh," Jonas said to Max. He didn't want any more trouble tonight. After he thought it over he spoke softly. "There might be one of him on the wall at the café. Why?"

Joe motioned to Billy and he began beating the drums again rhythmically.

"Something's not right," Max felt like he was drenched in dread.

"What's not right?" Jonas was getting worried.

"I'll tell you later."

Jonas was frustrated. He hated when people would bring something up with urgency and then not explain.

"Now, boys," Joe addressed the teens. "It's time to place the pachamama sticks I gave you earlier into the fire." Max and Jonas witnessed the teens—one by one— place what looked like pieces of tree branches that were decorated with herbs of some sort into the bonfire. Smoke piped out of the bonfire and they were all engulfed in a powerful aroma that was hypnotic.

Max was surrounded by a haze now. He felt woozy. He couldn't see Jonas, Joe, or anyone. He could hear some chanting. Joe must have instructed the teens to do so at this point of the ceremony:

GUARDIAN OF THE NEXUS DRAW DOWN THE
MOON
IT'S YOUR SPIRIT I COMMAND TO COMMUNE.
APPEAR WITHIN THIS CIRCLE OF LIGHT
COME TO ME IN THE MOONLIT NIGHT.

There was a flash of white light. Max walked toward it. Then he noticed a figure in the smoke just out of his reach. He wasn't sure if the person was cloaked or just had a hazy outline from all the soot. The white smoke now turned black.

"Identify yourself spirit," the voice grated from the hazy figure.

Max knew that voice. And the figure did seem to be hunched. "Glenda? Glenda Grimm is that you?"

"Indeed it is," she cackled. "And indeed you are the Guardian of the Nexus to possess such knowledge."

What was she talking about? Max still couldn't see any detail. *What was she doing out here?* Then something occurred to him. "Are you in Ravencrest?"

"Nay…we have only learned of it recently. Are we to go there?"

"Yeah," Max was confused. Then he had an impossible suspicion. Even though he couldn't make out any detail of Glenda he looked to the sky and saw the aura of a *full* moon.

"Time is of the essence spirit. I command you to breathe into this bottle."

Max thought that was an odd request. *Oh, what the heck.* He breathed into the bottle that was held in front of him.

"Fortune," she quickly stoppered the bottle. "And now Guardian is there something I can do for you in return?" Her cloak flapped. "A request?"

Max wasn't about to pass this up. He knew Jonas would've wanted him to ask about whether he was poisoned or not. But Max's gut told him he wasn't. "There's a boy that's been murdered—Jack."

"Jack who?"

Good question. Max didn't know his full name. "He is a scarecrow and lives at the castle."

Glenda gasped. "Ambrosius' pupil? It can't be."

"He can't get past the door in Yggdrasil."

"As the Guardian of the Nexus you can't allow him access?" Glenda said suspiciously eyeing the bottle she just stoppered.

Oops Max thought. And what would happen if the *real* Guardian of the Nexus showed up? "His soul is trapped," Max improvised.

"Oh," Glenda sounded concerned. "Binding a soul takes magickal expertise. Murder is the main ingredient. That's very dark magick." She pulled back her hood. "Show me what you see."

Max had images of his visit with Jack while he was in the Nexus fly through his mind including the Knightmare. He shook it off. "And how do we unbind him?"

"You can't use the usual herbs and incenses to reverse that kind of magick. You would need to kill the spell caster or..." her eyes fell back on the bottle in her hand "...something else..."

The words screamed in Max's head. "The Elixir of Life." That's what was in the bottle! It would free Jack! He grasped for the bottle. Glenda pulled back and made a sign in the air with her hand.

"Give it to me!" Max screamed.

Jonas' mouth dropped open in shock. He noticed this seemed to happen a lot since he met Max. All of the swim team had Jonas' same expression and Chance and Derek had a look like Max was a spoiled brat.

"I'm all out of pachamama sticks, Max" Joe said slowly. "Sorry, maybe next time I'll have enough to let you throw one on the fire," he patted him on the shoulder.

Ugh, Max thought to himself. *I look like such an asshole!*

Joe continued, "Our new moon ceremony is complete and I release all spirit guides back to their realm." He looked among the teens. "The rest of the fire ceremony will take place on the full moon..."

"That's Halloween," Jonas whispered to Max.

"Did I piss myself?" Max asked Jonas thinking he just had a seizure.

"I'll let you check," Jonas sounded disgusted. "Would you be quiet you're gonna get us in more trouble."

"I just had a serious hallucination."

"You mean vision?" Jonas was talking in a hushed whisper.

"Oh, I like the sound of that better. Yeah, a vision."

Max could barely contain himself. He wanted to blurt out to Jonas that he just saw Glenda Grimm.

"The tribal council wishes for me to assume my new role as Chief and Shaman at the full moon. You are all invited," he was sure to look and Max and Jonas. "The council will be here to witness. Please, no one disappoint me," he looked at Max and Jonas again. "That's all."

The teens gathered drums up and put them in Joe's van. Others were leaving.

Jonas was about to run up to Joe and thank him for inviting them when Max grasped his arm. "I saw Glenda Grimm!"

"What?" Jonas looked around. "Here?"

"No, in my vision, but we were in England."

"Did she recognize you?"

"No, because she was in England, so that meant it was in the past. So she didn't know me. Plus, there was all that smoke from those sticks so she couldn't make me out too well I think."

"This is phenomenal," Jonas was excited. He

grabbed his phone making notes on it.

"You're documenting this?" Max looked offended.

"Of course, are you kidding me? You do realize what this means don't you?" He didn't give Max a chance to respond. "That you can astral project yourself! I could probably do my whole thesis on you before I get to college. I'll call it the *Nexus Files*."

"Really?" Max looked at him berating. "How about the *Max Files*?"

"I don't know," Jonas made a sour face. "That sounds kinda lame."

Max was suddenly seized by the neck of his shirt and yanked in front of Derek wearing a pissed look. "Why are you wearing my shirt?"

"It's not yours," Max answered defensive. "It's Chance's. He gave it to me."

Derek turned to Chance who followed behind. "Why did you give him my shirt?"

"Look," Chance sounded like it wasn't a big deal, "he needed something to wear he was practically naked."

"It's true," Jonas nodded thinking he was helping.

Derek's eyes bulged out of their sockets as he looked at Jonas and then back to Chance. He let go of Max.

"Wait," Chance rescinded. "Shit. No. That came out wrong."

"Fuck you!" Derek pointed straight at Chance and tore off into the woods.

"Derek!" Chance called after him but he didn't stop. Chance turned to Jonas and Max. "Thanks a lot guys." And he took off into the woods after Derek.

"I'm wearing Derek's shirt?" Max picked at his shirt disgusted.

"Oh, who cares," Jonas blew the whole incident off. "You said you had something to tell me earlier. That something was wrong."

"Oh, right. During the ceremony I saw an Indian

next to me."

"Native American or curry?"

"Native American, oh my gosh, if that was Joe's father then that wasn't the head I saw in the pumpkin patch in my vision."

"Holy shit!" Jonas exclaimed. "That means someone else is dead."

"Or going to be."

CHAPTER 15

The tree's branches parted like bony hands opening.

Max saw two naked bodies in the Shadow Lake Forest. Their forms were toned and their skin light, one pale and the other slightly tan.

The tan one was behind the pale boy thrusting into him. It was Chance and Derek. Chance's fingers dug into Derek's buttocks. Max now understood why Cassandra kept going on about Derek's ass. He had to admit…*It was amazing!*

Their muscles popped from their skin. They moaned with ecstasy when they suddenly looked up to see Max staring at them through the trees.

"Get up! Get up!" Lindsey pounced up and down on top of Max and the bed. "Ew," she screamed. "You peed in the bed. Mom!" She yelled jumping off the bed and running out of his room, "Max peed in the bed!"

Oh shit! Max sat up in bed and scurried to bunch up his blanket when his mom rushed in.

She saw him breathing hard and sweaty. "Did you have a seizure?"

"No, I'm fine mom!" He tried to make for the bathroom that he was thankful for having in his new room.

But she yanked the covers from him checking him and the blanket to make sure he was okay. She yelped when she realized it wasn't urine. "It's okay, honey," she tried to regain her composure.

Max moaned in frustration and embarrassment and scampered in the bathroom slamming the door shut.

"It's perfectly natural," Evelyn leaned against the door. "It's called a nocturnal emission."

"Gross, Mom! That sounds like I'm polluting the ozone! I'm not talking about this!" His voice bellowed through the door.

"Well...breakfast is almost ready. Lindsey and I went to the store early for groceries."

Max's heart puffed against his chest. "I'm scarred for life."

He stepped back into his bedroom after taking a shower. His bedroom in Burlington wasn't this nice...or this big. Judging from the looks of his room it was obvious the house was Pueblo style. *He had his own fireplace!* The fireplace coned out of the wall in smooth white stone. In front of the fireplace was a Native American style rug. Next to the window Max's mom had set up his computer desk with his video camera. Along the wall, shelves were placed, that displayed his horror masks. Max was impressed and felt a little guilty about giving his mom a hard time recently. Then he looked at his huge king size bed...and noticed the sheets were stripped off. *Ugh!* He got dressed and stood in front of the staircase working up the nerve to go to breakfast. *The walk of shame!*

Max felt immediately at home as he descended the stairs. The house was cozy. His mom was really good at that. He looked around and saw a huge fire roaring in the fireplace and Lindsey in the large living room making every effort to mess up the place. *Please don't bring it up! Please don't bring it up!* "Smells good," he said cheerfully. "I can't believe we just moved in yesterday." Max plopped down on a stool at the kitchen island.

"Thanks...all the boxes are in the garage," she confessed with a smile. She sat a plate of bacon, eggs, and pancakes in front of him and looked to see that Lindsey was still busy. "It's nothing to be ashamed about. It's what boys do."

Max slapped his hands over his face. "Please stop talking."

"Well, if you're uncomfortable talking to me about it, I can call your father."

"No," Max put his hands out to stop her. "I'm fine, okay. I'm fine."

"Well, I'm sure I know what got this all started. You were over at Jonas'. I know he has the internet," she explained. "I'm sure you two were looking at...stuff."

"Stuff?" Max had no clue what she was talking about.

"Yes...you know...titties!" She said in a harsh whisper.

"MOM!" Max screamed gagging on a pancake.

"Now, I know you're almost twelve and you're probably starting to get some...urges..."

"Mom," Max objected, "I'm eating," he said with food stuffed in his mouth.

"You do know what titties are don't you?" She asked calmly trying to be helpful and instructive if need be.

"Oh my gosh, Mom," he was mortified at the

thought of his mom talking to him about sex.

"What are titties, mommy?" Lindsey had scaled up on the other stool at the island.

Evelyn screamed in shock quickly covering her mouth. She hadn't seen her come over.

"Do I have titties?" Lindsey screamed.

"Yes!" Max screamed hysterically.

"Max!" Evelyn scolded him.

"Where are my titties, mommy?"

"Look what you did," Evelyn continued scolding Max.

"Me? You started it," Max was still laughing.

"Lindsey," Evelyn put some food down. "Mommy's going to help you eat your breakfast," she was trying to change the subject.

"You gonna breast feed her?" Max snorted.

"Max, stop it!" She slammed a bottle of pills in front of him. "Don't forget your medicine!"

After forcing breakfast down Lindsey, coloring in her books, and taking her on a search for aliens in the backyard, Evelyn was finally able to get her to stop asking about titties. She was also able to get Max to agree to getting his haircut. She reminded him that tomorrow was their first day at school and Max was all too eager to go into Ravencrest.

Cobblestone streets lined Ravencrest's downtown. Main street led up to a steepled building with a white crest and large clock set in it that told Max it must be some sort of official and important building. He had already seen a bit of downtown since Joe's was in the area. His mom was marveling at the streets and architecture and could tell she was feeling better by the minute about moving to Ravencrest. The shops were eclectic and the architecture definitely New England. It wasn't too different than Burlington. Max liked it. And Lindsey apparently did too. She couldn't stop pointing and saying, "Let's go there," by every place they passed.

Evelyn was glad to finely find a designated parking space for CUSTOMERS ONLY right in front of WICCAN'S WEAVE & OM DAY SPA because the downtown parking was surprisingly scarce. "Here we are," she declared. Max got out of the SUV cautiously not knowing what to expect. Evelyn grabbed Lindsey and shuffled them all inside enthusiastically.

"Welcome!" They were greeted immediately by an excited lady with large oval glasses and beads around her neck. Her fingers were plump and adorned in flamboyant rings that varied from geometric shapes to butterflies. They were speckled with silver and colorful stones. She wore a scarf around her head and her entire outfit looked like it was some sort of wrap or several silk scarves wrapped around her. It flowed as she moved and she wore open toe sandals. "I'm Angelica Saffron. I own this place. You're new to town aren't you," she beamed at Evelyn and the kids.

"Yes, yes we are," Evelyn smiled courteously not knowing what to think.

"I thought so. We kind of know everyone here in Ravencrest."

"Do you know Jonas?" Max thought he would test her.

Evelyn gave Max a disapproving look but Angelica was already answering. "The Lee boy? He's so smart. He's a doll. Oh sure, I know him. He just never comes in here."

"He doesn't," Max said perplexed. He thought for sure Ravencrest wasn't big enough to have more than one place to get your haircut.

"Oh no, he usually goes over to Buzz's. All the boys do. I'm so glad you're here," she bent over smiling broadly at Max. "C'mon," she grabbed his hand while handing Evelyn a menu. "This is going to be fun. I haven't had a boy in here forever."

Max looked back at his mother for help but she was enthralled with the menu of services. "Oh, he needs a haircut, he can tell you," she waved him off not looking up from the brochure. "Oh, look Lindsey, they have hot rock therapy!"

"Yes, we do," a dark skinned lady with a weaved hairstyle approached. "The stones are placed along your energy centers called 'chakras.' The stones are then used during the deep massage for exceptional stress relief."

"Exceptional stress relief is just what I need," Evelyn's eyes were filled with yearning. "Can we do it now?"

"Actually, Angelica does the hot rock therapy. My name is La' Wanda Shikita Witta. I do manicure's, pedicures, body wraps, and facials," she smiled brightly. "Would you like a manicure while you wait?"

"How about a facial? I think Lindsey would like one too."

"Mommy, what's a facial?"

"You get to put mud on your face," La' Wanda said eagerly.

"Yeah," Lindsey cheered. She loved the sound of that.

"Great, follow me." La' Wanda led them to a very tranquil room with large plush sitting chairs and loungers. There were a couple of cozy looking beds with white fluffy covers and rose petals sprinkled on them. Candles were lit on dressers that were decorated with stones and glass jars filled with colored beads and flowers. Patchouli incense and harp music flavored the air.

"There's a changing room through there," La' Wanda pointed. "Why don't you put a robe on and we'll get started."

"Do I get a robe," Lindsey pouted knowing the answer would be no.

"I insist!" La' Wanda declared. "I have some that

will fit you," she smiled at Evelyn.

Lindsey jumped up and down excitedly cheering. "Where's Max?" She asked.

"He's in good hands," La' Wanda answered her.

Max doubted his decision to get a haircut. He couldn't be in worse hands he thought. This lady didn't arouse confidence. Just the way she dressed. And she didn't even show off her own hair, probably because it was horrible. Maybe her hair was brown instead of auburn. Ugh, his mother was in his head.

"So I see your hair has grown out a little, so you're not going for an early Bieber style, so more the dyke shorter version then?" She smiled.

"Uh," Max was startled at her commentary.

"Oh no, I said the B-word," She chuckled. "Oh, I'm teasing sweetie. He's a cutie no matter how you cut him," she laughed more. "But you are going for a little shorter right?"

"Right," Max said still doubting this idea.

"Well, we'll make it cute so all the girls will like it," she smiled almost loudly.

"Uh okay," Max was having a bad feeling.

"Or boys," Angelica took his hesitation as something else. "We don't judge here at the WICCAN'S WEAVE. As long as your money is green, plastic, or electronic," she laughed at her own joke. "Here," she handed him and electronic tablet. "I have some boy's haircuts you can look at. Why don't you pick something out?"

This technology made him feel a little better, but not much. After all, it wasn't the tablet doing the haircut. As Max finally picked something he pointed to a round table in the corner with a deck of cards. "What's that?"

"Those are tarot cards." She smiled. "I do readings for people." She read the confusion in his eyes. "You know, like telling fortunes."

"Like in the movies."

"Right," she giggled. "But without the background music. Well, unless of course I put some on," she began cutting his hair.

"That's when they pull the DEATH card out?"

"In the movies," she winked. "Yes, there is a DEATH card, but it typically means a transformation or the death of one aspect of your life as well as change and transformation; like you moving to a new town. It wouldn't surprise me at all if I did a reading for you right now you would see the DEATH card," she smiled.

Max wouldn't be surprised either but it wasn't making him smile.

"You should come back and get a reading sometime."

"Oh, you look adorable," Evelyn screamed seeing Max after his haircut.

Great, it's worse than I thought! Max thought to himself getting out of the chair.

"We got mud on our face!" Lindsey yelled thoroughly delighted.

"Can I have some to go?" Max said thinking he didn't want anyone to see him. He just knew the swim team would be at Joe's and Derek would probably seize the opportunity to call him a dyke.

"Oh, he's so funny," Angelica smiled.

"C'mere, little handsome," La' Wanda seized Max's hand immediately and escorted him past a little table between two chairs facing each other. Toward the corner was a sitting massage chair. She took him to a line of big cozy looking armchairs lined against an exposed brick wall. In front of the chairs were large copper bowls. "Your mother insists you get a pedicure."

"A pet-icure?" Max had no idea what she just said or what tragedy awaited him next.

"No, but that's a great idea!" La' Wanda's mouth

dropped open. "Did you hear that Angelica? We can do doggie pedicures. But we'll call it *PET*-icures like Max said. We need to jump on that!"

"That is a fantastic idea." Angelica agreed enthusiastically.

"Aren't you a gem," La' Wanda squeezed Max's cheek. "Take your shoes and socks off. Have a seat in that big chair." She took his feet and quickly filed and trimmed his nails. "Well, your feet are darling."

Max blushed he didn't know how to respond.

"You're ticklish too aren't you?"

Max got a worried look.

"Oh, don't you worry I'm not gonna tickle you on purpose. It was just an observation."

"Oh," Max relaxed.

She poured a mixture into the copper bowl. "Now, put your feet in this bowl. I'm gonna let you soak there for a few while I get your mom started on her manicure." The mixture in the bowl was fizzing.

Can this day get any worse, Max thought. He dipped his feet in. It was warm and very soothing. It had a pleasant scent. It kind of tickled too. He decided he was actually enjoying this but he didn't want to make it too obvious. He heard his mother talking to Angelica about the parking and how crowded it was.

"Is it always like this in downtown Ravencrest?" Evelyn was making reference to the difficulty she had finding parking.

"Oh no, not usually, but a lot of people are stopping by Joe's to pay their respects."

"Oh," Evelyn acknowledged. "I understand."

"Did you know him? I know you're new in town."

"No, I don't know Joe or his father, but Max met Joe just yesterday and went to some ceremony he had for him I guess."

"Oh yes, we heard about that. Well I'm glad Max

got to go. Joe keeps those ceremonies very private. He must think a lot of Max and especially for just meeting him." Angelica said admiringly. La' Wanda started on Evelyn's manicure. "Watu—that was Joe's father—was such a great soul," Angelica continued on talking. "He was deeply spiritual. Such an inspiration," she grasped at her heart.

La' Wanda finished up with Evelyn and was now almost done with Max's pedicure. "Here at the OHM DAY SPA I finish off the pedicure with a little reflexology." She massaged his foot.

"What's reflexology? Ohhhhhh," Max's face flushed as he was hit by a wave of pleasure in his groin area as she put pressure about a third way down from his third toe.

"Whoops, sorry," La' Wanda smirked at him. "Here," she put a bottle of oil next to him. "When you find someone special, you just tell them to massage there."

"Uh," Max was embarrassed, "so what's reflexology?"

"Basically it's putting pressure to relieve blockages in your Qi, or life force. It radiates throughout your body relieving stress and pain."

Max's face said it all. He barely heard La' Wanda's explanation. He was completely relaxed and in a euphoric state.

"Is he finished?" Evelyn asked hovering over Max.

"I believe so," La' Wanda smirked. "Here," she said to Max as he finished putting on his socks and shoes. "Don't forget this," she handed him the bottle of massage oil.

"Thanks," Max said very appreciative. Then a thought wiggled into his head that slipped right out through his lips, "Are you a master of something?"

La' Wanda gave a grin, "Why, yes I am. I'm a Reiki Master."

"Ray-key?" Max tried to repeat what she just said.

She nodded and leaned in close to him. "I see your mom's in a hurry so I'll give you an explanation the next time you come in. Free session on me since you gave us a great idea on the *PET*-icure thing," she smiled. She offered a quick description, "It cleanses your aura."

Max thought that sounded great. He needed all the cleansing he could get.

CHAPTER 16

The line was around the building.

"Max," Jonas yelled and waved from the entrance of the CONUNDRUM CAFÉ.

"Wow," Max ran up to Jonas, "so everybody in town really is stopping by to pay their respects," he couldn't believe the line. "It wasn't like this yesterday."

"It's a good thing my dad dropped me off when he did," he said gratefully. "I got us a table in the comic shop," he said pulling Max through a jam of people at the door. "Cassandra's holding it right now," he added begrudgingly.

Max smiled. He liked Cassandra.

"I got us a table right in front of the double-sided fireplace," Jonas continued talking over the crowd and pushing his glasses up on his nose. Max hadn't noticed the fireplace yesterday. But a lot was going on.

"Hey cutey," Cassandra greeted Max as he plopped down in the cozy couch. The fire was burning warmly. "Look at your hair!" She said delighted.

"Oh, you like it," Max ran his hand through it, "I wasn't sure how Angelica did."

"Is that where you got your haircut?" Cassandra squealed. "I should've known. Buzz is a butcher! It's so cute! I get my hair done there."

"I can't believe you went there," Jonas said in horror. "Only girls go there," he warned.

"Whatever, it just means he's *progressive*."

"*Whatever*, you're a girl. Of course you would think that. I'm talking about the guys from school. They're going to tease you for sure! It's social suicide!"

"Says the most popular guy in school," Cassandra rolled her eyes.

"My point exactly, if anyone knows what constitutes social suicide it's me!"

"You go to BUZZ'S BUZZ CLIPS and you're still a social retard!" She looked at Max fascinated, "I think it's awesome."

"I ordered you a Monster Macchiato and a Philosopher's Scone," Jonas said to Max.

"Oh, Jonas," Max just remembered, "the picture of Joe's dad."

"Oh, right," he grabbed Max's arm, "come with me. Stay here," he commanded Cassandra.

Jonas weaved Max through the crowd bringing him to a wall with several pictures. He showed him one with Joe and his dad.

Max studied it seeing an elderly man with braids down the sides of his face. "Yeah, that's him. The one I saw last night."

"That's Joe's dad. But that's not the head you saw

in your vision?"

"No," Max said and they rejoined Cassandra.

"What's going on?" Cassandra insisted on being included.

Before Max could respond, Jonas jumped in again. "Max had a vision and thought he saw Watu's head at Yorick's farm but he had another vision last night at the new moon ceremony and saw Joe's dad but that wasn't the same face he saw at Yorick's so we think maybe there are at least two headless bodies in Ravencrest."

Max and Cassandra looked at Jonas in amazement.

Then Max turned to Cassandra in an effort to seem less like a freak, "Or it was all a hallucination."

"That's probably it," she slapped his knee. "Especially if Joe's new moon ceremony includes any...you know...peyote or some other kind of hallucinogen...I hear those Native American ceremonies are fond of that."

Max considered the pachamama sticks. *But was that before or after he saw Joe's dad?* He couldn't remember.

"Oh, and he is epileptic," Jonas added.

"Would you just stand up and tell everybody!" Max was tired of Jonas announcing it to everyone they met.

"I can," Jonas was genuinely trying to be helpful and stood.

"Sit!" Cassandra commanded pointing down.

"Here's your drink, Max, and your scone. Sorry about the wait. I've never been this busy." Joe handed Max his items and put a salad in front of Cassandra. "And your salad," Joe said remorsefully. "But to make up for the wait and since you're here in front of the fire," he sat a large round plate down with graham crackers on a pool of chocolate. On the crackers were large toasted marshmallows drizzled with more chocolate. "I brought you Sasquatch Smores!"

"Yes," Jonas' eyes came alive. "Tell Max," Jonas demanded as he grabbed one of the Smores.

"Right," Joe agreed. "They're not called Sasquatch Smores just because they're colossal, but also because it's said to be Bigfoot's favorite delicacy. Oh yes, it's true," he read doubt in Max's face. "Many a weary camper has had an unexpected and frightful encounter with Bigfoot while making Smores by the campfire!" Joe laughed ominously. Then he looked at Cassandra, "And you better eat one missy! I don't want to hear any of this diet stuff! There are some skewers and extra marshmallows, chocolate and crackers if you want to toast some more. Chomp," he looked at Max remembering the sandwich he ordered yesterday. "Champ," he looked at Jonas. They both nodded eagerly, "Great, coming up!"

"So Max," Cassandra warned, "don't buy into all this Ravencrest mumbo-jumbo or more importantly what the Lord of the Dweebs over here is trying to convince you of."

"Hello," Jonas retaliated. "This is Ravencrest. What town *do you* live in? The paranormal is the norm around here."

"Oh, you mean like chicken-bone-licking and tarot cards and runes?"

"It's not chicken-bone-licking! What's wrong with you?"

"Uh, I have a life."

"Stalking is not a life."

She shot Jonas the finger. He stuck his tongue out at her.

Cassandra had already scarfed down her salad. "He knows I can't eat that," she pointed enviously at the Smores.

"Sure you can," Jonas insisted. "We're kids. We're supposed to eat like this while we can enjoy it. My dad tells me that all the time."

"I'm not a kid," she watched Max devour the Sasquatch Smore. "I'm a teenager. And the chocolate will not only make me fat but break out in zits," she said disgusted. "I need to go to the restroom," she got up and left.

Jonas watched her walk away from their cozy setting then looked at Max and pointed his finger down his throat.

"What?"

"She's probably gonna go throw up that salad she just ate."

"On purpose; you're kidding right?"

Jonas shook his head *NO* gravely.

"Why would someone do that?" Max asked trying not to think about it as he grabbed another Smore.

"She has image issues."

After a few more Smores, Cassandra came back and joined them.

"Sasquatch Smores! No Way!" Chance was standing by Max.

Max's insides jumped.

"Have one!" Cassandra offered.

Jonas looked insulted.

"No, but thanks," Chance grabbed his abs, "I have a swim meet this Saturday."

"Oh, and Derek will be there?" Cassandra salivated.

"Yeah."

"Yeah, I can't have one either." Cassandra sounded like she was getting ready for prom.

Chance tried to ignore that and looked at Max. "Dude, you hair is super cute," Chance ran his hand over his own head enviously. "No way Buzz did that. Where did you go?"

"WICCAN'S WEAVE," Jonas vomited the

information immediately.

Cassandra gave Jonas a *sell-out* look. She thought it was cool that Max went there but she knew most guys wouldn't understand and even though she joked how progressive Max was being she wasn't about to readily divulge that information as to spare Max any humiliation. She couldn't believe Jonas just did that to his friend.

Max looked at Jonas in disbelief as well.

"Oh, right on," Chance smiled not catching on that there was any tension. "Angelica did that right?"

"Yeah," Max admitted sheepishly.

"She's awesome. She made herself available to me and my brother when my mom passed away from breast cancer. Angelica is a breast cancer survivor herself. But it came back. She's back on chemotherapy I hear."

"That make people's hair fall out right?" Cassandra asked.

"Yeah," Chance answered.

"That has to be rough for her," Cassandra said. "Being in the hair business ignorant people probably make stupid jokes about her being a bad hair stylist."

Max realized that's why she was wearing the wrap around her head. He felt like an asshole yet again!

"Well, I feel bad for never going over to get my hair done after all she did for me," Chance said. "But now I think I'll go there."

"Go where?" Derek walked up looking like he just got sick when he saw Max.

"Max got his hair done at Angelica's. Doesn't it look good?"

Derek laughed berating. "Only girls go there!"

"Then you know it!" Max opposed.

Derek shifted his weight to lunge at Max but Chance stopped him and held his hand up to prevent Max from getting up just in case, "Give it a rest you two! Can't you just shake hands and move on?"

"You shake his hand!" Derek gave Max a disgusted look. "I got our drinks to go, it's too crowded. You coming?" He walked away looking at Chance as if to say *you better*!

"So you two make up in the woods last night?" Jonas asked.

"Yeah…what? What do you know?" Chance looked terrified for a moment.

Jonas sat back defensively, "You two tore off into the woods after the ceremony that's all."

"Yeah…right," he seemed calmer, "none of your business. I'll see you guys later," he waved to Max and Cassandra.

"Geez, psycho much?" Jonas muttered when he left.

"Well, that was pretty personal," Cassandra lectured him. "Just like Max's epilepsy."

Max realized her voice was really angry. Not like before when Jonas and her had a more playful exchange. This was more serious.

"And just like you tried to embarrass him in front of Chance about where he got his haircut," she continued. "You knew he would be ridiculed—"

"I was just trying to prove a point," Jonas didn't seem to get her serious tone.

"What, that you're stupid?"

"I didn't bring up you barfing up everything you eat in front of him."

"Screw you, you little shit-turd."

"That's redundant."

"You're retarded. You're a social retard! Did it ever occur to you that's why you don't have any friends? The only friend you have here you tried to alienate on his second day in town. Good going you redundant shit-turd!" She flipped the empty plate of Sasquatch Smores off the table and into his lap. "I didn't want any anyway!" She stomped out of the entrance to the comic shop.

Jonas and Max didn't say anything for a little while and just looked at each other in bewilderment. Joe brought them their sandwiches and they began to eat. Jonas finally spoke. "I hope she paid for her salad."

Max looked at Jonas in shock. "If she didn't I think I have enough money."

"No, I'll get it," Jonas said heavily. He took his glasses off and started cleaning them. "You know, I wasn't trying to embarrass you in front of Chance."

"I know," Max initially didn't think anything of it. But after Cassandra had said it, he had to wonder. "So about everything I told you...you don't think I'm crazy?"

"Not at all, I think you're clairvoyant. I just never met anyone that had visions and interactions like you. I haven't even talked much to the Sisters Grimm until I met you. I think you're the real thing!"

"Speaking of the sisters...when I was talking to Glenda Grimm in my vision at the ceremony last night she had me breathe into a bottle—"

"Why?"

Max shook his head, "She thought I was Guardian of the Nexus. Do you know who or what that is?"

"No, but I wonder if it's something like Cerberus: the three-headed dog that's supposed to guard the gates to Hades."

"Uh, well that sounds scary. Anyway, the bottle she had was the Elixir of Life and I think that will free Jack."

"Why do you feel so compelled to help Jack? You don't even know him."

"Because his soul is trapped, Jonas, he's in torment. I can feel it. I saw it in his eyes. I can't leave him there like that. And I suspect there are others that are just like him. It's the right thing to do. I *need* to do the right thing."

Max told Jonas how Watu was unable to speak and that it seemed painful when he tried. Jonas pointed out that he had been beheaded, but Max countered that Jack was beheaded too and he had no problem talking to him. Jonas offered that perhaps it was because Max was in the Nexus at the time.

"So what's the Elixir of Life?" Jonas asked through his food.

"I was gonna ask you!"

"Hmmmm," Jonas thought. "I don't know, but I think I might know somebody that will."

CHAPTER 17

"Water!"

A tall thin woman said from behind the counter with a strong Ukraine accent. Her lips were raging red and her skin was milk white. Her bobbed-hair was jet black that matched her outfit. "You don't drink water you die! Water is the elixir of life. Do they not teach you this in school?"

Max gave Jonas a discouraged look. Jonas brought him to UVA URSA'S APOTHECARY assured she would know the answer. There were shelves lined with bottles, herbs, lotions and soaps. The floors were a dark cherry wood. Incense was burning making a very pleasant atmosphere. This was obviously Uva Ursa herself. "Uh, well I was hoping for something more…dramatic."

"Such as?" She asked in a tone to say she was not a mind-reader.

Max looked at Jonas again for help but Jonas' shrug told him he wasn't going to get any, "something to free a trapped soul."

"Ah yes," she popped her finger out like an idea just came to her. "I get this all the time at Halloween. You want to talk to the dead, yes?"

"Sort of," Max thought he would probably have to see Jack again and wasn't entirely sure how to do that.

"What else?"

"Set them free."

"You need to banish a spirit?"

"Oh no, that's already done."

"An exorcism then?"

"Uh," Max looked at Jonas and this time he shook his head. "No."

She kicked her weight to the side that told Max she was getting impatient...well...more impatient. She seemed impatient naturally.

"You have a loved one that has passed and you are having trouble moving on?

"What?" Max sounded unprepared.

Jonas leaned in and said, "That's probably the closest we're going to find. I still think Jack just needs to move on maybe this will help."

"Sure," Max surrendered to Uva. "That sounds fine."

"And for talking to the dead?" She double-checked.

"Yes."

She turned and went to the shelves behind her and throughout her shop.

Max dug for money in his pockets his eyes following Uva with doubt. "We may just have to go back to see the Sisters Grimm," he said to Jonas. "I know they have the Elixir of Life."

"Are you crazy?" His voice raised and he immediately brought it down seeing that there were only a few customers in the shop and they were turning their attention to him. "You wanna go back there when we don't even know if you've been poisoned. Hey what happened with that anyway? Weren't we supposed to do a spell?"

"When have you seen someone *get better* when they've been poisoned? I don't have a scar." Max just knew he wasn't poisoned.

"Well, I'm in no hurry to go and see old crazy bird-eyed lady!" Jonas pushed his glasses up on his nose. "I really think you need to just convince Jack to move on. That's the answer."

"But Glenda thought it was a spell that is keeping him bound. Oh!" Max shouted to Uva, "How about something for spell-breaking too!"

She waved in acknowledgement while she was plucking ingredients from jars.

"But," Jonas hissed through his teeth, "Glenda thought you were the Guardian of the Nexus! That's why she thought Jack had to be bound by a spell because *you*," he poked his finger at his chest, "*a.k.a* 'The Guardian of the Nexus' couldn't allow Jack access through Yggdrasil!"

Max thought about that for a moment. Jonas was right. He looked at Uva and she looked hurried and bothered gathering items. He wasn't about to tell her to forget his spell-breaking request. "I'll get it just in case."

Jonas looked at Uva and got Max's meaning. "I'm not talking about the spell-breaking. That could actually come in handy some other time. I'm talking about us not going to see the sisters again!"

"Here you go!" Uva slammed several items down on the counter in front of the boys causing them to jump. "Ah coach," Uva smiled ostensibly looking past the boys. "I have your special concoction, yes."

"Great," coach said without enthusiasm as he zoomed in from the front door to the counter. He looked at the boys for only a split second not paying much attention to them.

Max noticed him from the night before at the fire ceremony. He had muscles like Chance.

"Hi coach," Jonas smiled at him.

The coach glanced down at Jonas for a moment. "Do I know you?"

"Yeah, it's me, Jonas Lee."

The coach just blinked at him.

Jonas' cheerfulness left his voice. "I'm in your lockers a lot."

"Right. When are you gonna stand up to those boys?"

"Well, most of them are on your swim team," Jonas didn't think he'd appreciate any retaliation against his team.

"So?"

Jonas didn't know what to say.

"Here it is," Uva handed the coach a plain white paper bag. "You have this made a lot. I am curious what you use it for." Uva gave a prying smile.

"I bet," the coach said indicating he wasn't going to answer. Without as so much as an expression he handed her money and left.

Uva watched the coach leave with an impressed look in her eye. Then she gave an indifferent shrug. "Okay boys, before you I have several incenses. This first one is Angelica—"

"Oh, I met her today. She cut my hair." Max said excited.

"How nice," she said not the least bit excited. "I am in coven with those two pleasant ladies. They are most efficient."

"You're a witch?" Jonas wasn't aware of that.

Uva waved her hands up and down her body at her appearance. "Does this really surprise you?" She didn't allow a response. "Now, where was I? Oh yes, Angelica. This will be most conducive to breaking a spell. You can also use to dissipate unwanted spirits and is good for healing and can bring visions."

Max and Jonas looked at each other excited as though gold was just placed in front of them.

"I think this next one will be much to your liking. It is perfect for the season...wormwood. It is ideal for speaking to the dead. It is best if you use in the cemetery of the deceased you choose to speak to, but not necessary...especially if you do this Halloween night. Doing this at midnight on October 31st just before the clock turns November will yield the best results. Remember that Halloween is All Hallows Eve: the Eve of Samhain. And November 1st is the Day of Samhain. This is very important. Most people make this error when they try spells or to talk to the dead at this time. It is essential you do this just before midnight when it goes from October 31st to November 1st."

"That's when I was born," Max exclaimed.

"You're birthday is Halloween?" Jonas asked dazzled.

"11:59 right before midnight." Max gleamed. He actually thought it was awesome.

"You know that?" Jonas sounded impressed. Most people he talked to didn't know their birth time unless they were into astrology and Max didn't seem the type.

"Yeah, my dad made a big deal about it for years," Max smiled. "My dad's the best. I'd be with him now if it weren't for my mom," his eyes sank. He just knew she was the one keeping the marriage from working and refused to let his dad have custody of him.

"That is most amazing," Uva actually sounded genuinely enthused as she commented on Max's birthday.

"It is said that those born on Hallows' Eve have the gift of second sight." Again she didn't give time for more commentary. "And this last one is Cypress." She placed a sprig down and a powder. "Burn this as an incense to help you get over a death and you can place the sprig in a grave to help the dead move on."

Max picked up the sprig and sniffed it. "I know that smell!" He leaned away from the counter to Jonas. "That was a scent I caught in the morgue at the hospital."

Jonas' face looked muddled. "How could you tell? All I smelled was chemicals for the bodies," his eyes almost popped through his glasses as he was annoyed that Max took him in there to begin with.

"But I smelled something else too." He turned back to Uva. He remembered the name that sounded in his head. "Do you have Calamus?" He asked unsure if he said it right or if it was even real.

"Oh no," she shook her head. "That is poisonous."

"What about Belladonna or Deadly Nightshade?" Max asked noting so many plants and herbs in containers of all kinds. He heard of them in a movie once and thought he'd just ask for fun.

"They are the same thing. Some call it Belladonna and some call it Deadly Nightshade. And it is poisonous. So I do not have. UVA URSA'S APOTHECARY does not carry anything poisonous," she said rather loudly as if making a proclamation of her innocence to the few patrons mulling around.

"Do you just have incenses? Do you have any potions?" Max was thinking of something more comparable to the Elixir of Life to help Jack.

"Oh yes, I have many concoctions."

"No potions?"

"Yes...concoctions and potions."

"What's the difference?"

"None. Some say potions, some say concoction,

some say draught. It is all the same. Yes, I have very nice sleep concoction made with some passion flower, valerian, and a hint of lemon. You will like very much."

"Well, do you have a potion that will help the dead move on?"

"Oh no, this would do you no good. They would have to drink it. They can't do this. They are dead."

Max turned back to Jonas. "She's right! How would I even bring it into the Nexus?" He looked at Uva again, "But then how would incense help?"

"I get your meaning," she waved her finger in the air. "Incense travels easily into the spirit realm. It is not solid."

"Oh," that sounded good enough for Max but he was disappointed he couldn't use an elixir of some sort. "We're still gonna have to see the sisters," he looked at Jonas conclusively.

"The Sisters Grimm?" Uva asked overhearing Max.

"Yeah," Jonas answered. "I bet they come in here a lot."

"Pshaw," she spat. "They do not favor me. They think me and my coven of witches are...how do you say...inferior. You see boys, there all kinds of witches and ways to approach the craft. Some like to dance around fires, or walk in nature, or have meetings in their home and cook. They call us *feel-good* witches. I think they mean it as not so complimentary. But...I actually like the sound of it," she smiled a little at them. "But I won't tell. It is all fine. But those Sisters Grimm seem to believe we don't have enough...umph," she pumped her fist in the air. "They don't think we are real. It's okay. We are not here to please them."

"Okay," Max jumped in. "I'll take all this," his eyes wandered along her shelves of herbs as he pulled money out of his pockets. "What's that?" He pointed to a bottle with a cork in it. A word on the label had caught his attention.

"Ah, this is powdered Skullcap."

The boy's mouth's dropped open as they looked at each other. "What's it for?" Max asked feverishly.

"Many things; you can treat allergies or headaches. Some use it for reducing symptoms of Diabetes or Hypertension…"

"What about epilepsy?" Jonas blurted.

"Oh yes, there are those that believe it is most effective for reducing…how do you call it…seizures."

Jonas' mouth was agape. "The sisters were trying to help you." He couldn't believe it.

"Would you like to purchase?" Uva seemed aloof of their enthusiasm.

"No thanks, just this." Max's voice dropped to Jonas. "We have to see them."

Jonas felt sick to his stomach. "Now, I'm actually looking forward to school tomorrow."

CHAPTER 18

Ravencrest Academy Founded 1777.

Max noticed Ravencrest Academy looked like a New England college campus. The buildings were large with red brick and large pane windows. The lawns were trim with perfect hedge work like Mr. Lee's yard. Trees stood guard like centurions. Numerous vehicles were dropping off their kids as others were parking in a lot along one of the sides of the campus. Max figured Chance probably parked over there somewhere.

"I'm taking Lindsey to class. Max, you're supposed to meet with your counselor first."

"I'll take him," Jonas offered as he had been waiting for Max to arrive.

"Oh thanks, you're such doll," Evelyn grabbed

Lindsey's hand and walked her up to the entrance.

Lindsey waved enthusiastic to Max, "bye!"

Max waved back to his little sister.

"C'mon," Jonas motioned Max to follow him. He led Max in through the main doors. "So I think we should plot our Halloween costumes."

"Halloween costumes? Aren't we a little old for trick-or-treating?"

"No," Jonas spewed quickly. "Yes," he retracted it just as fast so Max wouldn't think he was a child. "But there's other things to do besides that. There's the Ravencrest Halloween Bazaar. Everybody in town pretty much dresses up."

Jonas and Max arrived at the entrance of the Administrative offices when a group of teens brushed by him quickly.

Someone slammed hard against Max's arm. "Where's my shirt you little bitch? And stay the fuck away from Chance." Derek had hate in his eyes.

Max almost fell over from Derek's body-shove. Max took his backpack off, still holding it, and whipped Derek's shirt out. "You want it?" Max's voice almost lit on fire. "I'll give it to you!" Max was overcome with so much anger he charged Derek.

"Watch your balls!" Billy warned Derek.

"Oh, I'm ready," Derek said audaciously. Derek was going to savor his revenge. As Max got closer running at full speed Derek simply brought his leg back and went in a full kick to nail Max right in his groin.

Just before Derek's foot connected, Max pounced up slamming his backpack down on Derek's shin blocking his kick. The he immediately shoved the shirt up like a clothesline around Derek's neck and yanked him down to the ground with his force and weight. Derek and Max hit with a thud as Max strangled Derek. Derek managed to shove him away and Max immediately grabbed one of his huge textbooks that fell out of his backpack and whacked Derek square in the face punching his fist into the book. Blood sprayed across the floor.

Max was yanked off Derek by the coach.

Derek was screaming in pain. "My nose! You broke my fucking nose!"

Jonas was standing there in shock.

Max was smiling until he saw Chance standing in the distance with the same look of horror that Jonas had.

"You! Get your ass in that office!" Coach yelled at Max. "And you," he pointed to Derek. "Get your ass to the nurse. Billy, help him." He turned back to Max. "Inside now," he opened the door to where Max was supposed to be going to meet his counselor. Instead, Max was meeting with the principal.

CHAPTER 19

Flashing clouds spilled out along the night sky flicking lightning bolts and reverberating thunder.

Howling winds and rain engulfed the town. Doctor John Lambe descended the stairs where he lived and made his way to the front door of his shop. The shop was dimly lit with candles as he was expecting company. He bundled up his cloak and was thankful for his wool cap on this cold wet night. A banging at his door had stirred him from packing. As he opened the front door he was greeted by a flash of lightning and a shimmering sword. He stumbled back startled.

"Doctor Lambe, sir," a man in a helmet and leather armor said. "We have been sent to escort you," he spoke in a French accent.

The startled doctor opened the door more to see two other men with drawn swords.

"Abbot Conleth sent us. Please, sir, you must let us in," he continued as he stepped into the dwelling. He turned to the third man and said, "Stay out here and guard the front door." He looked back to the doctor, "Is there another entrance?"

Doctor Lambe shook his head.

The second man was wearing a horned helmet. He was tall and brawny with a large beard and moved about the flasks, bottles, spices and herbs of the apothecary searching the rest of the ground floor. "We're with the town guard," the first man answered. "My name is Lamorak," he was in his late twenties and had a large bushy mustache. "That's Kay," he pointed to the brawny man who was a little older and had an air of an experienced fighter. "Dagonet is outside. Abbot Conleth insisted that your life is in danger this evening and we have strict orders to protect you and escort you to the monastery."

"Aye, I know," the physician was an aged man. He and Conleth had gone through the priesthood together and spent decades in the monastery. During that time Lambe had focused most of his energy and studies to curing and caring for the sick. The governing belief of the Roman Catholic Church had been sickness was a manifestation of a person's sins. To intervene was to interfere with God's will so the only cure to administer was to pray for the person's sins. To administer herbal remedies or potions was viewed as witchcraft. Lambe felt all healing comes from God including medicine and was not an intrusion on God's will. Abbot Conleth permitted Lambe to administer his treatments to the sick. Conleth informed Rome of what was transpiring. The powers in Rome decided to influence the king in this region only to permit the clergy to practice medicine as opposed to the folk medicine that was being rendered by townspeople.

He and Conleth had a disagreement concerning the role of clergy practicing medicine. Lambe felt in order for him to make any real progress in the field of medicine he would have to explore it away from the Church and its influence and oversight. Lambe expressed to Conleth he needed to leave the priesthood and operate outside the monastery in the town. Conleth was concerned for both of them if he allowed it. Conleth was angered. He asserted that the Church had bent many of its own rules to accommodate Lambe and that he seemed ungrateful. Conleth also suspected some in Rome might retaliate against one or both of them. But Conleth held a deep respect for Lambe as well as a long friendship and he knew Lambe would leave the priesthood and continue to practice medicine with or without the Church's approval so Conleth worked diligently with the papacy to allow this transition.

It was finally agreed that Lambe could operate outside the monastery and not as a priest only if he would integrate prayers and elements of the Catholic faith into his treatments in place of pagan incantations. He agreed. However, he long suspected it would be a matter of time before the Church would retaliate and withdraw its approval of his practice.

"Who wants me dead?" He walked over to a locked cabinet pulling a key from his cloak. Before leaving the priesthood and setting up his practice he had made acquaintance with the head of the local druids and the king's trusted adviser Ambrosius. He and Ambrosius had been trying to bridge a noticeable gap between the Church and pagan beliefs. Lambe had thought of himself as the middle-man between the Church and the druids. He and Ambrosius had an amicable relationship at first until Ambrosius found out about the deal he had made with the Church on integrating Catholic prayers and beliefs into his treatments. Ambrosius was furious. Things had been tense between the two. Was Ambrosius the one that wanted him dead? The messenger took the elixir for Ambrosius. But perhaps he discovered it was a substitute. Perhaps he simply did not need him anymore as Conleth warned. Lambe unlocked the double-doors to the cabinet. He opened one of the doors revealing several books. He began pulling them out. He was going to take these with him to the monastery. He couldn't leave them. It was part of the deal. He was about to open the other side of the double-doors and hesitated. Maybe the Church was going to have him killed for leaving the priesthood and going against their laws. Maybe the Church sent these men to kill him. Lamorak was French. That did seem suspicious. And he said one of their comrades was named Dagonet. *Wasn't that French as well?* Lambe didn't open the other door to the cabinet and turned back to Lamorak. Thunder shook the shutters.

Lamorak noted the doctor's hesitation. "Abbot Conleth said you might doubt our presence. He said to give you this," he outstretched his hand.

Lambe held his hand out palm up. Lamorak dropped a ring into his palm. The ring had a runic "R" on it. Lambe understood. He was about to open up the rest of the cabinet when he was interrupted by a venomous howl. It was like nothing he had ever heard. "That didn't sound like the wind," he whirled around to Lamorak. His hands were trembling.

"It came from outside," Lamorak shouted charging the door with his sword ready. He flung open the front door and saw Dagonet standing there on the covered entry in disbelief staring toward the muddy road. Lamorak followed Dagonet's eyes out the front of the apothecary to see a flaming steed hissing from the rain drops pelting it. Its eyes were red coals smoldering in the night.

"Where's the rider?" Lamorak yelled over a clap of thunder. Lambe and Kay had moved up behind Lamorak and peered over his shoulder to see what the men were marveling at.

"I don't know," Dagonet answered Lamorak with a French accent. "I never saw him. It just appeared out of the night."

"How could it just appear out of the night? It's on fire!"

Dagonet turned around in a flare of lightning, "Perchance the same way the rain isn't putting it out!"

"Stay here!" Lamorak slammed the front door shut and turned to the doctor. "We need to go upstairs now!" He wasn't going to take any chances at being ambushed.

"Wait," the doctor rushed to a table of herbs. "That thing out there looks like something Ambrosius would conjure," he fumbled about several jars looking for salt.

"You've seen this thing before," Lamorak grasped the doctor's wrist.

"Aye...nay. Let me go you damned fool, I'm trying to save us," he struggled against the young man's grasp.

"What is that thing out there?" Lamorak demanded letting go of the physician.

"I don't know precisely," Lambe continued looking through jars. "I've seen...things. I don't know. It just looks like something Ambrosius would be capable of conjuring." Now, he was certain Ambrosius sent this thing to kill him and not these men.

"I know what it is," Kay stepped forward.

"What?" Lamorak insisted.

"It is an Arabian horse."

Lambe and Lamorak looked at each other in a moment of silent disbelief. "I don't think so," Lambe almost laughed but was trembling too much.

"Yea, I've been to their world across the Dead Sea. The people there boast and tell tales of magnificent horses that are powerful and fast. They say they are gifts from the Jinn."

"Jinn?" asked Lamorak.

"Found it," Lambe declared checking the last jar. "It's always the last place you look." He ran over to the door and poured a thick line of salt along the floor in front of it. Thunder shook the side of the abode. Then all three men realized it wasn't thunder. Something was outside the shop and it sounded as though it was moving up the wall.

Dagonet was studying the horse intently from the covered entry. It hadn't made any threatening movements. Even as bizarre as it had looked, the thing that caught his attention was a saddlebag. He caught glimpses of it in the flashes of lightning and the light burning from the horse itself. The saddlebag appeared stuffed. He wondered what this elusive rider might be carrying. He inched out into the rain and onto the muddy road. The steed didn't seem to take much notice of him. Dagonet kept his hand on the hilt of his sword ready, just in case, and squashed through the mud a little closer.

Inside, the men heard the splintering and snapping of wood from the level above. Lambe ran for the stairs. He was going to pour more salt when Lamorak caught him by the arm and spun him around. "Get outside, now!" Lamorak pushed the doctor toward the door knocking him down and spilling the salt across the floor.

"Oh, this is harrowing," the doctor whimpered; his hands still trembling. He rushed to his knees scooping salt and hobbled over to the table. There was a long thin flask with a rounded base that he dropped the salt into.

Lamorak and Kay reached the foot of the stairs. Kay ascended cautiously then stopped as all the candles in the shop whooshed out simultaneously. There was a green hue emanating from the top of the staircase. The physician rushed to his feet and darted over to another table along a wall. In the light emanating from the top of the stairs he grasped at a pitcher of water; looking up over his shoulder to the balustrade. Then, all the men in the apothecary saw the Knightmare standing at the top of the stairs.

The Knightmare looked down to the physician below and snatched the skull adorned battle axe from its side. The doctor rushed back to the first table just as the Knightmare hurled the axe down below. The death axe spun through the air like a circular saw just missing the doctor as he moved and jammed deep into the wall. He grasped the flask of salt and dumped water into it as his entire body quivered in fear. "A cork!" He screamed. "I need a bloody cork!" He was hunched over the table and flipping his hands about trying to search for one. He heard the Knightmare draw its sword. He gave up looking. He didn't have time. He stood up seeing the Knightmare start to descend the staircase toward Kay. The physician hurled the flask up at the Knightmare. Water sprayed about as the flask struck the Knightmare directly; shattering and spilling only a little water and salt onto it. Its green glow flickered in and out for just a moment, and then it began back down the stairs. The doctor yelped and bolted out the front door.

Dagonet was contemplating taking the saddlebag off the fiery steed when he was startled by the door to the apothecary smashing open. He spun around drawing his sword. The horse jerked its head toward Dagonet and opened its mouth. A jet of liquid flame shot out and onto the man sticking to his entire body. Metal, leather, and flesh were instantly melted. He only had time to let out a brief horrific scream before being completely reduced to a black sludge.

John Lambe witnessed Dagonet's horrific death. His mouth froze open in a silent scream as he stumbled back through the door to the apothecary tripping on his cloak and falling backwards inside the shop.

Kay charged up the stairs at the Knightmare sweeping his mace in an uppercut fashion striking the glowing knight. Kay was intent on taking off the

Knightmare's head and that's exactly what happened. The Knightmare's helmet flew over the staircase bouncing off the wall and landing on top of the physician below. Kay glanced down to see the doctor yelp and toss the helmet off. It was difficult to see down there in the shadows, but the helmet didn't appear to be leaking blood or guts. Kay looked back to the ghostly knight to see it still standing erect. Its brilliant glow had not faded and in the place where its head should be was an empty space. There was no flesh, blood, or skull. Indeed, the Knightmare was headless. But that didn't stop it. It stabbed the brawny guard in the center of the chest with its silver sword searing through him. Kay let out a gurgling scream as smoke rose from his front and back. Kay knew he was going to die. After the countless battles he had fought and prevailed it took this unearthly entity to take him down. It would be a good death, but he was still concerned for his longtime companion Lamorak. He had no intention of going easy. He used the last of his energy grabbing the Knightmare and pulling it through the balusters of the staircase to the shop floor below.

Kay and the Knightmare smashed on the floor between the front door and the doctor. Lamorak scrambled over and pulled the doctor up to his feet and back to the stairs. Kay lifted his head slightly—the ground floor dimly lit by the Knightmare's glow—and saw in the shadows of the far corner of the shop a tall figure looming with a broad-brimmed hat and a flowing cloak. "The Jinn," Kay declared softly with his last breath and died.

Lamorak was pushing the physician up the stairs. Doctor Lambe struggled as he kept tripping over his cloak. The Knightmare stood up quickly and in one continuous motion yanked its death axe out of the wall and up at the physician. The axe shrilled—sawing through the air quickly—and before Lamorak could react it flipped the doctor's head off his body and over Lamorak and down the stair case. The doctor's body fell back onto Lamorak sending him and the decapitated corpse tumbling down the stair case after the head. The headless Knightmare turned to the front door; the line of salt still across it. It held its palm out to retrieve its helmet—nothing happened. The Knightmare turned and walked to the staircase. Lamorak was pinned down by the corpse at the foot of the stairs and was struggling to get free. "You bastard!" He shouted. "I'll kill you!" Lamorak tried to get out from below the corpse. The Knightmare ignored Lamorak's cursing—bent down retrieving the physician's head—and stepped over Lamorak and the corpse and ascended the stairs.

A burst of lightning reflected the pouring rain outside and lit the open door to the apothecary. A man holding a lantern stepped inside cautiously. Another man came up behind him and pulled him back a little. "Father, what are you doing? Let me go first," Percy said with a stern whisper. His sword was drawn. "The demon's horse is outside. He's probably still in here." Thunder followed rattling Percy's nerves. "Stay out here," he instructed Father Gregory.

"After what we just saw, I'll take my chances inside." The priest answered firmly. He and Percy had made their way into town on horseback and quickly met up with three men-at-arms that were brave enough to accompany them after witnessing the Knightmare blaze through the main gate. As they were following the trail of burning hoof prints they witnessed Dagonet's gruesome death by the Knightmare's fiery steed. They secured their horses far enough away so they wouldn't be spooked by the supernatural forces and approached the apothecary warily; certain not to get too close to the steed while keeping an eye out for the Knightmare.

"Very well," Percy said. "But give me the lantern." He stepped inside the dark dwelling slowly and heard something by the staircase. He shifted quickly pointing his sword in that direction. Father Gregory jumped as the three men-at-arms came up behind him. Percy jumped at the priest's reaction then shook his head in annoyance.

"Who goes there?" Lamorak called certain it couldn't be the Knightmare as there was no green glow.

"We're here to help," Percy exclaimed crossing quickly over to Lamorak.

"It's too late. Doctor Lambe is dead. I'm pinned down."

Father Gregory was busy relighting candles.

"Was it a glowing knight?" Percy asked Lamorak as the other men came to assist moving the body off him.

"Yea, he's still here!"

Percy stood up immediately his sword ready.

"He's outside by now," Lamorak said crawling out from beneath the doctor's body as the other men lifted it up.

"We just came from outside." Percy refuted.

"He went up and most likely out the window." Lamorak ran to the front door of the apothecary. All of the men save the priest followed. Sure enough, they saw the Knightmare mounting its ominous beast and gallop down the muddy road in the rainstorm.

"We must follow," one of the men-at-arms barked. He was tall. He was even taller than Kay. He was also very muscular and handsome.

"Agreed," Percy answered. "Meet me outside I must check something." The men-at-arms ran outside to get the horses. Lamorak stayed and followed Percy. Percy raced to the body of the physician. "I do not expect you to follow us," Percy said to Lamorak knowing he almost lost his life this night.

"Oh, but I must. I must avenge the death of my companion, Kay," it suddenly hit him that he would never share his boisterous company again. He felt as though his insides were weighted down. He looked to Kay's lifeless body and his horned helmet that lay beside him. Many thought that Kay was cruel and crass. However, Lamorak knew him more as a loyal friend and dedicated soldier. Kay was not French; they met on one of his many travels and struck up a friendship after Kay saved his life. They were inseparable ever since…until now. "He deserves a pyre. He was like a brother to me."

"I understand," Percy looked at Lamorak consolingly. "I have lost all my fellow knights. They were like brothers to me as well. They too deserve pyres."

"There will be much fire this evening I am afraid," Lamorak spoke grievously.

"We will come back later and tend to those rites. For now, time is precious and others may die. Look!" Percy turned to Father Gregory. "He has the same ring as the king."

"Abbot Conleth had a ring like that as well. He had us deliver it to the doctor to prove our sincerity," Lamorak stated.

"So Abbot Conleth is no longer in possession of his ring," Father Gregory was thinking out loud.

"That's good," Percy said. "It might save his life."

"The doctor struck that green knight with something. It was a mixture of salt," Lamorak explained hoping it could be helpful to Percy. "It seemed to affect it for just a moment."

"Do you know of something else that might assist us?" Percy asked.

"Alas, I do not. The doctor didn't have any time to explain his actions or reasoning."

Percy had a dumbfounded look on his face and glanced over his shoulder. "What are you doing?" Percy noticed the priest had collected the physician's books.

"The good doctor has compiled many years of his dedication and research to curing and aiding the sick. We cannot let his hard work go in vain. The Church must continue his work and make good use of his accumulated knowledge."

Percy nodded in agreement as Father Gregory packed the last of the books in a sack. Percy made his way to the door. "We are going now." He turned to Lamorak, "I gather you are going with us?"

"Indeed," Lamorak said vehemently.

Father Gregory hurried ahead outside to the men-at-arms who had gathered the horses. Lamorak was outside under the covered entrance when Percy halted at the door. "What do we do about this?" Lamorak pointed to the Knightmare's helmet at their feet.

Percy studied it curiously. He smelled Chrysanthemum and Sage inside the apothecary. His mother used to call it Mugwort. She used it as a spice in meat to ward off maggots. It was as if someone had nudged his brain and he turned back to look inside the apothecary one last time. In a flash of lightning he jumped at the sight of a small boy. He was pointing at a cabinet in the corner and as quickly as the lightning flickered in the gloomy apothecary the image of the boy disappeared. "Jack!" He thought he recognized the boy. He didn't want to believe it earlier, but now how could he deny it. The body of the beheaded boy in the castle belonged to the protégé of Ambrosius. He went to the cabinet and opened the side that was closed. There was a jug and a sack. Percy grabbed the sack and rushed back out with it.

"Be careful," Lamorak suspected what Percy was up to.

Percy threw the sack over the helmet and snatched it up.

As they mounted their horses Lamorak looked about. "Where is Dagonet?"

There was silence among the men.

Percy spoke up, "As we approached we saw the demon horse breathe fire. He was reduced to ash."

There was another silence among the men and this time Lamorak spoke. "It was an honorable death." His horse swashed back and forth in the mud. "I am Lamorak. I thought you should know my name for I am certain I will not live through this night."

"I hope that is not true. I have lost enough brothers this foul night. I am Percy. That is Father Gregory and these other bold men are Bedivere," he said pointing to the handsome muscular man, "Gwalchmai and his younger brother Gareth," although that was something of an understatement. Gareth was thirteen years old.

"If the king's knights—save you—did not live, I don't expect to fare any better," Lamorak said undoubtedly.

"The king's knights are dead?" Bedivere shouted over the storm.

"As is the king," Percy answered Bedivere. "He was beheaded by this demon rider."

"You are looking at Sir Percy. The last of the king's knights," Father Gregory said proudly.

"Aye, I am the last of the king's knights," Percy said, "and I will make him proud in the next world by avenging his death. And I would be honored to ride into battle with you brave men." And with no objections they all charged through the streets of the town on horseback to the monastery…fiery hoof prints leading the way.

CHAPTER 20

"Homeschooling, Mr. Dane!"

The principal sat across from him behind her desk with a large pane window behind her that looked onto the front of the school. Eastern Hemlock trees poked around at the window with help from the wind. Max found it immediately interesting that her desk nameplate read:

ALARICE HEMLOCK
PRINCIPAL

The principal had frosted blue eyes with numerous bags under them that she wore as a badge of honor for her years as an educator. She was elderly but looked quite capable. Her white hair was in a tight bun as was her demeanor and outfit. She wore a clean and crisp neutral colored woman's business jacket and skirt. "Let me emphasize," she looked firmly at Max, "that I deplore homeschooling. I find it does not equip our youth with the proper socializing and integration of the various lifestyles and backgrounds that one will have to cope with in today's society. I feel it obstructs their ability to communicate with other people in real settings and dynamics. I also feel the same way about cell phone usage and texting. I can't count how many students I see carrying on a texting conversation while standing right next to each other. It is despicable. I applaud your mother's forbiddance of a cell phone to you...but...I digress. My other problem with homeschooling is that I doubt the standards of academic quality and comprehension are met. However, I deplore violence and disruption in my school even more. And I understand you had an altercation yesterday at the coffee shop with Mr. Reid. So I suggest homeschooling as a viable option for you, Mr. Dane, if I feel you are not able to overcome this violent pattern you have. I will neither tolerate nor allow such behavior in my school! Do I make myself clear?"

"Yes," Max answered immediately.

"Do I? What did I just say?"

"That you won't tolerate violence of any kind."

"Very good, and what is violence?"

"Uh," Max struggled for an answer. He wasn't expecting a pop-quiz on social behavior, "a form of aggression."

"Correct. Aggression. Excellent! And does aggression always have to be physical?"

"No, it can be verbal."

"Correct again, very good," she took her China Rose teacup from its saucer and sipped. "Yes, aggression can be verbal such as name-calling or bullying. I will not tolerate this either."

Tell that to Derek!

"Max!" Evelyn was shown into the office by the secretary. "I haven't even left the school before getting a phone call from the principal!" She was visibly enraged.

"I was just discussing with Max the homeschooling option I had mentioned to you on the phone."

"Could I possibly have a moment alone with my son?" Evelyn said apologetically to the principal.

"Of course," she gave a small bow of her head. "Do not leave," she said to Max. "I am not done with you yet." She closed the door to her office.

"It wasn't my fault," Max protested as he squirmed in the leather upholstered armchair.

"Stop!" Evelyn walked around the principal's office admiring the decor momentarily. "She told me about how you attacked Derek—stop—don't say anything—you listen! And apparently some of the students saw you attack him yesterday at the coffee shop! And now this! I've had it with you mister. I mean I really have," she stopped in front of Max. "You want honesty? You want the truth? You ruined my marriage!" She pointed her finger at him.

Max was frozen in his chair.

"Your father doesn't want you. That's why we're having a custody battle, because I don't want you either. So this homeschooling thing is not an option. I can't deal with you at home all day. I have too much work to do. And I'm not about to hire a tutor. You are not going to ruin Lindsey's life or my life here. You have an appointment with that therapist today at 3. If you mess that up like you have with the others I'm not going to defend you anymore. I'll let them lock you up or whatever the hell it is they do with delinquents. So you decide now what it is you want and you better think hard and you better think serious. You can be locked up in a cell or you can try and have some friends here in school and get to do fun school activities and boring school work and be free. I'm picking you up at

2:30!" She stormed out.

Max didn't want to cry in front of his mother, so the tears just rolled out. He heard muffled talking outside. He knew the principal was talking to his mother. He didn't blame his mother. She was right. She had every right to hate him. *But dad? Dad doesn't want me either?* She had to be lying. She was just angry. Max knew though. He knew just like he knew other things to be true without a shred of evidence. His dad didn't want him. Max wished he had died that day. It would have been easier for everybody.

The principal came back in carrying a folder. "I have your file," she sat back at her desk.

Max looked away and around her office trying to get his tears to dry. He couldn't help the sniffling. She had a fireplace in her office too. *Ravencrest sure did like its fireplaces.*

"So now I'm going to be your counselor. Look at me, Mr. Dane."

Max looked at her through liquid-eyes.

"Do you know what this means?"

"No."

"No, what?" She demanded.

"No, ma'am," he hoped that was the right answer.

"It means I have taken responsibility for you. This does not mean though that I will cover for you. So your attitude and actions better improve or we are both in for it. There are those here at this school who think my time is over; that my principles are outdated. In every walk of life in every career there are those that are constantly plotting against you. So if you fail then I fail. Your fate is now linked with mine, Mr. Dane, and believe me I will not have you tarnish my superb record."

"Yes, ma'am."

"Did your mother ground you?"

That was a good question. "I don't know."

"Did she take away your video games?"

Max chortled. "I don't have any," he wiped his nose.

"I see." She studied Max's face and handed him some tissue. "Then it must have been severe. Sometimes words are far more damaging than anything physical." She crossed over to a little table with cups and a pot. "Would you care to discuss it over some Mugwort tea?"

"No...but thanks."

"No to the tea or no to discussing it?"

"Uh...to discussing it, thanks."

She was unaffected. "Tea then," she poured him a cup. "You must have some honey in it," she insisted pressing on a thumb lever from a beveled glass container with a honeycomb design. She handed him the cup and saucer. "I must get some more Mugwort leaves from the Sisters Grimm. I am almost out," she said aloud to herself.

"You know the Sisters Grimm," Max hesitated drinking the tea.

"Oh yes, everyone in town knows of them. Not necessarily likes them, but that's true of anybody. Too many people waste their time trying to win favor with every person they meet. It is a futile and senseless task...but that doesn't mean we should fight them in the halls at school," she wanted to clarify in case Max took that as it was okay to start fights with Derek. "Yes, these tea leaves are exceptional that they obtain for me. I understand the sisters reap it during the day just after the full moon when the plant has absorbed the moonlight energy and thus allowing for the leaves to yield the plant's finest attributes to an exceptional tea." She refilled her tea cup. "So here is your locker combination and your list of classes. I am sure your friend Mr. Lee will be more than happy to direct you."

"How do you know that Jonas is my friend?"

"Oh, I know a great deal, Mr. Dane," she whipped

a silk cloth off an object on her desk. "I have a crystal ball."

She sure did have a crystal ball on her desk!

"Don't you know everyone in this town is a witch, wizard, or shaman?"

Max was sure he heard sarcasm in her voice. He took a sip of his tea. He didn't like tea but the name Mugwort sounded intriguing so he had to try it. It was surprisingly good. The aroma massaged his nostrils. He closed his eyes savoring the flavor. The gutter ball that was consistently in his stomach rolled away. Max felt his skin get cool and opened his eyes seeing what he thought was UVA URSA'S APOTHECARY. He saw bottles, jars, herbs, and spices thrown along shelves and tables. The floor was wood but not the polished cherry wood he had seen at Uva's. It looked like an apothecary, but not the same one he had been in. This place was old and worn. There was a window where he could see daylight. On a table in the center of the room were many bottles boiling linked together by various tubes. There was a red stone that was melting down and set to drip into another bottle.

Max found he could move in slow motion closer to the table. It was as if he was trudging through mud. His vision was hazy like he was trying to see through a migraine headache. The bottle that the red stone was going to drip into had a small etching of a dragon into it. Max heard knocking and then a man descended the staircase that was across the table from him. The man was old and wearing what looked like a medieval cloak. Max was suddenly reminded of his encounter in the woods with the teen and the men on horseback. The man checked on the bubbling bottles as he passed by the table to open the door.

"Ah, Abbot Conleth my friend," he greeted an equally old man wearing a brown robe and allowed him entrance.

"I wish I were here under more congenial circumstances," he shook his hand eyeing the active table.

"So you are going through with it?" There was concern in his voice.

"Ambrosius is most adamant he needs this tonight. I dare not disappoint him. It is essential for their ceremony."

"I don't trust him. I fear he will kill you as soon as he gets what he wants."

"Do you really think so? But he has been working with me and you for so long trying to establish peace between our people and the druids."

"He has wheedled your cooperation into completing this task for him. He could not do this without you. I am guilty equally. I have allowed him to use me as well, I see that now. Everything he has worked for has been for this night; the night he resurrects their Lord of the Dead." He saw doubt in Dr. Lambe's eyes. "I have seen it for myself in his grimoire. It is some sort of dragon he is attempting to resurrect! We must stop him."

Dr. Lambe looked to the table. The collection bottle with the dragon on it was given to him by Ambrosius. He was starting to believe his good friend. He scampered to a cabinet in the corner and grabbed another bottle and quickly switched it for the one with the dragon etching. "Do you truly think it's possible for him to do this?"

"I do not know. But *he* believes it and once he has what he wants you will be of no use to him. *That* I do know!" He put his hand on his friend's shoulder. "I have a way for us to return to Rome safely."

"Can you trust the Holy See?"

"I will bring Ambrosius' grimoire and the detailed notes I have made on the Table's meetings and rituals. *You* will bring the true elixir," he pointed to the melting stone. "You must also bring your writings on your work with ailments. It will be our penance. God forgives us."

"What if Ambrosius comes before it is done?" He

was worried the stone wouldn't finish melting in time for him to make the switch.

"I will send some men to protect you. They will bring you to the monastery. I have arranged travel for us back to Rome. We will be guarded. We will be safe!"

Max turned to the window and saw the sky move by quickly like a time lapse video. It was later in the day but not quite dark yet. Doctor Lambe was sitting at a table now by the cabinet in the corner. He had a quill in hand with a couple of books open and was writing in one. Max saw that the stone was almost done dripping in the bottle. Suddenly, there was a knocking at the door causing the doctor to jump. He scrambled to the table as the elixir was complete. He quickly put it with his books in the cabinet in the corner and clambered to the door. He looked at the substitute elixir on the table with the dragon etching. Ambrosius was powerful and smart. He had seen his magick at work. There was no way he was going to be fooled. He would be dead within minutes. He hoped Abbot Conleth's guards would soon arrive. It could be his only chance. He took a deep breath and flung open the door. He was immediately drenched in relief.

"Sir Percy?" He was shocked and abated. He peered over the young knight's shoulder convinced he was going to see Ambrosius. "Did Abbot Conleth send you?" He motioned him in.

Max saw the young knight with a little bit of facial hair and thought immediately that he reminded him of someone. *Maybe it was an actor?*

"Nay, I come on behalf of the king for Ambrosius."

Doctor Lambe hesitated. This was almost too good to be true. God answered his prayers. He had to be certain he didn't hear wrong. "Ambrosius is not coming?" He looked anxiously at the door as he expected him to walk in at any moment.

"Nay, I am supposed to acquire his package."

"Oh, of course," he went to the table without hesitation. There was no way that Sir Percy would be able to discern a fake. Guilt splashed over him. He had always liked Sir Percy. He struck him as an honorable young man. He was concerned what might become of him if the fake was discovered. He was sure he himself would be on his way to Rome before Ambrosius could do anything against him. Doubt crept in about making the switch. "Sir Percy these are your people. Let me ask you, what is this need-fire?"

"Ambrosius has been planning this for some time. He says now is our great time of need. My people across the land douse the fires from their hearth. A large central fire is lit by our religious caste."

"The druids?"

"Aye, this need-fire is lit by them and they believe that it is from this fire they can have access to other points in time."

That sounded ominous enough to Lambe. He was resolute in his decision to go ahead with the switch. He handed the fake to Percy. "You are to deliver this to Ambrosius?"

"Nay, my instructions from the king are to give it to the sisters."

"The ladies of the lake?"

"Aye, but from what I hear they are no ladies. They are witches."

"The Isle of the Dead is a dreadful place to take up residence. Be careful most noble Percy." The least he could do was offer him some assistance in case the sisters discovered his treachery. "I have something for you. To help you in case the witches turn on you."

"I have something that is supposed to guarantee my safety," he had Ambrosius' ring with a runic "R" on it. He then noticed quickly that Doctor Lambe had a similar ring. Indeed he must have been working closely with the wizard.

"You can never have too much protection," the doctor insisted as he walked back to the cabinet and fumbled through bottles and jars and papers.

Percy followed behind the doctor. "What's that?" He pointed to a large jug.

"Oh, that…" he smiled. "I call it Godspeed. It will make your horses run fast. Nay, I'm thinking of this," he pulled out a small clear jar and poured red wine into it. He took a small pair of pincers and plucked an attractive hood-shaped purple flower from a bottle. "This is Wolf's Bane," he dropped the hooded flower into the jar with the red wine, "the slightest skin contact can cause numbness." He corked the jar and handed it to Percy. "This will render you invisible to the witches."

Percy didn't believe that. But he was thankful for the gesture. "What do you call *this*?" Percy eyed the Wolf's Bane soaking in the wine.

"A witch bottle."

"That would seem logical," he tucked it away and bid farewell to John Lambe leaving the apothecary.

Max didn't understand exactly what was going on with this shell game with the Elixir, but his gut told him that Percy should have the real one. He yelled at him to stop. But he didn't hear him. He wanted to follow him but suddenly time must have passed again as the room was darker and lit with candles. Condensation huffed from his lungs. Max saw a headless body on the floor. He noticed his attire. It was Doctor Lambe. The other body looked to be a large Viking. Percy was here again with another priest and others that looked like warriors of some sort. Max's heart jumped. He waved and jumped around trying to get his attention. *Concentrate! Maybe if I concentrate!* Max breathed deeply and steadily and tried to let go of his tension.

Percy was leaving! That agitated Max. *Focus! Focus!* Max needed to let Percy know that the real Elixir was in the cabinet. The gutter ball was huge in his stomach. Max decided to focus his breathing there. He took a deep breath in through his mouth pulling the air into his diaphragm. He held it for several seconds and then exhaled. *Percy stopped!* He inhaled again this time through his nose and held it in his diaphragm again feeling the gutter ball disappear. He exhaled again slowly. Percy turned and looked back at Max. *Does he see me?* There was a flash of lightning and Max quickly pointed to the cabinet. Percy looked at the cabinet. *He saw me!* Percy opened the one door that was closed on the cabinet. Max approached behind him. *It was gone*! The Elixir wasn't there! *How?* He saw the doctor put it in there! Percy looked about the cabinet confused not knowing what he was looking for. He opted to take a sack from the cabinet using it to grab a helmet off the floor as he left the apothecary.

Max followed in slow motion outside watching Percy and the others leave as his hopes sank in the mud and rain. *Ugh.* Max thought. *At least he could have taken the jug.*

"Spirit! Spirit!"

Max turned. There were two older ladies looking at him. *Is she talking to me?* He looked around quickly to see if there was anyone else around. The rain had stopped. There were lights around people's houses, not that he would call them houses, they looked more like shacks. The lights looked like Jack-O-Lanterns flickering. But they weren't pumpkins. They were much tinier. Time must have passed again, he didn't see these when he came out into the rain. And if these were some version of Jack-O-Lanterns then it was still the same night. Max looked back at the lady that called him 'spirit,' and she waved him over to a table in front of their shack.

"Prithee, join us." She pointed to some food on the table. The other lady smiled at him. "Ye are not familiar to me but ye are welcome at our table. Does thou family live here in the village?"

"No," Max answered, but still doubtful they were really talking to him. Their British accents were a lot different than the Sisters Grimm and Jack's.

"Did ye die in the alchemists shop?" She pointed to the apothecary. "We heard many screams and saw the glowing headless knight."

"Headless Knight?" When Max saw the Knightmare in the Nexus it had a head...or at least a helmet.

"Aye," the lady said, "it went in with a head but came out without one. The lack of a head did not seem to stop it."

"Well, it took the doctor's head." Max assumed. He didn't actually see it. "And Jack's," he wondered aloud. He wasn't certain but it seemed more than likely that the Knightmare took Jack's head.

"Wasn't Jack the name of the alchemist?" The second lady asked the first.

"Aye, I believe so." The first lady erroneously confirmed. "Perchance, the knight was named Jack and since it lost its head it seeks to replace it with another head named Jack!"

The second lady nodded eagerly as though that made perfect sense. "Then it is good we cut these little substitute heads out of turnips."

"Oh," Max said, "Those are Jack-O-Lanterns?" He had never seen any cut out of turnips before.

"Aye," the first ladies eyes widened with joy. "Thank ye spirit, that's what we shall call them. Aye, Jack Lanterns! So the headless knight will take these."

"And perchance guide the poor soul to its head." The second lady said hopefully. She pointed up the road in horror. "Tis coming back!" And she fled inside one of the shacks.

Max and the first lady saw a man galloping toward them on horseback. However, he was not glowing and as he got closer they both saw that his head was intact.

The warrior tied off his horse and the lady called out to him. Max had stepped away as he approached. He didn't seem to notice him. Max could hear a little bit of their exchange as he questioned the Jack Lanterns. Then Max heard him say that he was here on behalf of Sir Percy. Maybe he could point this man to the Elixir. Max followed the man into the apothecary as he carried one of the carved turnips the lady gave him. The man obviously couldn't see him. He didn't know why the ladies could. Max followed the man as he looked around inside with the Jack Lantern. Max concentrated like he did before with Percy and controlled his breathing. Suddenly, the man whipped around and held his sword at Max's neck. Max looked startled. *Could he hurt me?* He didn't want to find out. The man dropped his sword and asked about the Elixir of Life. Max was trying to concentrate. He could feel a pulling at the center of his stomach. He didn't have much time. He just knew it. He pointed to the cabinet. The man peered inside. He looked at Max confused.

"The jug," Max instructed for him to take.

The man asked what it was for.

"It will make the horses go faster." Max hoped he would find that useful.

Max looked down next to his schedule of classes; he had a tea cup in one hand. "Swimming?" Max just snapped back to being in the principal's office and saw his schedule of classes.

"Oh yes, I believe you have so much energy you better have a good physical outlet to work off that aggression. In fact, I have been toying with the idea of adding Martial Arts to the curriculum and now I am considering it even more seriously," she dropped a stern eye on him.

"Uh, Ms. Hemlock—"

"Madame Hemlock if you please."

"Right. Madame Hemlock, I don't know if I can swim. Well…swim good I mean."

"You're in a school. *Learn!*"

"Yes, ma'am."

"You have detention tomorrow after school with Coach Matthews as I understand you have an appointment with your therapist this afternoon. Now, shoo," she scooted her hand out. "My desk was full before you showed up this morning and complicated my life."

CHAPTER 21

"Did they kick you out?"

Jonas was buzzing around Max like a bee moving from one flower to another. "How bad was it? I've never been in Madame Hemlock's office. What was it like? I heard she has a crystal ball. Are you grounded? You were in there for a long time. You practically missed first period."

Max was putting his books in his locker while Jonas was ranting. He was just waiting for him to take a breath. "I drank Mugwort tea with her. I'm not expelled, but I have detention tomorrow after school...and I have swimming tomorrow."

"Really? Oh shit."

"What? What's wrong with that?"

"Well, all of those douche-bags from the coffee shop. Not to mention they're all Derek's friends."

"I thought they were sophomores. How old is Derek?"

"Fifteen, I think."

"They won't be in my class will they?"

"Oh, I don't know," Jonas shrugged. "I always expect the worst. That way I'm not so disappointed when shit happens."

"That's kinda pathetic, Jonas."

"Well, you're gonna have to wear a Speedo."

Max didn't want to think about it. "But I didn't tell you the crazy thing yet. I was back in the Middle Ages again. Like when I saw that teenage boy in the woods. What do you think?"

"Well...Mugwort tea is purported to produce prophetic dreams or visions and to aid in astral projection. I think that's what happened to you!"

"You don't think I had a seizure?"

"I don't think so."

"You don't think I'm crazy?"

"Oh shit, yeah...You only attacked a teenager at least three years older than you...Twice!" He smiled at Max. "But this stuff...I don't think you're imagining it. I think you astrally projected. Like you did that night at the new moon ceremony."

"What the fuck, Dane?" A voice yelled from behind them.

It was Chance.

"Oh shit, he called you, Dane," Jonas stepped away from Max.

"Yeah, what the fuck, Dane?" Cassandra came around the corner next to Chance. "You're seriously messing up my pretty-boy's glam. First, his undoubtedly flawless nut sack! And now his nose! Why, Max! Why?"

Chance looked at Cassandra sternly like he didn't

want her help.

"I'll talk to you later," she took off.

Chance gave the same look to Jonas.

"Uh, right, well I'll see you in English then." He couldn't miss the pissed off look in Chance's eyes. "Hopefully..." and then he disappeared as well.

Chance stood there fuming over Max not saying anything.

Max knew Chance was pissed. He had every right to be. *Wait a minute. No he didn't. Mom had every right to be angry with him. But not Chance. Not about Derek. Derek was an asshole!* He was just about to tell Chance that when he thought better of it. "Why do you like Derek?"

"What? What does that matter?"

"I was just curious why you think so much of him."

"Look, don't try and change the subject. I saw what you did Max. You attacked him, just like you attacked him yesterday." He took a deep breath. "You're a bully!"

Max opened his mouth to protest.

"It's true. I'm part of our awareness program here against school bullying. You may not see it, but that's exactly where you're headed. I want to like you, Max...but I'm not liking what I'm seeing in you, Dane." He walked away.

He fought the tears coming back in his eyes. His mom's revelation cracked him like a hard-boiled-egg. Now, he felt like his shell was being picked apart piece-by-piece. "Fuck me." Max felt his whole being slump. "Can this day get any worse?" He wheezed.

"Maximillian Aiden Dane."

"Yes," Max answered looking up. It was Sheriff Alahmoot.

"Come with me," he said sternly. "Let's take a ride." The sheriff insisted that Max get in the backseat of the cruiser, "Might as well get used to it." The trip was otherwise quiet except for a call back into the station. He escorted Max into the sheriff's department and into his office. "Sit down. I have a file on you."

Max rolled his eyes. *Who didn't?* "Isn't my mom supposed to be here?"

"Well, it's not like I'm charging you with anything." He looked at Max for a long moment that made Max uncomfortable. "I don't need to charge with you anything do I?"

"No," Max blurted like somebody that was guilty of something and completely ready to deny it.

He watched Max squirm in his chair a bit before continuing. "You seem to think you have some psychic ability. I get that a lot around here in Ravencrest. It actually happens to be true for the most part. Now, in the case of Watu Warakin you lead me to believe you saw his head in Yorick's farm. I didn't find anything. I pulled a lot of strings to get a search party because the Federal Bureau of Investigation happens to have taken over this case. Do you know what any of this means that I'm telling you?"

"No," Max really had no clue. He was still trying to believe he was pulled out of school by the cops.

"It means I put my ass on the line because I thought you might actually have had some ability or insight into this murder. Not again. Don't you ever go around spouting gossip about police matters—especially someone's death. If Joe found out about this he would be devastated and hurt to know that you were spreading false information about his father's death. This is serious stuff and I should have just consulted a real psychic. I see in your file you're epileptic and I know epileptics have hallucinations. So you remember that the next time you talk to the dead or whatever it was you think you saw. I know you have an appointment with Dr. Evans this afternoon and I hope it goes well." He said in a tone that told Max he was actually demanding it went well.

Before Max could say anything the door to the sheriff's office opened and a short middle-aged round woman swept in followed by two men in dark suits that towered behind her. She was homely looking with large round frame glasses and her light brown hair poofed out coming to her shoulder. Max was certain it wasn't auburn. A sickly sweet smile was plastered on her face and she had the demeanor of someone that instructed people how to cook comfort food on a website.

"Deputy Mayor," the sheriff greeted her more insulted at her entrance than welcoming.

"That's *mayor*," she corrected him with a sweet smile, "with Watu's passing."

"*Acting* mayor," he rebutted without a smile in return.

She gave him a sly smile and motioned to the two men behind her. "You know Special Agent-in-Charge Tom McCoy with the Federal Bureau of Investigation and Assistant Special Agent-in-Charge Troy Knight?"

"Yes, we've already met. What's this about?"

"Then you know," she smiled sweetly again, "that they're in charge of the investigation into Watu Warakin's death."

"Yes," he answered annoyed. "Get to your point I'm pretty busy."

"Yes, you have been busy," Tom McCoy stepped forward. "Tell me why it was you decided to investigate Yorick's farm?"

"Well, last I checked I was the sheriff—"

The mayor gave a haughty laugh.

Tahamont gave her a sideways glance and continued "—If I feel I need to investigate a lead then I'll do that."

"What lead was that?" Tom insisted.

Sheriff Tahamont eyeballed Max for a mere moment.

Here it comes! Max thought.

"An anonymous tip," the sheriff said.

"Right—well—as you know the FBI is in charge of this now. So you're interfering with an official investigation."

"Into Bigfoot?"

"What?" Agent McCoy sounded annoyed and confused.

"Is the FBI in charge of investigating Bigfoot? That's the lead I was following up on at Yorick's farm. There was a sighting."

Max had to stop himself from laughing aloud.

Agent McCoy didn't look as casual about the comment.

Sheriff Tahamont read the agent's face. "That's why I got the dogs out there. We take that sort of thing seriously here in Ravencrest. I would hate to see Bigfoot hurt," he said almost threatening.

Agent McCoy stared at the sheriff for a moment seeming to take in what he said. Then he looked at the mayor shrewdly and back to the sheriff. "That's some creative bullshit about your hunt for Bigfoot. Except," he opened a folder, "that we've already talked to some of your volunteers that went out there with their dogs and they informed us you told them you were looking for Watu Warakin's head."

"And..." the other agent finally spoke, "we know you went into the hospital morgue to see Watu's body after we gave orders not to."

"Watu was a friend of mine," the sheriff said heated.

"Is there any chance you would be made Chief of the local tribe here after his death?" Agent Knight asked.

"What? What are you talking about? Are you accusing me of something? This is nonsense!"

"What *isn't* nonsense Sheriff Tahamont," Agent

McCoy took back over, "Is that you are now under investigation into impeding, interfering, and possibly planting or tampering with evidence into a federal official's death."

The mayor had a pleased look on her face as though she were enjoying the best tasting dessert bite after bite. "Effective immediately you are suspended *with* pay—"

"And you're lucky she's giving you that." McCoy interjected. "You better hope," he pointed his finger aggressively down at him as he was much taller than the sheriff, "that interfering with a federal investigation is all you get accused of."

Troy Knight opened the sheriff's door and waved in Deputy Sheriff Roy Drake.

Roy slinked in looking weathered. "I'm sorry Alahmoot," he held his palm up. "I'm gonna need your badge and your gun—"

"And his sheriff's hat," she pointed victoriously to the cowboy style hat on his head. "It's yours now." She looked at Alahmoot Tahamont gloating. "Roy is now...*acting* sheriff," she said savoring her sweet revenge.

"Alahmoot is a good man," Roy said to the mayor.

"Agent McCoy and Agent Knight's investigation will let us know for certain," she said snide. "What's he doing here?" She belted suddenly, jabbing her finger at Max sitting down.

Max was starting to wonder himself if he was having another hallucination as no one had taken notice of him till just now.

Agent McCoy looked at Tahamont demanding an explanation.

Tahamont answered his look. "You're the Bureau of Investigation. Or is that Men in Black? You figure it out."

McCoy snatched the file from Tahamont's hand and flipped it open reading with shocked eyes. "You're not investigating this boy are you?" He handed the file over to the mayor who was trying to grab it for a glimpse like an impatient child.

"That's no boy," Tahamont replied gravely. "That's Max Dane."

"Yeah, I see that," McCoy sounded unconcerned. "You did read the last entry I take it." He looked at Roy.

"Frank," Roy opened the door yelling to one of the deputies. "Get this kid back to school before I arrest him for truancy."

CHAD W. EVANS, M.D.
NEUROLOGY
FORENSIC PSYCHOLOGY

Max read the door as the receptionist opened it; finally letting him in. He had been waiting for quite a while.

"Max, come in, sorry about the wait," Dr. Evans greeted him. "Have a seat," he offered a leather couch.

Max felt as if his insides were sloshing about. *Don't screw this up! Don't screw this up!* Max repeated in his head.

"Max, do you know what I do?"

Don't call him a psycho-babble! "Uh, you're a psychologist."

Dr. Evans laughed. "True, but it's a little more complex than that. You're a smart guy, Max. I'm going to give it to you straight. I'm going to evaluate you. As a forensic psychologist I apply psychology to criminal investigation and the law. I assess the mental competency of criminals which includes juvenile and adult offenders. I assess the competency of victims as well and provide psychotherapy to them. I investigate reports of child abuse. And when it comes to divorces I perform child custody evaluations and conduct visitation risk assessments."

"Does that mean Lindsey is going to be evaluated?"

"She is."

"Why? She didn't do anything."

"You're protective of your sister."

"Yes."

"Interesting," he clicked his electronic pen on an electronic tablet he was holding.

Max watched wondering if he just said something wrong. "Has the evaluation started?"

Dr. Evans just smiled back. "Tell me about your dreams."

"My dreams?" No psycho-babble asked him about his dreams.

"Yes, your mom said you have terrible nightmares."

"I do, well, I don't sleep well."

"Because of the nightmares?"

"Yeah, I guess."

"What do you see?"

"Well…" Max didn't want to answer. "It's kinda hard to explain." Dr. Evans just leaned back in his chair as though he had all the time in the world. *Maybe that's why he was running late.* "Lately I've been dreaming about the Middle Ages—one night in particular—it's Samhain…Halloween."

"Interesting," he clicked on his tablet, "that you used the word Samhain—Devil's Night—also the name of the Celtic Lord of the Dead. Why do you think you dream of this night?"

That was a good question. "Well, I met a boy."

"How old is this boy?"

"About eight, I'd say." *Did it matter?*

He clicked on his tablet. "And does the boy have a name?"

"Jack."

He clicked. "And this boy lives in the Middle Ages?"

"Yeah, he does. Except...well...he's dead."

He clicked several times.

"Naturally, the Middle Ages was a long time ago."

"Yeah, but I mean...he was murdered."

Click, click, click.

"And how does that make you feel?"

"Angry...upset...confused..." Max looked at Dr. Evans' eyes. He was trying to figure out if he was judging him. Max waited for him to click on his screen.

He didn't.

"...I want to help him, but I don't know how."

"If he's dead, how can you help him?"

"His soul or his...being...I don't know. He's not at rest."

"You need to make it right somehow."

"Yes, exactly," Max was glad he understood.

"Do you just see Jack when you're asleep?"

Max felt that gutter ball again. He looked at his feet embarrassed. "Actually...I haven't seen him while I've been asleep yet."

"During the day, while you're awake?"

"Yeah."

Click.

"Even on days when you've taken your epilepsy medication?"

Max had to think about that. "Yeah, I think."

"Interesting," he clicked away again.

"Do you have lots of patients that see and talk to people that aren't really there?"

"Do you think Jack really isn't there?"

"No. I mean...he can't be...right?"

"Are you asking me or telling me?"

Max looked around his office. It was simple. His desk was in the corner next to the couch. Behind Dr. Evans was a glass window corner with a sliding door that opened to a balcony. Max had a view of large pine trees and mountains. It eased the pain of the gutter ball. He stared at his hands. They were cold and trembling. "How do you know…that you're crazy?"

"Do you think you're crazy?"

"That's just it! How would I know? I mean I'm sure you have some sort of mathematical formula or phone app that tells you. But how does the actual crazy person know they're crazy? Because to them they probably think things are normal. Or it seems normal to them. But everyone else is going 'CUCKOO! CUCKOO!' I feel horrible inside. I feel like there's some caged animal inside me. A dangerous caged animal! And I'm scared all the time. I feel like I have to keep a watchful eye on it to make sure it doesn't get out. I'm scared if I let my guard down for even a moment it's going to get out or someone's going to do something to set it free. I want to help Jack because I have to do something good; for someone other than me. I'm tired of being scared all the time! It hurts!"

Dr. Evans stared at Max silently.

He finally spoke. "I think we're done for the day."

CHAPTER 22

The flames flashed crystal blue.

Max wanted to call his father to ask if it was true what his mother had said; about not wanting him. But he had no way of calling him. He would have to borrow his mother's phone. Maybe he should have convinced her to get pizza for dinner and he could have "placed" the order. Why didn't he think of that earlier? But Max knew it was true. He didn't have to ask his dad. His dad would've never admitted it anyway. He would lie. *Why is it that parents expected their children to be honest but can't do it themselves?* Besides…what parent would admit they didn't want their kid? *Oh, right…mom.* Dinner was awkward with his mother. Fortunately, Lindsey provided plenty of distraction ranting about aliens and Mr. Creeps and how he had lunged at her their first day in town.

He was now in his room marveling at his fireplace. It was amazing enough to Max that he was just wearing shorts the other day and now found it quite necessary to have a fire blazing in his room. He was admiring the flames and realizing he would need more wood and hoping his mother was in bed so he wouldn't have to ask permission to go outside when the flames turned a fluorescent blue.

Cold slithered over his skin. Chilled air escaped from his lungs. In place of the gutter ball in his stomach was queasiness. His insides were squirming. His head flicked to the side as he noticed he wasn't alone in his room.

Standing next to him in front of the blue fire was the dead Indian with braids down the side of his head—Genuine Joe's father—looking more grotesque than he did the night before at the bonfire. He looked like a decomposing corpse. Even though he was dead, when Max saw ghosts before they always looked as they did just before they died, mainly…alive.

Max stepped away from Watu. Watu stumbled toward Max. His skin was bloated and blistered.

Max continued to back away toward his bedroom door, "I don't know what you want." Watu staggered closer to Max, grasping his greenish-blue neck. His face was so swollen Max couldn't recognize him from his picture, but the clothes were the same that he saw on his body in the hospital morgue and he recognized his braids, otherwise he wouldn't know who he was. Max could smell him now. He reeked of rotting meat. He had never smelt a ghost before either. Watu struggled to speak again. "I can't help you," Max said desperately. "I don't know how," he opened the door to his bedroom, his heart was flipping around in his chest. Watu lurched pointing out Max's window with one hand and pulling at his cheek with the other. His face burst shooting out pus at Max. Max flung himself out his bedroom door and rushed down the stairs.

Max continued down the stairs and right out the front door into the brisk night. He didn't even grab a jacket he was so scared. His heart was whizzing around in his chest. *I needed to get firewood anyway*; he validated his escape outside. He looked at his house trepidly. *Maybe I should sleep downstairs tonight...or...forever*. He didn't see how he would ever go back in his bedroom. What was Watu pointing at outside his bedroom? He walked to the side of the house where he could see the light from his window. He studied the trees outside his room. That didn't seem right. Then he looked across the street to the view he would have from his window: The Grimm's house. Their lights were on. Well, he wanted to talk to the sisters. And he wasn't getting any warmer. He took a deep breath and walked across the street noticing an SUV parked on the street in front of their house.

Max was working up the nerve to knock on the door when he heard a growl echo behind him. He spun around. It was now that he noticed there wasn't much street light on Shadow Lake Lane like his suburban neighborhood in Burlington. It was still a new moon so there was no light from the moon either, just a New England lamppost at the end of the lane. His eyes scurried through the dark. *Was that a dog?* It had to be a dog. *What else could it be?* Jonas would probably think it was a werewolf. *Right*, he tried to chuckle to himself but couldn't as fear swelled in his eyes. Did he just see movement? It came from just across the street in Jonas' front yard. *Wait, it had to be the stack of pumpkins Mr. Lee was carving. That was it. Was it crouched down? Or was it just a dog standing taking a leak on the pumpkins?* Then he saw two glowing yellow eyes. His breathing stumbled as it tripped over his skipping heartbeat.

The front door flung open.

"Shit," Max yelled. His heart should get a gold medal for gymnastics tonight.

"You have a foul mouth on you," Glenda squinched at him.

"You should talk," Max glared at her.

"Ha," Glenda popped in veneration and pushed the door wider allowing him entrance.

Max shot a glance over his shoulder making sure they weren't about to get eaten. He didn't see anything. "Were you on your way out?"

"No, I saw you dillydallying at the door." She pointed to the strange-eyed raven perched on the porch, and then flipped her patch up exposing her huge raven eye.

His insides winced. "You can really see through that...eye?" That freaked him out. *It couldn't be real...could it? It had to be a Halloween contact lens.*

Glenda cackled and waved him in.

Max rushed into the low-lit living room. There was a cozy fire burning. Martha stood from a plush armchair with a drink in hand. Across from her on the couch sat Sheriff Alahmoot with a drink as well. *That must have been his SUV parked outside.* Max was surprised to see him. Was he investigating the sisters or staking out his house? Maybe he was just friends with them.

Martha looked alarmed. "Where is your jacket?" She asked seeing him in only sweat pants and a t-shirt. "You'll catch your death."

"Too late for that," Glenda crowed.

Martha objected with a look. She patted the chair she stood from offering it to Max so he could warm himself by the fire. Max eagerly accepted. Dorothy appeared at his side almost out of nowhere with a plate in hand.

"Cookie?" She offered him more Halloween shapes with a smile.

Is she always baking?

"I promise there's no skull," she encouraged.

"Skullcap you mean, right? You were trying to help with my epilepsy."

"Oh, he catches on quick!" Dorothy took a delighted bite out of a witch-shaped cookie.

"Why didn't you tell me that in the first place?" Max griped.

"Well, where's the fun in that?" Dorothy offered him the plate of cookies again.

Max took a pumpkin shaped one.

"How did you figure it out? About the skullcap," Dorothy was still smiles.

"Oh, I saw some in Uva Ursa's shop. I asked her about it."

"Oh, that hack," Glenda grumbled.

"Yeah, she mentioned you guys didn't care for her. Just because she practices witchcraft different than you guys doesn't make her less credible." Max felt he needed to defend her.

Glenda looked as though she was about to challenge what he just said but Martha gave her a *now's-not-the-time* look.

"I'll get you some warm milk," Dorothy offered. "It's past your bedtime I'm sure. It will help you sleep." She walked to the kitchen.

"I'll never sleep again," Max shuddered taking a bite out of the cookie. "Not that I slept much to begin with."

"What happened?" Martha said concerned. She cradled her crystal stemmed cordial glass in her palm. It looked like a miniature wine glass. "It must have been alarming for you to leave your house without your jacket or shoes," she looked at his bare feet.

Glenda watched Max carefully waiting for the explanation she sensed was coming as did Sheriff Alahmoot. She tossed him a blanket from the back of the sofa. "Those piggies are cold."

Dorothy returned from the kitchen and handed Max a glass of warm milk. She observed everyone's attentiveness and remained quiet. Max felt more comfortable as his body warmed beneath the blanket and by the fire. Then that reminded him.

"Have you ever seen a fire turn blue?" Max asked the sisters.

They exchanged knowing glances. Glenda spoke. "Have you seen those TV programs where they look for ghosts using some electromagnetic detector?"

"Sure," Max lied. He was sure Jonas would know what she was talking about.

"Well, that's a bunch of horse-shit," Glenda continued. "You want to detect a ghost you light a fire. Ghosts make fire turn blue. Where did you see the blue flame?"

"In my bedroom."

"You had a candle lit?" Glenda asked.

"No, my fireplace."

"You have a fireplace in your bedroom?" Sheriff Alahmoot finally spoke sounding jealous.

"You must have Watu's old room." Martha said.

"Was it Watu you saw?" Glenda sounded hopeful.

"Yeah, but what…wait…Watu's old room? What are you talking about?" Max was confused.

"That used to be Watu Warakin's house that you live in. He moved about a year ago," Martha explained. "What did he tell you? Did he say anything about his death?"

"He didn't say anything. He couldn't speak. And his face exploded."

The house was quiet.

Alahmoot was frozen in mid-drink.

"That's what scared the hell out of me," Max finally continued. "I've seen plenty of ghosts, I guess is what you would call them, but none of them looked dead…or exploded."

"Looked dead?" Glenda asked curiously.

"Yeah, in movies they always show ghosts how they were when they died—you know part of their head lopped off or whatever wound killed them—but I see them how they were before they died; when they were still reasonably healthy. But I saw Watu at Joe's new moon ceremony and he looked like he was dying. And just now in my bedroom he looked all nasty and rotten like he was decomposing on the spot."

"And then his face exploded!" Dorothy tossed the rest of her cookie in her mouth.

"Yeah," Max inspected the warm milk.

"Was it green and disgusting pus?" Dorothy asked enthralled.

"Yeah, I almost hurled."

Dorothy looked thrilled.

"Dorothy, please," Martha fretted. "And you say he couldn't speak?"

Max nodded and took a sip of his milk. It was surprisingly good. Warm milk always sounded nasty to him. It tasted almost like pudding.

"It takes some deliberate magick to silence the dead."

"Aye," Glenda agreed. "And know-how."

"Why would someone do that?" Max asked.

"And how?" Alahmoot's question followed.

"Dead men do tell tales," Glenda answered Max.

"I don't know of any spells that can prevent the dead from talking," Martha pondered Alahmoot's question aloud.

"Ambrosius probably would," Glenda offered.

"Well he's dead—"

"But his grimoire isn't."

"It hasn't been recovered—"

"That we know of."

"I thought you were keeping an *eye* out for it."

"I have been," Glenda dropped her head in failure.

"Is there some other way besides a spell?" Max interrupted what looked like an uncomfortable subject.

"Cypress and Calamus," Dorothy beamed.

"Yeah," Max exclaimed. "Calamus is poisonous right?"

"It can be," Dorothy's smiles never seemed to fade. "Where did you hear that?"

"Uva told me. She knows all about that stuff," he said excited.

"Ha," Glenda shot Max's enthusiasm down, "I use Calamus in the Absinthe."

Alahmoot looked at his glass questionably.

"It depends on what part of the plant you use," Dorothy explained. "The dried root like Glenda uses is just fine."

"Cypress and Calamus," Max said. "That's what I heard in my head when I was in the morgue with Watu's body!"

"You were in the morgue?" Glenda asked Max praiseful.

Max nodded taking another drink of milk. "Uva also told me about Cypress. I thought Cypress was supposed to help the dead...you know...move on."

"Well, true...unless you use them in combination with each other."

Martha and Glenda's eyes bobbed back and forth between Max and their sister in complete astonishment. "Do elaborate sister," Martha insisted that Dorothy explain.

"It's an old technique, but the green pus is a tell-tale sign of Cypress and Calamus poisoning."

"Watu was poisoned?" Alahmoot almost stood, but fell back in the couch slightly inebriated.

"Well, not physically...just his spirit. The ancient Egyptians used Cypress for coffins," Dorothy smiled. "The trick is using more Calamus than Cypress, but it has to be the concentrated essential oil of Calamus. It also has to be infused. Oh, and it must be administered on the new moon relatively close to the time of death. So done properly, like it sounds it most certainly was, the spirit will struggle in pain whenever it attempts to speak and the more it insists the more painful it will get. The spirit decomposes like the body in life until it explodes!"

"Dissipate," Martha sounded like she was correcting her sister.

"Looks like he exploded to me," Max said supporting Dorothy.

Dorothy pointed at Max with a commending smile.

"So Watu wasn't killed by a bear," Glenda insisted. "I knew that was horse-shit."

"Why do you say that?" Max asked.

"Because obviously his death is being covered up if someone is going to this much trouble to keep him from talking," Alahmoot said as though it were plainly obvious. Glenda and her sisters looked as though they agreed.

"Maybe they're not trying to cover-up the way he was killed. Maybe they just don't want him talking about whatever he knows about someone or something."

Glenda squinched her eye at Alahmoot. "That's smart."

Alahmoot countered. "But if this potion had to be administered on the new moon then Watu had to die that day, hence someone planned his death. He was murdered."

Glenda squinched her eye at Max. "That's a good point."

"Maybe they didn't plan it. Maybe they just had a...premonition...so were ready."

"I have a headache," Glenda sat on the couch.

"So," Martha was clarifying, "we can agree that

someone didn't want Watu's spirit speaking from the dead—"

Everyone nodded.

"—and we know that whomever did this had precise magickal knowledge and aptitude."

Everyone nodded.

"—and they didn't want him speaking about…something."

Everyone nodded.

"So, why do you care exactly what he had to reveal?" Max thought he would play devil's advocate.

"Because someone could've killed him," Martha explained softly. "We have to know. He was a close friend to all of us. And if his spirit came back to speak then it is something worth knowing and we owe it to him to find out. His spirit will not be at rest until it is; even though," she looked at Dorothy, "he has dissipated."

Max understood Martha. She wanted to help. Just like he felt compelled to help Jack because he knew he wasn't at rest. And if Watu was in the same state, or even worse, then Max wanted to make it right. He looked at Dorothy, "You said the Calamus and Cypress mixture would cause the ghost pain as they tried to speak. How can they feel pain if they're dead already?"

"Oh," Martha cautioned, "the Otherworld is just as complex as this one. Don't believe the fictional stories of books and movies to explain death and the beyond so simply. The Otherworld is bound by Universal laws like this one."

"Heck," Glenda pitched in, "even the medical community can't agree if death is the ceasing of the heart or ceasing of brain activity. How can anyone even begin to grasp the complexity of the afterlife?"

"Suffice to say," Martha continued with her gaze upon Max, "that ghosts and spirits are not completely exempt from feeling pain, at least not in the Otherworld."

"Is Watu in the Desert of the Dead with Jack? Is that where the unsettled spirits go?"

"Can't you tell us, Max?" Martha asked slyly. "You've been there."

"He's *communed* there," Dorothy attempted to correct her sister. "It's not the same as *actually* being there."

"Oh no, I believe he has." She took a long sip from her glass, "Haven't you Max," it was a statement rather than a question. "You died the other day when we brought you here. Maybe for just a moment—time has no measure in the Nexus—but you were dead."

Dorothy looked at her shocked. More so that she didn't realize it at the time. It had to be because she was so focused on her cookies. Glenda looked as though she knew too. Alahmoot almost sobered up and stared at Max as if he were some weird alien creature.

"I don't know," Max's voice trembled at the thought. His insides fluttered with stress. "I've been dead before. It felt different that time if I was."

"You've died before?" Glenda was more captivated by Max as the night progressed.

"He has," Alahmoot slurred.

"How?" Glenda asked Max and quickly scowled at Alahmoot, "And *how* do you know?"

"I read it," his speech didn't improve. "I read all about it in his file—"

"I don't want to talk about it," Max asserted making it clear to the suspended sheriff that he didn't want him to say anything more.

"That's fine, Max," Martha intervened giving a steel eye to Alahmoot, "we don't need to know the details. Perhaps some other time when you feel more comfortable...or not at all. It's your choice."

"Oh, but I want to know," Dorothy said deflated knowing that Max wasn't going to spill the details now that her sister gave him permission.

"So if time has no relevance…you could be there for what seems like years and only seconds go by here in your physical body?" Max was making sense of what Martha said and thinking about what he experienced.

"Yes, or vice-versa," Martha watched Max's reactions closely as did everyone else in the room. "You could be there for seconds and minutes or years have passed here in the physical." There was a definite reaction in Max's face that everyone observed.

"But…" Max was finding this hard to believe. On one hand it made perfect sense. It would explain his absence seizures. It would seem like he was somewhere for a long time but mere seconds had gone by like when he was in the principal's office. *How could it be true?* How was it these grown-ups in Ravencrest were discussing witchcraft and the Otherworld like it was real and not some fairy tale while every other grown-up in his life would say it was just that. "…I'm epileptic. I have seizures and hallucinations."

"Tell me, Max. Did your epilepsy begin after you died…the first time?"

"Yeah…" Max suspected where she was going with her question, "…but my doctors said that epilepsy can develop later in life or even after trauma. Are you about to say that my hallucinations are a result of my dying?"

"I'm saying that you most likely had a natural gift for clairvoyant sight which scopes the past, present, and future. When you died you stepped over to the Nexus. I think you keep one foot there now. So I think your visions…not hallucinations," she said pointedly, "…have been augmented from your…stay in the Nexus."

"You make it sound like a Holiday," Max fussed.

"It does sound smashing, doesn't it?" Dorothy wringed her bat mitt with excited hands.

I keep one foot there now. That resonated with

Max. Was that why he saw dead people? It wasn't as cool as the movie made it seem. Was he really seeing dead people or was it hallucinations? The sisters and Jonas seemed to think it was real. Maybe he should believe it too.

"You don't believe your visions do you, lad?" Glenda seemed to read his mind.

"They seem almost like dreams," Max explained.

"You are more correct than you can know," Martha said.

"And you said you don't sleep well?" Glenda remembered what he said moments ago.

"No," Max scoffed. "How can I when every time I shut my eyes I know I'm going to see some horrific scene or know that something traumatic is going to happen to someone? I wish I would never dream again."

"Oh, don't be silly dear," Dorothy wiped one hand on her apron. "You'd die…" she glanced around the room, "…again." The others frowned at her. "I'll get you some more milk," she walked back out to the kitchen.

"So is there anything I can do to help with figuring out what happened to Watu?" Max asked Martha eagerly. And he was thinking whatever the sisters came up with might help Jack too.

Martha called out to the kitchen after Dorothy, "The Calamus and Cypress had to be injected into the body?" Martha asked for clarification.

"Yes," Dorothy replied.

"Plenty of syringes in the morgue," Glenda reasoned.

"If that's in fact where it was done," Martha said. "Did you see anyone else in there Max?"

"Yeah," he pointed to Alahmoot. He remembered seeing the black pants to his uniform when he was under the table hiding.

Martha and Glenda looked at Alahmoot questionably.

"Oh, c'mon," he said. "Of course I visited the body. He's my friend. And I'm the sheriff...*was* the sheriff," he took the last gulp of green liquid from a cordial glass similar to Martha's and looked as though he were about to throw it. "That bitch fired me!"

"Which bitch?" Dorothy chuckled at her rhyme returning from the kitchen. She handed Max another glass of milk taking his empty one.

"Bernice Dinah," he stood up swaying, "the *acting mayor*," Alahmoot made fun of her propriety. He finished off his small drink. "Hit me," he demanded a refill of Glenda.

"Oh, I think he's had enough Absinthe," Martha cautioned.

"Hell, if he got canned, why not?" Glenda grabbed the decanter of green liquid and poured him another.

"You do make that particularly potent," Martha continued to object to the refill.

"You can thank Doctor Lambe for that. He gave me his recipe before he croaked."

"I thought you didn't trust him," Martha said debatingly.

"I didn't trust his motives. But I trust his proficiency. He was damn good at mixtures of all kind; none of us can deny that."

"Why did she fire you?" Dorothy asked Alahmoot almost amused.

"He can tell you," he pointed at Max. "He was there." But he didn't wait for Max to comment. "I was suspended with pay—"

"Suspended with pay?" Glenda barked flabbergasted. "Well hell, that's like being on vacation," she snatched his drink back.

"Like hell—" he plucked it back and plopped back down in the couch. "They're trying to pin Watu's death on me, just like you three," he waved his glass around in the air. "Dinah has two agents with her: Men in Black."

"Men in Black," Dorothy sounded concerned. "Are you sure?"

"They say they're FBI, but you know how that works. I recognize their M.O. So I'm suspended with pay as a bribe...I can read in-between the lines. If I go poking around anymore with Watu's death, then they're gonna pin this thing on me." He emptied his glass in one shot and put his hand out for another. Glenda didn't hesitate to refill it.

Everyone was quiet as they absorbed what Alahmoot had told them. Max noticed Martha looking particularly weighed down by the news as she stared out the window of their living room contemplating the repercussions. "The VEIL is closing," her eyes did not avert from the window.

"Like the veil between this world and the Otherworld?" Max asked. It was close to Halloween and everything he had experienced and everyone he met in this town seemed to be talking about this veil.

"Oh, that veil has been closed a long time...well..." she moved her eyes from the night sky to Max. Her finger traced the rim of her glass. She glanced at her sisters and pondered Max. "Maybe it's not entirely closed...*perforated* would be more accurate." Her eyes followed her finger around the glass as she mused. "Perhaps you may be able to help us in some way."

"Incense," Max suddenly remembered why he had wanted to talk to the sisters again. "I bought some incense from Uva Ursa—"

"Hell she sells everybody incense that's the only *sense* she has," Glenda cut in.

"She said some of these incenses," he tried to ignore Glenda, "could help the unsettled spirits...well...settle. Maybe we can use them to help Jack and Watu. She wasn't specific on what to do exactly—"

"Ha," Glenda guffawed, "imagine that."

Again Max tried to ignore her commentary as he wanted the sister's instruction "—I thought you all would know."

"Of course we know," Glenda growled.

"So what do I do?"

Dorothy chipped in now, "What you need to do—"

"No," Martha interjected with her palm up halting Dorothy's explanation. "What *WE* need to do. *We* will do this together," she gave a look to her sisters that said it wasn't up to debate.

Glenda and Dorothy looked confused. Alahmoot looked drunk. Max smiled.

"Halloween then," Martha said settling the matter. "Be back here with your incenses. We will have to do it Halloween night."

"Great," Max was ecstatic. Then he had a confused look. "So is that actual Halloween night? Or should I be here like right before midnight on October 30th? Or right before midnight on October 31st right before November 1st?"

"What in the Universe are you talking about?" Glenda snapped.

"Uva said something about the timing of spells at Halloween and that people made mistakes with the date...or time...or something."

"Hrmph," Glenda growled, "amateur. Samhain technically starts Halloween right after dark. They just let anybody open a magick shop and delve out horse-shit." She saw that Max didn't appreciate her talking ill of Uva so she attempted to correct herself. "She's probably getting confused from all that religious mumbo jumbo. All religion has done is confuse the hell out of people and get 'em killed. Look laddie, it's real simple. All Hallow's Eve is just that, the eve before Samhain: The night we honor our loved ones that have crossed over; the night we honor our ancestors. Samhain is November 1st: The witch's New Year and Celtic New Year. Some call it the Day of the Dead, which I'm okay with 'cuz that makes sense, but now some say it's the 2nd, but don't get me started on that, again that's just Christianity latching its parasitic teeth into a host belief system feeding off it and poisoning it until it stifles it all together killing it but not before breaking off transforming itself into some completely new life form like one of those face-sucking aliens you see in the movies!"

Okay I'm glad I didn't get her started. And everyone else in the room looked as though they had the same thought. "So," Max eased the words out of his mouth trying to make sense of somewhat of what he just heard, "I should be here Halloween night right after dark?"

"Ha," Glenda said congratulatory. "Yes! Smart kid, I knew he'd get it. I'm starting to like this lad," Glenda smiled to the others.

The fire belched a ball of flame up the chimney spewing smoke and ash out into the cozy living room. Max and Martha jumped up to get away from the disturbance and found themselves standing next to the others as Glenda and Alahmoot even managed to vault from the couch. Dorothy stepped closer to the others with a concerned look.

"What the hell was that?" Alahmoot spoke less slurry.

"Yes, what was it?" Dorothy asked Glenda softly with concern.

She was silent for a moment staring at the fire. The others moved their eyes quietly from the fireplace back to Glenda and back to the fireplace again.

"This is *the* Halloween," Glenda said gravely to her sisters.

The Sisters Grimm looked as though they just had the life sucked out of them.

"What does that mean *'this is the Halloween'*?"

Max asked anxious.

"Yeah," Alahmoot agreed with Max, "What does that mean?"

"It means," Martha said slowly and surreptitiously looking at her sisters, "that this Halloween," Glenda and Dorothy returned timorous faces, "we'll be at the Halloween Bazaar!"

"What?" Glenda and Dorothy said together with shocked reaction.

"You gals are always holed up in here on Halloween night." Sheriff Alahmoot sounded surprised as well. "You've never been at the Bazaar on Halloween night only during the day."

"Right," Martha said. "Change in plans, Max. Meet us at the Bazaar on Halloween night instead. I think you have probably warmed up enough and should get to bed before your mother misses you."

Max's heart sank. He felt so cozy right there in their living room and by the fire that he wished he could just sleep there instead of going back to his bedroom.

"You should be fine to return to your bedroom don't you think, Dorothy?"

"Oh sure," Dorothy smiled. "Watu is toast."

Glenda rolled her eye and drank.

Max looked to the window wearily. He remembered the...*dog*. At least he seriously hoped it was a dog. *It had to be*. But just in case, "Sheriff, can you walk me to my place?" He was so embarrassed to ask, but he was even more embarrassed to ask an old lady to walk him even though he thought they would be more capable if there was any real danger since the sheriff was drunk.

"Sure thing, partner," Alahmoot agreed a little too fast Max thought as he grabbed his shoulder with his plump hand and whisked him out the front door.

Max barely had a chance to set his glass down before being shoved outside by the sheriff.

"And then get back here," Glenda cautioned Alahmoot. "You're in no condition to drive."

Alahmoot had his hand at the base of Max's neck as he walked him through the cold air. Max's eyes scanned the fog hoping there wasn't anything sinister in it. The chilled ground soaked into his skin through his feet only adding to his trepidation. "Max," Alahmoot spoke his name like a warning, "those sisters aren't sweet old grannies. My advice to you is to stay away from them. They're involved in some serious shit." He stopped at the end of the walkway to his front door. "And you don't need to go drawing any more attention to yourself."

Though he was grateful for the escort the fact that Alahmoot hadn't let go of his neck was unnerving. Max looked longing at the two vases that were taller than his sister that guarded the entrance to the front door. He felt a jerk in the center of his stomach. He suddenly saw Alahmoot in the hospital morgue standing above the headless body of Watu. He was in his sheriff uniform. He took a small bag out of his pocket that Max recognized immediately as one of the bags that Uva had put his purchases into. Out of the bag Alahmoot pulled a small pouch with ground herbs in it. He took a small censer from another pocket and poured the herbs into it and lit it at the neck of the body. As the incense burned and wafted to the body he began chanting. Max couldn't understand the words. The sheriff let go of his neck awkwardly as though he sensed that Max was just somewhere else.

It was Alahmoot!

Alahmoot was about to say something when his eyes aimed past Max. Max spun his head around to see what drew the sheriff's attention. There was a tall figure looming in the fog. *Or was there? Was it an optical illusion from the mist swirling and drifting?* Max didn't see it anymore.

"You better get inside," the sheriff told Max still

looking in the direction of where the figure was.

Max wasn't going to argue. He rushed up the walkway and grabbed some firewood from the porch and went inside. He was about to try and peek out the window when he sensed something else. He turned and saw his mother standing in the dark staring out the window into the open backyard. He knew just beyond the fog and trees was Shadow Lake.

"You're thinking about *him* aren't you?" Max asked forgetting about the sheriff.

Evelyn didn't even turn her head in recognition. It was as though she were expecting Max's intrusion. "I'm sure your father is just fine," she said dismissively.

"I didn't mean *him.*"

Evelyn now turned her head slowly as though insulted. "What were you doing outside?"

"I ran out of firewood," Max displayed the wood in his arms.

"Get to bed," she said coldly.

CHAPTER 23

Everyone whispered as Max walked by them in the lunch room and got out of his way.

Apparently, Chance wasn't alone in thinking he was a bully. In the movies it seemed glossy to be the bully. Max felt the gutter ball in his stomach.

Jonas scooched over making room for Max at the table he sat at. Jonas had a huge grin on his face as he watched everyone cower at Max's approach. He seemed the only one to be enjoying this.

"Why do you look so happy?" Max asked sitting down next to Jonas.

"Are you kidding me? This is awesome. All these people pick on me in one way or another. I'm finally a bad-ass by association."

"But nobody wants to talk to me."

"So, nobody every wants to talk to me either, I'd rather have them fear me than pick on me."

"Nobody fears you dork," Cassandra dropped her lunch tray on the table sitting across from them. "First, I'm taking a huge risk sitting here at this table with you."

"Whatever, nobody likes you either," Jonas laughed.

"Shut up, dweeb. Second, Derek looks perfect as usual. You couldn't tell anything happened. So I guess you're off the hook, Dane."

"Don't call me that, please," it reminded him that Chance was pissed at him.

"Fine cutey," she smiled at him. "I forgive you."

"Thanks," Max was genuinely thankful that he had at least two friends. "Why is it that if you just let people pick on you then you're a wimp and if you stick-up for yourself people call you a bully?"

"It's the *Kobayashi Maru*," Jonas sighed. He read Max and Cassandra's muddled faces. "The no-win scenario," he translated.

"Well I'm still pissed at about what you said at Joe's," she pointed her finger at Jonas severely.

"You mean the truth—"

"Jonas," Max stopped him from saying anything more and making it worse. He was an expert at making things worse and didn't want Jonas to do the same. "I think you owe Cassandra an apology—"

"Like you owe Derek one," Jonas countered stubbornly. "You *owe* me for your sandwich," Jonas said to Cassandra.

Max couldn't believe it. Jonas just wasn't getting it. Cassandra was right. No wonder he didn't have any friends.

"Look—" Max was trying to get Jonas to concede.

"No," Cassandra waived her hand at Max. "It's

okay, thanks for trying. Here," she pulled out some cash and tossed it at Jonas. "I'm square with you. But you're not with me," she warned. "Got it?"

"I met with the Sisters Grimm last night," Max blurted in hopes of releasing the stifling air.

"When last night?" Jonas found it hard to believe that Max was out past dark.

Max explained everything that happened from the blue flame and Watu exploding to suspecting that Sheriff Alahmoot killed Watu.

"Oh," Jonas pieced together what Max had related. "You had a vision of the sheriff doing that incense thing to prevent Watu from communicating after he was dead. And you had the feeling he was going to attack you last night after leaving the Sisters Grimm. I think you're right, Max."

"Whoa," Cassandra being the eldest felt compelled to bring a halt to the conversation. "Max, you have to be careful about starting a rumor like that. And you," she looked at Jonas revolted, "you believe anything, for fuck's sake. Hell, you believe in lake monsters, werewolves, ghosts, and aliens and who knows what else...don't even think about elaborating!"

Max fanned the air shushing her. "Something's going on," he pointed to the shocked reactions of the teachers. Jonas and Cassandra turned to see what he was talking about.

The teachers stood and then Principal Hemlock sailed in. She quieted the lunch room. "Attention students! Attention!" she called. "Sheriff Drake has an announcement."

"Deputy Sheriff," Jonas said to Max correcting her.

"Students," Roy Drake began by removing his hat and holding it over his chest, "it's my unfortunate duty to inform you that my boss and good friend Sheriff Alahmoot Tahamont died last night in a car accident."

There was a ubiquitous gasp from the room. Max

felt the color drain from his face into the gutter of his stomach. Jonas and Cassandra looked at him with alarm. *I was just with him last night!* He felt sick.

Sheriff Drake hesitated for a moment regaining his composure before continuing. "This comes at a difficult time right on the heels of the death of Mayor Watu Warakin. In most cities this is something you would simply read about in the paper, but not in Ravencrest, not in our town. We care about our citizens. The mayor and sheriff were good friends to many. They deserved better. I'll be making the rounds to several businesses that they frequented and passing this saddening news. Be sure to tell your parents." He put his hat back on and left with Madame Hemlock.

"There, you see," Cassandra said definitively to Max. "The sheriff couldn't have killed Watu."

"Just because he died in a car accident doesn't make him innocent," Jonas griped at her.

"Well he's gone in any case and you can't go starting rumors about someone when they're dead...it's not polite."

"It was Mr. Creeps," Max said to them. "I saw him in the fog standing in the street—"

"Our street?" Jonas was terrified.

"Yeah, he was there for a second and then I didn't see him again. But the sheriff was there too. I think he saw him."

"And now he's dead!" Jonas' eyes were so big they practically pressed against his glasses. "I knew it! Mr. Creeps is a portent! A harbinger!"

"A harbinger of what?" Chance stopped at their table.

"Death," Jonas hadn't noticed he was answering Chance. "If you see Mr. Creeps then your death must be imminent. I bet Watu saw Mr. Creeps before he died."

"What are you talking about?" Cassandra said

annoyed. "I see Mr. Creeps all the time. I'm not dead."

"Yet," Jonas said hopefully. "I meant if you see Mr. Creeps outside the pumpkin patch he guards, then you're going to die."

Chance looked as if this disturbed him.

"That's ridiculous," Cassandra refused to be sucked in. "You didn't see him, Max, it was just the fog playing tricks on your eyes, but for the sake of dork's argument here then Max should be dead too."

I have been dead—twice!

Cassandra crossed her arms and pointed her eyes at Jonas daring him to counter her point with some kind of bullshit. He remained silent.

Max seized the silence to tell them about Sheriff Tahamont getting suspended. Jonas finally realized Chance was there and joined in giving Max awkward looks as Max revealed that Chance's dad was sheriff before Tahamont's death. He saw that Chance became uncomfortable about his dad being brought into the conversation so Max mentioned that Tahamont called the FBI agents Men in Black in hopes of changing the focus. It worked, because as soon as he mentioned them Jonas went into a rant.

"Men in Black in Ravencrest? That can't be good," Jonas glanced around the lunchroom worried that he was about to be whisked off and never heard from again.

"How can that be bad, dork? Celebrities in Ravencrest are a good thing."

"No," Jonas let out a moan of frustration. "I'm not talking about that lame movie. I'm talking about *real* Men in Black. The real Men in Black aren't the good guys. They work for some government organization and cover up UFO sightings. They threaten and interrogate witnesses."

"I haven't heard about any UFO sightings in Ravencrest. So why would they be here?" Cassandra pushed her now soggy salad away with depressed eyes.

"I've always suspected the Men in Black also get involved with paranormal cases. They were bound to get around to Ravencrest eventually. The paranormal is the norm in this town."

"I think I saw a UFO once," Chance offered.

"What, an Unidentified Fucking Object," Jonas said skeptically.

Cassandra busted out laughing. She was immediately angry at herself because she was trying to stay pissed at Jonas. But it was funny. She attempted to cover it up by flapping her eyes flirtatiously at Chance. "Did you need something beautiful?" She was questioning why he stopped by their table.

Chance looked immediately at Max. And then he looked off in the distance to where Derek was sitting with the swim team. "Catch ya later," he said to Max and left.

He didn't call me Dane. Does that mean he's not pissed at me anymore? Max hoped that was the case. Chance was a senior. Why would he even be interested in being his friend or hanging out with him? Max watched Chance join the swim team at their table. That reminded him. He had swim class today.

CHAPTER 24

"Ow, fuck coach, that hurts when you jam it in like that!"

"You always say that."

Jonas crept down the locker room listening to coach and Chance. He was trying to get in and change for his dance class before the other boys got there and teased him or stuffed him in a locker and even more importantly, before Max found out. As Jonas approached the end of the lockers he had a partial view into the treatment room. He wasn't sure he wanted to see what was going on but his curiosity wouldn't let him turn around. He saw Chance bent over a treatment table facing him, but he was looking down. His pants were pulled down around his ankles and coach was standing behind him.

"Are you almost done?" Chance winced.

"Yeah, I'm done." Coach pulled back exposing a syringe.

Chance peered his head over his shoulder. "Great, and since I'm in the position…," he hinted with a grin.

"Nice try," coach smacked Chance on the ass and walked away to dispose of the syringe.

"You think I'll be ready for the meet?" Chance turned to face coach and pulled his pants up.

"I hope so."

"I'm getting stronger."

"I noticed! I could barely get that needle in your ass."

"Use more lube," Chance joked.

"I got class," Coach started to strip off his clothes.

"Oh, I see," Chance looked at coach admiringly, "you're a tease." Chance winked and walked away.

Jonas quickly jumped into one of the lockers to avoid Chance. Then he realized he couldn't get the locker open from the inside. *Shit, I did it to myself!* He didn't want to scream out. It would be so embarrassing. Yet, it wouldn't be the first time. Suddenly, the locker door whisked open. Jonas screamed.

Max screamed. "What the hell? You scared the shit out of me. What are you doing in here? Was it Derek?"

"No," Jonas climbed out of the locker looking slightly embarrassed as there were more boys in the locker room now. He glanced around quickly not seeing Chance. "I'll tell you later," he rushed off leaving Max standing there stupefied as the other boys laughed at Jonas.

Coach Matthews was in a Speedo waiting by the pool for the rest of the boys to get out of the locker room. His body was tone like Chance's. He just wasn't as lean and tall as Chance. Coach blew his whistle and ordered everyone at the shallow end of the pool. Max was surprised how easy he was with the boys. He expected him to be mean and nasty since he looked rough and bossy. Coach assisted and showed the boys how to tread water and float. That took up all the class time. Max was glad he didn't see Derek or any of the swim team. "Go get some clothes on, Dane." Coach barked at Max. "You got detention."

Max stepped into the school shower reluctantly. His heart was racing. This was not anywhere near like the shower he had at home. This was a huge square room with shower nozzles along the wall without much space between the next nozzle and a large cylinder in the center of the room with nozzles around it. All in all it equaled *zero privacy.* He was procrastinating going to detention and now he had even more reason. All of the boys in his swim class stripped of their swim briefs and were rinsing off. They must be used to this. He hated being the new student. Where was Jonas when he needed him? Max thought about just leaving his swim briefs on but then he would look like a super dork since everyone else was naked. But then he didn't want to get naked. It was the Kobayashi Maru. *Damn Jonas!* He was feeling dorkier by the second. And as if everyone had read his mind the boys were done at once and left the shower with remarks.

"See ya, Max."

"Good luck in detention," a boy named Hunter said snidely. Max knew he didn't mean it. He was in several of his classes and though Max didn't talk to him much he got a bad vibe from him.

Max brushed it off and stripped quickly. He wanted to get this over with before anyone else came in. He chose to get behind the cylinder in the middle of the room so that his view was blocked from the entrance into the showers and so no one coming in or passing by could see him. And no sooner had he completed his thought a naked body came around the cylinder. It was Derek. His body was just as milk white and toned as it was in his dream. What jumped out at Max—that he didn't see in his dream and though he tried to resist looking but couldn't help himself—was his bright red pubic hair above his penis. It reminded him of a circus clown.

"You wanna touch it?" Derek asked roughly.

"What?" Max's eyes jumped, meeting Derek's.

"My dick. You're staring at it hard enough."

"No." Max didn't want to touch it. It was Derek.

"Liar," Derek seemed pleased with himself. "Touch this," and he slammed his fist in Max's gut.

Max didn't have time to react he was so distracted by nudity and embarrassment. He felt his stomach on fire and his whole body came off the ground. He splashed face down on the floor and slid across the shower room. His ears were ringing. He heard the coach in muffled tones coming in after Derek. Max couldn't breathe. All his air was gone. He kept opening his mouth trying to catch air. He thought of fishing with his father and how the fish would struggle for air when they were pulled up on the pier. Max decided right then he wasn't going to fish anymore. He was drowning. He was drowning on a shower room floor. Darkness seeped into his vision.

CHAPTER 25

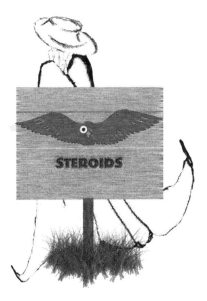

Max's eyes flung open with a pungent smell.

He sat upright immediately. He was in a hospital bed in a private room. Coach was standing over him holding a smelling salt packet. "Your mom will be here any moment. I need to talk to you first."

Max grabbed at his stomach in pain but was listening as he realized he woke in a hospital room…again!

"Derek didn't hit you. I made you do laps around the school on a bike for detention. You hit a cement barrier and impacted with the handle-bars."

"Are you kidding? That's not what happened."

Coach sat on the bed next to Max and put on a smile. "You're a tough kid," he patted his shoulder. "I can respect that. Not many kids can take a punch from Derek

Reid."

"I didn't," Max had a sick look. "I blacked out and ended up in the hospital."

Coach laughed. "Right...look...we have a swim meet this Saturday. I need Derek. He's the star of my junior varsity team."

"So you want me to lie so Derek Reid can be in your swim meet?" Max thought that was a stupid reason.

"No Max, I want you to lie because this isn't just about you...and it's not just about Derek. There are other boys on this team that have worked hard. But they need Derek to win this. He's good. And they've worked too hard to have Derek screw this up because his brain is swimming in testosterone." Coach's eyes drifted from Max, "Sometimes we have to make sacrifices for the greater good."

"Are we still talking about swimming?" Max knew coach wasn't. Max wasn't going to push it. He was almost bought, but he had to find some way out. He wanted Derek to pay. "Chance can't win it?"

"He's on my varsity team. Derek's junior varsity, he would be on varsity but I don't have the room. He'll probably be the captain of my varsity team once Chance graduates." Coach eased back. "You have some talent out there in the pool. I can see it early. That's my job. There'd be room for you on my junior varsity team once Chance moves on and Derek moves up." Coach could see the wheels spinning in Max's eyes that told him he was getting through to him. "If it makes you feel any better...you did kick Derek's ass twice."

He was right about that. Chance was right. He could've killed Derek. Maybe he did deserve to get punched and end up in the hospital. "Deal," Max stuck his hand out.

"You're a team player, Max," coach shook his hand. "And I consider this a personal favor to me. I won't forget this," he smiled at Max.

Max took his hand back rubbing his stomach more. "Let me ask you something?"

"Sure."

"Why is it in the movies people can get hit with pipes and bats and keep getting up to fight and I take one punch in the gut and I'm in the hospital?"

Coach chuckled, "Because real-life is more complicated."

"And more painful."

"Fair enough."

The doctor and Evelyn Dane walked into the room. *At least it wasn't Dr. Evans. This must be another doctor that's on-call.*

The doctor broke out in explanation immediately. "Your test results came back: no broken ribs, no ruptured spleen or internal bleeding. You'll be bruised but otherwise just fine. I'd like to keep him overnight for observation."

"Oh, Max…" Evelyn blurted in a sobbing tone and went to his bed-side with consoling eyes.

The doctor and coach took their cue and left the room.

Evelyn's eyes turned to razors as they left, "…why don't you just die."

Max refused to let his tears out. He wasn't going to give her the satisfaction of hurting him. "I guess we're stuck with each other for a little longer," the words pressed through his lips.

Evelyn considered her son for a moment with a glimmer. She leaned over him, "well done," and kissed him on the forehead. "Enjoy your hospital food," she said drably. "I need to go get your sister from daycare. I had to pay extra thanks to you…again. But since it was an accident I guess I can't get too upset. I'll see you in the morning," she walked out.

Max was at a loss of what to do. His dad didn't want him. His mom didn't want him. And he died twice and that didn't work. He wished there was a way he could just stay in the Nexus. He thought about that hard. That made him feel better. *But how can I do it?*

"Contraband!" Cassandra barged into the room holding a take-out bag.

Jonas followed. "Wow, look at this room," he spun around taking it all in. There was a flat screen behind Max on the wall with his vitals. There was another flat screen on the wall across from his bed for watching TV. The floor where his bed stood was laminate hardwood that came to an s-curve edge where the rest of the room was carpeted in a therapeutic blue. There was a lounge area with a sofa and an inlet with a mirror and wood cabinets. The room looked like it belonged in a luxurious hotel with the exception of the large hospital bed that Max was lying on.

Jonas' comment made Max take notice of it for the first time. It was very extravagant. He was surprised his mom didn't mention it but she was probably too distracted spewing venom.

"That bed's a little bigger than I thought it would be," Cassandra marveled. "I bet I can squeeze in there next to you! Are you naked under these?" She pulled at his hospital gown.

"Uh, I don't know," Max said as though that were a good question. He hadn't noticed until just then that he was wearing a gown. He peeled them away looking down the front.

"Oh my Universe, *Creepy* give it a rest! I'm sure he feels sick enough already." Jonas snorted. "You're clothes are over here, Max." Jonas opened some drawers in a dresser. He held up a pair of superhero briefs. "I have a pair of these!"

"Okay and I'm the creepy one," Cassandra argued. She turned to Max. "But those are soooooo cute," she squealed.

Max felt his face turning as bright red as Derek's pubic hair. His mom was right...*why couldn't he just die?*

"The food, Cassandra," Jonas reminded her closing the drawers.

"Right," she blurted. "I stopped by the CONUNDRUM. I know how bad hospital food is. I've stayed here enough times."

Max and Jonas looked at Cassandra expecting her to elaborate.

"But I don't remember the rooms this nice. Anyway, here you go," she pulled out a sandwich trying to deflect the focus off her, "the Chomp and a Philosopher's Scone compliments of Joe."

"That was nice of him," Max started with the scone. It was scrumptious.

"Joe's a nice guy."

"Yeah, he's the best," Jonas finally agreed with Cassandra on something. "So what happened to you?"

"Yeah, we heard there was some sort of accident."

"Right," Max was trying to remember what his story was supposed to be. "I hit a cement blockade."

"Those darn barriers they have out by the track?" Cassandra grasped Max's arm in sympathy.

Max nodded and decided this was a perfect time to stuff his mouth with the Chomp.

"How did you run into those?" Jonas was confused.

"Coach..." Max gulped some food hoping they would be disgusted with him talking with his mouth full so they'd stop asking questions. "...had me doing laps on a bike."

"Coach Matthews is crazy," Cassandra resolved thinking that was a silly thing to do for detention.

"Coach Matthews *is* crazy," Jonas agreed again with Cassandra. "He's giving steroids to Chance."

Cassandra's mouth dropped open as she spun to

look at Jonas like he was the hub of gossip. "How do you know that?" She asked eagerly.

"I saw him right before your swim class, Max. Chance was bent over naked and coach was giving it to him."

Max chortled his food and Cassandra chuckled.

"Oh, c'mon, you know what I mean."

"Are you sure it wasn't a direct deposit of testosterone," Cassandra sniggered.

"Ha, ha very funny," he shrugged her off. "Max, that must have been the 'concoction' that coach got from Ursa."

That did seem likely to Max.

"That's why I was in the locker. I had to dodge them. And Chance asked about being ready for the swim meet this Saturday."

"Oh no," Cassandra clasped her cheek. "The coach is a cheat," she said devastated.

"And Chance," Max sounded devastated too.

"The whole swim team I'm sure," Jonas added. "That's probably why Derek is such a dick. He's all roided out."

"No, not my Derek," Cassandra pounded Max's bed in a feeble protest. "That can't be true," she said mostly to convince herself rather than disagree with Jonas.

"That explains a lot," Max was thinking out loud. He looked at Jonas and Cassandra who had his attention. "Derek punched me! That's why I'm here."

"What?" Cassandra was in disbelief.

Jonas couldn't say anything. His eyes were bugged out.

"Coach asked me not to say anything—"

"Yeah, I bet," Jonas found his voice before grabbing the last of Max's Philosopher's Scone and popping it in his mouth. "He's trying to protect his job."

"And secure the win this weekend," Cassandra

reluctantly agreed with Jonas.

"We have to tell someone," Jonas looked at Cassandra.

"Principal Hemlock," she suggested.

Max felt compelled to defend the coach...or was it Chance he was defending? "What do you two even care? You're not the ones that had your guts punched out your ass."

"Did you shit yourself?" Cassandra turned her attention back to Max.

"Probably pissed himself," Jonas said impassively.

"Maybe, I don't know. I was in the shower, I was already wet. And I blacked out. No, I didn't shit myself," Max just realized what Cassandra asked first.

"I bet you have a cute pink winker," Cassandra grabbed at his hospital gown.

"What?" Max deflected her hands.

"Holy shit, you were punched in the shower. So Derek was naked. How big is it? Does the carpet match the drapes?"

"Yeah, bozo red."

Cassandra's mouth dropped open and face lit up like she just won the lottery.

"Anyway," Jonas attempted to get them back on track, "we can't let this go. We're talking about steroids and cheating. It's more than you getting punched."

"Look," Max said desperately setting his Chomp on the nightstand, "you can't say anything to anyone about this."

"Then why did you tell us?" Jonas looked put out.

"Because you're my friends and I have no one else to tell," Max was suddenly overwhelmed with emotion. He couldn't help it. "No one else cares about me." *Don't cry! Don't cry!* "My mom doesn't want me. My dad doesn't want me. I can tell by your faces you think I'm exaggerating, but my mom told me herself she doesn't want me. I'm the reason my parents are getting divorced." *Don't cry! Don't cry!* "They're having a custody battle because neither of them wants me. When have you ever heard of that? I can't even call my dad to find out what he's thinking. I don't have his number. I don't know my own dad's phone number because he wouldn't give it to me! I have to see a psycho-babble because I'm fucking crazy and I see scary shit all the time whether I'm awake or asleep or having a hallucination or premonition or whatever the fuck anyone wants to call it. So my mom is constantly worried that I'm gonna hurt my little sister. And now I'm mixed up in some steroid scandal. I'm tired. I'm tired of the drama. I just want to go to school and maybe get on the swim team and hang out at the coolest coffee and comic shop I've ever seen with my two best friends." The tears flowed out his eyes. *So much for not crying!* He tried to force it back but ended up choking and snorting which made it worse. He couldn't look at his friends anymore he was embarrassed.

Cassandra smothered Max burying his face in her chest. "It's okay, Max." She was panicked and trying to console him patting him on the back. "It's okay, we won't tell anyone," she looked at Jonas for him to agree.

"Whatever," Jonas was clueless. "Just because he had a drama queen episode doesn't change the fact that there's some serious illegal stuff going on at school."

"You're *best friend*," she looked at Jonas for him to desperately get a clue as Max's face was still hidden, "doesn't want to get involved. Besides, I'm sure they do some kind of testing at the swim meet. They'll get busted eventually," she gritted her teeth and contorted her face as if to say *work with me Jonas*.

It was the emphasis on *best friend* that got Jonas' attention. No one ever admitted to being his friend, least of all, their best friend. "Yeah, Cassandra's...right," he made a face like he just ate something sour. "They'll get found out eventually."

Max sat back as Cassandra patted his chest. "You feel better?" She asked.

He nodded wiping his eyes; still embarrassed about breaking down in front of them.

"Are you serious about your parents?" Cassandra was shocked that a parent would tell their kid they didn't want him.

There was a knock at the door and Chance peeked his head in. He was surprised for a moment that Max wasn't alone but recovered quickly, "Room for one more in here?"

"We were just leaving," Cassandra answered before Jonas could say something negative. "And you be nice to him," she warned Chance pointing a stern finger at him. "C'mon troll," she yanked Jonas from the hospital room.

Chance watched them leave before turning to Max and holding up a to-go sack. "I see I was too late," he said a little disappointed seeing Max's half-eaten Chomp. "I got you the Champ," Chance sat on the bed next to Max pulling out the sandwich. "But I also got you Fenris Fries," he said hopefully taking out the huge potato cut wedges.

"Fenris fries?"

"Yeah, Joe loves mythology. Fenris was a monster-size wolf. He was supposed to be son of Loki I think...anyway...the fries are huge."

"I see that," Max was feeling hungry again.

"Oh, and I brought you this," he gave Max a blanket with bright colors and an American Indian design. "I know it gets cold in these hospitals and their covers are paper-thin."

"This isn't Derek's is it?"

"Ha, no," Chance became more serious. "It was my mom's. She made that for me. It's a wearing blanket. I was able to give it back to her when she was in the hospital."

Chance didn't want to think about that now. "Not that you're going to die," he made light of his story.

"Thanks, I'll give it back once I'm out of here. Your mom must have known a lot about Native American design," Max marveled at the colors and detail she put into it as he covered himself. It was much warmer than his hospital sheet.

"Yeah, well she should be, she was Abenaki."

"You're part Indian?"

"That's what they tell me," he smiled.

"Thanks by the way," Max indicated the sandwich. "If you haven't eaten; then why don't you have the Champ, I'll finish mine," Max leaned to get his sandwich and Chance immediately intercepted it and handed it to him.

"Share the fries with me," Chance insisted. "I have a swim meet this weekend…"

Max couldn't help but think of what Jonas saw. He wanted to ask him if it was true, but didn't think that was a good idea at all. He was enjoying being with him. Maybe he could get a read on Chance and find out if Jonas was wrong somehow. Max stared at Chance as he ate trying to look past his long lashes into his cocoa brown eyes. All he got was a warm feeling inside.

"So," Chance recovered from a bite, "speaking of the swim meet…," he ran his hand over his head indicating this was a ritual before a competition.

He got his haircut. That was putting it mildly. His previous short messy hair which Max really liked was now buzzed off. He barely had a hair on his head. Max knew he could never get his own hair cut that short it wouldn't look good on him. But Chance wore it well. Max decided there probably wasn't a hairstyle Chance could wear and not look good. He probably could even be in the hospital beat-up and still make it look sexy. Did he just think sexy? Well, his lips were definitely sexy. They were full and looked delicious he bit into his Chomp wondering what they tasted like.

"…I ran into coach before I got here. I know what happened to you—what *really* happened. Thanks for covering for…thanks for covering for the team. They should be grateful."

"Except they can't know about it."

"…Right. Well *I* appreciate what you did, and I'm sorry for what Derek did to you." Chance decided he wasn't upset with Max anymore and was trying to apologize for Derek but knew Max wouldn't accept it outright, especially not from him.

"I guess we're even," Max renounced reluctantly.

Chance's eyes said he knew neither Max nor Derek was in agreement on that, but he didn't say anything. He downed some more monstrous fries.

"Uh, okay…so how do you stay all muscly?" He asked watching him finish the fries and his sandwich. Then he just remembered—steroids!

"Well, I train a lot. I'm in the gym and pool almost every day. And it certainly doesn't hurt that I'm a teenager like you. You know…high metabolism, raging hormones…lots of sex," he winked at Max.

"Oh," Max said confused. "Well, I don't even know that I qualify as a teenager."

"How old are you again?"

"Eleven…I'll be twelve on Halloween."

"Hot…you're a virgin right," Chance knew he was. He didn't wait for Max's reply. "Maybe you'll get a spankin' and a treat with a trick for the night," he winked again at Max.

Max was completely lost.

"Ha, you are so innocent it's cute," Chance knew Max didn't have a clue what he just said. "You have some amazing green eyes you know that?"

Max was warm again and feeling flustered. He was having trouble speaking for some reason. "So…you wear a Speedo when you compete?"

"Yeah, I wish I could go naked that thing is so tight."

Max felt himself struggling for words again picturing that. "And you have a tattoo?"

Chance considered Max for a moment. "You must have seen me swim. Yeah, right above my butt."

How did I know that? Did he see Chance swim? No, it was in his dream, when he was with Derek. Max wanted to ask if that was real, but was too nervous.

A nurse barged in. "Sorry honey," she said to Chance. "Visiting hours are over," she smiled at him.

"Okay," Chance got up grabbing hold of Max's hand. When the nurse turned to walk out Chance turned quickly leaning in and gave Max a quick kiss on his cheek. "See ya tomorrow if they let you out," he smiled.

Wow, his smile is pretty too. Max felt a strange sensation in the center of his stomach watching Chance leave. It was the absence of the gutter ball. For once he felt…what was it? He felt…*Good!*

CHAPTER 26

"The Celtic Cross."

Max roused from his slumber. At first, he expected he was back in Burlington. Then he thought he was in bed on Shadow Lake Lane. Then the cold seeped into his pores and he realized he was still in the hospital and squeezed Chance's blanket closer to him.

Angelica Saffron sat on the edge of his bed wearing a hospital gown. In place of the scarf around her crown were bandages. "That's a nice blanket. Good idea. These hospitals are always cold. As I was saying the Celtic Cross is an excellent and popular tarot spread," she shuffled a thick deck of cards that were larger than the cards his dad played poker with. "It's time for your reading," she smiled brightly reminiscent of Dorothy Grimm. "Now, I must confess that my deck is a bit unconventional. Most people use a single deck, in fact, I don't know of anyone else that does readings like me. I use three decks from different types of tarot. I have an Arthurian one, a Hermetic one and a Mythical one. I just couldn't decide. I liked them all. So it's not uncommon in my readings to get multiples of the same card. But each deck tells its own story and speaks to the diversity and intricacies within each of us. And if you do get multiples of a card then the Universe or your Higher Self is really trying to send you a message. So what the heck, why not," she giggled.

"Okay," Max was groggy and could tell it was still night. That seemed fine to him, but..."what are you doing here?"

"Oh, I heard you stirring in your sleep from across the hall so I figured I could sneak out and visit. I don't like hospitals. I bet you don't either, so I thought you might like the company. I know I do," she patted his hand.

"No...I mean...what are you doing in the hospital?"

"Oh," her smile diminished. "Well, turns out that my cancer didn't really go into remission. It progressed. Which means it spread," she patted her bandages on her head.

Max grabbed her plump hand. "I'm sorry."

"Oh," she patted his hand again, "you're sweet."

"I'm really not."

"Now, hush, don't you talk like that," she frowned at him. "We've all done things we aren't proud of. We can't change what we've done. All we can do is change who we are now. Isn't that right?" Her smile inched back.

"Yeah, I guess." Max thought about that seriously.

"All right then," she spun the tray table from the side of the bed over Max's lap and smacked the deck of cards down on it. "Now, shuffle."

"I don't know how to shuffle. My dad was

supposed to teach me," *he was supposed to teach me a lot of things.* Max felt the gutter ball back in his stomach.

"You're not a Vegas dealer. Actually, they do shuffle more like this now that I say it," she spread the cards out on the tray. "Just mix them around."

"So how does this work?" Max asked mixing the cards all around. He did see that there were three different kinds of cards from the design work on the covers of them. "Are you psychic?" Max asked hopefully thinking that if she were maybe she could settle for him whether he was crazy or not. He always thought he was but since he moved to Ravencrest he was hearing otherwise from Jonas and the Sisters Grimm.

"Everyone's psychic," she said brightly.

"You're kidding right?"

"No, of course not. Everyone can draw, just not everyone's good at it. And being good at something is relative. There are plenty of artists that are critically acclaimed that I wouldn't pay two cents for their work but with enough practice someone could hone their drawing abilities and probably turn out some decent work. But some have a natural ability for drawing just like psychic ability. Everyone can practice honing their psychic ability but people don't because they don't believe in it or have been taught it's evil," she smiled like that was ridiculous. "Are you done shuffling?" She saw Max stopped mixing the cards.

He nodded.

"Perfect, now draw one from the mix; don't think about it."

Max picked a card that had a gold circle with twelve segments inside it. At the top of each segment were knights on horses. Surrounding the circle on the outside at the three, six, nine and twelve o'clock positions were Scutum shields.

"You picked an Arthurian card," Angelica said as

though that was something revealing. "The way this works, Max, is that I read the cards...or interpret them. Your higher-self chooses the cards, like you did just now. You can look at it as your subconscious mind is speaking to your conscious mind. And it has all the answers."

"Mr. Lee said something just like that about the higher-self."

"Oh, well that makes sense. He's a very spiritual person. And a dear," she smiled. "Now, gather up all the rest of the cards into a stack." She watched Max make the stack. "Now, are you right-handed or left-handed?"

"Right-handed."

"Okay, then take your left hand and cut the stack to the left." Max did so. "Good," she put the bottom cut on top of the other and held onto the deck. "Now, flip up the card that you drew."

Max did. It was marked with the Roman numeral *IV* with a picture of a man on a throne. At the bottom of the card it read: *ARTHUR.*

"This card is your significator. It represents you in the reading and represents you at this moment in time." She tapped the card. "Traditionally this is known as THE EMPEROR in other decks. So you think it would mean the same thing, but, as I said, each deck speaks its own language. So what does this card mean about you I bet your wondering?"

Max nodded eagerly. He was awake now and captivated.

"The emperor means a strong masculine force in your life...or lack there-of. That will probably depend on the other cards in your reading. This card resonates on a divinatory level. You are challenging the father principle within yourself—meaning you are trying to manifest a creative idea or even establish a structure of a home and family life. This card pictures the emperor enthroned. In this case more specifically—Arthur. Arthur was the guardian of the land. When he attempts to abandon his kingly responsibilities and lead a life of his own he comes to grief. When he fulfills his duties he is given the support and assistance of many people and mystical forces. He is a lone and withdrawn heroic figure. He is ambitious and driven and can achieve great victories and conquests but will always be complicated by strife."

Max's interest was piqued, especially the commentary about a father-figure. He didn't want to interrupt and break Angelica's stride.

"Are you ready for the reading?"

"Yes, please."

"I'm going to do a classic spread called the Celtic Cross. This is a popular and revealing tarot spread." She took the top card from the deck that Max shuffled (one from the Hermetic deck), turned it face up and placed it across the significator. "This crosses you." It was marked: *II THE HIGH PRIESTESS.* A regal female with long robes sitting on a throne holding a grimoire was pictured. The crescent moon was in the back. Angelica looked at Max deliberately. "You're not getting along with your mother."

"Right," Max confirmed pathetically.

"Obviously, you have an interest in the occult and esoteric which is why we're doing this reading but this card confirms that. Also, I'd say you have strong psychic intuition and even powerful dreams. There is some sort of…encounter…that awaits you in the shadow world." She looked at Max cautiously. She was trying to determine if any of this was making sense to Max. She could tell it was. She continued. She pulled the next card off the deck (another Hermetic card), turned it face up and placed it above the significator. "This is above you." It was marked: *XXI THE UNIVERSE.* The card was deep blue with the earth floating in the stars and surrounded by cosmic energy. "This represents how things appear to be on the surface." She looked at the card for a moment and then back to Max. "It would seem to many that things are wonderful and cheerful in your life, but I also see a journey into the Underworld: a journey inside yourself; inside your psyche. Are you seeing a psychologist?"

There was a flash of light in Max's peripheral vision.

"Lightning," Angelica said delighted. "That really sets the tone doesn't it? Okay, on we go," she put the next card below his significator. "This is below you. This is the deep reality." She turned over a card from the Mythical deck. *XVIII THE MOON.* The card pictured a face in the full moon looking down on a river in the night with two stone towers in the distance. "Hmmmm...," she looked at Max decisively. "You are dealing with some personal demons."

Max nodded.

"You doubt yourself and your intuition. Trust in your dreams, they may have the answers you seek."

That's what I'm afraid of.

There was a rumble in the air as she set the next card to the left of *ARTHUR.* "I set this card here because it's behind where your significator is facing. So this card represents what's in your immediate past." It was another Mythical card: *3 OF SWORDS.* Three swords intersected and pierced a column. She waved her finger over the other cards as she put the pieces of the puzzle together. "Your parents are going through a divorce."

Wow, she's good. "Yeah," he said solemnly.

Angelica patted his hand. "Well, that explains a lot. Now, dear, don't think that's your fault," she attempted to comfort him. "You probably think it's your fault but it isn't."

Okay, maybe she's not that good.

She saw doubt in Max's face. "Let's move on then. This next card is what's in front of you; your immediate future."

Please don't be DEATH. It's going to be DEATH. Please don't be DEATH. It has to be DEATH!

She flipped the card up and placed it to the right of ARTHUR. It was an Arthurian card.

Max sighed in relief. It wasn't DEATH! Then his heart fluttered with excitement at seeing the picture. The card pictured an ornate silver chalice bejeweled with heart-shaped gems and overflowing with blue liquid. *The Elixir of Life! I'm going to find it!*

"*THE ACE OF CUPS,*" a sprightly smile came across Angelica's face. "You have a love interest."

"What?" Max dug his fists in his blanket sitting up and shooting his eyes over the card as though he missed something. "No...I don't have a love interest." *She's wrong...again!*

"This is your immediate future," she reminded him, "so maybe not yet, but soon."

Max considered the blanket for a moment, and then brushed it off. *It has to mean the Elixir of Life.*

"You see," she pointed at the arrangement of six cards, "the shape of the layout is the Celtic Cross."

Max noticed it looked like the cross he'd seen on first-aid kits.

"But we're not done yet," she smiled. "There's more. The layout isn't complete." She pulled the next card off the deck. Max could see from the cover it was a Hermetic card. "This is you right now in this moment in time." She flipped the card and set it to the right of the Celtic Cross. *XIII THE REAPER*: a skull figure swept a scythe as it danced through a field strewn with bodies and skeletons.

Max grimaced. "That's *DEATH*, right?"

"Yes...but...it represents your psychological state," Angelica said hopefully. "It's not really that bad of a card. It doesn't represent a physical death per se..."

Wrong again.

"...it's more the end of one aspect of your life so that something else can take its place. But we can't forget the significance of this particular card. In other decks this is the *DEATH* card, however, this is *THE REAPER*. This means the individual is reaping what he has sown. Looking at your other cards this clearly indicates a great time of transition for you." She sat back taking in Max's whole aura. "Max, your parents are going through a divorce and you are blaming yourself for what's happening to them. You think that everything bad that happens to you is because you deserve it because you caused their divorce. Max...honey..." she patted his arm, "...you are not responsible for what is happening to your parents. Whatever *differences—*"

That must be a grown-up thing.

"—your parents are having is their doing. We can only be responsible for our own actions and subsequently have to account for whatever repercussions come from those actions. This is what *THE REAPER* teaches. We're each responsible for our own happiness."

That sounded smart. Many people did seem to blame others for their personal unhappiness. Maybe he did too. But he still thought the *DEATH* card referred to his own death or that he felt like the walking dead. She did say the card represented his current state.

Thunder growled outside the window. Angelica looked at Max delighted. "I just love rain, thunder, and lightning. Okay now," she pulled the next card from the deck, flipping it and putting it above the previous card. The card was a Mythological one depicting a skeleton in a cowl rowing a skiff across a river of stars. Just beyond was a three-headed dog on the shore: *XIII CHARON.*

"This card represents the reality in which you are," she looked at the card again. It made her consider her own situation momentarily. "Let me clarify," she amended her comment. "There's multiple ways to look at this. This is a

DEATH card again—"

Well I've died twice.

"—in this particular spot in the layout it also represents your house and home. You know, how others feel around you. Obviously, your parents think their marriage is dead."

Max could see that.

"Of course, we can also look at this card astrologically. This card is in position number eight and house eight in astrology is the house of sex. She looked at all his cards so far. "Are you a Scorpio?"

"Halloween is my birthday."

"Oh, how fun," she squealed. "Yes, you are definitely a Scorpio. And Scorpios are very sexual."

"So does that *DEATH* card mean my sex life is over before it starts?" Max asked grimly.

Angelica laughed. "Oh no, dear," she smiled looking around the dim empty room to make sure no one else was around, "the French refer to the orgasm as 'le petit mort' or 'the little death.'" She giggled. "You see the Eighth House places sex, death and rebirth all at the same level. We all experience death and rebirth in life and even on a daily basis: failed relationships—"

"—failed marriages."

"—exactly," she patted his leg. "But it leads to new things: a rebirth, new relationships in a new town, new friends, new hairstyles," she pointed to his head with a wink.

Max smiled.

Angelica giggled to herself some more and found her finger tapping the *ACE OF CUPS.*

Max noticed her looking at him like she knew something but didn't want to say. "What is it?" He had to know.

"Where did you say you got this blanket?" She tugged on the wearing blanket.

"Chance gave it to me. Well, he let me use it. It was his mother's."

"Oh," she patted his leg again. "Chance is such a nice boy," she smiled prudently. "But we're not quite done with this card. Just to give you some small insight since this card is *CHARON*. In mythology Charon is the ferryman that carries over the newly deceased souls across the River Styx—depicted here as stars. People would place coins on dead bodies because it was said you needed to pay Charon to take you across the River Styx. Those that didn't pay were left to wander the shore and not granted access to the Underworld: or the Otherworld; or the afterlife... whatever your fancy."

"So someone could be wandering the shore because their body wasn't properly buried. That doesn't seem right." Max was troubled for Jack.

"We can look at that metaphorically rather than literally. It probably means if you don't pay your debts...your karmic debts that is...meaning if you don't live your life in a good way or attempt to make amends for the things you've done wrong then in essence you haven't paid your dues and aren't allowed entrance to the next life."

That explained why he showed up in the Nexus when he died. "What if the River Styx is dried up?"

"What makes you ask that?"

Max thought about the Desert of the Dead. "Oh, I saw it in a dream once. There was no river, but a desert...well a cold wasteland."

"Maybe the desert was just the shore."

"Huh...I haven't thought about that. I also saw a mirror in my dream. It was a long mirror."

"Was this close to the wasteland?"

"Yeah."

"Well, some would say that a mirror could be interpreted as a body of water, because water reflects."

"So the mirror could be the River Styx?"

"Absolutely," she smiled. "Incidentally, running or moving water is an ethereal cleanser because it doesn't reflect. So that's why you will hear in many legends or folklore that evil cannot pass a moving body of water. That's simply because it will cleanse negative energy."

Wow, she is good. But that still didn't explain why Jack wasn't able to cross-over. If the River Styx was right there, why was he unable to get through the door? Unless, Jack did something horrible, but he couldn't have he was just a kid. But so was Max. Max didn't want to believe that about Jack. There had to be some other reason.

Angelica drew the next card from the top of the deck flipping it and placing it yet again above the previous. An Arthurian card: *XIII BANSHEE.*

Max noticed the Roman numeral immediately. "*DEATH* again," he said hopelessly, "of course."

"Now, now," Angelica read Max's face. "Don't panic."

Max studied the card furiously. There was a young woman in a rippling dress under the blue moonlight. She stood next to a river running over stones. Her hair flowed in the air and her mouth was elongated and agape in an open scream. He knew this reading had to be about helping Jack to the afterlife, but he couldn't ignore that he already died twice. *Did this mean there was going to be a third time?* He was sure Angelica thought this was about his parents getting divorced.

Angelica tapped her finger on the bed tray where the cards laid as she considered her next words carefully. Angelica looked at Max finally deciding what to say. "You have some serious mother issues." The room rumbled from the approaching storm.

No shit. Max chose not to say anything and waited for her to elaborate.

She did elaborate as Max suspected. "This card

represents your hopes and fears regarding this reading, or in this situation, your parent's divorce. Obviously, you are not hoping for death," she giggled. She noticed that Max didn't react and decided to continue. "So, clearly this card represents your fears. Now, back to what I said about you having mother issues. It would seem that your mother does blame you to a degree for her pending divorce."

"Yes!" *Now, we're getting somewhere.*

"Sweetheart," she grabbed his leg again. "Just because your mother may blame you doesn't mean it's your fault. Like I said earlier we are each responsible for our own happiness and even more so for our own actions." She pressed on his leg with her next words as to drive the point home. "This is not your fault."

Yes it is. But that's okay, Angelica doesn't need to understand. I heard what I needed.

"Now," she tapped the card, "let's examine the BANSHEE shall we?" She waited for Max to nod so she knew he was tuned in. "This is an Arthurian card so the *BANSHEE* relates to the Washer at the Ford which is an aspect of Morgana or Morgan or Morrighan. Anyway, it gets all confusing when you try to think of it like that," she waved her hand in the air as if clearing smoke. "The point is the *BANSHEE* weeps for her dead child…or children depending on the story…"

Max was listening as though his life depended on it. His eyes were getting wet.

"… and those that hear her wailing laments were foretold to die. King Uther, Arthur's father, allegedly heard the wail of the *BANSHEE* the night he died. She has been affected by death so tragically that she is cursed with the knowledge of other's deaths. The *BANSHEE* is the Dark Woman of Knowledge. She initiates us into looking deep into ourselves." Angelica looked at Max painfully. "Honey, you are so young to be putting so much emotional pressure on yourself." She could see the tears in his eyes but knew he'd be embarrassed if she brought it up. "One last card and the Celtic Cross spread is complete," she said merrily.

Max appeared anxious. Angelica looked equally anxious.

"What does this card mean?" Max asked quickly before she flipped it.

"It represents the final outcome."

They could both see the next card was an Arthurian one. They looked to each other as though the slightest disturbance would cause the room to explode. "Well," Angelica said softly, "it can't be a *DEATH* card," she said more to convince herself rather than reassure Max. Max pulled the blanket closer as he felt his body get colder. Angelica flipped the card and again placed it above the previous. Max could see his breath in the lightning that peeked around the blinds. *XV THE GREEN KNIGHT.*

Max had no idea what that meant. "What does that mean?"

"In other card decks it is known as *THE DEVIL.*" There was a crack of thunder that reverberated through Max's hospital room shaking the walls knocking one of the stock photos swinging. Angelica jumped looking at Max concerned. Max was startled as well. Angelica waited for the room to settle and regaining her poise before continuing. "Okay," her hands fluttered in the air flustered, "the *GREEN KNIGHT* is shown here headless and adorned in skulls. He stands in King Arthur's court during a Christmas feast. The GREEN KNIGHT challenged Arthur's knights to the Beheading Game stating that the challenger would have one chance to behead him and if he survived he would return the blow a year later. Gwalchmai took up the challenge and delivered a severing blow to the *GREEN KNIGHT.* However, the *GREEN KNIGHT* stood up retrieving its head and reminded Gwalchmai he would return again in a year. The *GREEN KNIGHT* is the champion of winter or the Otherworld. He stands for the old year as it cedes into the new. He represents the challenge that all seek on their quest. And in your case I can't overlook the association of *THE DEVIL*...which...represents..." she hesitated.

"What? What is it?" Max demanded. He had to know.

"Uh...sexual obsessions...or impulses..."

"What?" Max felt a sudden pulling from the center of his stomach that made him retch.

"Max!" Jack was next to his bed in a panic. "What did thou do? Thou did something!"

Angelica jumped at the sudden appearance of the boy.

"There you are!" A nurse stormed into the room. "Come, Angelica, I've been looking for you." She grabbed her arm.

"Nurse Fran," Angelica smiled getting up.

"But, wait...no..." Max was torn by Jack's appearance and Angelica being pulled away. "What does the card mean? What's the outcome? What's going to happen?" Max was still freezing and reached for Angelica but his hands got caught up in his blanket and fumbled stopping her.

"Well, maybe some sexual issues," she whispered back to Max so that Nurse Fran wouldn't hear. "Hold onto those cards for me." She winked as Nurse Fran pulled her out of the room.

"Jack!" Max turned a look of shock to Jack because he saw him come out of his body. "What...how...?" He was going to ask where he came from but he just saw where he came from. He didn't understand how. Max clasped at his chest and stomach. "Were you inside me?"

"I'm sorry, Max, but I was scared when the Knightmare appeared. I was afraid what horrible fate would await me. I don't think I can handle any more pain," his eyes were sorrowful. "So..." he looked guilty, "...I jumped inside thy body to hide. Thou didn't protect thy self before thou entered the Nexus so it was rather easy. I'm sorry. I should have asked but I didn't have time."

"Are those the protective glyphs and what-ya-muh-call-its you were talking about?"

"Protective circles, aye." Jack was catching on to Max's strange jargon. "And again," he pointed to the tarot cards, "you didn't protect thy self."

"I wasn't in the Nexus; I was just getting a...reading...or fortune...whatever."

"Nay, anytime thou access thy higher self or the occult thou are accessing the Nexus. Care must be taken. Thou don't go into the woods alone without protecting thy self."

Uh...actually I do. But Max decided not to press it.

"That woman should have known better...but...I guess she couldn't have done a banishing."

"Why not?"

"Thou don't know?"

"Uh...no."

"It is easy. Draw a five-pointed star in the air with thy hand and envision it in blue-flame. This star is called the pentagram. It is a protective symbol. If thou art banishing you would start at the lower left point of the star and not the top."

Max started to do it.

Jack put his hand out to stop Max. "Nay, thou will banish me."

"Oh, sorry, but aren't you kinda banished already? You can't get past that...door. And you're already dead. How much worse can it get?" *Wow, that sounded really insensitive. I am such an asshole.*

"Aye, thou are correct. But somehow I feel that if I were banished I would lose total control of my spirit; that I would be forced into doing unspeakable things."

Max saw Jack's eyes stare off into his mind's eye like he often found himself doing when he was trying to figure out if his hallucinations were just that or something real or a memory. "So why don't you use that banishing pentagram on the Knightmare to get rid of him?"

"It does not work that way. A spirit cannot banish another spirit. Not like this."

"Oh," Max said defeated. Then he remembered what Glenda did to him when he was at the campfire. He was sure that was the symbol she made in the air that snapped him out of the hallucination and back to Ravencrest.

"Max," Jack marveled at the tray that hovered above his bed. "Do thou see? Thou did do something," he pointed to the card layout.

"Oh, that's the Celtic Cross layout."

"It's more than that," he swiveled the tray turning it sideways in front of Max.

Then Max saw it too. It was the symbol he saw on the door of Yggdrasil. "So what does that mean?"

"Thou unlocked the door I think. I feel thou have done something."

Max could feel some kind of energy in the air. It was new. It was exciting. But he wasn't sure if it was the excitement he felt before something fun, or the excitement he felt out of fear, or just before he died. "But how could I have done that? All I did was get a tarot card reading."

"I am not certain," Jack answered excited. "Keys and locks work and look differently."

"So you can go now? You can cross over, right?" Max was ecstatic. This meant he didn't have to worry about getting the Elixir of Life.

"If that were truth I believe I would be gone already. I do not comprehend," Jack was disappointed.

"I don't get it either," Max said. *Nothing is simple.* Max saw another flash of lightning in the room. The green flicker is what caught his attention. His mouth froze open; air swirling out.

Jack whirled around seeing Max's expression. It was the Knightmare—standing there headless and glowing green. "Get out of here, Max!" Jack shouted. "It's after me!"

"No, I won't leave you! Get inside me! I can protect you!" *Can I? Why did I say that?*

"No Max, go! It's too dangerous." The Knightmare stepped toward Jack.

Max leapt off his bed and on top of Jack, and as he suspected Jack disappeared inside him. He could feel it. It was like a cold I.V. flowing under his skin. Even though the Knightmare was headless he could tell it was glowering down at him. The skulls on its armor looked poised to devour him in the green hue. *Oh shit! Oh shit! What do I do?* The banishing pentagram—it worked for Glenda Grimm, why not him? He envisioned blue flame as he etched it with the palm of his hand in the air in front of him. And as he traced the pentagram in the air Max couldn't believe his eyes. He saw a real blue flame form in the air. He drew a real burning blue pentagram hovering in the air in front of him.

"Max how did thou do that?" Jack's voice asked inside his head.

"I don't know. I just did you what you said."

The Knightmare stepped toward Max.

Max instinctively shoved his hands out at the pentagram like he was pushing a shopping cart down an aisle. The burning blue pentagram hurled into the Knightmare blasting into sparks. The Knightmare halted as several of the symbols on its armor lit up in no discernable sequence or pattern. Max wasn't sure if he stopped it or if it was just confused. *Well, I'm not waiting to find out.* Max turned and ran for the door. Just as he reached for the handle his body flew back feet first. He did a belly flop on the hospital floor knocking the wind out of him.

"It's him," Jack's voice echoed in his head. "He's too well protected. The pentagram didn't work."

Max's body started sliding back toward the Knightmare. Then Max felt himself retch again as there was a pulling at the center of his stomach. Max managed to flip himself over onto his back as he was sliding and grabbed the bed ceasing his motion. He saw the Knightmare standing where it was before with its arm reaching toward him with an open palm in the air.

"Let me go, Max!" Jack pleaded. "He's too strong!"

No, I won't let him have you. He'll have to kill me!

"Max, don't do this, please!"

Max couldn't stop retching as he felt Jack being pulled from the center of his stomach. Max was retching so much he couldn't catch his breath. Everything started to get dim when he suddenly saw Jack fly out of his body and into the Knightmare.

The Knightmare vanished in a burst of flame with Jack.

The door crashed open and Chance bolted in with a nurse in hot pursuit protesting that he was there at 3 a.m. Then she saw Max on the floor struggling to breathe and in a puddle of his own urine. "Oh my! Stay with him!" She yelled at Chance. "I'll get the doctor." She ran back out of the room.

Chance knelt down sitting Max up. He was sure Max didn't even know he was there.

The nurse returned almost immediately with Dr. Evans. "What happened?" He took out a muscle light checking Max's pupils. "What are you doing here?" He demanded of Chance.

"Does it matter?"

"Check his vitals," Dr. Evans instructed the nurse

as he continued to examine Max.

"Here, hold this here for me," the nurse asked Chance to keep an electronic thermometer against Max's neck as she put an electronic ring around his arm.

Chance patted Max on the back gently trying to comfort him.

"His B/P is normal." She took the thermometer from Chance. "So is his temp," she was looking at the readouts on the large flat-screen mounted on the wall behind Max's bed.

"He must have had another seizure and fell out of bed." Dr. Evans took his tablet and ran it from the top of Max's head to his toes. "Do you think you can stand him up?" He asked Chance.

Chance nodded and assisted Max to his feet.

Dr. Evans repeated the scan on Max's backside and then flipped through his screen. The nurse looked to the monitor on the wall as Dr. Evans synced his tablet to it. "I don't see any broken bones. Okay, get him cleaned up and back to bed. I'll call his mother," he ordered the nurse and left.

"I'll do it," Chance told the nurse.

"I can't let you do that."

"He's my brother," he lied.

"No, he's not Chance. I know you. I know your mother…I *knew* your mother…" the nurse embarrassed herself thinking about his mother's death. "Okay, fine…but if you need me press that buzzer," she pointed to a button on the wall. "And make sure he gets some sleep," she smiled at Chance. "I'll clean this floor."

"C'mon, Max" Chance walked him to the bathroom. Chance started the tub filling and pulled Max's soiled gown off him sitting him on the edge of the bathtub. "You okay? You're not gonna fall over are you?"

Max shook his head. He didn't really care he was naked in front of Chance. He felt cold, groggy, and like the life had been sucked out of him. He was having trouble concentrating and focusing, but then he saw Chance start to strip his clothes off. Max's brain was almost frozen but he was able to marvel at Chance's naked body. Max could see every muscle. And his body was smooth like his. Even his penis. *Wow, his penis is huge! How did he fit it in a Speedo?* Max could almost feel his body warm just a tinge. Chance's body was perfect with the exception of some bruises on his torso.

Chance towered over Max. "Okay, in we go," he stepped into the tub and guided Max in; sitting him down in front of him. Max was shivering. "You're gonna be okay, buddy." Chance said reassuringly and put his arms around Max and pulled him against his body.

Max closed his eyes. He warmed up against him and was calm. For the first time...in a long time...he felt...safe.

CHAPTER 27

Max's eyes flapped open.

Chance's arm was around him. He was in bed. He didn't remember getting out of the tub and to bed, he must have been totally zonked out. He couldn't believe Chance spent the night. That was nice. Max examined Chance's hand that was next to him. He could hear he was still asleep. He ventured to grab his hand gently and squeeze it. His hand was warm. He looked closer at his fingers. *Does he get manicures?* Then Max's eyes drifted to the side of his bed and he sat up with a start, "MOM!"

She was sitting by the bed with her legs crossed and arms folded and gave him a distinct *uh-huh* look.

"Max is up! Max is up!" Lindsey's head popped up and down from the bedside.

Chance bolted up in bed at all the commotion. His eyes met Evelyn's. "What time is it?"

"Almost eight a.m.," she didn't look at her watch.

"I'm gonna be late for school," he leapt out of bed darting for the bathroom.

Evelyn got a clear look at his nude body. "Well, he seems to be in good shape. Who's that?" She pointed toward his exit.

Max looked guilty. "That's Chance."

"That's his name? Is he a stripper?"

"No," Max's eyes bulged. He didn't know how he was going to explain any of this to his mother. "He's on the swim team," he hoped that would suffice for now.

"How does he fit in a Speedo?" Evelyn gasped, and then waved the air clearing her thoughts.

Chance hopped out of the bathroom with his pants on and pulling on his last shoe while trying to yank his t-shirt over him at the same time.

"Are you Max's friend?" Lindsey asked coming around the bed.

"That's right, cutey," Chance smiled at her.

Lindsey smiled back deciding instantly that she approved of Max's new friend. Evelyn stood up and moved Lindsey back, "go pester your brother," she commanded. "Can I talk to you outside," she demanded of Chance rather than asking.

They both stepped into the hallway as Chance finished putting on his last shoe.

"Well," she gave him a calculated look. "I'm not blind you know. Don't think I don't know what's going on."

Chance got that *oh shit* look, but chose to say nothing.

"Did your father give you those?"

"What?" Chance was totally expecting her to say something about him having to stay away from Max.

Evelyn looked to make sure no one was standing in ear shot. "The bruises, dear, I saw them. Your father did that?" She was concerned. "You know, I've been around law enforcement. I can talk to the sheriff."

"Actually, the sheriff's dead."

"Right, of course, I meant the…current sheriff."

"That would be my dad."

Evelyn's mouth dropped open.

"Thanks for the thought. I'm fine."

"Why would you put up with that sweetie? You definitely look…capable enough."

"If he takes it out on me he leaves my little brother alone."

Evelyn clasped at her chest. "Well, if you need to…get away…you can stay at our place. And your brother too of course," she offered motherly.

"Thanks," Chance smiled at her. "It's nice to know we can stay somewhere safe."

"Well, *thank you*," she returned the smile. "Nurse Susan told me what you did for Max last night. Thank you."

"You're welcome. He seems like a good kid."

Evelyn forced a grin.

"Well, I have to get to class," Chance turned and went down the hall.

"Mrs. Dane, or is it *Miss* Dane, now?"

"Evelyn," she pressed the politeness out of her mouth. She spun greeting the familiar voice and face of Dr. Evans with yet another forced grin.

"I'll cut to the chase," he took out his *mi*Pad. "I believe Max had another seizure last night. I'd like to keep him a couple of more days," he clicked on the tablet. "Plus, it would give me a convenient opportunity to continue his therapy."

"Oh, I see," Evelyn said maliciously, "as long as it's convenient for you. How much is this going to cost me? I've seen that five-star room he's in."

"I *am* the doctor," he enforced.

"Exactly, so it's not really up to you is it? It's the insurance company that's going to make that call."

Dr. Evans threw her threatening eyes through his square lenses.

She put her hand up resigning that this was a losing battle and stormed back into Max's room with Dr. Evans in her wake. "Max, dear, apparently you are going to be staying here a couple of more days," she waved her hand aggravated indicating Dr. Evans' entrance behind her. "I'll ask Jonas to bring your homework," she kissed him on the forehead. "He seems the type that would just love that," she grabbed Lindsey by the hand and glared at Dr. Evans on her way out.

"Charming lady," Dr. Evans plopped down on the couch in Max's room and stretched out. "Shall we get started?"

Max couldn't understand why he wasn't going home. "What's this all about?"

"You tell me, Max. What *is* this all about? Let's start with last night." He made a couple of clicks on his tablet.

Max wanted desperately for that *mi*Pad to explode in his face.

"What were you doing before Nurse Susan found you on the floor?"

Max was hesitant to answer. He didn't like opening up to people and didn't want to be judged. But his mother did insist on making things work with this psycho-babble. "Jack was here."

"The boy that was murdered?" He flipped his finger through some notes on his tablet.

"Yeah," Max confirmed sheepishly.

"So you were asleep and then you saw Jack?"

"Yeah…no…I was awake and then I saw him. He

leapt out of my body."

"Jack is inside you?" *Click. Click.*

"Well, not anymore. He was. He was hiding inside me."

"Does Jack talk to you?"

Max thought about seeing Jack in the Desert of the Dead and of course just last night. And then how Jack was able to talk to him in his head when he was inside him just before the Knightmare yanked him out, "yeah, of course."

Dr. Evans looked up from his tablet and directly at Max. "Was it Jack that told you to attack Derek Reid?"

"What? No…" Max became flustered. "It's not like that."

Dr. Evans took note of Max's increased heart rate that was registering on the monitor behind him.

"Jack is real."

"You said he was murdered."

"Well, he's *really* dead…he's a ghost." Max saw the tarot cards still on the tray swiveled away from his bed. "Angelica Saffron was in here. See," he pointed to the tarot cards. "She gave me a reading last night. She saw Jack too. So did Nurse Fran."

"Not Nurse Susan?" Dr. Evans looked at him skeptically.

"No, it was Nurse Fran. She came and took Angelica out of here. Just go ask her."

Dr. Evans stood up and crossed to Max's bed and pressed a button on the wall and then sat back down on the couch. In a few moments Nurse Susan came in.

"Did you need something, doctor?"

"Yes, I thought I told you to stop telling patients about Nurse Fran," his voice was scathing.

"I…I did." Nurse Susan admitted ashamed.

"Max here seems to know all about her. So I seriously doubt it."

Nurse Susan looked back and forth at Max and Dr.

Evans in confusion. She didn't understand.

"No more," Dr. Evans warned her. "Now, go."

Nurse Susan left irritated.

Dr. Evans saw Max's puzzled face. "I know your mind is quite fragile right now, Max. So I'll indulge you. Nurse Fran worked here many years ago when I was still a baby. She took it upon herself, albeit she called it her higher calling—her angelic duty—to bring mercy to those that were about to die." He saw puzzlement still in Max's eyes. "She assisted patients she thought were suffering in passing on."

"Oh," Max understood now.

"This is quite illegal, Max. We in the medical field are to help patients live...not die. I could go on forever about the moral implications and debates on both sides. In any case, it was illegal and she had been found out. So after assisting her last patient to die, Nurse Fran hung herself in that patients room in this very hospital. Some of the staff here insist she still wanders the halls visiting the terminally ill and offering guidance."

"But...so..." Max's lips trembled as he was fitting the pieces of his puzzlement together. "...You mean that Nurse Fran couldn't have been here last night. But Angelica saw her too. Just ask her."

"Max," Dr. Evans took his glasses off and rubbed his eyes. "There is such a thing as patient confidentiality that prevents me from going into great detail or even revealing certain things. But since I believe this directly affects your own mental state and well-being I will allow a minor divulgence." He leaned on the arm of the couch making it appear he was inching closer to Max. "Angelica Saffron's cancer metastasized to her brain. I did the operation. Max...she did not survive. She passed away yesterday afternoon before you were even admitted here. You couldn't have seen her in your room last night."

Tears streamed out of his eyes as he looked at the

tarot deck. "But...that can't be right." Then he remembered what Jack had said: *"Thou don't know?"* He must have been talking about her being dead. That's why she couldn't do a banishing. And that must have been why the room was so cold the entire time she was there. Max didn't want to believe it, but knew it must be true. "Her tarot cards," Max insisted on Dr. Evans believing that Jack, Angelica, and Nurse Fran were all there. "How did they get here?"

"Obviously, that's what you were doing up and out of bed. You got them from her room. She was just across the hall." He looked at Max sternly, "I presume you were sleepwalking and this is related to your seizure and this wasn't a case of theft."

"But Jack was really here, so were the others. Don't you see? Maybe I'm not epileptic. Maybe I just see ghosts. Everyone else seems keen on the supernatural in this town, why not you?"

"Max, most people are mindless cattle and follow the herd or latest trend just because everyone else is. I suspect you're much smarter than that. To answer your question most people in Ravencrest *do* believe in the supernatural, but that doesn't make it true. Remember, most people once thought the world was flat. The American Indians are a very superstitious people and they have a strong influence here in Ravencrest. Perhaps with a new mayor that will help...mitigate things. In any case, I see now that my usual methods of therapy just won't do with you. Since you have an affinity for the metaphysical how about we try something else? Will you try a guided meditation with me?"

Max wasn't sure if this was a trick. But it sounded okay and interesting. "Sure."

"Excellent," Dr. Evans got up and left his tablet on the couch. "We're making progress already," he smiled and pulled the plush chair from the lounge and over next to Max's bed. "I want you to close your eyes and take some deep breaths." After Max did this he continued. "Continue your breathing and picture yourself barefoot on a white beach."

"I don't like beaches," Max's eyes were still closed.

"What surrounding would you find calm?"

"I like the snow."

"Very well," Dr. Evans said calmly. "Picture yourself standing on the snow in your bare feet but you are not cold. You are completely comfortable. You can hear the wind and feel it blowing through your hair. You are on top of a mountain range and before you is the top of other mountains and..." he wasn't sure what Max would like so guessed if he didn't like warm sunny beaches he probably wasn't drawn to sunny blue skies either "...gray clouds. Can you see it Max?"

"Yes," Max sounded calm.

Dr. Evans was looking at Max's heart rate and pulse on the monitor. He was satisfied. "Now, look down at your feet. In the snow you can see that you have made prints. There are footprints behind you from where you came. Step back on one of those footprints so as not to make new ones. And now step back with the other foot doing the same. Now, turn around Max. What do you see?" Dr. Evans saw Max's pulse and heart rate increase.

Max was in his swim trunks. He was on a wood pier of the lake. It was foggy and cold. "I don't wanna be here," he opened his eyes with tears.

"What do you see, Max?" Dr. Evans coaxed him.

Max's eyes were open but he was still on the pier. His heart rate increased. "Don't make me do this," he shrunk back into his pillow. His breath huffed on the pier. His heart struck at his chest as he forced his eyes to look out into the water. "I don't want to see this," the fear choked his words.

"What do you see, Max?" Dr. Evans insisted even though he saw the monitor registering dangerously high numbers.

"I see..." Max's eyes turned from the water and to an area of fog on the land.

"Yes?"

"I see..." Max's breathing struggled. As the fog rolled he was able to see it. It was standing there not like the crucified figure he had seen in the pumpkin patch. It was just...standing there...its oak face pointed toward the lake. "I see...Mr. Creeps." Then inexplicably Mr. Creeps' head turned to face Max.

The alarms went off on the monitor. Max's eyes rolled back in his head as his body started to convulse. "Max! Max can you hear me? Turn away. I want you to turn away from where you are."

The alarms stopped. Max's body subsided. Dr. Evans took his cue, "Max where are you this time? Can you tell me?"

Nurse Susan busted into the room. Dr. Evans put his hand up stopping her from speaking. He waved his hand dismissively indicating that he didn't need her. She again gave an irritated look and left. Dr. Evans turned back to Max and thought he saw cold air come out of his mouth but decided he was mistaken. "Max what do you see?"

Max passed through the mist as Dr. Evans insisted he turn away from Mr. Creeps. He stepped off the pier and onto the grass and muddy ground. Then he noticed it wasn't grass. "I see hay and mud."

"That's good," Dr. Evans was hovering over Max in his bed. "Can you tell where you are? What else do you see?" He clicked on his tablet and then put it in Max's hands. "Perhaps you can write it."

"I'm in a stable of some sort," Max looked around seeing stone walls. It looked medieval to him. There were a few horses. They were all neighing and shuffling about in their stalls disturbed. He wasn't sure if he was in a castle or some other place. His answer came urgently through an arched wooden door.

A monk in his thirties with brown curly hair, blue eyes, and light facial hair walked urgently into the stable leading another older balding monk with a scraggly beard. The younger monk led the other past Max and around to an empty horse stall. "It's over here, Abbot Conleth," he pointed on the ground of what Max thought was an empty stall.

"I have many important things that must get done this day. You felt you had to bother me Brother John, with a matter of a dead horse?" Conleth brandished the tome he was carrying at the younger monk annoyed.

"Nay, of course not Abbot Conleth, look again. The horse has been murdered...mutilated." There was an obvious panic in the young monk's voice.

Abbot Conleth's demeanor changed immediately as he actually looked at the horse this time. The ground beneath its body was soaked in blood. There was a hole in its chest where its heart was carved out. There was a design painted on its white coat with blood...no...he approached the dead horse and leaned in closer...the design was etched into the horse's skin. He looked at Brother John and saw his eyes trembling.

"What does it mean?" The younger monk's finger trembled too as he pointed at the horse, "that symbol." It was a triangle with a circle in it.

"Uh," Abbot Conleth's voice stuttered with uncertainty. He felt fear grasping at his chest. "I've seen that before, aye. Aye, in this book," he showed the tome again to Brother John as he opened it and began searching the pages frantically.

"What book is that?"

"It belongs to Ambrosius Aurelias. It's his grimoire."

"A grimoire...what is that?" His voice was mixed with horror and confusion.

"A book of spells."

"Witchcraft! What are you doing with it?" The monk objected.

"I...confiscated it," he lied.

"But..." he was overwrought..."to have such a book is treason against the Church. It's treason against Rome."

Abbot Conleth lifted his eyes from the pages of Ambrosius' tome realizing he said too much to the young monk. "Aye...aye it is. We must not let any of the villagers see this horse. It would cause a panic and raise too many questions." Then he suddenly had a question of his own. "This isn't one of our horses. Whose is it?"

"The young squire."

"Jack?"

"Yes."

"Where is he now?"

"Out in the fields I believe; chasing birds."

"You must not let him see his horse. Tell him it's sick and that we'll take care of it. We can kill two birds with one stone."

"I don't understand, abbot."

"There is something I need you to take to the castle. It is for the king: a suit of armor. Take one of our wagons and take Jack. Conceal the armor and the horse under a tarp. Don't let him look under it. Drop the boy off, take the armor to the king, and leave this poor horse's corpse in the stables. We must get through this horrible day. I will take my leave and warn Doctor Lambe."

"Why Doctor Lambe?"

"He was working on something for Ambrosius, something to do with tonight, and I think this horse is part of it. This symbol," he found it in the book, "is a symbol of evocation."

"What does that mean?"

"It means manifesting a spirit. I believe Ambrosius and his druid brothers are attempting to resurrect something this devilish night. Something none of us should ever see."

"You think he did this?" The monk asked in a frenzy indicating the mutilated horse.

"Aye, I do. I must leave. Go! Do what I told you and be careful!"

Max sat up in bed hyperventilating. He looked at Dr. Evans as he pulled his tablet from Max's hands. Dr. Evans looked from his tablet to Max with bewilderment. "Was it you...or... *'Jack'* that mutilated a horse?"

CHAPTER 28

"Maximillian Aiden Dane."

Sheriff Roy Drake entered the hospital room followed by the same two men in black suits that Max had seen at the sheriff's station a few days ago.

"Am I under arrest?" Max plopped back on the bed as he had just finished dressing and was sure that Dr. Evans told them something incriminating about his therapy session.

"Not today," Sheriff Drake answered without enthusiasm and sat down next to Max. "Could you take your shirt off, please?"

Max looked confused.

"It's okay, Max." Dr. Evans walked in. "Thanks for waiting," he said sarcastically to the sheriff.

"What's this about?" Max asked freakish.

"Just take your shirt off, please," Dr. Evans instructed.

Max went ahead and complied feeling weird.

"See…as I said…nothing," Dr. Evans pointed.

"Okay," Sheriff Drake seemed satisfied.

"You can put your shirt back on, Max." Dr. Evans looked at the acting sheriff and the two mysterious agents with disapproval.

"Can you give us a moment?" The sheriff said to Dr. Evans more as a command than a request.

"But he's my patient."

"If I have to perform surgery I'll call you."

Agent Knight grabbed Dr. Evans and shoved him out of the room despite his protests.

"Max," Sheriff Drake said as soon as the doctor was out of the room, "we talked with your friend Jonas Lee. He says you both had an encounter with the late Sheriff Alahmoot Tahamont in Shadow Lake Forest," he opened a folder to check something, "five days ago."

"An encounter?" Max thought that sounded ominous.

"Yes, Jonas claims you were attacked—"

"–or clawed," Agent McCoy, the one Max remembered as large and bulky, suggested.

"Uh, yeah, I was…clawed…by the bear that you guys hunted down, right?"

"You heal fast," Agent McCoy said insinuative.

Max was getting a read on the bulky agent. His mere stature was intimidating. He could tell that he was testing him. He just didn't know what the right answer was.

"And remarkably well," Agent Knight added.

"Or maybe you weren't attacked at all," Sheriff Drake appended.

"You think I'm lying?" That's why they had him

take his shirt off. They were expecting to see a scar. Of course they thought he was lying. But he wasn't about to tell them that witches healed him.

Sheriff Drake looked to the two agents as though he was waiting for some sort of approval or indication of resistance before continuing. "I believe Jonas Lee said that you had a vision of Watu Warakin's head being in Yorick's farm."

Oh shit. That's what this is about. He could feel the panic in his eyes.

"Did you tell Sheriff Tahamont about your vision?"

"Yeah," *actually Jonas did...but whatever.*

"And it was after that...that you were attacked?"

"Uh..." Max was trying to remember. "Yeah, that's right."

"Then two days later," Agent Knight said, "he brought you into the station from school?"

"Yeah," Max was wondering where they were going with all this.

Sheriff Drake pulled out a metal band with spikes that had a patch of fur on one side of it. "Have you ever seen anything like this, Max?"

He shook his head.

"They're called Shuko hand claws."

"Also known as tiger spikes," Agent Knight said. "They can be used for climbing, or attacking someone."

"They're a martial art device, you see," Sheriff Drake demonstrated by putting his hand inside the band. "This one has fur on one side." He looked at the two agents and then back at Max, "Fur that could be easily construed as a bear's paw when your adrenaline is pumping. We found this pair of Shuko claws in Sheriff Tahamont's belongings."

Max's mouth dropped open a bit in hesitation. "Are you saying that Sheriff Tahamont attacked me?"

"We are," Sheriff Drake confirmed.

"But...but...why?" Max knew the late sheriff wasn't fond of him. Would he really try and kill him?

"We think that you spooked him with your vision. So he attacked you. You see, Max, the Native Americans are a superstitious people. They believe people can have visions, such as you. And we think that Sheriff Tahamont believed he could transform into a bear. He kept these Shuko claws as part of his *'transformation.'*"

"Was your wife superstitious?" Max remembered that Chance said his mother was Abenaki.

"What?" Sheriff Drake was caught off-guard.

"Did you start beating Chance in place of your wife or did you just beat them both?" Max glared at him.

Sheriff Drake stood up violently. "You little shit!" He rolled his fist at Max. "Shut the fuck up—"

Agent McCoy's large hand shoved against Roy's shoulder halting him, "Agent Knight why don't you take the good sheriff for some donuts. I'll finish up here."

Sheriff Drake directed knives, bullets and a whole arsenal of deadly weapons at Max with his eyes as the young agent forcibly escorted him out of the hospital room.

Agent McCoy loomed over Max looking at him with either a hint of admiration or deciding the best way to shut him up permanently without leaving a trace. Max wasn't certain. Max figured the man could squash him flat with his thumb. His heart was thumping in his chest. The only time he really felt alive was when he was certain he was about to die.

"I would re-think your strategy son," Agent McCoy cautioned him with a drawl in his voice. "I could get away with a stunt like that, but I don't live in this town. You do. And he's your new sheriff like it or not."

"So..." Max wanted to change the subject fast. "You think Sheriff Tahamont was trying to kill me? You made it sound like he was the one that killed Watu Warakin. But there was a news report; you guys killed the bear that killed him."

"We supplied that cover story. Sheriff Drake insisted on keeping Tahamont's reputation intact. Some sort of allegiance I assume. I could care less. I just want to nail the guy that killed Watu."

"And you think it was Alahmoot Tahamont," Max asked in shock. That would explain why he saw his legs leaving the morgue. He used the Cypress and Calamus to prevent Watu from speaking from the dead to reveal him as the murderer.

"Yes I do. I don't necessarily share Sheriff Drake's postulation that Tahamont's superstitions made him believe your vision. I think it was more likely he thought you saw him murder Warakin. We think he was devising a way to off you next. That's why he went to the school to pick you up that day. Fortunately, Sheriff Drake called him in to the station because of our arrival. You might actually owe him your life."

Was that true? Max couldn't get a read on the agent. But it would explain why he was at the sisters that night. Was he really plotting to kill him? He was sure that Tahamont was contemplating to do him harm when he escorted him home. If that was true, what made him change his mind?

"We were hoping that you or Jonas actually saw Tahamont attack you. Or that you at least would have a scar that we could compare to the Shuko claws. Then we could pin this thing on him easy. But no such luck. So I guess Sheriff Drake gets to uphold his friend's reputation with an unblemished career."

"You mean you aren't gonna tell people?"

"You see, Max...what we have now is circumstantial evidence so the cover story is going to have to hold. My suggestion to you is to keep this to yourself.

No one can prove Tahamont murdered Watu. And you don't want to be the one to tell Joe or anyone else in this town."

"Sooo…why tell me then?" Max shifted uncomfortably as he sat on the bed.

Agent McCoy was careful to keep a guarded distance between him and Max. "As it turns out, Max," he paused as he considered his words, "we did find Watu Warakin's head. We found it where you said it was: On Yorick's farm."

How can that be? Watu's head wasn't the head he had seen in his vision. Max's eyes searched the bed for answers. Maybe his visions were like dreams, where things weren't exactly as they seemed. Things always were jumbled up in dreams and his visions did seem a lot like dreams. His mom and the doctors seemed to think so. So maybe it was Watu Warakin's head he saw in his vision when he was standing in front of Mr. Creeps.

"Look, since your tip paid off I felt you deserved to know the whole story: The truth. But in my line of work, Max Dane, I've learned that people insist on knowing the truth but resent you when you give it to them. I saw your file. I think the last thing you need is to bring your family into more legal red tape by blabbing about the truth concerning Alahmoot Tahamont. Seeing that he's dead now…I'm satisfied knowing that my man got what he deserved even though I didn't actually get him. You should be satisfied too and just leave things alone."

That actually sounded great. Except…Max kept trying to leave things alone but somehow he found himself always getting smacked in the face with drama. But there was something he didn't like or trust about the tall, stocky agent. "Deal," he put his hand out to shake. Maybe he could get a vision or a read on him if he touched him.

Agent McCoy leered at Max's hand as though it were rigged to explode. "Son, I've been doing this too long. I know better." He put on his sunglasses and stopped before turning to walk out. "It was impressive that vision you had. That was pretty accurate." He shot his finger and thumb at him as though it were a gun, "I got my eye on you."

CHAPTER 29

"A ghost gave you a tarot reading?"

Max was sitting with Jonas and Cassandra on the CONUNDRUM CAFÉ's side of the crackling fire. On the café's side of the double-sided fireplace was a coffee table and a couch with side tables and armchairs positioned in front of it. Jonas was discussing the assignments Max needed to make up, one in particular that wasn't due yet which was a story or report (student's choice) he had to write for English class on Halloween, when Max told the pair what had happened in the hospital room after they left and that he found out this morning that Angelica Saffron had died that same day earlier.

"That is so amazing!" Jonas continued in his exhilaration wiping Chupacabra Chai spittle. "I've never had a tarot reading, let alone one done by a ghost!"

"There is nothing amazing about someone dying, doofus." Cassandra lectured Jonas. "And…" she turned her tone on Max, "there's nothing funny about making up you saw a dead person." She then softened her tone, "You were probably just medicated."

"Why is it that you are the only person in Ravencrest that doesn't believe in the paranormal?" Jonas asked insulted.

"I'm not the *only* person," Cassandra prodded her spinach salad and then guzzled water defensively.

"Cassandra," Joe was at their couch without warning, "rabbits are starving because you're eating all their food. What else can I get you?"

Cassandra objected with her eyes.

"A compromise then," he scraped slices of blackened seasoned chicken breast into her greens. "Now, it's a Thunderbird salad," he smiled.

"Fine," Cassandra realized there was no point arguing.

"You boys okay?"

Jonas and Max nodded. Max gulped his Monster Macchiato attempting to shut himself up. He wanted to tell Joe about seeing his dad and what Agent McCoy told him about Sheriff Tahamont. But something in his head rattled around indicating he shouldn't. It was hard to resist the temptation. What did McCoy say about people resenting you for telling the truth?

"Joe Warakin?" The short round lady that Max had seen at the sheriff's station appeared behind Joe.

Joe spun around. He greeted her with confusion. "Bernice, you know it's me. I remember when my father appointed you deputy mayor."

"Well, it's *Mayor* Bernice Dinah now," she said poisonously.

"*Acting* Mayor Bernice Dinah," Joe returned a

dangerous smile. Then he squared his posture and amended his face. "What can I do for you?"

"I was wondering if I might be able to steal a moment of your time."

"I am rather busy," Joe indicated his customers.

"As am I," Bernice smiled sweetly.

Joe looked at her trying to figure out if she was insulting him or not. "Of course, well it's probably not going to let up. It always gets this way as we get closer to the Halloween Bazaar."

"Which is why I chose to come to you, it's about the Halloween Bazaar. As...*acting* mayor..." it looked as though it was painful to say "...I am now the master of ceremonies. But I know many in Ravencrest would naturally see you as the person to take over affairs of this tradition as you will no doubt have a seat on the tribal council..."

"I will be the Chief and Shaman."

"Precisely," Bernice said excited as though that were the point she was trying to make, "and as the Chief and Shaman your approval would make things much easier."

Joe looked back at Max, Jonas, and Cassandra as though he missed something and then when he saw they didn't have a clue either he shifted toward Bernice. "Approve what?"

"A new tradition," she smiled ever so sweetly.

"Oh," Joe said revolted. "We're not changing the Halloween Bazaar—"

"Heavens no," Bernice giggled bubbly. "No, I meant an addition."

"Oh," he looked again at Max, Jonas, and Cassandra surprisingly shocked. Ravencrest was a haven from Christianity and most organized religions. His father suffered a lot of criticism from the council and town members for appointing Bernice Dinah as his deputy mayor because of her strong Catholic beliefs and affiliations. But his father thought it would be a good melding for those in Ravencrest that did desire something more orthodox. Joe was certain she was about to propose changing the Halloween Bazaar altogether. She never made it a secret that she disproved of the festivities. So he was shocked to hear otherwise.

"I was thinking a parade perhaps," Bernice said cheerfully.

"Oh," Joe said again, but with confusion. "Well there sort of is a parade already during the Bazaar."

"I am proposing the next day."

"The Day of the Dead," Jonas blurted. "That's a great idea. The pagans celebrated for three days, we should too! We should incorporate the Mexican traditions of dedicating November 1st to infants and children that have passed and the 2nd to adults that have died."

Joe smiled at Bernice in agreement with Jonas.

Bernice Dinah made a face as though someone just raked their fingernails across a chalkboard. "No, not like the pagans and not the Day of the Dead; we don't need another parade of gallivanting ghouls, goblins, zombies and skeletons. I meant All Saint's Day. But now that the young man has mentioned it, we should celebrate All Soul's Day as well." She grabbed Joe's arm ushering him away from the couch of interfering children. "Please...what I had in mind..." her voice trailed off as she pulled Joe through his café.

Jonas looked like he had just been slapped in the face. "Well, now I know what I'm going to do my Halloween report about," he grumbled.

"And Jack showed up at the end of my tarot reading," Max continued with his story.

"Who's Jack?" Cassandra asked taking a bite of her newly converted Thunderbird Salad.

"He's a dead boy from the Middle Ages," Jonas

explained. "Max think's he was murdered." He looked at Max. "What did he want? What did he say?"

"He says I opened up something with the Nexus. I'm not sure, everything happened so fast. He was hiding inside me."

"Hiding inside you," Jonas said rather disgustingly. "Like Freddy Krueger?"

"What?" Cassandra asked exasperated.

"You know… like *Freddy's Revenge.*"

"No, nobody knows that but you dillweed."

"And then the Knightmare thing showed up," Max pushed through their bickering.

Jonas' mouth dropped open in mid-drink of his Chupacabra Chai. "The glowing green knight you saw in the Desert of the Dead?"

"Yeah, except now he's headless."

"What nightmare are you talking about?" Cassandra was lost.

"Not a dream," Jonas explained for Max again, "a headless green glowing medieval knight." He gulped his Chai anxiously. "Did it have the skulls?"

"Yeah," Max said. "It was all covered with skulls."

"Real human skulls?" Jonas asked macabrely enthralled.

"No, they were etched into its armor…like a design."

"Oh," Jonas seemed a bit disappointed.

"Uh," Cassandra interjected, "are you saying you actually saw this…in the hospital?"

"Yeah," Max was feeling a little better about it since Jonas seemed so interested and not treating him like he was crazy.

"So how did Jack get inside you?" Jonas was still a bit disgusted at the thought.

"When I was in the Desert of the Dead; I guess he kind of…jumped on…or in."

"Oh yeah," Jonas explained to Cassandra as though he had been there, "the Desert of the Dead isn't like a real desert it's more of a frozen wasteland." He thought about what Max just said about Jack stowing away. "You know, that's probably why you are supposed to cast protection circles or perform clearings before you explore the astral plane...you know...like Joe did at the full moon ceremony. I've always read you're supposed to do that but didn't really think it was important. I guess it is."

"I just can't figure out what the Knightmare wants with Jack."

"Oh," a thought struck Jonas. "Maybe...maybe the Knightmare is the Guardian of the Nexus. You know...what you were pretending to be with Glenda. So maybe this Knightmare thing retrieves wayward spirits or ghosts."

"Yeah," Max was actually impressed. "That makes sense."

Cassandra looked at Jonas concerned he was fueling Max's delusions. "Are you seeing a psychiatrist?" She asked Max with caution in her voice.

"Yeah," Jonas answered yet again. "He's seeing Dr. Evans. Just like you are...or were...a lot of good that did with your eating disorder."

Cassandra's face went hot as she was about to lash out at Jonas when Derek Reid slammed his fist down on the coffee table in front of them.

"Hey cow," Derek jammed his finger threateningly at Cassandra. "I have a swim meet tomorrow so don't go stalking around my house. I need to get sleep."

"Afraid your parents might think you're dating a girl," Jonas tried to defend Cassandra. He didn't know why, it just came out.

Derek slugged his fist into Jonas' shoulder knocking him over into Max on the couch. "Watch it you little shit! Coach told me not to hit him," he pointed at

Max, "but not you. Oh, wait...coach isn't around anymore is he?"

"What does that mean?" Max asked propping Jonas back upright as he grabbed his arm in pain.

"Oh, that's right...you were all passed out in the hospital because you're a pussy. Coach got suspended."

"No one knows that for sure," Cassandra said hurt about Derek calling her a cow. "But probably," she looked at Max. "Someone mentioned something about steroid use to Principal Hemlock," she focused accusingly at Jonas.

"I knew it was you," Derek rolled his fists at Jonas. "You're always perving in the lockers."

"So it's true," Jonas cringed and grabbed at his arm anticipating getting punched again.

Derek looked stumped for a moment. "Stay away," he barked at Cassandra.

"Hey," it was Joe's wife. "I saw you hit those kids," Meredith snapped at Derek. "My husband may put up with you because you're in his boys club, but I'm not going to stand for it," the tall dark-haired young wife loomed over Derek. "You apologize."

Derek looked her up and down not the least bit threatened. "I don't think so." He walked away.

Meredith leered at Joe across the café. She was indicating to snatch Derek as he walked out but Joe was still being bombarded with ideas from the mayor as he was trying to take orders from customers and get orders ready.

"I can't believe you," Cassandra hit Jonas with a pillow from the sofa. "I told you to shut up about my...bulimia...and Derek heard you. That's why he called me a cow!" She beat him with the pillow. "It's your fault!"

"I thought you were gonna shut up about the steroid use," Max chimed in standing up. "And you keep telling everyone I see a psychiatrist and piss myself!" A table of students next to them looked at Max horrified. "Ugh," he grabbed Cassandra's hand. "Let's go!"

"You're leaving?" Jonas sounded scared.

"We're drumming," Max said dragging Cassandra to the stage. Max yelled to Joe. "Hey Joe, can we hit the drums?"

"Absolutely!" Joe waved him up there enthusiastically. "Go hit it!" Joe always enjoyed when people utilized his stock of drums.

"What?" Cassandra asked nervously. "What are we doing?"

"We're gonna drum our anger out," Max said with a determined smile. Max looked at the multitude of drums and decided on the large round frame drum. Cassandra grabbed the Junjun drums that had a tribal sun etched into the frame.

Max was scared as people started to look at them. He paused looking at everyone looking at him and shut his eyes. He breathed in slowly from his nostrils feeling his lungs get full. Then he exhaled slowly back out through his nostrils. He did this a few times feeling himself calm and with his eyes still closed he grabbed a beater and struck the drum hard. Max felt the vibration move up his arm and resonate through his whole body. It was an interesting sensation. He struck the drum harder and then softer to experience the difference in the vibrations. Then he opened his eyes while he drummed. The vibrations made the crowd kind of jump. He smiled. Cassandra smiled as well and started beating the Junjun. The crowd went back to talking and weren't as focused on them. Max closed his eyes again and kept drumming. His whole body shook but not like when he had a seizure. He could feel it in his ears. Then he suddenly got a waft of frankincense and cinnamon.

CHAPTER 30

"The war drums sound."

Ambrosius stepped through a cloud of frankincense and cinnamon that billowed from a censer as he positioned himself outside the salt circle. He traced the last of the sigils in the air with his finger.

"I hear nothing."

"It is not your gift," he looked out the window arch of the castle to the setting sun. "The portent is there, nonetheless."

"...Meaning?"

"We have a great battle ahead of us. A battle this very night: Samhain."

"We have already fought a great battle, Ambrosius...Nay a war!" The king spun on him infuriated,

"Lest we not forget the Valhalla Wars! That was no small feat," he said contemptuously. "Why are you bent on bringing war back upon us?"

"We have a grave error to correct. You know this to be true."

"Yea, at what cost? Look at all that we have built and accomplished." He drank from his goblet.

"In time it will cost us far more I fear."

"So you have warned The Table over and over. You alone believe this to be truth."

"Nay, not me alone, the Sisters Grimm are assisting. Am I to understand that you are wavering in your resolve? Are you not coming to the ceremony?"

The king looked into his goblet momentarily misplacing his courage. "How can you be so convinced Ambrosius that this is the thing to do? After all we have done to set things right—"

"Nay, not right—"

"We already prosper and you would cast us back into chaos!"

Ambrosius pointed to the salt circle. "Let us get the truth together."

"Ah...thy...demon," the king said unimpressed.

"Demon?" Ambrosius was offended. "Since when have you referred to entities as Demons? Father Gregory has gained your ear."

"It does not matter. I will neither accompany you to the ceremony nor will I send my men to the Giant's Ring."

Max was drumming one moment with Cassandra and now he was here. He watched as the silence was threatening. The king looked uneasy and Ambrosius looked as though he were contemplating the different ways he could kill him.

"I will see this ceremony through, with or without you!" Ambrosius grabbed a dagger from a table. "Don't even think of standing in my way," he pointed the blade at the king. "I am warning you." He flipped the dagger around, "I will need your blood."

"Very well," the king snatched the hilt of the dagger from Ambrosius' hand. He sat his goblet on a table and put his hand over an empty flask. He sliced his hand letting the blood dribble into it.

"That may not be enough," Ambrosius examined the flask.

"Then you know where to find me!" Mead splashed as the king snatched his goblet up and then pointed behind Ambrosius in horror.

Ambrosius turned around and saw the king was pointing at a peculiar eyed raven. He turned back to the king without an ounce of concern in his face. "That is nothing to fear. It is but a *familiar*."

The raven spat out a gurgling croak.

"That...that is a *portent* if I ever saw one," he spewed at Ambrosius. "My death is near. All of our deaths are near if you persist with this madness!" He threw his goblet at Ambrosius and stormed out of the room.

Ambrosius sighed as he turned his attention to the corner of his chamber. "You however," he gripped his oak staff tight, "are most certainly a sign of something," he looked at Max.

Max's mouth popped open. As usual, he had no idea how he got where he was at or what exactly was going on. But obviously he was facing the great wizard Ambrosius that he had been hearing about. Max was nervous. Not only was he facing Jack's murderer, his murderer was fully aware of his presence and could see him. His heart thumped in his chest. "You...you can see me?" Of course the ladies in the street in front of Doctor Lambe's saw him too. He shouldn't have been that surprised...it was bound to happen again.

"I see a great many things," Ambrosius looked at

Max inquisitively. "And so do you. Which is why I summoned you." He pointed to the censer and then the floor.

Max looked to his feet. He was standing on a triangle. And around him was a circle outlined in salt. Max stepped off the triangle. There were symbols on it that he didn't recognize. "You didn't summon me," Max's fear left him as he was overwhelmed with anger at Ambrosius' presumption. "I came here on my own." He rushed at Ambrosius. He didn't know why or what he was going to do. But as he approached the edge of the salt outline there was a sharp pain all over his body, from his scalp to the soles of his feet, like he was being cut with razors. He was punched back with a force. His hands, arms, and legs flickered for a moment, like he almost vanished. His head vibrated with a powerful pain that felt as though it would literally explode. He couldn't cross the salt outline. As his head vibrated he noticed some symbols in the air above the salt outline. They were like smoke. He had seen these symbols before. Was it the Knightmare, Mr. Creeps, or both? He traced over them in the air with his finger and they shimmered as he touched them. It reminded him of when the symbols lit up on the Knightmare after he tried to banish it. Maybe if he found the images like the ones he saw on the door of Yggdrasil or traced the Celtic Cross layout from his tarot reading he could unlock the circle and get out.

Ambrosius looked alarmed and pointed his finger at Max authoritatively. "I command you to identify yourself spirit!"

He retracted his hand. "Maximillian Aiden Dane," he didn't know why he answered. No one called him Maximillian. He saw that Ambrosius had confusion in his face. Max thought maybe he had an upper hand. He displayed a haughty smile.

Ambrosius became irritated when he saw that

smile. "Very well then…write your name in my grimoire," Ambrosius turned to a table. And then stopped, confused yet again. He looked about his chamber as though he misplaced something. Then he swung his eyes upon Max with severity.

Max just returned a blank stare at the wizard wondering what his next move was going to be.

Ambrosius circled Max urgently looking at the salt outline for a break in it. Once he seemed satisfied it was secure he faced Max magnanimously with a firm grasp upon his oak staff. "You take the guise of an innocent child. Yet, I see that you are truly a clever and dangerous entity. I seek answers. Is your land commanded by a king?"

"No."

"Who then?"

"Uh, the President."

"And your religious caste: Is it headed by wizards, druids or witches?"

Max chuckled. "Do you mean priests? There really aren't any wizards or witches. Well…maybe the place I'm from…that's debatable. I'm starting to think it could be a safe haven for witches."

"What is this place?"

"Ravencrest."

Ambrosius looked to the arched window at the human-eyed raven. "Ravencrest," he repeated to it. "What religion do you follow?"

"Me? None."

"What religion do others follow?"

"I don't know…there's a lot."

Ambrosius seemed a little relieved for the first time since he started throwing questions at Max. "And are there many gods?"

Max laughed. "Uh…no…nobody believes that. They pretty much just believe in one."

"Hex!" Ambrosius' anger returned as he talked to himself. "Something goes wrong. What went wrong?" He shouted at Max. "What went wrong?"

"I don't know what you're talking about," Max shouted back. "Now, let me ask you something."

"What," Ambrosius looked offended. "You dare!"

"I dare anything...murderer!"

Ambrosius stepped back. "One man's murder is another's self-preservation."

"And what self-preservation came from Jack's murder?" Max was outraged.

"You lie!" Ambrosius' temper flared.

"I don't lie! I know!" Max pointed at the triangle that he had appeared on. "I've seen your symbol etched into Jack's dead horse—"

"Where?"

"At the monastery."

"Enough! Begone!" Ambrosius waved his hand in the air.

Max felt a pulling in his stomach again and the familiar scent of frankincense and cinnamon.

CHAPTER 31

"Fire is the true creator."

Abbot Conleth mused as he looked from the fire to his metal chalice. "It forges, mends, and cauterizes. It births idea and spirit," he swirled his Mugwort tea in front of the library's hearth.

It was the old balding monk with a scraggly beard that Max had seen in his vision while at the hospital. Though unexpected; Max was grateful for the scene change even if he didn't get his answer from Ambrosius. He stared at the two men waiting for some kind of reaction to his appearance.

Nothing.

"Your words are blasphemous," cautioned the middle-aged man wearing black robes that sat at a table of open books.

Max saw that the books were all thick and old; composed of uneven pages of parchment. The priest was thin and had a hooked nose. He was beginning to feel more certain they couldn't see him like Ambrosius, but was afraid to move about just in case.

Conleth stood adding more frankincense and cinnamon to the thurible. "Father Gregory," he patted the air dismissively about his commentary on fire being the creator; "I am merely preparing myself and this space to receive visions."

"Now?" Father Gregory asked as if he were to be an accessory to a crime. "With me present?"

"It's already done," he snatched a dagger from the table and pointed it at the priest.

Gregory pursed his thick red lips defensively and recoiled on the bench.

The abbot smiled with satisfaction; apparently achieving his desired result. "Did you know that I received my first vision while forging this very dagger?" He pointed the end of the dagger to the ceiling focusing his eyes on the steel and away from the priest.

Father Gregory collected himself once he decided the abbot wasn't going to attack him. "I have heard of your...premonitions." Gregory's long tapering fingers flipped the pages of a manuscript. "Tell me...your...visions...have you documented them all?"

Conleth took his seat again in front of the hearth. "At first I thought it was from the steel that I received my vision. But then I realized it was from the fire. By gazing into the fire I have been able to receive advice, guidance...and premonitions. I have even discovered that by opening myself to the spirits—allowing them to take over my body—and with a quill in hand, will find that when I come out of the trance I have written down their wisdom. Aye, to answer your question, I have documented my premonitions just as I have documented my rituals and the rituals of Ambrosius and his Round Table Society."

Gregory slammed the book he had open and stood abruptly. Max could see now that the thin man was tall. "To what end have you done this?" He crossed hotly to the abbot. "What possible good can come from these acts?"

The abbot shifted in his seat, turning to the younger priest, "Why knowledge of course."

"What knowledge can you get from dabbling in these pagan's rituals? What knowledge does our Holy Father not already provide you?"

"I was 'dabbling' as you say in these practices long before I came here and met the likes of Ambrosius. In fact, I think it was my knowledge in these matters that drew him to me. He knew I would understand their ways. And may I remind you, that you too are consorting with these pagans. Why…you even take up residence with the king of the pagans!"

"By orders of our Holy Father I will remind you in turn. And yet even though I have taken up residence with them I have had much influence on their life without indulging in their heathen practices. In fact, my influence has been so positive that I shall suggest a service tonight at the castle."

"Tonight?" Conleth laughed. "Samhain? Their sacred night," Conleth laughed more drowning it with a drink from his chalice.

Father Gregory looked embarrassed from Conleth's laughter. "I only said suggested. Perchance I will suggest tomorrow for a service instead. But your involvement with this Society of theirs…these rituals of yours…they are heresy. It is no different than the practices and concoctions that Brother Lambe delves in."

"Aye, and it got him excommunicated. He is Doctor now…not Brother. I know that my assistance has marked me. We are both marked men: Lambe and I. I know your true purpose here Father Gregory. The pope has sent you to relieve me of my post here and put you as abbot of this monastery." Conleth read the shocked look on Gregory's face. "It is okay. It is the least of my worries."

"I should hope not. I should hope you don't take excommunication and breaking your vows so lightly. Yea, I said excommunication. You are very well headed down that path yourself."

"Nay, I do not take that lightly, but when you weigh it to your own life it is of little consequence. I have foreseen it. This devil of a night will be our end, for myself and Doctor Lambe. I will not live through this night to see my excommunication or any other punishment that awaits me on Earth."

"I hope you are not attempting to deflect attention from your serious...misguidance." He heaved a great sigh. Gregory's anger subsided. "Clearly, you have spent too much time among these pagans, you and Brother Lambe both. I will propose to our Holy Father that in the future we should not leave our monks and priests in one place for too long so they can remain anchored in our core beliefs and not become susceptible to the locals." He sat at the chair next to the abbot in front of the hearth. "I have a proposal for you and Lambe both to get you back to Rome. That is...if that is what you want...an escape from this night; if you seek redemption."

"Aye, indeed I would...but...I know my fate is sealed."

"Perchance..." Father Gregory knew he would have to resort to the part of the abbot that had embraced this pagan witchery "...your fate is sealed if you stay here. Perchance...the end of your life here in this village is all you saw. If you come back to Rome, you and Brother Lambe can start anew. Redemption does await you both. Doctor Lambe can become a Brother again."

Wasn't Doctor Lambe dead? Maybe they didn't

know. Max could see from the look on the abbot's face that he was considering the priest's offer.

The abbot exhaled weighted. "I don't think we would be welcome back in Rome. I fear there are people there that would rather see us dead. I have heard whispers of *THE VEIL.*"

"What veil?"

The abbot waived his hand withdrawing the comment; deciding not to elaborate.

"I certainly hope you are not suggesting that our Holy Father is an assassin or in league with such individuals. I will admit that the path back to Rome could be complicated. But if you truly believe that your life will end here this night...then what do you have to lose?" Gregory stood and went back to the table where some books were still open. "If you renounce these ways...this fire gazing and spirit invoking...and bring back your books on the rituals you have recorded at this Society, and if you can convince Brother Lambe to do the same and bring his books on the illnesses and treatments he has recorded then I believe Rome will find that valuable enough to give you both a renewed life. I can arrange for you and Lambe to be escorted safely to Rome."

"Why would you do this for me?"

"You shouldn't even have to ask. We are a brotherhood. Your instruction of monks on writing and ornamentation of missals and manuscripts is admirable and meritorious," he tapped the tomes. "You have done much for handwriting and scripting. I believe you have much still to offer. There is even your metal work," he pointed to the chalice. "Your gift for the craft is known wide. Did you make that as well?"

"Aye," he held the chalice up. "In fact, that's how I received my calling," his eyes flickered throughout the room. "Sister Bridget of Kildare had asked me to construct vessels for her convent. Eventually, she encouraged me to enter the brotherhood...which I did." He smiled nostalgically.

Gregory's blue eye shifted to the shadows. "What is that abomination?" He gasped pointing.

Max looked to the shadows as well gasping also. It was the Knightmare! It was laid out on a table in pieces.

Father Gregory approached the corner with caution. The pieces of armor were laid out barely perceptible in the flames of light from the fireplace.

"Aye, speaking of my metal work...Ambrosius had me construct that for the king."

"Ambrosius!" Father Gregory denounced.

"Aye...it is for the king," Abbot Conleth felt the urgency to reiterate. "It is to be presented to him at their ceremony tonight."

"It has skulls on it! Why would the king desire such a thing? Won't he be insulted?"

"Nay, Father Gregory. The skull is resistant to decay. It is often all that remains of the dead so in their culture the skull is a symbol of power and the gateway to etheric knowledge."

Father Gregory grabbed a candle off a table and held it to the corner. "And why is it green?"

"Ah that," Conleth smiled. "That metal was made by Doctor Lambe. He calls it Green Gold. I understand there is some gold in it along with other metals; quite unique. Nay, I rather think the king will be most pleased with this suit of armor, even though I didn't finish the helmet."

"Is that...writing I see inlaid in the armor?" Gregory eyed intricate etchings that were imperceptible from a distance.

"Aye, it is...some magickal and esoteric symbols..." he read the sour look upon the Father's face..."Ambrosius gave me the designs," he pulled some parchment from a table. Father Gregory inspected the parchment. "He says it is supposed to protect the wearer from ethereal energies and through the Nexus should they happen to travel."

"The Nexus?"

"The land between our world and the next."

"We would call that Purgatory or Limbo. Do I really have to remind you of that? And need I remind you that we are to convert these heathens and not indulge them in their fantasies? And here you constructed a physical representation of their delusions."

"We will need the king's permission to continue to operate in this region. And if this pleases him then I should think it's a pittance."

Father Gregory's face cooled. "Your craftsmanship is remarkable," he examined the armor. "I can understand the appeal. The written word is the most powerful; more powerful than most would or could understand."

There was a knock at the door and Brother John stepped in, a monk in his thirties with brown curly hair and light facial hair, "My apologies for interrupting, but there is a messenger here for you Abbot."

Percy entered from behind the monk.

"That is no messenger," Conleth scolded the monk, "that is Sir Percy, the king's finest knight." He waved the monk out of the room. "My apologies, they do not get out much and wouldn't know the difference from a knight, squire or mercenary."

"I took no insult. And in his defense I am a messenger today. Perchance more of a delivery than a message," he hoisted his saddlebag atop a table and paused looking at Father Gregory.

"It is okay," Abbot Conleth motioned for Percy to continue.

Percy took out a large heavy object wrapped in silk. "It is from the king." As Conleth reached for it Percy noticed the runic "R" ring on his hand; the same ring he was traveling with. He was about to remark on it when Conleth caught him looking and his eyes darted to Father Gregory. Percy understood that the abbot did not want him to say anything about it in front of the priest. Instead of remarking on the ring, Percy said, "I need not stay to see you open this. I must take my leave. I have one more stop and a journey ahead of me still this day."

"Oh, where is it you are going?" He sat the object down on the table.

"The banks of the Isle of the Dead."

"You must travel through the Wild Forest, am I not mistaken?"

"Aye."

"That could be treacherous," Conleth warned.

"I spent my childhood in the Wild Forest. That is not what concerns me…"

The Wild Forest? Max had heard that before. The teen he saw just before he was attacked told him they were in the Wild Forest. Then it hit him! *Was it really? That was Sir Percy as a teen.* That explained why he looked familiar to him when he saw him as an adult. Max felt an even stronger connection with Percy.

"Please allow me to give you a blessing; for a safe journey."

"Me too," Father Gregory insisted.

Percy hesitated. He wasn't faithful in his own people's beliefs. He wasn't keen on embracing these priests' faith either. He felt he was only trading one superstition for another. However, he could see how important it was to them. "Aye," he agreed. "Will it hurt?"

"Nay," they chuckled and Father Gregory and Abbot Conleth laid their hands upon his armor and said a brief prayer. Father Gregory commented retracting his hand after the prayer, "That is a most peculiar feeling leather armor you adorn."

"I would not think you versed enough in combat wear to know such a thing." Percy smiled and gave a polite nod to the abbot and priest and left.

Abbot Conleth unfolded the silk wrappings revealing a tome with a gasp.

"What is it?"

Conleth collapsed on the bench by the table. "It is Ambrosius' grimoire."

Max decided that's what Ambrosius must have been looking for. The king must have swiped it before he left. But he had already seen Abbot Conleth with the grimoire in the stables. *Oh wait,* now Max got it. He was seeing pieces of the past out of order, like a jigsaw puzzle that wasn't put together.

"What does that mean? I do not understand."

"It means the king is against Ambrosius. And I or whoever possesses this book is in mortal danger."

"But what is it?" He pointed at the heavy book.

"It is Ambrosius' book of spells. And probably other writings I imagine." He hesitated from opening the pages as though it were caustic. "He will stop at nothing to regain this."

"More witchcraft," Gregory scolded Conleth yet again. He failed to see the significance or ramifications of Conleth having the grimoire. "This simply must stop! That armor needs to get out of here. And you have yet to answer me on my offer to you and Doctor Lambe."

"Aye…of course!" He didn't hesitate with his hand twitching upon the grimoire. "I will see this armor is taken away and I will go deliver the news to the doctor myself."

"Very well, and bring all of this." He scooped his hands over the tables. "Even those…drawings…and that book of Ambrosius'. I must go and make preparations. I take my leave of you," Father Gregory swept from the library.

Conleth finally gained the nerve to peruse the

pages of the grimoire. He stopped and read. His eyes were aghast. "I may have been wrong. *None* of us may live through this night."

CHAPTER 32

"Did you see your power animal?"

Joe took the beater from Max. Several people in the café stared at Max. "Oh shit, did I piss myself?" Max checked quickly.

Joe chuckled. "No…maybe you got a little zealous with the drums. But that's okay," he didn't want to discourage Max. "That's what they're here for," he called out to the annoyed looking patrons. Joe held the beater he took from Max out to one particularly miffed lady. "You wanna go next?" She didn't find it in the least bit amusing and returned her attention to picking out bits of her Chomp sandwich. "She looks like she could use a few minutes on these drums," Joe winked at Max and Cassandra.

"Thanks, Max, that was awesome. I needed that,"

Cassandra said gratefully. Her hair frizzed out even more than usual from exploding on the drums following Max's lead. She pushed her auburn hair out of her eyes and face and grabbed Max's hand leading him off the stage and back to the couch. Jonas wasn't sure if he was about to get beat next by his two friends. "That was fun Genuine Joe," she said to Joe as he accompanied them enthusiastically to their spot in front of the fireplace.

"You know little missy, I believe that was your first time since I've known you that you got up there!" Joe beamed.

"Yeah, it was. I should do that more often," She smiled at Max sitting next to him on the couch. Not letting go of his hand.

"We need to get you up there next, Jonas," he patted him on the shoulder hopefully.

Jonas chose to remain silent for the moment.

"So I was right, huh?" Joe smiled nudging Max's shoulder. "You were on a vision quest! At some of these ceremonies I hold with the swim team that happens. I've seen that look in their eyes before. The same one you had while drumming."

Jonas' attention perked.

"Vision quest, huh?" Max grinned. "I like the sound of that instead of hallucination or seizure." He smiled at Jonas and Cassandra (who still held tightly onto his hand).

"Did you meet your power animal?" Joe was excited for Max.

"Oh right," he remembered Joe asking something about that. "What's a power animal?"

"Also called a spirit animal," Jonas interjected fanatically.

Cassandra narrowed her eyes at Jonas as if to say *shut up and don't interrupt.*

"That's not entirely correct," Joe smiled at Jonas

and knelt down by the couch bringing himself to their level.

Cassandra stuck her tongue at Jonas. *Ha ha.*

"I tend to think of your spirit animal as representing your nature and state of mind. And your power animal represents how you walk in life, how you act, and how others see you in general."

"So is that the same thing as a familiar?" Max remembered Ambrosius referring to Glenda's raven as one.

Jonas and Cassandra looked at Joe intently to hear the answer to Max's question.

"Not exactly," Joe realized he opened a big can of worms. "It gets confusing I know: Spirit Animals, spirit totems, spirit guides, power animals, and familiars." He looked over his shoulder at his customers gathering. "Familiars are spirit helpers in human or animal form. Power animals and spirit animals are spirit guides and aren't physically present."

Joe's wife—Meredith—walked by him, "Continue," she smiled. "It's slow in the comic-shop right now," she walked up to the counter to help.

"Thanks honey," he patted her leg as she passed. "I still have to make this quick," he said to the three. "Shamans of long ago were said to have the ability to walk the threads or intricate web of this world and the invisible world. These shamans helped people remember that all life, plant and animals, have energies that resonate in this world and the invisible world, and that by adopting their energies we can learn from them and learn about the spirit world as well as the natural world. So power animals are spirit guides in animal form. By working with your power animal you are working the qualities or energies of that animal to guide and teach you for the current path you are on in your life."

"So how do I know if I saw my power animal or a

spirit animal?"

"That is an excellent question. Usually, only you can answer that because you instinctively know. Your power animal will stay with you for a long time. Sometimes even your whole life, although it's not uncommon to have more than one power animal as life is always changing. But for me, I really only have a sense of my spirit animals that are influencing my life whereas your power animal comes to you in a vision quest."

"So what animal did you see?" Jonas asked excited.

Max shrugged. "I saw a raven."

"That's great," Joe sounded thrilled. "The raven is a powerful Spirit Totem. They are similar to the crow. They are everywhere squawking out to everyone reminding us that magick is always around. If we just know how to look for it."

Jonas looked at Cassandra vindicated. She didn't take note of his look as she was enthralled with Joe's narrative.

"Birds in general are a powerful Spirit Totem because they symbolize the soul and departed souls. They hold the key to communicating with other animals and thus other energies. To have a bird as a power animal means your perceptions are open to energies of the past, present, and future. A bird as a power animal means you are invoking the energies of a guide and teacher."

Max was listening intently.

"And the raven is the pinnacle of bird totems when it comes to magick. It is bathed in mysticism and magick. The raven can mimic the calls of other species so it is also attributed to shape shifting. It is said to hear the croak of a raven is an omen of death or the outcome of a battle."

Max's mouth dropped. *That's what the king thought.*

"Anyway, I can go on forever. You two," he

pointed at Max and Jonas, "need to come to the fire ceremony for my pow-wow. We're holding it the night before Halloween because of the Bazaar, but it's technically the first night of the full moon, so it works out."

"Oh, so Halloween Eve!" Jonas laughed at his own joke.

"Right," Joe didn't get Jonas' joke.

"Nobody gets that," Jonas said exasperated. "It's like saying Christmas Eve Eve," he felt compelled to explain, "Because Halloween is actually Hallow's Eve. And that's how..." he was barraged by silent stares from Joe, Cassandra, and Max. "...Forget it...I need to put that in my report too."

Cassandra cleared her throat to Joe waiting for her invite to the fire ceremony.

Joe frowned at her. "Sorry, it's a guy only thing."

"Don't you think that's a bit discriminatory?" She asked with not too harsh a tone.

"Oh sure," Jonas piped in quickly. "It's okay for women to have female groups or meetings and it's called 'empowering women' or something lame like that, but if males do the same it's 'discriminatory.' Don't be such a hypocrite."

Cassandra almost gave Jonas an ounce of respect. She turned to Joe and waived her hand inconsequentially, "I'm sure Meredith will give you grief for the both of us."

He pointed his finger at her assuredly, "You know it. Okay back to work!" He commanded himself and charged off.

"So...uh..." Jonas looked back and forth at Max and Cassandra almost afraid to ask. "Does this mean you guys aren't mad at me anymore?"

"Oh right," Max had to think about that. "You know, the more I think about it Jonas, you did the right thing telling Principal Hemlock." He looked down at his feet. "I never do the right thing. Besides," after the vision quest (that did sound better than a hallucination) it seemed pointless to stay mad at Jonas, "that was like ages ago."

"Wow, that drumming stuff really works," Jonas was impressed.

Cassandra couldn't believe what she was hearing from Max. "Boys...so forgiving!"

"Girls...so grudge-bearing!" Jonas retorted.

Cassandra flipped her head away from Jonas ignoring him. "You guys are gonna be at the swim meet tomorrow, right?" Cassandra looked right at Max squeezing his hand.

Jonas looked at Max waiting for him to decide. And Max looked at Jonas thinking he was going to jump in with an answer as usual. Max finally figured out that Jonas was waiting for him. He wanted to see Chance compete. "Yeah, we'll be there." Jonas looked relieved so Max figured he picked correctly.

"That's great, see you then," Cassandra finally let go of Max's hand then grabbed his face and gave him a quick kiss on the lips and got up and left.

Max looked at Jonas as though he had just been slapped.

Jonas' mouth and eyes were wide open in shock. "She wants to have sex with you!"

"What?!" Max just about came out of the sofa. "No! What?"

Jonas nodded his head like it was a done deal. "You're gonna be doing adult website...salami slapping!" He declared with a startled enthusiasm.

"What?" Max looked genuinely worried and grabbed his chest finding it hard to breathe.

"You know what to do, right?"

"No!" Max was petrified. "What? No!" He looked around the CONUNDRUM CAFÉ worried people were watching. No one was paying attention to the boys at all.

"You're gonna need lessons!" Jonas concluded.

"That's fine," he waved his hand in the air. "The internet is the best way to learn these things anyway," he took out his phone. "My dad has that stuff blocked on my phone, but he doesn't know that I found his password," he opened the web browser.

Max got up to get a closer look. He was nervous but curious since he'd never been to one of those websites as his mother kept the internet at bay from him.

As the web browser reached the scandalous site the phone started to ring. Both the boys screamed in terror standing upright.

"It's my dad!" Jonas dropped the phone on the plush chair he was sitting in. "How did he know? How did he know?" Jonas babbled—panicked.

Now, some of the patrons were watching the boys seeing them dance around like they were on hot coals.

"Answer it," Jonas ordered Max.

"Me? It's *your* dad!"

"It's *your* fault! You're the one that's gonna boff Cassandra!"

"I'm not boffing anyone!"

"Hello, Mr. Lee," La' Wanda Shikita Witta, the large lady with weaved hair, picked up the phone from the chair and answered.

The boys screamed again startled at her abrupt arrival.

"Oh no, your boys are fine. They just never seen a scary black lady before," there was a smile in her voice. "Oh, that's right, you only have one son. I thought you were snatching up all the white boys," she chuckled. "No, no, they're here at Joe's. I just came over to get a bite to eat." She paused listening to Mr. Lee. "That's very nice of you to say," she said quietly. "She was fond of you as well. Here he is," she handed the phone to Jonas and crossed to Max drawing him over to the sofa and sitting down with him.

Jonas took the phone reluctantly like it was a plate of veggies. His eyes were pressed flat against his glasses with horror at what his dad was going to say. He looked to Max for support, but he looked equally uncomfortable taking a seat next to La' Wanda. Jonas' eyes took on relief after his father talked for a moment. "Yeah, he's here." He pulled his head away from his phone. "Your mom is with my parents," he told Max. "Yeah, we can do dinner here," he looked at Max for confirmation.

Max nodded to Jonas trying his best to avoid eye contact with La' Wanda.

"That's great dad," Jonas was alleviated his dad didn't mention anything about the website. He ended his call. "My dad's gonna pick us up later. We get to spend Friday night here!" Jonas had always wanted to spend a Friday night at the CONUNDRUM CAFÉ, but never had a reason since he didn't have any friends. "This is great!" He couldn't contain his excitement. "We can read the new issue of *TALES FROM THE CAMPFIRE!*"

La' Wanda motioned for Jonas to retake his seat in the plush chair. Then Jonas remembered, "I'm so sorry about Angelica," he said to La' Wanda.

"Thank you, honey." She smiled.

Max couldn't believe what good spirits she seemed to be in for someone that just lost their…friend…business partner…he finally looked at her trying to get something. *There it was.* Lover? Was he reading her right?

La' Wanda looked down at Max sitting next to her almost as if she detected his scan. "These are yours I believe," she smiled setting down the deck of tarot cards that Angelica had done his reading with.

Max looked at the cards on the coffee table. "I didn't steal them!"

"I know you didn't, sweetie."

"Well, Dr. Evans seems to think so…or that I had a seizure…"

"She did a reading for you, right?" La' Wanda asked purposely.

Max nodded his head slowly. "I know that makes me sound crazy." His heart was racing. "But it was real to me!" That didn't make him sound any less crazy he realized. It's been easy to avoid the question since he moved to Ravencrest with so many people like Jonas believing in the paranormal. But fear and doubt oozed into his psyche, yet again, and he wasn't able to suppress the question: *How does a crazy person know they're crazy?* His hand trembled at the thought. He knew his mom and dad believed it. He knew his mom was convinced he was going to hurt Lindsey…and he wasn't entirely certain he wouldn't.

"It's Halloween," La' Wanda patted his leg. "This is the time of year when the dead are supposed to be able to make contact with the living…" she suddenly felt a flurry of cold air enter the CONUNDRUM CAFÉ which was uncanny as they were toward the back of the café by the fireplace.

"Indeed it is," Martha Grimm stood regally next to La' Wanda, accompanied by her two sisters, "but it has been a long time that such contact has occurred with any regularity." The conversations in the café became softer with the entrance of the Sisters Grimm. "However," Martha shifted her focus from La' Wanda to Max, "I suspect this Samhain may prove to be quite…active."

"We're honored to have you here," Joe had made his way over. "You've never come in," there was a welcome surprise in his voice.

"We have come to pay our respects." Martha returned her eyes to La' Wanda. "Angelica Saffron was a seasoned soul. Her departure is not lost on us," she offered her hand which La' Wanda took and stood. "If only it were a different time and a different place we may have been able to alleviate her condition."

La' Wanda smiled. "Angelica and I both believe that everything happens for a good reason; even seemingly bad things, such as death."

"It would appear, like and learned souls attract," Martha squeezed her arm implying the union between La' Wanda and Angelica. She turned to Joe. "We also have come to venerate Watu Warakin and commemorate your passage to leader and shaman of your tribe. You will no doubt prove to be as impartial and enlightened as your father if not more."

"How about a candle ceremony..." La' Wanda clapped her hands together elated "...to honor the passing of our loved ones."

"Don't you usually do that on Halloween?" Jonas asked.

"This is Ravencrest," Joe said enthusiastically. "It's always Halloween here."

"I have candles," Meredith leapt from the comic shop with a box. The CONUNDRUM CAFÉ was completely quiet now as all the patrons seemed eager to participate. Meredith began to hand-out white candles from the box. Max followed Jonas' lead as he grabbed a handful and helped give the candles out. Jonas actually regretted that Cassandra wasn't there to be a part of this.

The Sisters Grimm were amazed at the camaraderie in the CONUNDRUM CAFÉ. "Shall we join hands," Martha grabbed Max's hand as he stood. Her other took La' Wanda's.

Everyone in the café began to join hands when Meredith bursted, "I need a lighter or matches." And then suddenly, all the candles in the CONUNDRUM spontaneously lit. Everyone jumped in surprise except for Martha Grimm who smiled down at Max. Glenda and Dorothy dropped their mouths open in shock, looking at Max with admiration.

"Just like the good old days," Dorothy elbowed

Glenda.

"Okay then," La' Wanda looked about at all the lit candles and joined hands. "May these candles light the way for all our dearly departed in the next world..."

Max's eyes flickered over and met Martha's. As he held her hand he had to wonder if she was able to get impressions off him like he could with people.

"...While we mourn their passing we can be comforted in their birth into a new beginning in the afterlife."

Max had his doubts about that statement. He looked at Martha. Her eyes still touched his. He felt she was of the like thought.

"...So mote it be," several patrons muttered after La' Wanda's closing words. Everyone let hands go and extinguished their candles returning to their previous activities.

"I thought I'd keep it short and sweet," La' Wanda said. "I didn't want to take away from the Halloween Bazaar," she smiled at Joe.

"This is the best Friday night ever," Jonas belted.

"You think so, little man?" La' Wanda patted Jonas' head affectionately. She looked around the CONUNDRUM. "Oh, I see someone I need to chat with. Don't forget your tarot cards," she told Max stepping away with a wave.

"We didn't know you possessed a tarot deck," Martha said as though quizzing him.

"It sounded as though you didn't know much about the occult before arriving to Ravencrest," Glenda followed up.

"Angelica left it for me," Max replied.

"She bequeathed it to you?" Dorothy asked.

"She did a reading for him...as a ghost," Jonas bounced on his chair.

Silence visibly struck the sisters as they stared at

Max. An uncomfortably long moment passed before Martha finally spoke. "I lit those candles spontaneously. That is something I haven't been able to do in a long time. It would seem you have unlocked some part of the Nexus with that reading you had from Angelica Saffron..."

"Really?" Jonas was having difficulty grasping that concept. "A tarot card reading could unlock something in the Otherworld?"

"It was a tarot reading from a ghost," Dorothy related. "That's no small potatoes."

"Just think if Jesus himself absolved a Catholic of their sins personally," Glenda commented. "Why they'd probably wet themselves."

"Tarot cards are esoteric and contain much occult knowledge," Martha attempted to answer Jonas' question. "They are a meditative and divinatory tool. A long time ago it was foreseen by some, but not believed by all," she admitted rather guiltily and looked to her sisters, "that ethereal energy and occult knowledge would eventually be suppressed. To avoid that knowledge from disappearing altogether some decided to create tarot cards, in an effort to save the wisdom of the ages hidden in a deck of cards, through a series of imagery and symbolic underpinnings."

"Uh okay," Jonas looked at Martha and then Max, "I guess I missed the part where a tarot reading can unlock something in the Otherworld."

"Don't be such a smartass, laddie," Glenda growled at him. "She's getting to it."

"You both must understand," Martha continued her attempt at an explanation, "that other planes work different than our physical plane we are in here and now. So what would pass for a simple door, lock, and key here; may look and operate completely different in the Otherworlds. These realms vibrate and resonate at a higher energy frequency than most people are able to perceive. You would have to bring yourself in tune with that in order to communicate with these other realms."

"You're talking about magick now aren't you?" Jonas was on the edge of his seat.

"Oh, he catches on quickly," Dorothy smiled. "When you received that tarot reading from Angelica you were in tune with the Otherworld. I told you before that I think you hold one foot here and another in the Nexus. Like a key that is fingerprinted you were able to unlock something that hasn't been open for a very long time.

"Part of it," Dorothy said affably.

"Right," Max failed to see the relevance. "Jack mentioned something about the tarot cards unlocking something too," he was trying to work it out. "He showed me the Celtic Cross layout, when turned on its side, matched the symbol on the door of Yggdrasil."

Martha's eyes widened in astonishment. "Is this the same Jack you spoke of before?"

"Yeah, he was Ambrosius' apprentice. He says Ambrosius murdered him."

"He's a ghost too," Jonas said excited.

The sisters exchanged looks of pointed interest. "Just as you said sister," Dorothy spoke to Glenda.

Glenda shifted her patch like it was a pair of glasses. "Maximillian Aiden Dane," Glenda squinched her eye at him in realization. "He was there...in Ambrosius' chamber," she decreed to her sisters.

"That was your crazy-eyed bird there," Max looked in disbelief at Jonas. Jonas had an equally shocked face as he understood what Max was getting at. Max was also thinking of how he saw Glenda in the past during the new moon ceremony. "But that was in the Middle Ages. I mean...I know you guys are old...but you can't be that old!"

Glenda smacked Max's shoulder in retaliation!

"Well, seriously. How you can be that old?" Max

wasn't going to let it go. Jonas looked anxious to hear the answer as well.

"We're witches," Martha said simply, refusing to elaborate.

Joe appeared clapping his hands together. "It's Friday night. So who's ready to eat? You're staying right?" He pointed at the sisters.

The sisters looked at each other as though faced with the most difficult conundrum of their life. Though the majority of people in Ravencrest were accepting and open about mysticism, paganism, and witchcraft; they themselves had rarely received the same unbiased courtesy.

"You have to stay!" Jonas wasn't about to let the Sisters Grimm not hang out with them. He was usually scared of them, but here in the CONUNDRUM CAFÉ, he wasn't worried. "You've never been here!"

"That settles it!" Dorothy plopped down on the sofa next to Max utterly delighted. "What are you having?" She asked Max.

"Oh," Joe handed them menus.

"I usually get the Chomp," Max told Dorothy.

"And I get the Champ Club," Jonas blurted.

"Oh…named after the Lake Champlain monster," Dorothy said to Joe. "Very clever, I'll have that too."

Jonas was flattered that Dorothy picked the same sandwich as him.

Glenda dragged herself over to Dorothy and Max and slumped in the sofa. "I'll take that Chomp thing."

"Do you have anything light?" Martha remained standing for the moment.

"I can do you a salad. I can get you the Thunderbird salad. It's excellent. My wife added that one to the menu," Joe smiled.

"That sounds…excellent. Do you have any tea to drink?"

"I have a Chupacabra Chai Tea or a latte." He saw that Martha didn't look excited about that. "Of course...You look like you would enjoy my Haiku hibiscus tea."

"Indeed I would," Martha smiled at him, "as would my sisters."

"Guys," he said to Max and Jonas, "you probably shouldn't drink something that's gonna keep you wired all night. Your parents will never let you come back in here. Let me suggest Will-O'-Wisp water or Pegasus' Nightcap."

"Pegasus' Nightcap," both boys answered enthusiastically. They liked the sound of that.

"It's warm milk with honey," he whispered to Martha. "Done and Done! Sit down, sit down...relax."

Martha waited till Joe left and was back behind his counter. "So do you know the location of the Elixir of Life?" she asked Max. "Ambrosius provided us a false one."

All eyes were on Max.

"I..." Max wondered if he should tell the sisters what he knew. He was struck with a sense of doubt. The sisters, including Jonas, leaned in edging him on with yearning faces to know what he knew. "I saw Doctor Lambe make the switch. I saw him give a substitute to Sir Percy—"

"Ambrosius didn't make the switch and Ambrosius didn't deliver the Elixir," Glenda's eye darted between her sisters.

"I thought you guys had the Elixir of Life."

"We don't possess it," Martha answered.

"What do you need it for? I need it to free Jack."

"Why is that so important to you, dearie?" Dorothy asked sincerely.

Max looked into the fireplace feeling the gutter ball in his stomach that was always there if even a hint of it when he was actually enjoying himself. He remembered not seeing his reflection in the mirrored wall of Yggdrasil. "Because maybe freeing his soul will remind me of what it's like to have one."

They all looked at Max severely not taking that comment lightly. "We told you we would help you Halloween night. We still intend to do that. There's other ways besides using the Elixir," Martha sought to ease him.

Max was starting to doubt the sister's sincerity. He felt they only wanted the Elixir for themselves and had no intention of helping Jack.

"So where exactly did you see Doctor Lambe put the Elixir?" Dorothy decided to press the issue.

Max was reluctant to answer, but decided to test the waters, "in the cupboard in his apothecary. What does it matter anyway? That was a long time ago."

"Now, we have a point to work from," Martha answered. "And time is not linear. It is a web."

Max wondered if that was why he saw things out of order during his vision quests.

"She's right," Joe arrived with their orders. "Time is like a web: woven and intricate. Not linear. Native American shamans knew this and knew that people could visit other times readily through dreams. They believed that is where nightmares came from: seeing into other timelines and possibilities. That's why dreamcatchers are web shaped. And the feathers or beads represent the individual having the dreams."

Jonas' confused look returned, "I thought dreamcatchers were supposed to confuse the bad dreams and only let the good ones come down to the dreamer."

"We just tell the white people that. Here you go ladies," he gave them their food and tea. "Boys," he handed them their sandwiches and drinks.

Max and Jonas looked at their white drink suspiciously. "It looks like milk," Jonas said disappointed.

"It's Pegasus' Nightcap," Joe put his hands on his hips. "Try it."

They sipped it cautiously.

"It's good," Max was surprised.

"Of course it is," Joe said genially. "Enjoy," he departed to take care of his other customers.

Dorothy nibbled at her Champ sandwich delicately. Glenda took a hefty bite out of her Chomp and Martha pecked at her Thunderbird salad before setting it down and engaging in her Haiku Hibiscus tea.

"So," Max asked after a few bites, "what exactly do you mean by *'time is not linear'?* How is that significant?"

Martha sipped her tea thinking of the best way to explain. "It means time is very complex. It's not a simple line to trace as history books would make it seem. And it also means that time is not as fragile either. Like a web, there are many strands that comprise and support the web—"

"So forget that horse-shit of killing yourself before you were born and such," Glenda piped in.

"At the most you would create some alternate realty much like an additional strand in the web," Dorothy giggled. "Time is changed frequently. Most perceptive people only remember it as déjà vu or a dream."

Jonas and Max mulled that over their plate of food. Then Max got a sneaky sensation. Despite the amount of people in the CONUNDRUM CAFÉ Max was surprised to get the feeling of being eyed. He whirled around and it wasn't hard to spot them with the only black suits among a sea of students and casual wear: Agent's Knight and McCoy. "I thought they were leaving town," Max mumbled.

"What is it, laddie?" Glenda turned to where Max was looking. "You see something?"

"Yeah, the Men in Black," Max thumbed over

Martha's shoulder toward the entrance.

Jonas spotted them immediately sitting at a table with beverages. "Holy shit, those two are Men in Black? I thought they were FBI."

"You don't think they actually have badges for that do you?" Glenda snarled.

"Men in Black? Where?" Dorothy peered around Martha to where the boys were looking and pointing.

"I don't see them either," Glenda said more worried than annoyed.

"Nor do I," Martha sounded concerned, turning in her chair.

"How can you not see them?" Jonas complained. "They're right there," he pointed. "How long have they been there you think? I didn't notice them come in. They questioned me about Alahmoot. I'm on their radar!" He was in hysterics.

Max and the Sisters Grimm stared at Jonas incredulously, quieting him down.

"And why were they questioning you about Alahmoot?" Martha asked.

"Oh, they were asking me if Sheriff Alahmoot was there right before Max was attacked by the bear, which he was, and if I actually saw the bear, which I didn't."

"Why would they care about that?" Glenda grumbled.

"Did they question you?" Martha asked Max.

Max considered telling them what Agent McCoy said about Alahmoot attacking him and killing the mayor. He was their friend. Then doubt crept in under his skin filling him with ick. If he was their friend then maybe they had a role to play in the mayor's death. Maybe they were all in it together. And if that were the case, then telling them what Agent McCoy revealed would only make him a target. "Oh…yeah, they asked me the same thing."

Martha scrutinized Max like she saw completely

through his lie.

Max squiggled in the couch. Then he noticed something and now was the perfect time to mention it as a distraction. "I think I know why you can't see them! I can't believe it works."

"What?" Glenda growled impatiently.

"A witch bottle," Max noticed a corked jar on the table between the agent's beverages.

"How do you know about witch bottles?" Dorothy was impressed.

"I saw Doctor Lambe make one."

"What's a witch bottle?" Jonas was actually hurt he hadn't heard of one. He thought he knew everything paranormal.

"It makes someone invisible to witches," Max explained. "It's made with Wolf's Bane and red wine."

"There's a little more to it than that, dearie," Dorothy patted his hand. "Well…the red wine needs to rest under a full moon for four cycles, and then you add the Wolf's Bane, but yes, that's pretty much it."

"Alahmoot was right," Martha said wringing her hands. "They know their stuff so they must be Men in Black."

"I knew the Men in Black investigated paranormal stuff," Jonas said loudly.

They all shushed him.

"Hey boys!" There was a loud clap that made everyone jump. It was Mr. Lee. "I see you are consorting with the enemy," he said playfully. "You better get started on your pumpkin carving," he wagged his finger at the sisters. "I'd hate to win by default," he chuckled. "C'mon guys, time to go!" He swept his hand for them to follow him out.

"I think we will take our leave with you," Martha stood and her sisters followed suit.

As they were all exiting, Max noticed at another

table in the CONUNDRUM was La' Wanda sitting with Chance. *Oh, man!* His spirit sank. How did he miss him? He really wanted to talk to him some more and be with him. Max's thoughts were distracted by crashes and screams. A huge rush of wind blew in the CONUNDRUM knocking over some people's drinks and other items that were close to the entrance.

"C'mon, Max," Mr. Lee waved him out the door as Jonas was already outside.

Dorothy and her sisters held the door open for him. "Ah, now we see," Martha said. Max glanced over his shoulder and saw that the witch bottle was one of the items that crashed on the floor.

Dorothy whispered to Max, absolutely tickled. "There's always a work-around."

CHAPTER 33

Chance was virtually naked.

He launched from the starting block and sailed through the air in his tight swim briefs; standing out—as did the entire Ravencrest team—against the competition's speed suits. The Ravencrest crowd roared as Chance plunged in the water much farther along than any of his competitors.

Max found himself shouting, along with the rest of the Ravencrest Academy, cheering Chance on. Cassandra grabbed his hand, and held it in the air, as they flailed along with the infectious school spirit. Even Jonas couldn't help but look more than mildly interested. Max watched excitedly as Chance's chiseled arms cut through the water, his hairline cresting the surface: He was a torpedo shooting the length of the pool.

"You see how fast he is?" Max yelled enthusiastically. "He's so far ahead of everyone else!" He jumped up and down. "I can't believe how fast he is!"

"It's the steroids," Jonas said obviously.

"Will you stop that," Cassandra snatched her hand away from Max so she could properly scold Jonas. She hesitated briefly. Deciding that the students around them weren't paying attention to Jonas' remarks, she continued, "Look," she pointed to the deck. "Coach is here, which means there were no steroids found, and means the team is clean. Now, shut up or cheer!"

Jonas peered through the crowd to the deck where all the officials, swimmers and coaches were. Sure enough there was Coach Matthews. "How did I miss him?" Jonas said to himself. "Look, I saw what I saw. That doesn't change anything. The fact that coach is here only means he's smarter than I suspected—meaning he was able to cover it up."

"He's past the flip turn," Max yelled as Chance bolted through a continuous motion of flipping forward and launching off the wall with his feet—starting the final lap. He was still ahead of everyone else in the pool. Max couldn't help but think how inhuman Chance looked slicing through the water. He was fast in the relay too, but seemed even quicker in this individual meet. Max and Cassandra's voices raged until they were raw as Chance touched the wall finishing in first place.

The Ravencrest Academy crowd erupted with emotion and cheers that echoed through the natatorium. The Ravencrest Ravens came in first place over the Sleepy Hollow Horsemen—winning all the events.

"Wasn't that fantastic!" A bubbly blond girl, named Stacy, turned to them joining in on their enthusiasm. "The medley relay was definitely the best! Wasn't Derek just amazing! He totally pulled the team ahead with his backstroke!"

"Well, that's no surprise," Jonas said sarcastically, "he practices it all the time!"

"I know! He's so dedicated!" Stacy didn't get Jonas' derision. "I know you're a fan," she said rather harshly to Cassandra.

"Well...I don't know..." Cassandra said sickly thinking of how Derek called her a cow.

"Did he finally get a restraining order against you?"

Max decided that Stacy was nowhere near as friendly as her face looked and that her blue eyes were made of ice. "Derek's never going to take an interest in you and padding your bra is not gonna help."

Stacy's eyes popped, and mouth fell, as she covered her breasts shielding them from Max's words.

Cassandra snorted a laugh at Max's off-hand comment completely thrilled.

Stacy glared at Cassandra as though the insult came from her and still covering her chest. "You've been stalking me too, I see. Well, while you're at it you might as well pick up some pointers from the most popular girl at Ravencrest Academy," she unguarded her chest. "It's no secret you need all the help you can get," she made a face at Cassandra's red frizzy hair, braces and outfit. She flipped her head around and pranced through the bleachers after her friends.

"Don't pay any attention to her Cassandra," Max said. "She's insecure so she lashes out at others to bring them down in order to make herself seem better, but actually she's just left a void in the center of her being because she doesn't know how to make herself happy."

"Wow, okay...you really do see shrinks don't you."

Max decided now was the perfect time to make an exit. "I need to give Chance his blanket back." He brought the bright colored wearing blanket that Chance's mom made.

"Okay," Jonas said. "I'll catch up with you later at your house to plan our costumes!"

"Sure," Max said.

"I guess I'll see you guys later," Cassandra sulked down the bleachers.

Max was sure Cassandra was looking for an invite but he didn't have time to deal with her moodiness. He needed to get to the locker room if he wanted to catch Chance.

"You know what," Jonas spun around. "I'll wait for you here," he plopped down on a bleacher.

"Okay," Max didn't care. He just didn't want to miss Chance. Max approached the deck when a security guard stopped him.

"It's okay," Coach Matthews waved him through.

Max approached gripping the wearing blanket, weary that coach was going to blame him somehow for his suspension. "Uh, welcome back, coach."

"Welcome back to both of us. I understand you were in the hospital a few extra days during my suspension."

"Right," *so I wasn't the one that accused you of roiding the swim team.*

Coach studied Max as though he were contemplating that same circumstance and turned his head to examine Jonas in the bleachers.

Even from far away Max could tell that Jonas was crumbling in guilt from coach's stare. He finally stood up and yelled, "It's okay, Max, I changed my mind. I'll catch up with you later at your house," and fled.

Coach turned his attention back to Max. "So you ready to join the swim team?" He said cheerfully. "Did the meet inspire you? My offer still stands."

"Yeah, actually I am," he couldn't believe he just

said that. His mom might actually like that. She might actually think of him as a normal kid. And the more he thought of it...he actually liked the idea too. Max gave coach an eager grin.

"That's terrific news, Dane! You'll have to start though in November." His eyes just discovered that Max was holding a colorful blanket.

"Oh, I'm returning this to Chance. He brought it to me in the hospital."

"He saw you in the hospital, huh?"

"Uh...yeah," Max wasn't about to elaborate.

"I think he's still in the locker room," he shot a thumb to the entrance. "If Derek's in there you tell him *I* said no fighting!"

"Right," Max forgot about Derek. *Damn!*

A large group of the swim team—having changed into their street clothes—were exiting. Max rushed down an aisle of lockers after them, presuming that Chance was in the group, when he heard smacking sounds like someone eating rather loudly. He stopped and turned going along the middle walkway that cut between rows of lockers. He followed the sounds toward the therapy Jacuzzi and showers. He walked through the entrance-way to see Chance and Derek in their Speedos eating each other's faces!

Well, that's what it looked like to Max but he didn't see any blood. There was gnashing and twisting of tongues and lips. Max froze in awe of the spectacle. His stomach twirled with emotions that he couldn't identify.

Derek pulled away from Chance realizing Max was there. Both boys turned to face him with their Speedos tenting. They both stretched their suits to capacity. Max felt his jaw slack and his eyes pop out of his skull. He knew he should try to ignore the whole thing but he couldn't budge his eyes from their swim suits. His brain was fog. He was trying to think of something to say or do because he knew he was staring for too long, but he couldn't think. What was he doing here?

"What are you doing here?" Derek was pissed. "What's that sissy blanket?"

Chance punched Derek in the arm. "That's my sissy blanket. My mom made it."

"What's he doing with it?" The words flung at Chance.

"Hey, it wasn't your blanket." Chance knew that wasn't going to save him.

"Fuck you! Why do you even bother with him? He's like ten."

"Twelve. He'll be twelve on Halloween," Chance winked at Max.

Max felt his face blush. He was surprised Chance remembered.

"You've got to be fucking kidding me," Derek said disgusted. His voice dropped so that Max couldn't hear him. "What is it with you and younger guys?"

"You've never objected before." Derek turned and bent over picking up his gym bag. Chance smacked his ass. "C'mon, why do you hate him so much?"

Derek bolted straight-up, more than annoyed. "You've been hot for him since you pointed him out that day before he walked into Joe's…" His face suddenly went taut as he glanced past Max. Chance looked and Max spun around to see Agent McCoy.

Max's head searched frantically for Agent Knight. He figured he had to be close. *This guy meant it when he said he was going to keep an eye on me. First he was at the CONUNDRUM and now he's here.* "What are you doing here?" Even with Agent McCoy's sunglasses on Max could tell that question ruffled him. He was about to speak when another voice interrupted.

"Yes, what are you doing here?" It was coach. "Students only," his voice was authoritative.

"Ah," Agent McCoy flipped out his badge, "Coach Brent Matthews, congratulations on the win," he looked down at coach.

"Thanks," Coach wasn't convinced of his sincerity. "So really? The FBI investigates *alleged* high school sports doping?"

Agent McCoy was a statue. Then he re-animated. "I understood that was all cleared up, which is why you're back from your suspension. Oh yes, we know about that. Since we're in town indefinitely, I'd like to talk to you about a little program the FBI does from time to time. We educate young athletes on federal statutes regarding gambling and corruption in the sports industry and make them aware of bribery and drugs and how organized crime may attempt to corrupt them."

Coach drew in the quiet, attempting to decipher if there was a hidden message for him.

"I'm outta here," Derek shattered the silence. He grabbed his duffel bag and charged toward the lockers.

"Yeah," Coach called over to the boys. "Why don't you get along to the CONUNDRUM, the rest of the team is celebrating there. I'll talk to Agent…"

"McCoy."

"…McCoy."

"I understand you served some time in the military Coach Matthews…"

Max followed Chance to his locker still curious what Agent McCoy was doing here. He didn't buy that story at all. His suspicions quickly were forgotten as Chance whipped off his Speedos. Max admired every ripple of his back muscles as he twisted to retrieve a pair of designer underwear from his locker. Chance looked at Max with a smirk as he slowly put his underwear on in front of him. Chance couldn't stand it anymore and laughed. "You are so cute! Your eyes are so big!"

"So is your…" Max pointed and was immediately

ashamed. "Here…" he handed the blanket out.

"Oh right, thanks." Chance took it with a smile, stuffing it into his gym bag, and then plopped down on the bench in front of Max still in just his underwear. "So what did you think of that kiss?"

"Kiss? Oh…" he must be talking about him and Derek. "That was a kiss?" His mom never kissed him like that. Neither did Cassandra.

"Yeah," Chance chuckled. "What did you think it was?"

"A mauling!"

"Ha!" Chance grinned. "So you mean you've never done anything like that?"

"To a cupcake!"

Chance laughed some more, pulling Max close to him. He was between Chance's really defined legs. "You are so freakin' adorable," he put his face right up to Max's.

Max could smell his skin. He only had a moment to gasp before Chance's lips latched onto his. Chance's lips massaged his, then his tongue flicked inside his mouth. Max was wrestling tongues with Chance. He didn't have a clue if he was doing any of this right, but it was such an amazing sensation he felt like his body soared out the top of his head. His underwear was tighter and the blood drained from his legs. Max grasped onto Chance's bare legs for support, but it seemed Chance could tell Max was losing balance as his hands tightened around his waist stopping him from falling. Chance pulled his face away slowly from Max's. Max's eyes fluttered in ecstasy.

"Damn, you're a good kisser," Chance stood up still holding onto Max.

"Am I?" Max asked dreamily.

"Look," he was back out of his underwear.

"Whoa," Max was shocked. "What happened to it? It grew!" He didn't think it could be any bigger.

"Same as you," Chance grabbed Max's crotch.

"It's called a boner...I'll show you how to use it sometime," he winked. He put on the rest of his clothes. "So hey, why don't you come over to the CONUNDRUM with us and celebrate."

"Oh..." Max shifted his crotch around trying to get more comfortable; "yeah..." he desperately wanted to go with Chance, especially since he invited him. If he said no, Chance might not ever invite him again. "Uh..." But Jonas was planning on coming over to plan their Halloween costumes and he'd been so excited about it. He was Jonas' only friend. "Jonas is coming over. I told him I'd be there." *Stupid! Stupid! Stupid! Stupid! Stupid!*

Chance grunted. "I got it, he's your friend," he grinned. "That's cool, c'mon," he grabbed Max's hand and walked him out.

CHAPTER 34

The raven perched above the abbey of the monastery in defiance of the tumultuous weather and blinked a small human green eye.

The raven watched as a man draped in a hooded snowy white cloak carrying a staff entered the church. The raven flew in behind him and took position in the dome. The hooded man had a vaporous aura. It soon dissipated after he entered the church evidently keeping him completely dry and immaculate from the storm.

Abbot Conleth had come from the library side entrance followed by three men-at-arms: Yvain, Erec, and Cador. The abbot was as tall and thin as Ambrosius. In appearance they seemed to be the same age. However, the abbot did not look as sophisticated. He was balding but his hair was wild and strewn. His beard was scraggly. If he weren't wearing a monastic cloak he could be easily mistaken for a hermit. Even in his cloak he looked quite disheveled. He fumbled with several scrolls and parchment and glanced from his collection. Seeing the main doors to the church wide open—leaving a plain view to the grounds and current cloudburst—he yelled to two more men-at-arms that were standing by the door supposedly guarding it. "Tristan! Dinadan! Secure those doors!" And that's when he noticed the man in white standing inside the church.

The man in white, still grasping his oak staff, pulled back his hood with his other hand: revealing an elderly sophisticated man with a bald dome and long silver flowing hair along the side with a matching beard and mustache.

"Ambrosius," Abbot Conleth was afraid that he would make an appearance. "Isn't tonight the festival? You're feast...you and your fellow druids." He struggled trying not to drop everything he was carrying.

"Samhain."

"That's the one, aye, aye. You've mentioned it before to the Table," he said regaining his composure and balance.

"Summer's end—the feast of all souls—the time when the veil between our world and the land of the dead, Tír na nÓg, is the thinnest; a time when the living and the dead can communicate; a night that exists outside of time itself; a perfect night for a murder!" He slammed the end of his oak staff against the stone floor causing a thunderous echo.

All of the guards drew their swords in response to his hostile display.

The abbot's heart was racing with fear. *Certainly Ambrosius wouldn't try anything now...not with five guards. Would he?* "Ambrosius, what the devil are you doing here?"

"Interesting choice of words," Ambrosius spoke with a crisp tone. "This Devil figure permeates your religious order. I knew it to be a simple metaphor for the evil that lurks inside men. But now I know this Devil to be true. Your people have talked so exuberantly of this Devil and written about it so generously you have poured the mental energies of your delegates, followers, and congregation into this figure and now have given it life. You have created your own Egregore. How hypocritical that your priests speak against the mysticism of my people, yet you weave your own. What have you done? What is your plan?"

"I should ask you that! We were in this together. You double-crossed me. I've seen what you plan to do. You are resurrecting your Lord of the Dead. The others at the Table told me not to trust you. You plot to annihilate us all!" Abbot Conleth's heart began to race again. He looked to the guards for support. They were standing alert with their swords drawn.

"Doctor Lambe is dead," Ambrosius said sternly.

Abbot Conleth dropped everything he was carrying as his hands covered his mouth. His fingers trembled as he let out a small cry. "John…" he muttered.

Ambrosius' eyes were drawn to the materials that tumbled from Conleth's hands. One item in particular ignited contempt within him. He pointed to a thick leather bound book with parchment pages. On the cover of the book was an image of a large cup engraved on it. "What is that doing here? How did you get that?"

Conleth's hands were still trembling in shock from the word of his friend's death. He glanced down at the strewn parchments and the book that Ambrosius was pointing at. Before he could get a word out Ambrosius was huffing again.

"How could I have been a fool…again,"

Ambrosius said in a gruff. "What was I thinking trusting you and your kind; thinking there could be some covenant between our people. You have betrayed me."

Conleth was snapped from his temporary shock by Ambrosius' words. "Betray? How dare you sir. I have put my own career at risk to bring understanding and compromise between your people and the powers in Rome. And most definitely put my own life in jeopardy. Do you think the Church would simply let Doctor Lambe walk away from his priestly duties to dabble in Apothecary if it weren't for me? I had to placate that. And aye, I had to impose concessions upon him, but it was better than him standing before an inquisition. If you are going to accuse me of betraying you, simply because I made a man use prayers outlined by the Church during his treatments, then aye, I am guilty. Aye, I am guilty of saving a man's life."

"But he's not alive anymore now is he?"

"I suppose I have you to thank for killing my long time comrade and friend." Fury grew in Abbot Conleth's voice. He motioned for Yvain, Erec, and Cador—who were standing behind him—to take action.

Ambrosius shook his head disappointed. Then a howling wind charged the doors to the abbey blowing them open with a thunderous echo as they had not been bolted. The piercing wind had halted the men-at-arms' approach. A whirlwind of leaves and rain entered the abbey.

Conleth's eyes widened with fear. "Ambrosius," he yelled over the wind, "I have foreseen what is coming. Retribution is upon us!"

"Foreseen?" Ambrosius shouted to the abbot. But the abbot wasn't paying attention to him. Instead his eyes and mouth were frozen open at what he saw behind Ambrosius: A headless green glowing knight standing at the entry doors.

CHAPTER 35

Jonas' ear peeled off.

"Perfect!" Max examined the silicone.

"I can't believe you make molds and masks!" Jonas jumped around Max's room. "This is going to be so awesome!"

"I'll have your ears done in time for Halloween." Max was distracted, as his thoughts drifted to the kiss with Chance. He almost asked Jonas if he ever kissed anyone. But then he'd probably have to explain that Chance kissed him. When Chance's lips were on his and their tongues touched the gutter ball in his stomach was replaced with twinkling excitement. He'd give anything to feel that all the time. *Kissing Chance doesn't make me gay does it?* He thought about asking Jonas, when Jonas just about pounced on him.

"You made a mold of my ears! I can't believe it!" Jonas looked at all the masks that Max had displayed along a wall in his room. "And your mom buys you the stuff to make all these. That's so cool of her."

Max felt guilty. He hadn't spoken much to his mom recently. "Well, I don't have the internet to play on. So she buys me these supplies instead. I want to use them in my films someday."

"Oh, right...your horror movies! Hey," Jonas grabbed Max's camera. "Have you recorded anything?" He started pressing buttons.

"Not really," he decided he should try and say something to his mom. "I'm gonna go get some more firewood," he went downstairs. His mom was in the kitchen decorating Halloween cupcakes with Lindsey as a cozy fire crackled in the living room.

"Look," Lindsey beamed holding up a green cupcake. "It's an alien!"

"It's an alien for a change," Evelyn worked on a spider cupcake.

Max marveled at all the designs on the cupcakes. His mom could design with fabric *and food.* She was good with all that kind of stuff. There were cupcakes that looked like mummies, skeletons, skull and crossbones, spider webs, ghosts, and eyeballs. "So..." Max said to his mom, "I'm going to join the swim team."

"That's great, sweetie." She added chocolate sprinkles for the body of the spider.

"I decided that I'm going to be good."

"Good at swimming?" She slipped black licorice in for the legs.

"Uh...being a human."

"Good luck." She plopped two candy-corns for fangs.

Max gave up and picked up some firewood.

327

"What are you boys up to?" She finally looked at Max.

"Oh, working on our costumes. Speaking of..." he explained their idea which would require an actual outfit. His mom wasn't only an editor of design magazines but also a fashion designer. He waited to be hit with how busy she was and there was no way.

"That's fantastic!" She leapt from the stool. "Asuka likes to sew. She's been looking for an excuse to show me her construction skills. We can work on this together for you boys. This will be a perfect bonding activity for all of us. That's what Halloween is about!"

Max was surprised and shocked and happy. His mom was so ecstatic it was a total one-eighty from how she had been acting. His gutter ball was buried for the moment. "Great, I'll go tell Jonas," he ran upstairs with the firewood.

"I'll call Asuka. Tell Jonas he's staying for dinner," she yelled after him.

"My mom's calling your mom she's gonna make us dinner," Max burst back into his room dropping the firewood. Jonas was covered with terror. "What is it?" He ran to Jonas and shook him. His face was the color of milk. "Are you okay?"

Jonas shoved the camera at Max. His hand trembled as he pointed to it. "Tell me...tell me...you...messed with that on your computer...special effects."

"I haven't done anything like that. What are you talking about?" He looked at the monitor and reversed to see what Jonas was so scared about. Max realized it was the footage from when they arrived at Ravencrest; when he had his seizure. His mom ran up to him and the camera dropped. Lindsey moved toward him and his mom, when suddenly, you could see a thick tree branch grab at Lindsey's backpack. On camera you hear Lindsey yelling,

"It moved, it moved. The scarecrow moved." His mother blocked most of the view. But Max knew who it was. He felt the color of his face match Jonas'.

"That's...that's Mr. Creeps, isn't it? I didn't really believe it, but...you're serious, you didn't mess with this footage?" Jonas' voice choked on fear.

Max shook his head violently plopping down on the floor by Jonas. "I...but...what did he want with my sister's backpack?"

"Nothing! He was trying to grab your sister! Holy shit! I can't believe this is real! This is really real! What do we do?"

"Maybe we should show the sisters."

"Yeah, maybe, they probably know something or what to do. You don't mean now do you? It's getting dark!"

"Okay, okay, we won't go there now." Max grabbed the logs he dropped and threw them into the fire.

"But that's an idea! Maybe you should tell the sheriff."

"They're not going to believe it. They're gonna think exactly what you did; that I messed with the footage," Max stirred the logs.

"No...I mean..." Jonas couldn't believe he was going to suggest this since the idea scared him. "...I mean Sheriff Alahmoot. You seem to have a knack for talking to dead people. Maybe he can tell you something. You said you saw Mr. Creeps right before he died."

Max smiled. "That's brilliant! Hey...maybe I should try fire-gazing."

"Pyromancy! Yes!"

"I need your help. You know about this stuff...meditation...and that. You need to help guide me."

Jonas felt honored that Max thought of him like that. "Okay," he sounded less scared. "We should use that incense you got at Uva's."

"Great idea!" Max snatched it from under his bed. "Okay, here we go. We have: Cypress, Wormwood and Angelica."

"Which do we use?" Jonas was trying to remember what Uva told them.

"Well, I had Wormwood tea in Madame Hemlock's office when I...went on a vision quest," he liked Joe's term. "And I think the priest I saw was drinking the same kind of tea."

"How would you know that?"

"The same way I know everything else that I shouldn't."

"Right, okay, Wormwood it is," Jonas grabbed two sticks and put the ends into the fire, igniting them. He blew them out propping the two smoking sticks on the hearth. "Maybe we should put some meditation music on to help set the mood. I have some on my phone. Do you have any *mi*Speakers? Oh..." Jonas was just reminded by Max's glare that he didn't have a cell phone so probably no accessories either "...right. Well maybe on your computer..." Max's face didn't change "...that's fine," he put his phone away. Jonas sat down next to Max on the floor in front of the fire. "Okay, take some deep breaths in through your nose and hold. Now, exhale out through your mouth...again...good. Keep doing that as you gaze into the flame. Feel the warmth of the flame in the center of your belly. See yourself standing in front of the fire watching the flames. Keep your eye on the dark radiance just above the flame as you walk around to the back...back...back..."

The flame blew...no...it was a torch that blew under the full moon. *It wasn't a full moon yet, how could that be?* Of course...it was Samhain again. *Jonas is good.* But he knew he wouldn't find Sheriff Alahmoot here. Max was standing in front of a castle in the night. There was an eeriness that blanketed his surroundings. The silence was stifling. As the moonlight sank beneath flickering clouds he heard a horse gallop away. He turned. In the torch-light he saw a handsome man with facial hair. It was Sir Percy! His heart leapt.

Max ran over to him when he saw fear grip Percy's face as he grasped the hilt of his sword. Max's eyes followed Percy's and then he joined in his fear. It was the Knightmare! Max was surprised to see it had a helmet again—it wasn't headless. It must not have lost it yet or maybe it found it. He needed to communicate somehow with Percy, but the glowing knight was headed directly toward them. Max wasn't sure if it could see him. It saw him in the hospital...but he wasn't on a vision quest then. But did it matter with the Knightmare? It seemed whenever he was having one of these visions it was because he was in the Nexus. And if the Knightmare was able to travel through it like it did to collect Jack, then maybe it could see him. In any case, it was definitely going to see Percy and Max wasn't convinced the knight in leather was going to stand a chance.

Max stood aside as the Knightmare approached, but Percy hesitated. Max was frightened for him. Why was he just standing there? Max saw his fingers tighten on his hilt. *He can't be seriously thinking of fighting this thing? He won't win.* "It's already dead you can't kill it," Max screamed. Percy's eyes flicked toward Max. "Move," Max's voice reverberated the panicked beating of his heart. And then Percy stood aside. Max didn't get a chance to confirm if Percy heard him or not as the Knightmare stood between them and stopped. Max's excited heart came to a halt. He was frozen waiting for the Knightmare's next move. It just stood there. Did it see Percy? Did it see him?

Then suddenly it raised its hand in the air and made a fist. The wind raised violently kicking debris about. There was a piercing scream in the night like Max had never heard, forcing him to cup his ears. As Max was defending his ears from the shrill he saw a ripple in the night air. The dark was bending and from the center of the distortion; out popped a blaze of light. No, it was a horse on fire! Then Max realized the horse wasn't exactly on fire. It was transformed as though comprised of fire. Its eyes burned red and flames flew off its hooves and tail. Its mane was rolling lava.

He watched the Knightmare mount its horrendous steed while throwing a drenched saddlebag across its blazing back. *What was in that bag?* Max had an impulse. Jack did it. Why couldn't he? Max plunged at the Knightmare before it rode off. He was going to enter its body. But as he jumped up, certain symbols on the Knightmare's armor illuminated; similar to what occurred in the hospital. Max was pretty certain it was a different sequence this time. As he was just about to make contact with the Knightmare, he felt a pulling sensation in his gut, yanking him back onto the drawbridge as the Knightmare road off in a trail of fire. The planks of the drawbridge didn't feel like wood. Max wasn't hurt at all when he struck down. It was like the ground was fluffy. He was definitely in the Nexus.

"I told you he is well protected."

Max got up. "Jack," he was surprised to see him.

"Why are you here Max?"

"I'm here for answers," Max didn't hesitate. He didn't know if it would work. He plunged inside Jack.

CHAPTER 36

Food and offerings outside dwellings were soaked in the rain.

"I do not understand why your people leave these things out." Father Gregory shouted to Percy as they galloped to the monastery.

Ambrosius could explain this better than he. Then Percy found himself angered at that thought. *How could Ambrosius betray them?* He wasn't as strong in his people's beliefs but never found a reason to challenge them. He didn't know if he believed these things. However, he would attempt to answer the priest's question. "Tonight is when the fissure in time is exposed and the living have access to the dead. The offerings are a gesture to welcome our loved ones who have passed on to

the Otherworld."
"They sit and eat with the dead?"
"Many claim so."
"And you have done this?"
"Nay," Percy confessed. "I never knew my father.
I don't imagine I would recognize him."
"And your mother?"
"Aye, I knew her, but my studies in Knighthood
have precluded my partaking of this ritual." Percy was
filled with guilt. His mother would have been offended he
never took part of the ritual. He never had. He convinced
himself it was superstition. But another part of him was
resentful that she sent him away with the king. He didn't
want to sit with her now that she was dead.

"Do you truly believe this?" The priest asked in
astonishment.

"Aye I do," he lied. "Is it any more difficult to
believe than this demon of yours we are following?" He
wasn't expecting an answer from the priest. "It is told that
sometimes when the dead visit they will do a good deed
for you."

"Have you had such a visit before?" Their horses
were approaching the monastery. The priest was sure none
of these people had ever had a visitation from deceased
loved ones and wanted to make a point.

"Perchance," Percy answered vaguely. Until now
he had never had an encounter. But after seeing Jack he
had to consider if all the astonishing tales and beliefs he
had grown up with were true. And yet, the priest had some
astonishing and sensational beliefs as well that could be
valid.

They crossed the bridge past the guest houses into
the monastery. Percy dismounted and realized for the first
time how large the monastery was. The grounds were
larger than the castle. The monastery was comprised of
several buildings together—branching off the abbey—

forming a square. In that conglomerate of buildings were the library, guest houses, smaller chapel, and the monk's dormitories. The monastery also consisted of separate buildings on the grounds that were: the abbot's house, kitchen, stables and workshops. There was probably more than he knew of. The monastery was almost a fortress. Percy pondered how he never perceived this before. Perhaps the atrocious events of this night had opened his eyes.

The grounds were ornate with cobblestone paths and vegetation. There were numerous gardens, farm fields and orchards; lush with vegetables, plants and herbs. There was a stone fountain at the intersection of the cobblestone paths in front of the main entrance to the church. The fountain was circular on the bottom level with water overflowing from the rain. There was another circular tier above; water poured out from protrusions evenly spaced all around. And from the center of that tier rose a stone block with four sides. To Percy it looked as if it were cut to resemble the shape of the steeple to the monastery. Abbot Conleth once told him the fountain was to represent the garden of paradise: A place where supposedly the first two humans were created by their god and then banned after the woman made the man eat some fruit that gave him knowledge. It seemed very much to Percy that this meant their god was intent on keeping his people ignorant. But he never expressed that to Conleth. The grounds of the abbey even had fish ponds. *Fish ponds?* It seemed obscene to Percy.

The men made their way to the stone church and halted their horses in the mud at the sight of the Knightmare's steed blazing at the main entrance.

Gareth grabbed Percy's arm tugging him back from the others. "I have a message for thou. I am to deliver it to the last of the king's knights." The night flashed. "A stranger came to me tonight," Gareth was thankful for the night's protection. He could feel his face flush at the remembrance of the exact details of making acquaintance with the stranger with strange markings. He pushed the carnal memory aside and continued with his promise to deliver the message. "Thou art not to trust the priest."

"Which priest?" Percy spoke offended. "Father Gregory? Abbot Conleth? Or some other priest altogether?"

Gareth looked at Percy with his pale blue eyes. He didn't know what to say. The stranger wasn't that specific.

"How can you trust this stranger? And how can I trust you when you are a stranger to me?"

Gareth couldn't reply to Percy's question. Percy turned and joined the others.

The men were standing in the downpour huddled by the fountain. "How do we get by that steed?" Gwalchmai asked in fear. Fire swirled from its nostrils in huffs. "Thy saw what it did to Dagonet."

"We don't even know if we can kill it," Lamorak asserted thinking of how the glowing knight dealt a death blow to Kay even after its head was taken off. In fact, it seemed as if the Knightmare didn't have a head in the first place. Lamorak thought it reasonable to assume the green knight's horse was just as indestructible.

"How do we know the abbot is even here?" Gwalchmai continued with his string of protesting questions.

"He's here," Percy assured. "That I am certain of. I left him here at the church, in the library at the back."

"Thy left him," Bedivere said accusingly. "Why didn't thy stay with him?"

Percy picked up on Bedivere's condemning tone.

"I didn't know he was in danger then. I DIDN'T KNOW THE KING WAS IN DANGER!" The words sprayed out of his mouth with rain. He was infuriated.

Father Gregory grasped Percy's arm in support.

"Nobody's blaming you," he said with a stern tone to the others that meant they should not be accusing Percy of anything.

"What does this...*thing*...want?" Bedivere demanded. "It must have some sort of purpose."

"It's after heads. That much is certain." Lamorak explained, "It collected Doctor Lambe's head after it killed him."

"Aye, I believe Lamorak is correct," Percy agreed. "The king's head was missing as well as Jack's."

"Jack?" Bedivere was trying to think of who that was. "I don't know Jack."

"Jack was Ambrosius' protégé, a young boy. He couldn't have been more than eight years of age."

"What warrior revels in claiming the head of an eight-year-old boy?" Gwalchmai was disgusted.

"It does not make any rational sense," Lamorak said. "I could understand taking the king's head. However, taking the doctor's head and leaving Kay's is confusing."

"I agree," Percy was contemplating Lamorak's words. He understood the point he was trying to make. It was common for their people to takes heads in battle as reverence to their personal victory, as well as out of respect for their foe, and the vigor they had fought with. But this was no war; no battle. There was no honor or reverence in these acts at all. "These were executions," Percy deduced. "Father," Percy turned to Gregory. "You say this thing is a demon..."

"Yea, brought here by your people's delving into mystical and magickal practices that you can't understand or control. It has allowed the Devil to send his legionnaire on this nightmarish night of yours. These festivities and rituals you take part in on this night have created and opened a gate allowing the Devil easier access to our world."

"And what is the purpose of this Devil?" Bedivere

asked curious. He had never heard of such a thing, yet he had never seen the likes of a glowing green knight and a burning steed either, so he was willing to learn more from the priest.

"The Devil's intent is to turn men toward evil. He will do this by corruption. To corrupt man he has given you his tools so you will do it on your own without even realizing it. Those tools are witchcraft, magick and mysticism. Your people have practiced these things for ages allowing him to gather strength. What you are witnessing tonight is the culmination of your ignorance and deceit allowing the Devil's power to come to full. Eventually, he will make our planet like his fiery realm called Hell. He is trying to bring Hell to Earth. Chaos, corruption, misery and suffering: that is his only goal."

All of the men were feeling a pit in their stomach. They felt as though they were each responsible for bringing this evil upon themselves. Percy in particular felt weighted down by the priest's words as he felt personally responsible for the events of this night. If he had never left the king, perhaps he would still be alive. If he was at the castle with the king, perhaps Jack would still be alive. And if he had stopped the Knightmare when he first saw it, perhaps the doctor, Kay and Dagonet would still be alive as well. Among these feelings of guilt, there was still something nagging at Percy. It was doubt. There was something about the Knightmare that wasn't making sense to him. It ignored him. "This demon's purpose is to destroy us all then, father?"

"That is what it does. It causes mayhem. And that is exactly what it has done tonight—lest we forget it killed all the king's knights save you. And you Percy, I believe were spared by the one true God—the mortal enemy of the Devil—that sent his only son to Earth to die for our sins: sins like witchcraft. God has saved you Percy, because you are pivotal in this battle tonight."

Percy was shocked. It was as if Father Gregory had read his mind. Could that really be the reason he was spared? Divine intervention saved his life? Some god he never heard of took an interest in him and spared him? That did explain why the Knightmare ignored him.

"I don't mean any disrespect, father," Lamorak interrupted. "However, none of this helps us in our current predicament. I believe Percy is attempting to deduce what the Knightmare is after to understand its goals and motives. This can give us a tactical advantage as it would seem our weapons are ineffective against this foe."

"Aye exactly," Percy snapped out of his thoughts, "Father, you have had dealings with these demons. Your knowledge is obviously expansive. Do you have anything that can assist us in this battle?"

"Yea," Father Gregory shook his fist with enthusiastic recollection, "now that you mention it I believe I have." He reached into the bag where he put the doctor's books and pulled out a silver cross. He could see from their faces that they didn't know what it was. Gregory didn't think this was the appropriate time to go into a sermon about Jesus dying on the cross. There would be time for that later. "It's a powerful symbol of my religion."

"Do you have more?" Percy took the cross from the priest with intrigue.

"Yea, I do," Father Gregory replied pleased at the men's interest. He handed the remaining crosses to Bedivere, Lamorak, and Gwalchmai.

"What do you do with it?" Bedivere looked at the cross confused. "Throw it?"

"Yea," Lamorak snapped. Of course, now he remembered. "Kay showed me one of these from his travels. It's called a throwing star."

Bedivere studied it with doubt. "It seems a mace or war hammer would be more effective."

"No," Father Gregory said irritated. "It's not a

339

weapon against man. It is used to ward off evil."

"Aye," Bedivere yelled. "I will throw it at the flaming steed driving it off."

The rain barraged the men as Bedivere turned poised to hurl the cross at the flaming steed when Gwalchmai yelled with a fervent urgency, "Come back!"

CHAPTER 37

Gareth disappeared in a blur.

Percy was standing with Bedivere, Lamorak, Gwalchmai, and Father Gregory on what truly had to be the most magickal night of the year Percy thought. Percy was watching Gareth. It didn't exactly look like Gareth but they all knew it was. Percy and the others watched as a smear moved through the rain at high speed. It was the same size as the thirteen-year-old. It was like a wave surging through the rain. And in a blink it snatched the saddlebag from the steed.

Immediately the steed snapped its head in the direction of the swell and blew a jet of fire with a piercing scream. The men covered their ears, but looked on in amazement. Fire plowed through the rain setting off large clouds of steam.

"Why would he do that?" The question dribbled out of Gwalchmai's mouth in disbelief. He was certain his brother was dead. Then he thought of how fast he moved. "How could he do that?"

Then everyone saw Gareth miraculously standing by the side of the abbey. He was unharmed and holding the saddlebag in his hands. The steed saw him too.

The flames from the steed blazed higher. Smoke billowed from its ember eyes as they glowed hotter. The steed snorted, then reared, and as its legs came down it charged Gareth letting out another piercing scream. A funnel of flame sprayed from its mouth heralding its charge. The flames engulfed the trees and brush outside the church. The steed did not hesitate in its advance and plowed through the ashen remains of the disintegrated foliage. Gareth was standing in front of the entrance of the abbey now and tossed the saddlebag after the steed.

Before Percy and the others could react at all, Gareth was standing beside them at the fountain. Gareth was bouncing on his feet from heel to toe with exhilaration. "We have a way in now, eh!" He declared with a large grin.

"Aye," Bedivere swept his sword from its sheath. "Our brave lad has given us an opening," he slapped Gareth affectionately between the shoulder blades seeing a clear path to the abbey. "Let's make haste!" And he charged the entrance of the abbey. With the exception of Gwalchmai, the other fighters drew their swords and rushed after Bedivere with the priest following.

Gwalchmai stood looking disappointed at his brother with his big grin. "What did that stranger do to ye? It's not natural." He followed the others, leaving Gareth standing alone in the rain and mud: with his grin gone and his spirit sinking.

CHAPTER 38

Max lifted up the tarp and saw the mutilated horse!

"Llamrai," he screamed.

"I told you not to look under there," Brother John pushed the tarp out of his hand while yanking the reigns.

Max bolted from the wagon. *He needed to tell Ambrosius! He would know what to do! He could save Llamrai!* He was running through the castle. His body felt smaller. His arms and fists were definitely smaller and he was wearing a green tunic. It worked! He was inside Jack. He felt his heart racing as he clambered up a stone staircase, charged down a hall, and pushed through a chamber door. There he was! There was Ambrosius, standing there in his white flowing cloak with his arms wide ready to embrace him, as if he knew what was the matter and was waiting for him. Max ran to him in tears. Ambrosius put a hand on his head and the other on his shoulder spinning him around. And for a moment Max felt a warm gush like bath water running down his chest. His view raised up as he saw his tiny headless body in the green tunic topple onto the floor as blood poured out onto a design similar to the one carved into his horse!

The fire was burning blue. Jonas was scared. He looked at Max who was breathing cold air. There was a knock at the bedroom door. "Max!" It was his mother.

"Oh shit!" Jonas stood panicked. What was he going to do? His eyes jumped from Max to the fire to the door. Jonas waved his hand in front of Max. "Get up," he said desperately. But Max was frozen and urinating in his pants. "Oh shit!"

Evelyn opened the door striking something, before she got a full view of Max's room.

"Hi, miss Dane," Jonas peaked his head around the door. "Max was working on my ear. For our costume…"

"Oh, of course, where's Max?" She tried to push the door more but Jonas' foot was locked down on the floor.

"Oh, he's cleaning up in the bathroom; messy stuff," he pulled at latex on his ear.

"Yes," Evelyn said a little disgusted. "Okay, well your parents should be here soon. So get downstairs," she yelled into the room so Max could hear. "Are you okay, Jonas? You look flustered."

"Oh," he searched the rug for answers. "I'm just so excited about having a buddy to go out with on Halloween."

Evelyn looked touched. "That is so sweet. You know, I'm excited too. It's going to be special working with your mother on your guy's costumes." She turned and went downstairs. Jonas heaved relief, slammed the door, and ran back to Max.

Max's skin was melting! The armor was grafted onto his skin from the fire. The pain was indescribable. It was as if someone was pressing down relentlessly on a sun burn that bore to his bone. Max looked down at his arms and saw a green armor with skulls. His vision was like looking through a blazing tunnel. Everything was some hue of red. A sword was thrust into his hands. "Kill them," Ambrosius commanded. "Kill every one of them that bears this ring with the symbol of their Round Table Society," he held a ring with a runic "R." "Kill them and bring me their heads. Kill any that try and stop you and any others I command. When you have brought me the ring bearers heads I will return yours and your soul. You will be free! Not a moment before!"

Max tried to swing the sword right there and then and take off Ambrosius' bright red head. But he couldn't move against him. Max looked at the sword wishing for a battle axe. He preferred the battle axe. And then suddenly there was a skull adorned battle axe in a cyclone of fire. Ambrosius didn't seem to mind the conjuration. Max grabbed the battle axe and hooked it to his side. He couldn't wait to use it on Ambrosius!

Jonas looked at Max in horror. He looked worse. His face was contorted in pain and the urine spot spread out more on his jeans. "I hope he doesn't get any on the carpet. That's why I have an octopus and not a dog." He looked frantically around the room for ideas of what to do. Then he saw the incense splayed on the floor. He dowsed the incense that was lit and grabbed the Angelica. "The spell-breaker," he said hopefully. He lit it and then sat purposefully in front of Max. "Max come back to me!" He uttered frightfully. There was no change. "Maximillian Aided Dane, I command you to come back to me!" He yelled dangerously.

Max ran into Ambrosius' arms and felt the blade sawing his flesh and then the bone. His body fell below him spilling out its contents. Max wanted to yell desperately but only blood came out. Max was infuriated.

"Nooooo!" He finally screamed.

Jonas jumped. Then he heard another scream downstairs. "Hold on buddy!" He patted Max's face and ran to the bedroom door. He opened it cautiously to hear that his parents had arrived and they were all screaming salutations. "Grown-ups are weird." He turned back to the fireplace. "It's okay, Max. I don't think they heard you." But Max wasn't there. Jonas panicked. Then he went into the bathroom to see Max with his face in the toilet retching. "Max," he ran over to him patting him on the back. "Are you okay? What happened?"

"He cut my head off!" Max cried into the toilet. "Again and again he cut my head off!"

"What? Who?" Jonas was confused.

Max slumped back from the toilet resting on his heels, "I jumped inside Jack's body. I lived Ambrosius decapitating him. Jack is living it over and over and I was too," tears flowed from his eyes.

It showed in Jonas' eyes that he pitied Max. "How many times did you live it before I got you back?"

"Six," Max's chest heaved trying to catch his breath. He looked at Jonas with sorrow. "Jack is the Knightmare."

CHAPTER 39

The glass cracked into a spider web.

Chance was slammed up against a window in Ravencrest Academy's atrium. Derek jabbed his finger in Max's direction. "You're next you little fucking cunt!" And before Chance could recover, Derek barreled into him hurling both of them through the window into the courtyard.

Max and Jonas, and every other student that was arriving to school, had their mouths stuck open in shock. They saw blood flying.

"I loved you! You fucking piece of shit and this is what you do!" Derek was on top of Chance hurling fists into him with ferocity. Coach came up behind him and then Derek slumped over.

"What happened?" Jonas was trying to see. "I think he did the Vulcan nerve pinch."

"No," Max saw the coach pull something out. "I think he gave him a shot. I think I saw a syringe."

"Are you sure?"

"No, he was too quick!"

Coach scooped up Derek into a fireman's carry. "Can you get up?" He asked Chance with blood and cuts all over his body.

"Yeah," Chance stood sweeping glass off his clothes and followed coach.

"Everybody get to class! Show's over," bellowed Principal Hemlock.

Max scurried over to Chance as he followed coach to the nurse's office. "Are you okay?"

"Yeah I'm okay," he had his hand on his face like he was holding it up in place.

Max could see he had cuts on his arms from the glass and his face was swollen and bloody. "What was that about?"

"Oh, someone told him I was holding your hand coming out of the locker room on Saturday. I'll catch up with you later," he grabbed Max's hand quickly getting blood on him.

Max stood there watching him follow coach. "Of course it's my fault." His spirit slumped. "Why wouldn't it be?"

Jonas joined him with Cassandra right on his heels. "Did you guys see that?" Her eyes and hair were big.

"Yeah, who didn't?" Jonas retorted.

"I didn't! I can't believe I missed it! Did you get it on your phone?" Then she remembered Max didn't have one and looked at Jonas reluctantly.

"No, I didn't get it. It happened so fast."

"I bet Sally did. She always has her phone ready for something to go viral! I need to go find her!"

"I just don't get it?" Max was confused. "I don't get why he's always so pissed. Why was he yelling something about loving him?"

Cassandra stopped from her pursuit of Sally and turned to Max. "Really?" She looked at Jonas who had the same expression she did. "You really are pretty aren't you?" She laughed. "I need to find Sally!" She ran off.

"Chance looked really bad didn't he?" Max asked worried.

"Yeah, well...I imagine he's used to getting beat up."

Max gave him an *I can't believe you just said that* face.

"It's true. Anyway, how are you feeling after last night?" Jonas asked him as they walked to class. "You didn't eat much."

"Well, after just about yacking up everything I ever ate, I wasn't much in the mood to replenish. I can't believe Jack is the Knightmare. He's in so much pain."

"I think the moral of the story is...don't go jumping inside ghosts! I never even heard of that. What would possess you to do that?"

"Ha...you kinda made a funny. I possessed a ghost."

"Oh yeah," Jonas smiled. "I guess we just need to wait until Halloween night and let the sisters help him."

"Yeah...well...I'm not entirely convinced of that. I think they're up to something. I don't know that I trust them."

"I'm so glad you said that. I don't either. They kind of freak me out. I mean that bird-eye and all. Who does that?"

"First, we have Joe's Chief...Shaman...whatever ceremony Thursday night."

"The fire ceremony, that's right," Jonas said excited. "Oh, and our Halloween essays are due on Friday remember."

"Yeah, Halloween day, how appropriate," Max sulked. He hadn't even started. "You know…maybe there's something we can do for Jack before Halloween; use the fire ceremony. I mean we've done fire-gazing and I hear fire is the true creator, seems kinda appropriate."

"That's a fantastic idea. We'll search my books and see what we can find."

Later that night they rummaged through Jonas' magick books. But mostly Max tried to get the octopus to show its colors while Jonas surfed the internet searching for possible solutions to freeing spell-bound souls (once he didn't come up with much in his books). The next day at school everything was business as usual: including Chance not only looking perfect as always, but Derek attached to his side like nothing happened.

Max pointed at Derek leaning on Chance at his locker. "Okay, I don't get that either. I guess that makes me pretty too?"

"No," Jonas had to agree, "I'm with you on that one."

"I told you boys are weird," Cassandra showed up. "All you boys," she included them with a roll of her finger. "So we should go on a date," she said to Max.

"Talk about weird," Jonas frowned at her.

"Shut up, troll."

Max's eyes bulged out of his head. He looked at Jonas for help. "Uh…uh…we have that fire ceremony tonight."

"Right, but…"

"And Halloween tomorrow."

"We'll figure something out cutey," she pinched his cheek and headed down the hall.

Max looked at Jonas. "What's a date? I mean what are you supposed to do?"

"I don't know. Watch a movie or have dinner I

think."

"Oh...then I went on a date with you and your family earlier this week?"

Jonas shrugged his shoulders. "I guess...we have more important things to worry about. Like what we're going to do tonight."

"Planning a date?" Derek rammed into Jonas' shoulder knocking him to the tile.

Max spun on Derek and before he could do anything Derek slammed his foot into his thigh and knee bringing him down into the ground in pain. It felt like his leg almost cracked.

"I haven't forgotten about you! You little fuck!" He threatened Max with a finger. "You stay away from Chance! If you don't I'll make sure you do! He's mine!"

"What the fuck is wrong with you?" Max struggled to get up but the pain shot through his leg; stalling him. "I don't even see why Chance is your friend. You're an asshole!"

Derek went to kick Max in the face when a foot intercepted; blocking him. Coach stood firm between the boys. "You," he jabbed his finger at Derek, "my office!" He turned to see Jonas was already up helping Max to his feet. "Are you boys okay? Do you need the nurse?"

Jonas looked at Max to answer. "I'm fine...we're fine," Max answered. He was more pissed than anything.

"Get to class then," Coach went after Derek.

"I want that fucker dead," Max boiled.

"Max, don't say that," Jonas was shocked. "That's bad energy."

"It's true! What possible use could that prick serve in the Universe?"

"You don't know that. Besides, it violates the witch's three-fold law: whatever energy you put out returns to you three times."

"I'm not a witch."

"It doesn't matter. Call it what you want—Karma, the Law of Return, the Rule of Three—it's true. Whatever energy you send out into the Universe returns to you. You shouldn't think like that."

"So what's the plan for tonight?" He just wanted to forget about Derek.

Jonas considered Max for a moment wondering if anything he just said sank in. "We take the Angelica, since we know it works for spell-breaking, and toss it into whatever fire they're using for the fire ceremony. I'm assuming Joe will start the ceremony like he did the new moon one with all the protections in place so we shouldn't have to worry about any ghosts hijacking your body or hiding inside you. So once we light the Angelica you concentrate on Jack and command him to be free from the spell and go to the light. That's going to be the hard part, because you need to signal me somehow that you've made contact with him, and when you do that I will toss the black salt into the fire giving a command for Jack to be free."

"I don't know how I'm supposed to signal you...I never know what's going on with my physical body when I'm in the Nexus."

"Oh...I know...you usually piss yourself. That will be my signal," Jonas said delighted.

Max stared at him. "Great," he said tepidly. "So what's black salt again?"

"It's used to drive away evil...or negative energy. It should do the trick."

"Did you get that at Uva's?"

"No, actually I found a recipe online. I made it myself! You need sea salt and scrapings from an iron skillet. My parents cook all the time so it was super easy," Jonas was pleased with himself.

"It's done! It's done! You have to come and look," Mr. Lee ran into the house telling everyone. The Danes were over at the Lees for dinner. Mr. Lee just finished his pumpkin carvings. "C'mon, c'mon," he yelled to the room waving everyone outside.

Asuka paused her cooking and joined Evelyn, Lindsey, Max, and Jonas outside in the front yard where Mr. Lee stood proudly by his pumpkin display.

"Dad, that's fantastic!" Jonas jumped up and down.

"Wow, Mr. Lee!" Max was excited too. There was a huge pumpkin as tall as Max and rounder than anyone. The rind was carved away leaving exposed pulp. In that pulp was an intricate circular design. It wasn't exactly circular; there were ellipses and points. It reminded Max of when his dad had him look through one of his childhood toys called a kaleidoscope. "What is it?" Max didn't want to insult Mr. Lee because it looked impressive. He just didn't know what it was.

"It's a mandala!" Mr. Lee roared. "Lindsey, you inspired me with your mashed potato art! And those," he pointed to seven smaller pumpkins that surrounded it, "are lotus flowers!"

Positioned around the huge pumpkin were seven smaller pumpkins with lotus flowers carved into the pulp and the tops of the pumpkins were scooped out with a candle sitting in it. Those seven pumpkins lit the larger pumpkin making the Mandala shimmering and luminous.

"It's absolutely beautiful," Evelyn proclaimed.

"Honey, it's quite spiritual. Your best yet!"

"It looks like you won, Mr. Lee," Max pointed across to the Grimm house. "They didn't put anything out."

"Oh, they will tonight. They always wait till the late hour before Halloween. They like to work in the dark. Okay," he looked at his watch. "Let's go eat so I can get you boys to that ceremony in time."

There were numerous older and elderly Native American men along with some boys from the swim team and other boys Max didn't recognize in the same spot where the new moon ceremony was held. And then there were Chance...and Derek. "This way, this way boys," an old man directed Max and Jonas into a circle handing them each a hand drum.

There was a fire pit in the center of the circle this time. Max was annoyed they were across the circle from Chance, but relieved he didn't have to be next to Derek. With any luck Derek would catch on fire. Anyway, they had a job to do and he couldn't afford to be distracted. He decided it was for the best.

"Hey," Max said to Jonas. "I just want you to know that whatever happens at this fire ceremony or on Halloween night...that I really like being your friend."

"Sure," Jonas was more scared than flattered. "Did you see something? Did you have a premonition? Should I be worried?"

"No...you'll be just fine."

CHAPTER 40

"Hand me my grimoire."

"Is that why you're here?" Conleth was distracted by the headless knight.

"Yea," Ambrosius yelled, "and to check on a horse. I need that grimoire, hand it over."

"This is my penance...and redemption. It is everything I need to attain my goals." Conleth was trying to ascertain if Ambrosius was in control of the armored creature.

"You don't really think you can keep me from it do you?" Ambrosius' words were not loud or harsh but the warning was glaring.

Conleth gulped. He didn't dare challenge Ambrosius' power. He bent down to retrieve the grimoire amongst the parchments and books he had dropped. At that moment a shrieking axe spun over him that surely would have hacked his head off had he not moved.

Erec's view of the hurled axe, however, was blocked by the abbot until the last moment. He only had time to yelp before his head and body hit the floor with a dramatic force.

Cador was on top of Erec. He just tackled him saving him from the axe. Erec was slightly in shock realizing what had just happened. He looked up at Cador. "Gramercy, my friend," he expressed.

Cador grasped Erec's wrist in an attempt to pull him up when Erec yanked Cador and kicked him down to the ground next to him just as the Death Axe passed back over them of its own accord as if on some invisible tether. This time Cador's head would have been lopped off. "Matched?" Cador asked slightly in shock.

"Matched," Erec declared pleased with returning the favor.

Abbot Conleth was now kneeling down clenched onto the leather book and parchments. He looked up in confusion at the axe that had passed overhead twice.

The Knightmare caught the double-headed battle axe at the belly of the haft. It flipped the axe deftly in the air and caught it again at the hilt ready to throw it again when Ambrosius raised his palm for it to stop.

Tristan and Dinadan had jumped aside from the main door at the Knightmare's entrance.

The green knight hesitated; almost throwing its Death Axe. Ambrosius squeezed his oak staff and was more forceful in his stopping motion. The headless knight was frozen with its arm raised; poised to hurl the axe.

"It's true," Conleth gasped standing upright. He took notice how Ambrosius halted the Knightmare. "You're in league with the Devil." Conleth's path was now resolute. He had to get back to Rome with the book and notes he had made of the Round Table meetings. He rushed back in the direction of the library for the passage to the night stairs—his robes flapping in his retreat.

Ambrosius turned to see the abbot fleeing and faltered just enough in his control over the Knightmare. The Knightmare cocked its wrist ready to launch its axe. Tristan saw this and reacted by knocking his composite bow and shooting an arrow at the Knightmare's hand to pierce it. His reflexes were nimble; his aim was perfect. However, the arrow shattered against the Knightmare's gauntlet. The Knightmare let its Death Axe fly again at the abbot. This time Yvain launched into action: throwing his spherical wooden shield at the legs of Abbot Conleth. Conleth toppled to the ground just as the Death Axe missed him again. This time everyone was ready for the axe's return trip.

Cador and Erec—back on their feet now—bolted at Ambrosius tackling him. All three men hit the ground hard, winding Ambrosius.

Yvain rushed after his shield and helped Abbot Conleth back to his feet as he scrambled to retrieve the book and parchments, yet again.

Dinadan grasped his sword and attacked the Knightmare. The Knightmare retrieved its axe just as Dinadan approached. It spun around clashing Dinadan's sword and forcing his blade to the stone floor. Dinadan's blade was caught under the axe's wing. The Knightmare twisted his axe with such force against Dinadan's attack that it snapped the blade of his sword. Dinadan stumbled back from the momentum of the Knightmare's counter move holding what was left of his sword.

Tristan was already in the air; his sword pointing down and in both hands ready to drive it through the back of the Knightmare. Tristan rammed the sword into the Knightmare's back. The sword's blade shattered against the Knightmare's armor and Tristan slammed against a skull that was designed into the back plate. He stumbled back from the impact as the Knightmare whirled its arm around striking Tristan with a force that he had never felt before. The hit catapulted him back into the air.

Tristan knew now that this headless knight was an experienced fighter and would go into an offensive move by bringing its axe down on him as he impacted the ground. Tristan also realized that his weapons were ineffective against this knight. So in a deft maneuver Tristan armed his bow in mid-air firing it off to the side at the wall of the abbey. The Knightmare had brought its axe up with both hands in motion to bring it down on Tristan as he predicted. The arrow struck precisely—cutting the rope that held a huge and heavy wooden chandelier. The chandelier crashed on top of the Knightmare in mid-strike smashing it into the stone floor and halting its attack as Tristan hit the abbey floor. Candles from the chandelier scattered about the floor splashing wax; some stayed lit. The lighting in the abbey dimmed but there were torches aflame along the walls.

Ambrosius was getting back on his feet with the aid of his oak staff and only managed to get on one knee before it was whisked from his grasp. Ambrosius was startled and found himself staring up at the last of the king's knights: Sir Percy. Ambrosius glanced to his sides and noted that he was now flanked by Cador and Erec. "What are you doing?" Ambrosius demanded of Percy as he strained coming off his knee and getting up on both feet.

Percy's eyes were wet as he thought of Jack. "You have shamed the king. You have betrayed us all." He took the oak staff in both hands. "I'm taking your magick," he slammed the staff over the splinted knee piece of his leather armor breaking it in half. Percy tossed the pieces away satisfied he rendered the wizard powerless.

"Foolish boy," he rumbled. "All you have done is robbed an old man of his walking stick. Magick comes from within!" He swept his arms out. A gust of wind emanated from Ambrosius' motion. Percy was knocked off his feet by the gale and back toward the entrance of the abbey. Erec and Cador were tossed aside as well—Erec against a wall and Cador back in the direction of Yvain and Father Conleth. The swell of air flipped the chandelier off the Knightmare, catching Dinadan off guard, and landing on him. He yelled as the weight of the chandelier crashed on his legs.

The Knightmare stood upright shimmering emerald green; it's Death Axe in hand. It was facing Ambrosius. Ambrosius in turn was facing the ghostly knight making "eye contact" where its head should be.

Yvain scrambled Father Conleth out of the main sanctuary of the abbey, up the night stairs, and across a passageway overlooking the cloister.

Percy recovered from Ambrosius' attack and was back on his feet with his sword drawn. He rushed at Ambrosius.

Bedivere and Lamorak had made their way over to the chandelier and were lifting it off Dinadan. They did not know him, but he was obviously in combat with their enemy so that made him their ally. Gwalchmai drug Dinadan out from under the chandelier as the Hellsteed charged. It reared and spewed a stream of fire at the men. Bedivere and Lamorak dove out of the way of the arc. Gwalchmai saw the flames coming and bolted—leaving Dinadan flopping along the floor on his back like a fish out of water. Dinadan could feel the heat pouring down on him. All he saw was flame, when suddenly, he was face to face with Percy.

Percy was in motion to attack Ambrosius when he caught sight of the Hellsteed stampeding toward his comrades. He did not know the downed man but he knew his fate would be the same as Dagonet. Dinadan didn't stand a chance against the flames of the Hellsteed. Neither did Percy, but he wasn't going to sit idly by and watch this man consumed horrifically. He just reacted—diverting his attack on Ambrosius and running toward the man—jumping in front of him with his back toward the arcing flame.

Percy now looked Dinadan in the eyes and knew that he would never see anything again. He couldn't help but think of this as his funeral pyre and hoped that his death would not be in vain; that Dinadan would be spared. The green-eyed raven dove into the flames.

Lamorak dive-rolled across the stone floor—dodging the arc of flame—coming nimbly back onto his feet, and prepared for a counter attack. He saw that the Hellsteed was not targeting them with its spew of flame, but rather the retreating abbot. The Hellsteed's flame ignited stone like hot oil as the stream shot up the night stairwell.

Yvain and Conleth were almost completely down the passageway when they heard the roar of the Hellsteed's fire travel up the night stairs behind them. They were well out of the way of the flames but Father Conleth and Yvain increased their step at the sound of terrible screams that followed the flames. Yvain couldn't help but cringe at the thought of which of his comrades had surely fallen.

Cador was almost standing again after being blown aside by Ambrosius' magick. However, he had landed by the entrance to the night stairs. He made an awkward jump back as the Hellsteed's flame made its way toward him. Part of the stream grazed his leather gauntlet. The fire stuck to his gloved hand like jelly and dissolved everything in its path quickly—like flame consuming paper. It ate away at flesh and bone; depositing black sludge in its wake. Cador ran frantically splattering sludge everywhere screaming in horror as he could do nothing to stop the fire eating away his arm and midsection until he was consumed completely into a pile of black muck.

CHAPTER 41

Yvain and Abbot Conleth crossed along a passageway by the cloister.

They continued on down a corridor that lead to a pathway outside in the rain. Before they reached the pathway they passed a chapel. There were candles lit inside and a faint sound of a person mumbling. Conleth stopped at the open door looking inside and saw a priest kneeling down and praying. "Father Gregory?"

Yvain tugged at the abbot's arm. "We don't have time. I must get you to the stables."

"But Father Gregory…we can't leave him."

"I'm sorry abbot, but my orders were explicit. We must go! Now! Those flames and that knight could be gaining on us."

"Very well then," Conleth agreed reluctantly. He and Yvain jogged down the pathway out in the whisking rain when Conleth stopped again and grabbed Yvain's arm. "Drat, I almost forgot—the elixir!"

"Elixir?" Yvain shouted over the storm.

"Ambrosius needs an elixir for a ritual with his druids tonight. Yvain, we must get that elixir. I believe Ambrosius is attempting to awaken some Demon of the Dead."

"I believe he already has," Yvain said obviously.

"No, not that knight. This is something far worse— A Lord of the Dead. His name is Samhain."

"Where's the elixir?" Yvain asked concerned.

"It's at the apothecary. Ambrosius was there earlier but couldn't find it. I'm sure the doctor hid it from him. But it must be there. We have to go there and find it before he does."

"Very well," Yvain said pulling the abbot down the path through the rain. A figure stood in the shadows and watched the two men enter the stables.

Upon entering the stables several mercenaries readied their weapons. Yvain raised his hand to show everything was okay. "I am Yvain, escorting Abbot Conleth on Father Gregory's behalf." The mercenaries lowered their weapons. "I thought there were more of ye." He didn't recognize any of them from his earlier introductions.

"The rest were dispatched to the ring of stones."

"That's where the druids are meeting," Conleth explained to Yvain.

"These men are Swiss," Yvain said as suspicion rather than an observation. "Could thou not gather enough men from the village?" Yvain wasn't entirely certain he trusted them even though Father Gregory obviously did.

"The Church sometimes employs mercenaries. It is quite common nothing to be concerned about." He tried not to sound doubtful. Yvain's suspicion stirred his own worries. He still wasn't completely certain how Rome looked upon him.

Most of the mercenaries were mounted on horses and ready to depart. Yvain noticed a cart lined with straw and a man lying in it. "What have we here?" He approached the cart.

"This is Jean-Luc. We found him earlier this evening."

"What happened?" Yvain asked in shock seeing he was covered in blood and wrappings.

"Attacked by witches," he said in broken English and pain. "They killed two of my men."

"Witches?" *What an unbelievable night this is turning into.* "Are they dead?"

"No…wounded one…they flew away screaming…must be banshees. They used broom."

"They flew on brooms?" Yvain was skeptical.

"Ja."

Yvain looked back to Abbot Conleth in amazement and disbelief.

"Headless knights, flaming horses, flying witches; I will believe almost anything after this night," Conleth admitted.

"Ye all have thou orders," Yvain barked to the mercenaries. Upon that, they all mounted their horses and brought a horse to Abbot Conleth.

"The apothecary—we're going there correct?" Conleth sensed this wasn't going to happen.

"I am. Thou art not. I told ye my orders were explicit. These men will get ye to Rome. Leave the apothecary to me." Conleth was about to protest but Yvain stopped him. "There's no use arguing. Go!" And the mercenaries, abbot, and cart took off into the night.

Yvain left the stable on horseback toward the apothecary. The figure in the rain darted after the departing mercenaries.

CHAPTER 42

Flickering faces in the night guided Yvain's way to the apothecary.

He tied off his horse and glanced down the road. Turnips hastily carved to look like faces sat in windows of the small houses, each with a candle lit inside of the hollowed out turnip. Yvain was a man-at-arms that did some mercenary work. He had never seen this ritual before. He stepped up to the covered entrance out of the drenching rain. He looked into the apothecary. The door was wide open with a line of salt across it.

"Don't go in there!" A voice behind him warned.

It was an old lady standing in the doorway of one of the houses across from the apothecary. "Ye should go in!" Yvain called. "It is not safe outside."

"It is even less safe in there," she pleaded. "There have been enough deaths tonight."

"What do ye know?" Yvain asked coming back into the rain and across the road.

"I know a man lost his life in the street outside the apothecary there. And that men inside died. We all saw the headless horseman galloping down this street and then disappear into the night. We are afraid it will come back for us."

"Is this why everyone lit these turnips?" He could see them more easily now. The turnip had slits cut into it to look like eyes, nose and a mouth.

"Aye, it is obvious it is a tortured soul searching for his head before he can rest. We along the row here decided to make these lanterns quickly in hopes that these will guide that poor man to his head in this world or the Otherworld. We will do this every year on this night."

"And hopefully he won't come for thy heads instead," Yvain reasoned.

"Aye," the old lady said wringing her hands, "that too."

Yvain grasped the old lady's hands. "That seems smart. I'm going over to the apothecary now. The things we've seen tonight have been the works of a dark wizard. I believe there is something in the apothecary that he is after. I come on behalf of Sir Percy," he figured that would give him more cooperation than mentioning the abbot's name as he understood the Church's precarious standing in this region. "Ye have any idea what might be so useful over there?"

"The alchemist healed a lot of us with his mixtures. They were all useful as far as I know. He was a nice man."

Yvain let go of her hands and started back to the apothecary.

"Here," the old lady handed him a turnip lantern. "Ye might need this."

Yvain stepped across the salt line into the dark apothecary and sat the flickering turnip on a table. The turnip's grimace glowed on the walls inviting Yvain to look around.

He cast his eyes along the tables and walls trying to make sense of the various bottles, jars, and plants. He tried to ignore the body of a large mercenary and the decapitated corpse of the physician. Suddenly, he sensed a presence behind him. He spun around drawing his sword and found himself pointing the blade at a young boy with green eyes in strange garb.

"What..." he stammered. "How did ye get here? What are ye doing here?"

The boy looked shocked that a sword was jabbed at him.

Yvain dropped his blade slightly embarrassed. "Do ye know the contents of this shop? I'm looking for the Elixir of Life."

The boy did not answer but merely pointed to an open cabinet.

Yvain walked over to the same cabinet that Percy was at earlier. There was a large jug and various contents that didn't look of much interest. He turned back to the boy looking for help.

"The jug," the boy finally spoke.

Yvain pulled out the large jug and read the label. "Godspeed? What is the purpose?"

"It will make the horses go faster."

He turned back to the boy, but he was gone. Yvain rushed around the apothecary searching the shadows for the boy, but he was nowhere to be found.

CHAPTER 43

The embers burned at 1,000 degrees Fahrenheit beneath Max's bare feet.

He had done some spontaneous things in his short life-span, but this had to be one of the most brash. What possessed him to do this?

The elders cleared the space with pachamama sticks and called in the four directions. The six Tribal Council members took positions around the fire pit and began the ceremony. "*Kwai*...hello...to all," the eldest council member spoke looking around the circle. "Welcome Abenaki members, distinguished guests and *Ne-Do-Ba*...friends; we have already voted before tonight that Joe Warakin shall serve as Chief and Shaman of our tribe—a position his father held. I can speak for all of us when I say that we feel secure in the future of our tribe's welfare and customs with Joe as Chief, as well as our relations with local and state governments. A chief should be modest, courteous, impartial, and fair. Joe encompasses these qualities as did his father. Watu Warakin did not die, he merely passed the torch of leadership on to his son, before embarking on his journey with the Great Spirit.

"We do not believe in coincidence, so it is no mistake, but by design of the Great Spirit, that tonight—this full moon—this Harvest moon should shine upon the powwow of our new *Sacmo*...Chief." He swept his arm out for Joe to step forward.

Joe was wearing traditional colorful Abenaki clothing much like the Tribal Council. He made a point to make eye-contact with Max and Jonas before standing in front of a path of smoldering coals. At the opposite end of Joe was another Tribal Council member holding a large feather adorned headdress that came almost to a point.

Max and Jonas, along with the spectators, awed as they realized Joe was to cross the burning coals to be adorned with the Chief headdress. Max whispered to Jonas, "Did you light the Angelica?"

Jonas nodded trying not to draw attention.

"To begin my new journey as Chief and Shaman I must cleanse my aura and begin anew," Joe addressed the crowd. "The best way to do this for such an honored and revered position is to fire-walk."

Joe stood at the start of the path of coals—barefoot. The eldest Council member motioned for the crowd to start using their hand drums. The drums beat softly. Everyone was mesmerized anticipating what Joe was about to do.

"I begin the path as a tribe member. I will emerge from the path cleansed and transformed as the new Chief and Shaman of the Abenaki tribe of Ravencrest, its leader in legal and spiritual matters. You all here are my witnesses. I ask for my father to smile upon me with his blessing." And Joe stepped onto the burning coals barefooted and walked slowly down the path of fire.

"Now," Jonas whispered to Max, "concentrate on the fire."

"There's not much fire. It's just coals. We were expecting a bonfire," he just knew this wasn't going to work.

"Look at the fire-pit then," Jonas was watching Joe walk the coals. He wasn't sure how he was going to throw the black salt into the fire-pit without being noticed, but hopefully the fire-walk would be over by then and people would be mingling.

Joe emerged from the end of the coals and then adorned with the Chief Headdress. He lifted his arms victorious to applause and loud drumming. Jonas was watching mesmerized. He wasn't sure if it was from the pachamama sticks or just the elation of the fire ceremony and being witness to Joe's passage. Then Jonas witnessed another marvel. Max had stripped off his shoes and socks and before Jonas could get a sound out Max was standing on the smoldering coals.

As Max took his first step on those coals his spirit ignited! It was like he forgot what it felt like to be alive until just now. Max stared at the coals, the heat pulsing beneath his soles. He froze for a moment. Then he heard Joe's voice. He wasn't yelling at him in admonishment. Instead, he was encouraging Max to come toward him. Joe coached him to continue walking. Max moved his feet and began to walk across the coals. The heat was in the center of his stomach. The spot where he usually felt a gutter ball rolling around was filled with excitement. While Max's feet shuffled along the coals the flames suddenly shot up surrounding him. He couldn't see anything but flames. He continued walking and noticed a figure in the flames just beyond. It had to be Joe. Then, he was able to see the figure plainly as he stepped closer. It certainly wasn't Joe. It was a handsome man. He looked like a knight in leather armor.

CHAPTER 44

Flames washed over Percy.

The image of Dinadan was choked away by fire. All Percy could now see was flame. But he didn't feel any heat. None at all! He didn't feel any pain. *This is strange,* he thought. *Perhaps I am dead.* He rose from his one knee into full stance. Looking all around he could see only flames. Above and below he saw the same. There was no perceivable sky or ground. No abbey—just flames. *Is this the Hell that Father Gregory spoke of? Didn't he describe something like this?* Then, suddenly, a figure stepped out from the flames. It was a boy. At first Percy thought it must be Jack. But as the boy approached Percy cautiously he saw that it was not Jack. He thought it was Jack he had seen at the apothecary too, but now realized it was this boy instead. This boy was dressed in strange garb and probably a few years older than Jack. And then it spoke his name.

"Sir Percy!"

Percy dropped to his knees astonished. "It's thou! The tree fairy!"

"Why does everyone think I'm a fairy? My name is Max."

"Many apologies," he stood up. "Max the tree fairy," he corrected himself. Percy was staring at Max in awe. "Thou came to me when I was a lad. Thou haven't aged a bit. Thou know my name. Thou even have green eyes! Thou must be a fairy!"

That confirmed it for Max. Sir Percy was the teenage boy he saw in his vision when he was in the woods. And now Percy was a man. *Time is a web!*

"Because of ye, the king took notice of me that day in the forest and took me in. Thou changed my life!"

"Hopefully for the better," Max was doubtful.

"Aye, of course!"

"That's great! At least I've done something good. Look," he didn't want to sound rude, and he was really glad to hear he had a positive impact on Percy's life, but he knew how this worked. "I don't have a lot of time. I'm trying to help someone else too. His name is Jack."

"Jack!" The pain swelled in his eyes. "I hope thou do not speak of Jack the young boy I was charged with guarding."

"Yes, that's the one."

His eyes answered for him, but he still managed the words. "He is dead."

"I know," Max understood his sadness. "But I can still help him."

"How can ye, his life is gone."

"It's his afterlife that I'm fighting for." Max saw the confusion in his face. "Jack is the Knightmare—the green knight."

The painful realization poured over Percy's eyes and face like a waterfall. "I taught him to fight," he fell to his knee. "I taught him so he could protect himself...not to become that...demon!" The words swelled in his throat, "Fairy, thy words art a sword through my heart!"

Max reached out and touched the young knight's face in consolation. He wondered if anyone would cry for him like that when he was dead...for good. He envied Jack for that.

"I see now that it was Jack's name—his full name—that was inscribed on the floor in Ambrosius' room." Sir Percy couldn't help but blame himself for this tragedy.

"The Elixir of Life—I believe it can free Jack from this spell."

"Elixir? A spell?"

"Yeah, Ambrosius killed Jack and turned him into that Knightmare. The Elixir—the one you were supposed to bring to the sisters—is what we need."

"Aye, I see, but I delivered it—"

"No, Doctor Lambe switched it. He gave you a fake one."

"How can thou know these things? Aye, thou art a fairy of course. Thou know many things."

"The Elixir is in the apothecary...oh, wait...no it's not," he remembered that it wasn't there anymore. He pointed that man to the jug instead. "I don't know what happened to it." He was deflated.

"If Ambrosius cast this spell...then killing Ambrosius might just release Jack."

"Yeah," Max sounded positive again, "do that!"

"I am afraid I have crossed over now," he looked around.

"Oh, you're not dead. You're in the Nexus. We both are."

"I do not know this word 'Nexus.'"

"Yeah, well me either really, till recently. But I think I'm starting to get it. All I can really say is that we're outside space and time right now."

Max could tell from the look on Percy's face that his explanation didn't help any.

"We're kind of in-between."

"Ah!" Percy exclaimed. "My mother told me that those from across the veil could help in practical and spiritual matters. And if they did it was a sign that thy afterlife would be elevated. I never believed her. Not until now." Percy's voice turned sad. "Only if she lived so I could tell her that she was right all along." Percy regained his composure. "If I am not dead then how do I get back to my battle?"

"Uh right," Max wasn't entirely certain. He just usually woke up somewhere drenched in piss. Suddenly, in the flames he saw Glenda's crazy looking raven buzz by. He had no clue how it got there, but it gave him an idea. "I know what to do," and he made the sign of the banishing pentagram. Percy was instantly pulled back through the flames and out of sight and that's when Max's leg felt hot. Max looked down and his pant leg was on fire.

CHAPTER 45

Joe yanked Max off the coals.

People were running around in the excitement. Joe and some of the elders threw blankets over Max as his jeans were on fire. Some ran up to scold him, while others were concerned for his safety, and other people were pointing at the night sky yelling in astonishment. Max could just hear voices as he was smothered in wearing blankets.

"Did you see that? Did you see it?"

"What were you thinking?"

"Show off!"

"The sky was on fire, did you see it?"

"Someone always ruins it for the rest of us."

"Max are you okay," Joe peeled back the blankets.

"Yeah," he was confused and embarrassed. He stood up exposing his bare leg, charred jeans, and superhero briefs.

"Are you sure?" Chance had rushed over with Derek in slow pursuit. Chance smiled at the sight of the briefs. "Is your leg okay?"

"What were you thinking?" Joe asked in desperation rather than admonition.

"I don't know what I was thinking," Max lied. "I'm eleven."

"Liar, Liar! Pants on Fire!" Derek slinked up laughing at his own joke. "It's his birthday; he's just trying to hog all of your glory, Joe. What a loser!"

"Like you never wanted to try fire walking!" Chance attempted to defend Max. "You live and burn right!" He winked at Max.

"Joe, did you see?" The eldest Council member rushed to him grabbing his arm.

"Well, yeah, I'm the one that put him out."

"No, not that boy," he said as if a person on fire was a mild nuisance. "The Thunderbird! It emerged from the flames as you whisked this young man off the coals." Several other members of the tribe came over claiming they saw the same thing, as well as some other boys. "There has not been a sighting of a Thunderbird since our people first settled here in Ravencrest."

"Did you see the Thunderbird?" Max asked Jonas.

"No! Yes! I just saw I flash. I was watching you burn!"

Max saw that everyone seemed more interested in the appearance of the Thunderbird than Max fire-walking, which was just fine by him. The Council members were acting as though it was some sign of monumental meaning. Derek pulled Chance away. He seemed to be forgotten by the crowd for the moment so he seized Jonas. "Did you throw the salt?"

"No! You didn't piss yourself!" Jonas said disappointed in Max.

"Good," Max said eventually, "just in case Percy can't come through, we still might need it for tomorrow night."

"You mean tonight," Jonas looked at the sky where people were still pointing claiming they saw the Thunderbird, "it's already Halloween."

CHAPTER 46

Percy rose from the flames.

Ambrosius was a gifted and learned wizard. His knowledge of the magickal arts and control of the ethereal elements were prodigious. He had seen things most could never glimpse or imagine; seen things men had only dreamt. Yet, even he was surprised and left speechless at what he saw.

After the Hellsteed vomited arcing flames across Percy and Dinadan nobody expected they could survive. Everyone in the abbey anticipated their tortuous screams. But instead, after the flames passed over them, Percy stood up. His leather armor was smoking but otherwise undamaged. Dinadan lied on the floor still alive— obviously blocked from the flames by Percy. Percy aimed his sword at Ambrosius and yelled, "Attack the wizard! He's controlling the Knightmare! Concentrate thy attacks on him!"

But Bedivere had already acted. He was set on destroying the Knightmare to avenge his comrades and was leveraged in an attack. He had started with his weight on his right leg while grasping a war hammer. He swung it with all his might as if he were going to knock the Knightmare out of the abbey. As he was in mid-swing the Knightmare reacted swiftly. For being so large and armored, Bedivere could not believe how fast it was and didn't have time to alter his momentum. The Knightmare dodged the oncoming war hammer and swung its death axe up hacking off Bedivere's hand. The axe sizzled as it passed through his flesh and bone cauterizing the wound with a searing heat. And without missing a step (and full of rage) Bedivere grasped the hammer from his own severed hand (now on the stone floor) and hurled it at Ambrosius this time.

CHAPTER 47

The dragon reared its head breathing fire!

Max, Jonas, and the rest of the neighborhood of Shadow Lake Lane, and even Mr. Lee, marveled at the pumpkin creation of the Sisters Grimm. Max was holding his sister's hand as his mom was still inside working on costumes. Max and the rest of the kids were on their way to school when they were drawn over to the Grimm's yard seeing the fire display shooting out the mouth of the Dragon.

Several regular-sized pumpkins comprised the body making numerous arches appearing as though it was undulating up and below the yard. The tail was spiked and the wings were clawed; both made from pulp and rind of the pumpkins. The head reached into the air and was carved from a large pumpkin. No one knew how they managed to get flames blazing out of the open mouth.

The Sisters Grimm came outside to greet the neighbors. Dorothy brought out her smile and plate of Halloween cookies. "Happy Halloween," she shouted so delighted. Martha and Glenda passed around plates of cookies as well.

"Congratulations!" Mr. Lee wasn't too proud to concede the victory to the sisters. "You managed to outdo yourselves yet again!"

"Oh, you are too kind, Haruto!" Glenda smiled at him, "your carvings…the best yet."

"Your hand only gets more deft with each Halloween," Dorothy smiled grabbing a cookie from one of her plates that was circulating through the crowd.

"A Mandala," Martha commented on his pumpkins as people were circulating across the street to checkout Mr. Lee's work, "truly inspirational!"

Max slinked up close to Martha and whispered. "Bring the ring with the 'R' on it tonight." Max knew they still had at least one.

Martha looked down at him quizzical.

"We'll need it to free Jack," he confirmed.

"Are you witches today?" Lindsey asked Dorothy grabbing a stack of cookies.

"Oh, we're witches every day, lass," Glenda answered. However, today they were dressed in dark cloaks. "Here take some more cookies, your teachers will be thrilled!"

"Oh, I should get punch," Dorothy beamed.

"We need to get these kids to school," Mr. Lee smiled. "But I'll come back for some!"

Max and Jonas frowned at each other. They wanted to stay and join the festivities that spontaneously broke out there on Shadow Lake Lane. And they still had a report to turn in.

"Max Dane," barked Dr. Ziwa the English professor. The students had an ongoing debate if he was Swiss or German, but no one actually had the nerve to ask and he never offered any personal information. "Come up here in front of the class and read your report or story. I decided that since this is actual Halloween day why not celebrate with oratory reports."

Max saw the rest of the class was just as shocked as he. None of them were expecting to have to read their reports aloud. And nobody else felt this was a great way to celebrate Halloween. "Uh...okay." He shuffled up to the head of the class. He looked at Jonas, who was the only person who didn't look scared. He gave him a thumbs-up and an enthusiastic smile. "Right...okay...the name of my story is 'Just Jack.'" No one laughed so he decided it was safe to continue.

"Once a long time ago in the medieval ages lived a boy by the name of Jack; just Jack. Jack was an orphan that worked as a stable boy in the monastery. Jack did other duties for the monastery such as working as a live scarecrow to chase off birds from devouring the monastery's crops.

"One day, a valiant knight took notice of Jack and with permission from the monks began to train him in the ways of Knighthood. Unfortunately, once the knight took notice of Jack it also drew the attention of a dark wizard. The wizard watched the boy secretly as he trained and became more proficient in his knightly skills. Then, one day, while Jack was scaring away birds in the cornfields the dark wizard attacked the boy cutting his head off as part of a twisted spell to make Jack his undead servant.

"The knight was sorrowed by Jack's death and felt responsible. He searched endlessly for Jack's head in hopes of freeing him from the dark spell. The longer his search went on he knew the longer that Jack was in torturous servitude to the wizard. The knight pleaded with the townspeople to help him fight the evil and break the spell that held Jack. The knight suggested carving a substitute head with a light inside to guide Jack to freedom in the afterlife. The townspeople agreed because they feared their own children would be taken in a similar manner.

"The knight drummed the story of Jack so that others would join the lighting ceremony. The knight drummed so fiercely that his plea was heard across the ocean by the Native Americans. They carved pumpkins while the Europeans carved turnips. They carved these faces and lit these lanterns every Halloween when the veil was thinnest between this world and the next, when Jack would have his best chance of crossing over led by the Jack Lanterns: now known as Jack-O-Lanterns."

Dr. Ziwa looked Max up and down from the back of the class, "Most excellent, Mr. Dane! I see you chose the path of blending fact into fiction. A desirable method of delivery as it does seem to bind to your audience's memory more readily that a simple shopping list of facts and bullet points. Your story differs from the *'Stingy Jack'* tale, and I dare say I prefer yours. Well done."

Max took that as his cue to sit down. He didn't know about all that psycho-babble that Dr. Ziwa spewed. He was just trying to tell Jack's story even though he did indulge a little.

"Speaking of bullet points, I will make one concerning Mr. Dane's story: young boys in medieval times were indeed employed to be living scarecrows; running about the fields clapping pieces of wood together to frighten birds that would eat crops. Due to the plague there were fewer children to fill these roles, so farmers used the makeshift mannequins that we associate with the scarecrow today. Okay, who's next?"

Jonas shot his hand up immediately.

"Very well, Mr. Lee, the floor is yours."

Jonas couldn't wait to get his report out thinking of the acting mayor. This was his moment of defiance.

"Halloween originated from the Pagan celebration of Samhain which translates to 'end of summer.' Samhain is not the name of a lord of the dead as is often erroneously recited in books and movies.

"Samhain marked the final harvest of the year when the weather grew colder and the daylight shortened. The Celts believed the worlds of the living and dead were closest at this time allowing the dead to visit the living once again. People left places at the dinner table and food and offerings to welcome their loved ones that had passed.

"Faeries were mischievous entities from the Otherworld that were thought to disguise themselves as beggars and go door-to-door asking for handouts. Those that gave them food weren't subjected to their mischief. The Celtic families would douse the flames from their hearths as the Celtic priests—called druids—would light a central bonfire—called a need-fire—in honor of the dead as thanks for the harvest; to appease the gods of coming winter; and to guide the dead, spirits, and entities back to the Otherworld.

"Hot embers from this need-fire were brought home by families in hollowed-out turnips to rekindle their hearths keeping their homes warm and free from evil spirits. This festival lasted three days.

"It's no mistake or coincidence that All Saints Day falls on November 1st and All Souls Day on November 2nd. In an attempt to take over the Pagan holiday Pope Gregory III moved All Saints Day from May 13th to November 1st and this was later commanded by Pope Gregory IV and the Romans systematically murdered the Druids seeing them as their major obstacle to the new order of things. But the Roman Catholic Church could not stomp out Halloween as the Pagans refused to let go of their supernatural beliefs about Samhain. So the Church was forced to incorporate

385

these Pagan traditions into the Catholic's new holiday. Children would now go door-to-door gathering 'soul-cakes' as a means of collecting prayers for the souls in Purgatory.

"The Eve of All Hallows Day became All Hallows Even and then eventually abbreviated *Hallowe'en*," he wrote in on the chalkboard. "And now known as *Halloween*. The true meaning of Halloween is celebrating the end of harvest and honoring the dead." He sat the chalk back down signaling the end of his report.

"Mr. Lee, straight and to the point as always...I like this too! Very informative and very accurate; excellent, who's next?"

CHAPTER 48

The halls of Ravencrest Academy were all a buzz about the Thunderbird sighting the night before.

Max explained to Jonas that he was sure it was Glenda's crazy-eyed raven. He also told him about meeting Percy and how he had seen him before when he was a teenager. Jonas explained that Glenda's raven probably got distorted in the flames which made it look bigger than it really was.

"I have a theory," Jonas continued. "Remember that Glenda's green-eyed raven is already here, and remember that old guy at Joe's ceremony said a Thunderbird sighting last happened when Ravencrest was first settled…"

"Right," Max knew he wasn't going to be able to

follow for very long.

"...My theory is: if someone witnesses a time-distortion it warps their visual perception because time and space are bending. So things can appear to vary in length, height and speed than they really are depending on their frame of reference."

"And..." Max could feel his brain slipping.

"So Glenda's raven was actually passing through time to the past; it passed through the flames you were in so everybody saw a huge flaming bird—a Thunderbird!"

"Wow..." Max actually kinda got that.

"It also can explain UFO phenomena. You know...how they appear to fly at great speeds, have strange warped lights, do impossible aeronautics, and then disappear."

"You think UFO's are birds?"

"No!" Jonas slapped his arm.

And then Max was slapped on the ass with a "happy birthday!"

He twisted around from his locker seeing Cassandra standing there with a satisfied grin and a gift bag with bats decorating it. He was slightly disappointed that it wasn't someone else, and then he felt bad for feeling that way. *It was selfish wasn't it?* "You remembered it was my birthday?" Max took the gift bag.

"Duh, of course," she kissed him quickly on the lips as he peered down in the bag.

Jonas rolled his eyes.

"Well, you have eleven more coming," Cassandra rubbed her hands together.

"I'll give those," Chance leaned in over them all looking down at Max.

"Whatever," Cassandra elbowed him in the abs. "You have Derek to spank and...everything else."

"I didn't realize you were a player, Max," he referred to the kiss he got from Cassandra.

388

"Go ahead," she urged Max. "Open it."

Max pulled out a square cell phone from the bat riddled bag.

"It's not a *mi*phone, but it has prepaid minutes and data so you can text me."

"Uh," he looked at Jonas and Chance's shocked faces. "I don't know that I can accept this. If my mom finds me with this—"

"It will be our secret!" Then she looked at Chance and Jonas with slit eyes. *"All of ours!"* She warned them.

"Happy twelfth," Chance decided now was the perfect time. "Here," he whipped out a ghost gift bag he was holding behind his back, "just a little something…to think of me."

Max grabbed it eagerly, pulling out a bottle of cologne.

"It's *SHRED*," Chance said. "It's what I wear. I like it a lot."

Before Max could thank him, Jonas threw his backpack to the ground. "Oh geez, you guys are making me look like a bad friend. I have a present for you too but it's at home because I was gonna give it to you later at your surprise party…" He reacted to Cassandra and Chance's faces, "Oh, whatever…it's not much of a party…just your family and mine. Oh…well…I was supposed to invite you," he pointed to Cassandra. "And you," he reluctantly admitted to Chance, "this afternoon at Max's house."

"How did you get an invite?" Cassandra frowned at Chance.

"I met his mom in the hospital," he nudged Max playfully. Then he smiled with his perfect white teeth and dimples, "She loves me."

"Wait a minute! *How did I get an invite?*" She looked at Max.

"Oh," Jonas confessed. "I told his mom you're his girlfriend."

"What?" Max decided he would never get used to whatever came out of Jonas' mouth next.

"Don't worry," Jonas said. "Your mom is thrilled...unlike my parents," his eyes dropped.

"What does that mean?" Cassandra asked and Chance seemed interested too.

"Forget it!" Max didn't want Jonas to blab that Asuka Lee thought they were boyfriends.

"Anyway," Cassandra grabbed Max's hand. "I have to help with the Bazaar so I can't make it."

"Neither can I champ," Chance put his hand on his shoulder and leaned into his ear. "I'll sneak by your place later tonight and give you those spankings," he patted him on the butt.

Max felt his face flush.

"But, hey..." Cassandra had an idea to help alleviate the bad news, "schools out at noon today. Why don't you both come and help me with the maze setup at Yorick's?"

Max's spirit was already brightened by the prospect of Chance coming by that night, but this sounded like great fun in the meantime.

Cassandra explained that the Halloween Bazaar extended from downtown Ravencrest to Yorick's farm. So it gave a variety of activities for people to partake.

Jonas, Cassandra and the other students were busy putting decorations in the corn maze. Max said he was going for more decorations but cut through the stables and was now standing a couple of feet away from Mr. Creeps on the grassy knoll. Here he was again, just like the first day he arrived in Ravencrest.

He stared at Mr. Creeps. "What do you want with my sister?"

A cool breeze ran through the high grass.

"I saw you move...I have it on video," he pulled his camera out of his backpack and held it up waiting for

Mr. Creeps to look.

He gulped.

The scarecrow posed with its arms outstretched—the roots of the two twisted trees anchored in the ground.

Nothing.

Mr. Creeps' disdain inflamed Max's fear. "You stay the fuck away from her!" He slammed his camera back into his backpack. "Don't hurt her!"

Max looked back over the grassy knoll and could see a small corner of the maze where the others were decorating. He knew they would miss him soon.

"Are you telling me or you?" A deep and harsh voice boomed.

Max whipped his head back to Mr. Creeps.

The scarecrow's cloak swished in the cool breeze; its oak face was unmoved.

Max stared at it.

Nothing.

"So…" his trepidation came back for a visit. "So you can talk?"

The breeze kicked by.

"I wouldn't hurt my sister!"

"What is it you seek Maximillian Dane? Is it salvation or redemption?" The abrasive voice echoed all around Max. But he didn't see Mr. Creeps animate.

Max spun around searching the high grass frantically for someone with a megaphone. Max brought his eyes back to the scarecrow. "What are you talking about?"

"Do you seek to assist Jack, or are you just trying to help yourself?"

The voice thundered as though it was in Max's head.

"Of course I want to help Jack. There's no…there's no help for me."

"Confronting the truth head-on is salvation and

redemption for the soul. It's so obvious as if it were under your nose. Yet, the simplest answer can be so difficult to pull-off."

"Max?"

Max jerked and saw Jonas standing there.

Jonas looked at Mr. Creeps guarded. "Are you okay?"

Max nodded. "Did you hear?"

"Yeah, I heard you talking to him." The scarecrow was fixed. "Did he answer you?" Jonas was ready to bolt at any second.

"Yes! He was talking to me! You must have heard him. He's really loud!"

"Okay," Jonas looked at Max and Mr. Creeps warily. "I only heard you talking. It's time to go home. Let me help you," Jonas reached down to pick up Max's backpack. "Oops," he pointed at his crotch.

Max looked down and saw he urinated in his jeans again. "Dammit!" Max had tears in his eyes.

"It's okay," Jonas said comforting. "We'll get you home before anyone sees."

"SURPRISE!"

Evelyn, Lindsey, Haruto, and Asuka jumped up in the kitchen as Max and Jonas passed by making for the staircase.

"HAPPY BIRTHDAY!"

"Max pee-peed!" Lindsey pointed at his jeans.

"He sure did," Haruto was shocked. "How old is he again?" He asked Evelyn as she was lighting candles on a round cake that had a huge cake skull resting on top of it that was decorated like a DAY OF THE DEAD skull.

"He's twelve!" Lindsey clapped. "We get to have cake!"

"No," Jonas decided to cover for Max. "I just spilled my Chupacabra Chai on him. I was gonna help him get his pants off."

Asuka grabbed her husband's arm with delight at hearing this.

Jonas shot his eyes straight up to the ceiling, "oh fuck," he whispered exasperated to himself.

"Never mind that now," Evelyn waved them over to the counter. "You can get out of those pants when you get into your costumes. Don't kill the mood. Come blow out your candles so we can have cake!"

"Cake! Cake! Cake! Cake! Cake!" Lindsey stomped around clapping and yelling.

They all sang happy birthday to Max. And again, Max found that when he was with Jonas' family and his, that he felt part of a real family again. Max closed his eyes and made his wish; blowing out all the candles.

Max opened his presents. From Jonas he received the complete collection of *TALES FROM THE CAMPFIRE* comics. And from Jonas and his parents he opened a digital movie slate clapperboard. "Wow…that is so awesome!" He didn't feel worthy. He gave them all hugs.

"You're welcome, Champ. Did you make this cake yourself?" Haruto asked Evelyn amazed.

"Yes."

"We should team up for next year's pumpkin carving!"

"Oh, you're too kind, Haruto!" She turned to Max. "Well, I'm sorry your girlfriend couldn't make it and that nice young man who's a stripper."

"Girlfriend?" Asuka asked defensively.

"Yeah, Max has a girlfriend!" Evelyn exclaimed. "What's her name again?"

"Cassandra," Jonas answered flatly.

"She's not my girlfriend!"

"I'm sure she's not good enough for your son," Asuka shook her head.

"Okay, it's time to get ready," Max pulled Jonas

upstairs with his slice of cake to escape the adults.

CHAPTER 49

"Captain Kirk and Mr. Spock!"

Cassandra screamed enchanted. "That is so perfect you two!"

"Max made my ears!" Jonas was just as excited. "I'm Spock!"

"No shit, troll!"

"Our moms made our outfits," Max said.

"They're fantastic!"

"So…" Jonas and Max both were examining Cassandra. "What is your costume?"

Max did notice she looked dressed exactly as she did every day.

"I'm the Wicked Witch of the East," she showed off her socks and red shoes, "before the house fell on her."

"I'm an alien!" Lindsey proclaimed holding up her backpack with one hand and holding Max's with the other.

Cassandra looked down at the little person with a green alien head.

"And who's this?" Cassandra was tickled.

"It's my little sister, Lindsey." Max said.

"Max made my mask!"

"Did you really?" Cassandra was impressed.

"Yeah, she loves aliens."

"And I see you brought your backpack," Cassandra laughed.

"It holds more candy," Lindsey yelled.

"Where's your mom?" Jonas asked rather annoyed they were stuck with Lindsey.

"She'll be here soon. She got a call from Dr. Evans," Max said not so thrilled. "He had something important to discuss with her." That worried Max. He didn't know if it was concerning him or his sister. He squeezed Lindsey's hand.

"Thanks for coming," Dr. Evans said as Evelyn Dane took a seat in front of his desk. "I know this was last minute as the whole town is occupied with the Halloween Bazaar and I'm sure you have activities planned already. But this simply could not wait."

"Who are they?" Evelyn asked of the two foreboding men in black suits.

"These are Agent's McCoy and Knight with the FBI."

"Oh," Evelyn drooped back in her chair. "This is about Max."

Dr. Evans pulled out a picture.

"Excuse me," Evelyn said before he could do anything with it. "Why is the FBI involved with my son?"

"We were investigating another case," Agent McCoy explained with his drawl. "When we came across this," he pointed to the picture in Dr. Evan's hand. "We were asking the doctor here for a profile on someone who would do this—"

"I thought the FBI had their own profilers." Evelyn crossed her arms smug.

"Exactly," McCoy answered.

It took a moment to sink in. "You mean..." she looked at Dr. Evans unbelievably. "You do profiling for the FBI?"

"I'm not just an ER doctor." He returned the smugness.

Agent McCoy waved his hand for Dr. Evans to give her the picture.

"Okay..." Evelyn was confused. "What am I looking at?"

"It's a mutilated horse." Dr. Evans answered.

"It has a satanic symbol carved into it," Agent McCoy said.

"I believe," Evelyn held back her disgust as she realized what the picture was, "that is a pentagram."

"Right...satanic," Dr. Evans continued. "And there is a triangle in salt surrounding the horse." As Evelyn opened her mouth to ask the next obvious question, Dr. Evans cut her off. "Max described this exact horse mutilation to me in one of our sessions. The satanic symbol included; exactly as this picture. This picture was taken today at Yorick's farm. There are letters along the points of the triangle. They spell a name."

Evelyn clasped her hand over her mouth muffling a small scream.

"In our session Max made it sound as though he or someone named Jack performed the mutilation."

Evelyn released her mouth. "Jack..." the words trembled off her lips. "I don't know a Jack," she folded her arms nervously. "I don't think he knows a Jack."

Dr. Evans looked at the agents. They stepped back to give more space. "That's the other thing I needed to talk to you about…before this came up," Dr. Evans took the picture back. "Max has difficulty staying in touch with reality. He hallucinates. He sees and hears things that other people don't; that simply don't exist. He speaks in strange ways at times. There's the self-urination…"

"I know all this. He's epileptic. He has seizures."

"Yet, he persists with all these symptoms despite being on medication. The medication doesn't work. The medication doesn't work…because Max is not epileptic."

Evelyn Dane looked at the agent's faces and at Dr. Evans. "I'm guessing…this isn't good news."

"Max is schizophrenic."

"What?" Evelyn stood in horror.

Dr. Evans stood as well. "He could even have a split personality, but it's rare for someone with schizophrenia to also have a split personality. It may be too soon to say schizophrenia definitively, but I can say for sure at this time, that Max does have some personality disorder."

Evelyn just stood with tears in her eyes.

"You know I'm right," Dr. Evans said. "I know you've suspected it."

"We need to find Max," Agent Knight said.

"He's right," Dr. Evans grabbed Evelyn's arm.

"He's with Lindsey at the Halloween Bazaar." Her face turned pale. "You don't think…"

"He could hurt her. He also may become suicidal."

"Eat me!"

Max, Jonas, Cassandra, and Lindsey yanked their hands back from the buffet table.

"Yes, eat!" Another head that was poking out of the table said.

"Mom?" Jonas said to the first head. There were five adult heads poking out along the buffet table, all with varying Halloween make-up.

"Yes, it's me," Asuka said. "Isn't this wonderful.

It's the talking head buffet!"

"How fun," Cassandra said.

Asuka scowled at her up and down.

"Where's dad?"

"He's at the Curious & Creepy animal display booth with your octopus."

"That's right, I forgot about that. We need to go check that out," he said desperately to the others. "I heard Lenny is bringing his tarantula and Sarah is bringing her python."

"I got your python!" Derek was there wearing overalls and a haughty grin. "What are you?" He looked down at Jonas.

"I'm Mr. Spock."

"He doesn't wear glasses," Derek sniggered.

"I can't wear contacts. I'm too nervous to put those in."

"You mean too scared. Of course you are! You're a pussy!" he laughed.

"You!" Asuka yelled. "You leave my boy alone! If I weren't trapped under this table I'd come out there and beat you!"

"Ha," Derek broke into hysterics. "You're a girl. Girls can't hurt guys except in movies because it's bullshit!" He started to walk away when Cassandra stopped him.

"What are you supposed to be? A farmer?" She looked him over like it was a stupid outfit.

"Oh, you wish, so I could milk you like the heifer you are!"

"Don't listen to him," Jonas said leering as Derek left.

"Ugh," Cassandra cocked her hip to one side, "except that sounded kinda hot."

"You're a fucking mess," Jonas adjusted his glasses.

"Language!" Asuka and three other heads screamed.

Max pulled his sister with her plate of food away from the table and walked with the others through the Bazaar.

"Boo!" Someone in overalls and an old man mask jumped in front of them from behind a crowd of people.

"Derek, you asshole!" Jonas almost choked on his food.

Chance whipped the mask off quickly. "Nah, it's me," he smiled brightly. "We have matching outfits."

"Why?" Cassandra asked annoyed.

"We're an old couple. What's scarier than getting old? You guys screamed."

"I choked," Jonas corrected him.

Max thought the mask looked familiar but didn't get too good of a look at it.

"So I guess you guys have seen him? We got separated."

"You should try that permanently," Cassandra twirled her curls with a sassy look.

"Great costumes," he told Max and Jonas pretending he didn't hear Cassandra.

"Thanks," Max smiled broadly. He liked whenever Chance took notice of him. And it was nice he included Jonas in the compliment.

"Yeah, thanks," Jonas offered reluctantly.

"I know you!" Lindsey was excited to see Chance.

"Lindsey!" Chance knelt down in front of her. "How's my favorite girl?"

"I'm an alien!" She put her mask on to show him.

"Oh, I see! Where's your UFO?" He winked at Max.

"It's in the shop."

Chance stood laughing. "Okay...I see you're as quick as your brother."

They explored more of the Bazaar together including a short stop at Alarice Hemlock's tent where she did a palm reading for Chance.

"You can't light it!" Mayor Dinah protested.

"We light it every year," Joe rebutted. He stood in front of the erected pile of wood.

"The bonfire is a tradition," the eldest Council member supported Joe.

"It's a tradition," Joe continued, "not only for our people but for the pagans and wiccans here in Ravencrest. It represents the tradition of the need-fire, when people across the land doused the fires from their hearth and a large central fire was lit by their religious caste, the druids. They believed it was from that need-fire they could have access to other points in time on this night."

Bernice Dinah's face expanded more than it already was. She looked like a great big toad gasping in air at the absurdity of Joe's speech. "And we all know the druids sacrificed people in those fires. That is not the sort of thing we should be celebrating, representing, or setting an example of for these children. And as far as accessing other points of time, that is just plain ridiculous. It is ungodly and it is not Christian."

"It's a tradition!" Joe contested yet again.

"Not this year!" She saw that Joe and the council member would stand firm on this. "It's a fire hazard. Sheriff Drake will confirm it," she looked at him.

"It's true Joe, sorry." Sheriff Drake agreed with the toad.

The council member challenged her, "neither Mayor Warakin nor Sheriff Alahmoot ever saw it as a fire hazard."

"Well, they're dead, and I'm in charge." Mayor Dinah said flatly. "This is not a tribal matter, this is a city matter. You have no authority."

"And your *acting* authority is borrowed from my

father," Joe said outraged. "I'm going to run against you when my father's term is up."

Sheriff Drake took a call on his cell phone. "Yeah, I understand." He put his phone away, "Has anyone seen Max Dane tonight? I understand he's here."

"Is he okay? Is something wrong?" Joe was concerned from the sound of Roy Drake's voice.

"I need to find him…now!"

"GHOST ROASTs," Meredith handed Max, Jonas, and Cassandra cups, "and a Philosopher's Scone for the alien," she handed it to Lindsey. "Max, this is your first time at our Halloween Bazaar. Joe makes his signature GHOST ROAST only for the Halloween Bazaar. You can only get it right here at our booth during this festival."

"It's excellent," Max sipped the drink with a half-smile as he watched Derek in the distance arguing with Chance.

"I want to finger paint," Lindsey pointed to another booth.

"Do you mind if I take her," Cassandra pleaded. "I always wanted a little sister."

"Sure," Max said and watched the witch and alien charge to the finger painting booth. "Hey, I have to ask you about something," he said to Jonas. "When I saw Percy last night, he mentioned that it was Jack's full name that was inscribed on the floor. Do you think I will need to know it in order to free him?"

"Yeah, probably, you said before that someone said it was a symbol of evocation. That would make sense since we now know Jack is the Knightmare. They used it to bind him and help turn him into that nightmare. No pun intended."

"Well I still don't know his full name. Percy didn't say."

"Do you remember the letters you saw?"

"Yeah," Max looked around for some paper.

"Here, type it on my phone," Jonas took his cell out.

"Oh," Max remembered, "I have one," he pulled out the one Cassandra gave him and then frowned.

"Yeah," Jonas saw what he meant. "It's not that fancy. You can't do notes. Just use mine."

"Okay, on one side of the triangle were the letters 'AR, J, PEN,' all on top of each other, and at the other side of the triangle were, 'TH, A, DRA,' again on top of each other and at the top of the triangle was, 'UR, CK, GON.'" Max typed it into the notes.

"Okay," Jonas studied it, his brain was processing. "Did they use one for the horse too?"

"Yeah," Max remembered.

"What was that sequence?"

"On one side, 'LL,' then 'AM,' and at the top 'RAI.'"

Jonas typed that in too. "You said the horse's name was Llamrai," then it clicked. "Okay, I got it, so back to Jack's name. We know he goes by Jack," he studied the pattern. "Jack is his middle name," Jonas figured it out.

"I guess he went by his middle name," Max said. And he saw the astonished look in Jonas' face. "What? What is it?"

"That can't be," Jonas looked at his phone in disbelief. "But he wasn't real."

"I didn't think witches and ghosts were real, but I've changed my mind since moving to Ravencrest. What's his name Jonas? I have to know."

"Arthur Jack Pendragon," Jonas looked at Max in shock.

"You mean...like...King Arthur."

"Except...he never lived to be King."

CHAPTER 50

"Kirk. Spock. We're ready," Glenda barked.

"We've been looking for you. This way," she walked them toward Martha and Dorothy who were standing just a little bit away from the crowd with a direct view of the erected wood pile.

"Listen," Max slowed up, pulling Jonas back. He looked briefly over his shoulder to one of the booths. "I don't trust the sisters to do, what they say they're going to do, for Jack."

"Why?"

"I said I wouldn't tell anyone," he remembered Jonas couldn't even keep his mouth shut about the steroid incident, "…but it's not going to matter much after tonight. Agent McCoy told me that Sheriff Tahamont murdered

Joe's father and then attacked me in the woods that day because he thought my 'premonition' was really an eye witness account."

"What?" Jonas screamed.

"Let's stand together," Martha instructed.

"What's going on over here?" La' Wanda strolled over with Uva. "Are you about to cast a circle?" She asked hopefully.

"As soon as that bonfire is lit," Glenda snapped.

"Max, we have to tell Joe," Jonas said.

"No, we don't. He'll ask you how you know, and then you're gonna have to explain about those agents and a cover-up that you really don't know all the details about. It's just going to upset Joe. When has telling the truth ever did anybody any good? Look, my point is that I think the sisters then had something to do with Sheriff Tahamont's death. Dorothy said that Watu couldn't speak from the grave because of a Calamus and Cypress mixture. Her recipe for Absinthe contained Calamus. That's what he was drinking at their house that night. What if the sisters used the Absinthe not only to get Alahmoot drunk and killed, but also to prevent him from speaking beyond the grave?"

"For what reason?"

"I don't know. For whatever agenda they have going on. Sheriff Tahamont tried to warn me about them that same night he died. He said they were involved in some serious shit."

"They will not light the fire," Uva said.

"They light it every year," Dorothy protested.

"No," Uva said directly, "that little...Christian mayor will not permit it."

"That's preposterous!" Martha exclaimed.

"If it were a different time, I'd just fireball the thing," Glenda growled.

"So, we join your circle, yes?" Uva said candidly.

Martha looked to her sisters who each had hesitant faces. She then looked to the abandoned pyramid of wood. "Very well, but we will not do a circle. Max…Jonas…over here, we will form a line."

"Jonas," Max whispered to him, "you're the only one I trust. I need you to make sure that Jack is set free."

"Me? What about you?"

"I may be…distracted."

"How am I going to do it?"

"Stick to the plan that we had that night at Joe's fire ceremony," he handed him the Angelica. "You brought the black salt?"

Jonas nodded.

"Then throw them both in the fire and release Jack."

"But, you heard, there's no bonfire."

"There will be," Max said confidently, "I just know it. If for some reason you need to improvise I know you'll think of something. You know a ton about this stuff. You're smarter than any adult I know."

"Max, you're at one end of the line," Martha directed, "and Glenda you're at the other." As Max passed by Martha he held his hand out for the ring with the runic "R." She looked at him with admiration, and dropped it in his palm.

"You do realize that we are putting ourselves in direct danger," Dorothy said softly to Martha.

"We can't avoid the Knightmare for eternity," Martha put her hand on Dorothy's shoulder. "It ends tonight."

"Take these," Glenda handed them each one of her charm bags, "for protection, just in case. But we're not going to do anything if we don't get that fire lit," Glenda grumbled as she huddled with her sisters.

"You're going to do just what you said you'd do," Martha said.

"How?"

"We have Max."

"Let me remind you that Mr. Creeps allowed for us to fly them," Glenda protested. "Max isn't going to be able to get us enough ethereal energy for what you're suggesting."

"The first seal to the Nexus has been broken. And remember, it's Samhain Eve," Martha smiled. "We'll simply borrow something from the past."

"Will not a line decrease the energy? A circle seems more empowering," Uva and La' Wanda barged in on their cluster.

Glenda rolled her eyes. "Amateurs," she muttered.

"If things go according to plan, you will not want to be in a circle believe me," Martha professed to Uva and La' Wanda.

Amongst the whispers and debate over whether to form a line or a circle, Max managed to scribble in the dirt without notice. He stood upon the spot at the end of the line. They all joined hands: Max, Dorothy, La' Wanda, Martha, Uva, Jonas, then Glenda at the other end.

"Max, hold your free hand out to the Universe," Glenda shouted from the other end. Max held his free hand up with the ring on his finger.

"We stand here on Halloween night..." Martha began, "Samhain Eve...New Year's Eve as it once was a long time ago. This night begins Samhain, a point outside of time, when trapped human souls can enter their new human incarnations..." she looked down the line to Max, "...where the living can have access to the land of the dead: Tír na nÓg, where the dead stay forever young. Normally, one must traverse the Nexus to reach it, but on Samhain it can be bypassed. We reach through time," she looked down the other end to Glenda, "like a long stretching arm to a point where we once had the energy, the power...to assist in this Ritual of Crossing."

Those words brought up images in Jonas' mind; images of Mr. Creeps stretching his long arm at Lindsey. Then a realization popped in Jonas' head. He looked down the line to Max, but he couldn't grab his attention.

Glenda took her sister's cue and focused on the point of time she was suggesting. She reached through the murky cloud of memory into another night of Samhain a long time ago when they were still strong in their power. When the sisters mustered and united the last of their ethereal energy and hurled it at attacking knights.

CHAPTER 51

THE GREEN KNIGHT

Flames shot up along the stone floor.

The Hellsteed was protecting the Knightmare's flank. It was jetting flames in defensive lines setting the stone itself on fire. Erec and Tristan were separated from the others by the lines of fire. They had considered doubling back through the library when they heard Percy's command to attack Ambrosius. Tristan knocked his bow faster than Erec had seen anyone in the land and let an arrow fly at the wizard. Erec charged Ambrosius with his sword ready to pierce his heart.

Lamorak was at the end of one of the Hellsteed's lines of fire and easily maneuvered around it to engage Ambrosius as well.

Gwalchmai ran up to Dinadan grabbing him and

pulled him back toward the wall out of the action. "Leave me," protested Dinadan. "Go help the others."

"Nay, I'm not going to let ye get killed," Gwalchmai insisted, pulling him the rest of the way toward the wall and out of the way.

"That didn't seem to concern ye moments ago," Dinadan grumbled thinking how he left him to be burned instead of pulling him back then.

"Thou art safe," Gwalchmai said satisfied with himself and ignoring Dinadan's commentary.

"If ye refuse to aid the others, find something to make a splint for my leg," he said angrily. Dinadan didn't think it was broken but wanted to be able to get up and around. Something told him there would be more fighting this evening.

There was now a line of fire between Percy and Ambrosius, not to mention the Knightmare and its steed, but it didn't matter to him. Percy was now resolved to put an end to the Knightmare's torture. He stepped right through the flames unaffected.

Bedivere's hammer, Tristan's arrow, Erec and Lamorak's swords all sped toward Ambrosius. He was still surprised at Percy's invulnerability to the Hellsteed's flames when he noted all of the other attacks coming at him. He could easily deflect them but he would have to divert his control over the Knightmare. He sighed. It had to be done. With a flick of his hand Bedivere's hammer ricocheted as though striking and invisible wall. Tristan's arrow splintered. Erec and Lamorak were knocked off balance and went sliding along the stone floor. This wasn't Percy's plan. However, the distraction worked another way after all, because immediately, the headless Knightmare swept upon Ambrosius like a bat consuming its prey. It drove its Death Axe at the center of Ambrosius' chest. Ambrosius had thrown his hands up in time and the Knightmare's axe collided with an invisible shield.

The Knightmare did not give. It held pressure on the axe not about to let up. The two were locked in a stalemate. The Hellsteed galloped behind Ambrosius and breathed a stream of flames that consumed both the wizard and the Knightmare.

Flames engulfed Ambrosius, yet he was not on fire. He was no longer locked in combat with the Knightmare. Instead, a blond-haired boy wearing a green tunic stood before him.

"Arthur? You're the Knightmare?" Ambrosius was shocked. "This can't be."

"What are ye talking about? I'm not the Knightmare. I couldn't have murdered anyone and decapitate people. Ye are the one that murders and decapitates! Ye were my mentor and my friend I thought." Ambrosius reached out to comfort the boy. "Don't touch me!" he screamed stepping back. "Ye don't ever get to touch me again!" Tears jumped onto his cheeks. "Nobody gets to touch me again," he said quietly to himself looking at the back of his hands; then turned them over examining his palms considering his own mortality. "Why?" He looked back up at Ambrosius. Tears were now flowing. "Why did ye kill me?"

Ambrosius was crying now too. "Arthur, I am so sorry," his hand still reaching out to the boy, "I am so sorry I wasn't there to protect you. I was so focused on tonight...the ceremony. I couldn't see. I didn't see it coming." Ambrosius wanted to explain more. He wanted to make Arthur understand. But there was such a great pain at the center of his chest the wizard found it hard to speak. The wizard looked down and saw the point of a sword sticking out of his sternum.

Percy yanked the sword back out of Ambrosius. He had ventured the flames of the Hellsteed one more time. Again he was unaffected. He was thankful for the diversion the flames caused. He was able to thrust his sword into the wizard from behind as the Knightmare had him engaged in a struggle. The flames of the Hellsteed ceased. Everyone could now see that Percy had impaled the wizard. As Percy pulled the sword out, Ambrosius grabbed his shoulder and choked out a whisper. Percy was bewildered at the wizard's words.

Suddenly, there was a burst of flames that shot up around Ambrosius as he was taking his last breaths. And as he disappeared in a ball of flame Percy and the others saw a horrific image: a large twisted looking scarecrow with its arms outstretched. The Knightmare and the Hellsteed were immediately engulfed in flames next. And Sir Percy yelled, "Arthur Jack Pendragon, be released from thy torment and slavery!" Then they were gone. But as the balls of flame flashed they created a plume of fire that shot up into the rafters of the abbey igniting the ceiling.

"We have to get out of here," Lamorak yelled to everyone as the fire in the rafters of the abbey spread rapidly. Father Gregory was now at his side. But no one moved as they were all fixated on Percy and the disappearing Knightmare.

A burning timber fell from the rafters. "We must go now," Lamorak yelled again.

Gwalchmai just finished putting the splint on Dinadan's leg and yelped at Lamorak's command. He ran out of the abbey. "He left me again," Dinadan growled. Despite having only one hand, Bedivere scooped up Dinadan in his strong arms and charged out of the abbey with Tristan, Erec, Lamorak, Father Gregory, and Percy.

CHAPTER 52

"Was that boy a Pendragon?"

Everyone was panting from exhaustion, pain, distress and shock. "Did we hear you right, brother?" Lamorak continued his question to Percy yelling above the downpour that seemed stronger than earlier.

"Arthur did ye say?" Bedivere rested Dinadan on the ground but still had his handless arm around him for support.

"Aye," Percy answered them both. "But he preferred to be called Jack."

"Was he the king's son?" Gwalchmai huffed drops of water in awe.

"Bastard son," Father Gregory answered and seemed to make it a point to clarify.

"How do ye know this?" Percy asked astonished.

Father Gregory hung his head low. "Abbot Conleth told me. The king divulged this in their Round Table meetings."

"Round Table?" Erec asked.

"Yea, 'The Round Table Society' they called it. Some secret society they put together," Gregory explained. "The members wore a ring with an 'R' on it."

"Of course," Percy said aloud to himself.

"Abbot Conleth said Ambrosius was acting obsessed and wanted the members of the society to use their influence so they could gain more power, but that the members didn't approve."

"So he had them killed," Percy realized. "He used the rings as markers so the Knightmare could find them."

"Why would a powerful wizard like Ambrosius need the assistance of such a wicked entity?" Erec challenged.

"To maintain his innocence," Gregory replied. "Many saw that headless knight charging through the village," Gregory continued with his explanation. "And with our deaths it would be a simple matter for Ambrosius to maintain his innocence."

The night flashed and thunder cracked the silence that came from the expressionless fighters. "Where were ye during the battle?" Bedivere asked Father Gregory suspiciously. "We could have used thy help."

"I was helping! I was in the chapel praying. Don't underestimate the power of prayer. We were victorious. We owe our thanks and success to God for answering my prayers."

"Can ye pray me a new hand?" Bedivere sounded annoyed.

"God works in mysterious ways," Father Gregory said consolingly. "And I gave you those crosses to assist you. Did any of you use them?"

There was a long silence.

"I did," Gwalchmai announced.

"And you survived," Gregory said proudly.

"I didn't use it and I survived." Bedivere countered skeptically.

"And you're missing a hand," Father Gregory said coolly. "But our Heavenly Lord helps even the ignorant."

"No offense to my brothers," Lamorak interrupted. "But I am more interested in what happened to Arthur."

"Aye, what happened?" Gwalchmai chimed in.

"I found Arthur's headless body in the chambers of Ambrosius," Percy answered. "There was blood and magickal writing."

"Obviously used to turn Arthur into this twisted green knight used by the dark wizard," Father Gregory added.

"It's truth," Percy agreed.

"Ambrosius must have given him dark powers and fighting skills," Tristan commented.

"Aye," said Percy, "the dark powers. But I'm afraid I was the one that gave him the fighting skills. King Uther secretly had me train Arthur in combat. He wanted me to prepare him for taking over the throne. The king gave me this armor and sword as gratitude. Ambrosius was to instill wisdom and education in the boy." Percy grew disgusted at the thought. "This is most grave because many in the village have seen the green knight this evening. Everything King Uther stood for and the good things he did will be wrecked. And the memory of Arthur will be tarnished."

"Only if people know the true identity of the green knight," Lamorak hinted.

"Aye," Bedivere agreed. "We must make a pact to never reveal this."

"What will we say?" whimpered Gwalchmai.

Percy thought for a long moment, the torrent rain

pelting them. "Jack was a knight of King Uther beheaded on this day by a dark wizard. He searches for his head throughout time. Arthur became King after his father was murdered but only briefly, before being killed by the same dark wizard that cursed Jack. We shall never reveal that Jack and Arthur are the same."

Bedivere stuck his fist out, "Agreed."

One by one the others put their hand on top of Bedivere's fist—one on top of the other—each replying, "Agreed." They all looked to Father Gregory. He was the last to comply.

"It is not in the nature of a priest to lie." He studied the men's faces. "However, this seems to be for the greater good. So I am sure God will forgive me this white lie." He put his hand on top of the others, "Agreed!"

"Our battle is not quite over yet I am afraid."

They all spun around to see Yvain atop a horse. "Abbot Conleth warned me druids are gathering tonight at the Ring of Stones. They are attempting to conjure up their Lord of the Dead."

"Then we must stop them," Bedivere shouted vigorously. You would never have guessed he just had his hand lopped off.

"The leader of their Church," he pointed at Father Gregory, "has already dispatched warriors to stop them."

"Aye, that may be truth, but if these comrades possess powers such as Ambrosius they won't stand a chance." Bedivere swept his arm out magnanimously in the rain in front of him. "But we have Sir Percy. The one who single handedly vanquished the dark wizard himself with his powerful sword. They will need him," he looked about at all of them standing in the rain looking exhausted and a grin formed on his face, "and us to prevail."

"You speak bold words my friend," Percy said. "But the Ring of Stones is far from here."

"Where is that?" Tristan asked.

"Badon Hill," Percy answered. "The battle will most assuredly be over by our arrival."

The men murmured in agreement.

"Aye, I believe I have our salvation," Yvain held up the jug labeled GODSPEED.

Percy smiled. "Let's get the horses."

CHAPTER 53

Riders of the tempest approached on horses with small wings flapping on their hooves.

Percy and his team's horses had wings that formed on their hooves after drinking the doctor's potion. The horse's speed increased dramatically. They galloped just above the terrain; their hooves never touching the ground.

The team arrived on the edge of the storm, just ahead of it. Bolts of lightning splintered the clouds followed by thunder. As they came up on Badon Hill they saw the Ring of Stones. And towering over the largest stones of the circle was the effigy of a man made out of wood. They saw the army of mercenaries engaged in battle. Bursts of light flashed on the battlefield. Bodies of druids sprawled about like lifeless ragdolls.

"What is that?" Bedivere screamed in amazement at the effigy.

"The druids were attempting to light that when we arrived," one of the mercenaries answered looking up at the Wicker Man. "We managed to hold them off. Some are more powerful than others."

"Have you used the Rowan wood?" Father Gregory asked him.

"Ja," he pointed around to dozens of spears in the ground about the Ring of Stones. "There have been no lightning strikes like you said."

"Did you use the Rowan arrows?" Father Gregory sounded impatient.

"Ja, we've barraged them. We were able to hold them at bay—"

"Hold them at bay? You're not supposed to hold them at bay," Gregory shouted. "They are supposed to be dead."

"They levitated boulders to block the arrows and had trees attacking us!"

"Trees?" Gwalchmai and the others watched curiously as Father Gregory and the mercenary's exchange continued.

"Then they started using fire," the mercenary apologized.

"Don't panic Father," Bedivere said stoutly. "We have a knight that's invulnerable to fire," he looked to Percy. "And we could use some drying off," he grinned bravely.

"That is truth," Father Gregory said as if he suddenly remembered they were there. "I do have my knights."

"We're not knights," Dinadan corrected the priest. He was saddled behind Bedivere due to his leg splint, "Only Sir Percy."

"Aye," Percy pivoted his horse to face the others.

"But, after what we have been through together this night I would not entrust my safety to any others. I would ride into any fray with you. I am honored to call you my brothers."

The wind picked up from the storm they out ran as it inched closer. Lamorak took out the cross that Father Gregory gave them. "Now, might be a good time to don these," he hung it around his neck. The others did the same as Father Gregory watched pleased. Tristan got some Rowan arrows from the mercenary and began firing at druids. The wind howled fiercely. Percy spun his horse back around and found himself facing three dark robed figures.

"Warriors of Valhalla you have arrived," the tall one stretched her arms out.

Percy glanced back over each of his shoulders to the others in confusion.

"We thought Yggdrasil was closed. How did you get here?"

"Sisters," the smallest whispered to the other two, "they are the riders of the tempest. They killed Ambrosius!"

Percy noticed the other two witches flinch at the small one's commentary.

"But their horses," the oldest protested.

"Ah," the tallest realized. "They must have found one of the doctor's potions."

"Your evil ends tonight witches!" Percy yelled. "We have already ended Ambrosius' treachery and life!"

"Then your mettle is worth a Vallhallan warrior! However, we are three! You face the coven of the Ladies of the Lake! You will not find us so easily dispatched!"

Tristan shot three arrows in succession at the witches. Percy was surprised at how fast he moved.

A druid waved his hands and a cyclone whooshed in front of the witches deflecting the arrows.

Mercenaries engaged the druids while archers took up flanks.

Father Gregory was nervous with anticipation. He could sense the end was near.

All around the witches saw their druid brothers being slaughtered by arrows and pikes. They put up a fight but were outnumbered and defeated by the Rowan.

"You have betrayed your own kind," the eldest witch called out to Percy and his team. "And for that," the witch continued, "by the Goddess Frigg we curse you on her day; this thirteenth full moon of the year. You will know death by her day and her hand!"

The tallest sensed them being targeted by archers and infantry. She knew the end was near. "Sisters," they put their hands on her shoulders. "You do realize this will consume the last of our power and we shall be defenseless afterward?"

"So be it," the smallest grumbled.

The hunched figure shot her arms out in front of her sending a fireball the size of a large boulder hurling toward the priest and the team. The witches stood transfixed from the shadows of their hoods waiting for the fireball to consume the men. The tallest took a step forward anticipating victory when Sir Percy charged through the fireball; smoke flying off his leather armor with his sword raised.

The boulder-sized fireball still charged at the others. Father Gregory stood muttering; holding his cross boldly in his extended arm when Gwalchmai practically jumped on him clenching to his robes. He shook the priest hard enough that he dropped his cross.

"Drat!" Father Gregory yelled.

"I'll help ye find it!" Gwalchmai whimpered loudly dropping to his knees patting the ground trying to find the cross with his hands.

"You're in my way. I can't see." Father Gregory

was now on his knees as well trying to find the cross among the grass and mud. "I need more light." Panic was in Gregory's voice.

"Oh, that's better!" Gwalchmai yelled able to see the grass better in the flickering light.

Father Gregory looked up and saw that the light was the immense fireball closing on them. He then saw the cross dangling from Gwalchmai's neck and yanked it in front of him, with Gwalchmai's frightened head facing the oncoming fireball. Father Gregory knelt in front of the charging fireball, his robes flapping violently in the winds, holding the silver cross defiantly. "In the name of our Father Almighty in Heaven, the one true God, I vanquish thee!" Gwalchmai's hands clenched his face.

As the boulder of flames rolled through the air at the priest and the others it shifted from a vibrant yellow to a pumpkin orange then a dull gray and dispersed in a puff. Gregory and Gwalchmai were smacked merely with smog.

"Ye did it!" Gwalchmai coughed shaking the priest praiseful. "Thank the gods!"

Father Gregory turned on him haughtily. "No," he corrected. "Thank *The God!*"

"I'm a believer!"

CHAPTER 54

Jonas and the others felt a vibration in their hands.

Jonas at first thought that someone was just getting restless when he noticed a glow about Glenda as she extended her free hand in front of her: and without another warning a huge boulder of fire erupted from her hand and rolled past people in the Bazaar and struck the pyramid of wood igniting the structure into a tower of flames.

Bernice Dinah screamed shielding her body with flailing arms as she trotted as fast as her fat legs allowed from the blast of flames. "Roy!" She yelled in desperation.

"He's gone to find Max," Joe said watching the bonfire in amazement.

"Did you see that?" The eldest council member gripped Joe's arm with a mixture of fear and exhilaration.

"Who didn't?" Joe was still in bewilderment.

"It was the Thunderbird!" The old man declared.

"That was a fireball! Not everything is a Thunderbird!"

"It was a fireball released by the Thunderbird!"

Joe smacked his forehead with his palm, shaking his head in frustration.

"You did this!" Bernice pointed an accusing finger at Joe. "People could get hurt! What an irresponsible stunt. And you want to run for mayor. I'll be sure the town of Ravencrest knows how you endangered their lives and the lives of their children!"

Joe tried his best to ignore the babbling old man and the blithering of Bernice Dinah as his eyes searched the scattering crowd for the origin of the fireball.

The wind whistled through the cool air and the sky rumbled.

"It's the wings of the Thunderbird," the old man persisted.

The line was broken as Uva cupped her mouth gasping from the sudden appearance of the fireball. La' Wanda let go of Dorothy and Martha's hands as she was startled by the fireball and panicked with the frenzied crowd.

"Hoo-we!" Glenda clapped her hands together pleased. "Just like the old days," she joined her sisters.

"It was from the old days," Dorothy congratulated her.

Jonas was stammering and tried to get to Max but couldn't see him through the people. Max broke out his phone and began to type a text as he bolted for the Curious & Creepy booth. The booth, python, tarantula and everything else were left unattended as the adults had vacated to find either their children or companions. Now, was Max's chance that he had been planning. He hit SEND on the phone, reached in the tank and grabbed Jonas' octopus, and charged back to where he scribbled in the dirt.

The cool autumn air turned turbulent. Then a fiery figure belched from the bonfire.

The old man went prostrate screaming about the Thunderbird. Joe and Bernice watched the figure in awe seeing the flames vaporize to reveal a glowing green headless knight atop a fiery mare!

The Hellsteed tapped its front hooves on the ground sending sparks from its fiery coronal band and galloped toward the origin of the fireball.

The old man tilted his head up toward Joe, "You can't deny now that it's the Thunderbird!"

"It's not a Thunderbird," Joe screamed at him. "It's the Headless Horseman," he couldn't believe those words just came out of his mouth.

"...Headless   Horseman...Thunderbird...," Bernice stammered in horror and confusion, "...You see what all your Wiccan, Witchcraft and pagan practices have done? They create nothing but horror and evil. Look what you have done to this great Catholic holiday."

"It's not a Catholic holiday," Joe pushed her out of his way, grabbing her walkie-talkie, and ran in pursuit of the galloping glowing knight.

Jonas couldn't see Max. He felt his phone vibrate and assumed it was his dad. He looked and saw instead it was a text from Max:

DON'T REVIVE ME. JUST SET JACK FREE. YOUR FRIEND.

Max opened his palm with difficulty. The blue-ringed octopus was bright yellow with blue-rings. It looked pretty. It was the prettiest thing he'd ever seen, next to Chance. That was his only regret about this—that he'd never see him again. He felt what little color his body already had, drop out below him. He heard his heart beating thunderously in his ears. His muscles cramped over his entire body and his breathing was shallow. Max saw the earth moving in slow-motion as he realized his body fell backwards onto the ground. He tried to admire the night sky as the pain in his muscles raced through him and his breathing stopped. He knew he would be dead again—this time for good—that was the plan.

The Hellsteed stopped in front of Max's body. The Knightmare drew its sword. The Sisters Grimm took positions next to Max. The Knightmare paused. It turned its torso toward the sisters as though it considered attacking them; however, the charm bags prevented it from taking action against them. It turned back to Max and raised its sword.

"Arthur Jack Pendragon, I release you," Jonas pelted the Knightmare with black salt.

The Knightmare's glow flickered. The Hellsteed's flames sputtered. The Knightmare reared its horse and hurdled in the direction of Shadow Lake Forest.

"Excellent work little wizard," Glenda patted Jonas on the back.

"Not really, I didn't set Jack free."

"That Knightmare was created with some serious magick. It's going to take some serious magick to set that boy free."

"Yeah, I thought you guys were supposed to help with that," Jonas argued.

"We were! But we need Max," she pointed to Max's body on the ground.

"What's that?" Jonas pointed to the dirt below Max.

"It's a bit messed up now, but it looks like a symbol of evocation. It seems the lad had other plans," Glenda sounded sad.

Cassandra and Lindsey screamed in alarm at the sight of Max's body.

Joe ditched his pursuit of the Headless Horseman and radioed for a paramedic when he saw a body on the ground. He pushed people out of the way and came upon Max Dane. "Oh no," he muttered. "What happened?" He asked the bystanders but then saw the octopus in his hand. He flipped it out and grabbed Cassandra. "Put pressure here," he indicated Max's palm.

The paramedic rolled up in an EMS cart.

"He needs artificial respiration," Joe told the arriving paramedic. The paramedic immediately broke out a bag valve mask respirator as Joe went to one of the nearby booths and grabbed some herbs, crushing up the stems and leaves. He rushed back to Cassandra, "press this into his palm," he pushed the mixture in Max's hand and began chanting.

"He smells really good," Cassandra sobbed. "He must be wearing SHRED."

Jonas needed to pursue the Knightmare. He snatched the runic ring off Max's hand.

"What is wrong with you, troll?" Cassandra yelled.

Joe continued chanting but opened his eyes watching Jonas in shock.

Jonas didn't have time to grieve for Max as much as he wanted to. He never had a friend before and he wasn't about to let him down. He knew now how he was going to free the Knightmare. He realized it with Martha's speech about reaching into the past. Max was right the first time they watched the video footage in his bedroom. Mr. Creeps *was* going after Lindsey's backpack. Jonas snatched Lindsey's backpack from her hand.

"My candy! My candy!" Lindsey screamed holding onto one of the straps.

"What are you doing?" Joe couldn't believe Jonas' audacity.

The Sisters Grimm looked at Jonas in shock as well. No one could believe that Jonas was trying to steal a little girl's candy.

Uva and La' Wanda looked toward Jonas but were

greeted by Angelica Saffron.

"Blessed be!" She stood in front of the two with a smile.

La' Wanda yelped. Uva grabbed La' Wanda's arm.

"How can this be?" La' Wanda couldn't believe her eyes. She almost didn't want to believe it. It was hard enough losing her the first time. She knew she would have to again.

"It's Halloween. It's the time of being reunited with your loved ones that have passed," she took La' Wanda's hand. "I didn't get to say goodbye. I couldn't go without telling you that I love you."

"I love you too. You know that," La' Wanda sniffed.

Uva, contrary to her typical bold exterior, was in tears.

Jonas ignored the condemnations and Lindsey's screams. He shoved his hand down in her backpack fishing. He finally yanked out a bottle. He was right. Mr. Creeps put the Elixir in Lindsey's backpack! "Ha," he dashed for Shadow Lake Forest.

"It's the Elixir of Life," Glenda couldn't believe it. "The lad wizard has it!"

Martha and Dorothy's attention shot from Max to Jonas who was in hot pursuit of the Knightmare.

"After him," Dorothy yelled.

"I wish we had some broom," Glenda huffed as the sisters ran as fast as they could.

"What is going on?" Evelyn shouted. She was accompanied by Dr. Evans, Agent McCoy, Agent Knight, Sheriff Drake, and Mayor Dinah. "Lindsey," Evelyn grabbed her. "Are you okay? Did Max hurt you?"

"Jonas tried to steal my candy," she complained.

"What?" Evelyn couldn't make sense of that.

"It looks like venom from a blue-ringed octopus bite," the paramedic explained more to Dr. Evans than

Evelyn Dane. "I have him on a portable ventilator now. I'm waiting on the ambulance to arrive before we move him."

"Excellent Sam," Dr. Evans agreed. "He's as stable as he's going to get here."

"Thanks to Sam and Joe," Alarice Hemlock arrived wearing a gypsy costume and moon and star decorated head wrap, "he's a shaman."

"Modern medicine is stabilizing this young boy," Bernice said, "and modern medicine will save his life…"

"…with the assistance of some good old fashioned herb magick and Esoterics. The science of Medicine can work with magick and the science of Esoterics."

"Medicine and magick working together?" Bernice patted her chest choking on the preposterousness. "Science? You think Esoterics is a science? I think we need to review the curriculum that is taught in Ravencrest Academy. That's just ludicrous," Bernice argued. "That's nothing but a bunch of tomfoolery and superstition."

"Angelica Saffron," Joe stood in amazement.

Everyone looked where Joe was. Even Sam the paramedic stood and took notice. They all saw Angelica talking with La' Wanda.

"That can't be," Dr. Evans would not believe it. "There's a lot of smoke from the bonfire," he reasoned.

Joe looked about the Bazaar and saw that most of the crowd had stopped running erratically. He knew practically everyone in Ravencrest. He was familiar with the losses they suffered over the years. So it was plain to him that families were gathered with their deceased loved ones. Joe scanned through the wafts of smoke for his father. He wished that Meredith was by his side right now.

CHAPTER 55

Red-hot hoof prints scorched a path through Shadow Lake Forest.

"What am I doing? What am I doing?" Jonas kept saying over and over as he ran through dirt, trees and foliage. He hated the dark; even with the full moonlight it was eerie. He had never been in the woods by himself. He was always too scared to go. He had only been in them with Max. Max made him venture in there. Max made him do things he would have never done alone or at all. Max was his friend. And now Max was gone. He only knew him for two weeks, but to Jonas that was a lifetime. For so long he was alone and now he would be again. If anything, he was mad at Max for leaving him alone yet again. Max had a strong connection to Jack so he would help him for Max.

He promised he would and Jonas decided right then he was
going to be someone that kept his promises.

"Where's Max?" Evelyn's voice broke through the
preoccupation.

Sam and everyone else turned, seeing the portable
ventilator on the ground without a patient.

The raven with one green eye flew above Jonas. He
knew he wouldn't catch up with the Knightmare on foot so
that's why he took the ring. He would make the
Knightmare come to him. What he didn't know was how
to use the Elixir. How could it drink it? It didn't have a
head. Jonas figured he would continue along the burning
trail until he worked the nerve up to put on the ring. Then
there was movement through the trees. Jonas came to a
halt; his heart crashed into his ribs. "What was that?" In
the moonlight he could see something moving fast through
the trees. It was coming at him, and it wasn't the
Knightmare! Jonas fled in the opposite direction which
took him off the path of the Hellsteed but he wasn't going
to worry about that right now. He just wanted to get as
much distance between him and whatever that was in the
woods.

He came to a clearing and stood in front of the lake.
There was a wooden pier just a few feet away. The
branches moved in the forest behind him. He ran for the
pier. He didn't know why. "I can't swim, I can't swim!"
But he didn't know what else to do or where to go. His grip
tightened around the Elixir of Life. The wood planks
echoed under his feet in the cool night. He reached the end
of the pier. His blue eyes stared at the water; the moonlight
flickered off its surface. He thought about trying to swim.
He watched the swim team. Maybe he could do it. His
pulse pounded through his veins. He just knew he would
drown. The pier vibrated below his feet. He spun around.

It was the Sisters Grimm.

Max stumbled through the forest.

He almost caught up with the figures. Everything moved in slow-motion and things looked slanted and elongated like a fun-house mirror. His breathing was shallow. He wasn't sure exactly who or what the figures were. He just had to get to them. He knew someone besides him was going to die.

"We're not going to hurt you," the sisters crept down the pier.

"You're going to kill me," Jonas shouted. "Max told me that you killed Sheriff Tahamont. You're psychos!"

"We're not psychos," Martha tried to assure Jonas.

"And even if we were," Glenda grumbled, "they never kill the neighbors!"

"That's true," Dorothy agreed with her sister.

"Just give us the Elixir," Martha said in a coaxing voice. "We didn't kill Sheriff Tahamont. He decided to drive home drunk."

"Josh!" A voice yelled.

The sisters turned around and Jonas looked past them. It was Max. He was stumbling toward them on the pier like a zombie. Jonas was stunned.

Max saw the blond boy at the end of the pier. "Josh, don't do it. You can't swim. You can't die again. I won't let you this time."

Silence fell among the sisters. Jonas knew Max had to be out of it. "It's me, Jonas. I'm not Josh." *Who was Josh?*

Max fell to his knees: his breathing slowing. "What? No…you're supposed to be Josh. Josh deserves to live. Josh is supposed to take over my body. That was the plan. That was my birthday wish."

The sisters were still speechless watching Max. Jonas waived the Elixir to show Max. "I haven't freed Jack, yet. The Knightmare is still out there."

Max understood now. He opened his hand.

432

Jonas rushed past the sisters before they realized what was going on and he handed Max the runic ring. He put it on. Jonas was about to hand him the Elixir when someone in an old man mask and overalls grabbed Max by the shoulder and yanked him back through the forest. At first Jonas thought it was Derek, but it was so fast that Jonas wasn't even sure it was human. It had to be what chased him onto the pier in the first place. Jonas charged after the swaying foliage.

"He still has the Elixir," Martha couldn't believe he got by them.

"Here we go again," Glenda fussed.

"After him," Dorothy yelled.

CHAPTER 56

Percy came down on the tallest witch—with his sword—in a death blow.

Before he connected she was yanked back with the other two witches. As he was still swinging he saw the witches towered by pearl smoke. In just a flash of a moment a large dark figure with a twisted face and broad brimmed hat stretched its twisted arms and hands out scooping the witches back into the cloud. And as quickly as the dark figure appeared—they all disappeared. There were no vapors left from the smoke. It was as if they had never been there.

"Ye did it!" Lamorak charged over to Percy. "Ye vanquished them! Ye truly are the king's finest knight."

"I'm his only knight," Percy said solemnly. "And

I'm not his anymore...he's dead. And I didn't vanquish the witches. They were taken."

"By what...was that a Jinn?"

"You are very astute, Lamorak." Father Gregory answered. He was there with the others now. "*What* indeed," he ignored his reference to the Jinn. "Their Lord of the Dead," he pointed to the Wicker Man. "The druids and the witches worship this demon. He snatched them back to Hell where they belong. I imagine as retribution for failing to bring him into our world completely." The rain caught up with them as it began to drizzle.

The sky cracked with lightning.

"Father Gregory!" A voice called from the moonlight.

Everyone spun around with their weapons ready and saw young Gareth standing there nude breathing heavily almost out of breath. His naked body was covered in mud and blood. A sword was strapped to his back and he was pushing a cart with Jean-Luc bandaged up inside it. The man grasped onto a large tome.

"What's this?" Lamorak asked in astonishment.

"It's how our people fight," Gwalchmai answered ashamed at Gareth's nudity.

"It's bold! I like it," proclaimed Bedivere.

"Nay," Lamorak shook his hands at Gareth's body to indicate the blood. "What's this?" He looked at Gareth. "What happened?"

"Abbot Conleth...the caravan..." his breathing stumbled.

"Wolves...we were attacked by a pack of wolves!" Jean-Luc screamed.

The sky ruptured releasing a cascade of rain.

"Who's this?" Bedivere asked annoyed at the man's ranting.

"His name is Jean-Luc," Yvain answered for him. "He is one of these Swiss mercenaries. He barely survived an earlier encounter this evening with those witches."

"And now this…" Bedivere was more sympathetic.

Gareth pulled an iron box out of the cart. He opened it revealing a severed head.

Father Gregory made the sign of the cross. "It's a boy."

Percy felt the sword of grief penetrate his heart yet again. "It is Jack."

"I thought you said Ambrosius beheaded him," Lamorak said to Percy.

"I do not know what this means." Percy was confused.

"I do," Father Gregory explained. "It means that Abbot Conleth and Ambrosius were working together. Now, I see their plan must have been to overtake the Church. And I played into it. I was offering Conleth a way back to Rome and I suspect he would eventually use that, along with Ambrosius' magick, to take over the papacy. I also suspect that they both succumbed to the evil of greed and had a disagreement over power distribution." He looked at the sullen faces that stared at him. "It also means that with the return of this," he indicated the iron box, "Jack can rest in peace." He attempted to lighten their spirits.

Gareth took the tome from Jean-luc and handed it to Father Gregory. "It's all I could save." It was difficult to distinguish if it was tears or rain in his eyes. "They're all dead," he hung his head.

Bedivere grasped Gareth's shoulder with his only hand and shook him confidently until the lad looked up at him. "Ye were brave. Do not blame thy self. Ye managed to save this man."

Father Gregory ran his hands over the image of a cup that was etched into the large leather-bound tome. He tucked it under his cloak to protect it from the rain. "He's right, Gareth. You were brave and you have done a great service to the Church." He put his hand on Gareth's other shoulder and looked the naked youth up and down.

"The Church is always looking for fine young lads such as you to join the priesthood." Gregory released Gareth's shoulder and waved his arm to the others. "In fact, all of you could be a great service to the Church. You already have by stamping this evil out tonight. You can be God's army: his gauntlet to clench around the wicked, his guard against the followers of witchcraft and Satan." The Swiss mercenaries that had survived the battle with the druids were now gathering. "You may not think so, Percy, but I believe you did vanquish those witches tonight. Those that are brave enough to stand against the corrupt, immoral, and malicious will always prevail. You alone have demonstrated that more than once on this evil night called Samhain."

Percy looked as if he wanted to say something, but couldn't find the right words.

"And ye Father Gregory, have demonstrated more than once this night the power of thy god," Gwalchmai spoke. "I am a believer. I think we should follow ye and thy god," he looked at the others in almost desperation. "We no longer have a king or an heir to the throne."

"Aye," Yvain agreed. "The Church does seem appropriate."

"But Percy should lead us," Lamorak insisted.

"Aye," Bedivere agreed.

"God leads us first," Father Gregory chimed. "But yea, your King is dead and his knights extinguished, except for you Sir Percy." The priest looked at him as did they all. "Percy, I believe your purpose is to rebuild a new knighthood; a knighthood in the name of God."

Everyone cheered with approval except for Percy. He stood there silent—butterflies in his stomach. *Is this my purpose? Is this why I was spared from the beginning?* He wished he could go back into the Nexus in hopes of getting some advice from fairy Max. Everything seemed to be pointing in this direction, but he had a sick feeling in his stomach. The rain stopped, but thunder continued rolling through the sky. "I don't think I have the authority to Knight my brave and most worthy brothers."

"You do if the Church backs you. And now that Abbot Conleth has passed I speak for the Church in this region. If you pledge your allegiance to the one true God, you will have the Church's blessing."

Percy looked into the faces of the men he fought next to on this dreadful night. He saw in the moonlight and the flicker of lightning they desired it. "Aye, we will pledge our allegiance to your God and to your Church."

Everyone burst into cheer again, but Percy motioned for them to quiet. "First, we must attend to a pyre for King Uther and King Arthur." He looked at the Wicker Man that towered behind them. "We shall make use of this."

"Hear, hear!" Father Gregory cheered. "I think it only appropriate to use what was part of that dreadful festival that Ambrosius boasted of for something good."

"Our steeds still have wings," Bedivere pointed out the Swiss mercenaries that were retrieving the horses, to Percy. "I will go retrieve the bodies of Uther and Arthur for the pyre," Bedivere continued.

"You're going to need a hand my friend," Lamorak looked at Bedivere's stub.

Bedivere stood taller than any of them and looked down at Lamorak with a blank face. Then he burst into laughter. "Aye, I believe I will."

"You remind me a lot of my friend Kay," he chuckled.

"I want to go with ye," Gareth spoke up.

"Indeed, of course," Bedivere shouted. "The lad shall go with us." And the three of them sped off on the winged horses.

Father Gregory stood next to Percy. "I wonder what the townspeople will think if they see the young man riding into town naked on a winged horse."

"I should think after tonight, not much." Percy smirked for the first time this evening. "It's not that uncommon around here."

"Winged horses?" The priest looked questioningly at Percy.

"Nay...naked warriors," he clarified.

Jean-Luc pulled Father Gregory to the side. "I think you may find this of interest and perhaps value," he handed him a cracked vial. "I recovered it from the site where I battled the witches."

Father Gregory took the vial with a much appreciative look.

Not much time had passed and the three returned with the bodies of the fallen Kings and their other comrades in a wagon.

"The potion wore off just before we got here," Lamorak sighed. "It seems our horses are back to normal."

Everyone gathered around the Wicker Man as the bodies were placed inside.

CHAPTER 57

Max felt the blood pumping out of his shoulder yet again.

It was definitely claws that dug into his skin.

"I should've fucking finished you off that first day in the woods!"

Max saw the dirt passing him by as his body clunked against rocks and limbs. He couldn't see his attacker but he knew the douche-bag's voice well enough now. It was Derek.

"I was supposed to run off with Chance tonight and his little brother. I was going to off his old man, that fucking abusive piece of shit! But no…Chance didn't think I was serious!"

Max saw his blood shoot by as Derek's claws went deeper.

He must have those Shuko claws.

"He didn't want me to really do it. Instead he told me he was going over to hang out with you later tonight. I know what that means! I was going to kill for him. Are you willing to do that you little shit? Are you willing to kill for Chance?"

Max felt the wind through his hair and saw the stars sailing above. He was flying. No…Derek threw him. Max hit the grass and slid for what seemed like a mile.

"It doesn't matter," Derek's voice echoed in the distance, "you're gonna die for him!"

Someone stood beside him. "Help," Max grasped for their leg. He looked up. It was Mr. Creeps. Once again, he was just beyond the pumpkin patch in front of Mr. Creeps. Max grabbed his cloak and pulled himself up. His vision was a mess. His breathing staggered.

"He's coming for you," Jack was there.

"I know," Max saw Derek in the grassy field. He could've sworn his eyes were glowing yellow through his mask, but Max was poisoned and most likely bleeding to death.

"I speak of the Fae. You need to take the ring off." Jack warned him.

"Jack, you can control him. You are the Knightmare."

"Nay," Jack said reluctantly. "I cannot be that monster." Ambrosius said the same thing to him. "That thing has killed people—innocent people. It has beheaded and butchered people. I cannot be that!" Tears were in his voice.

Max saw that Derek was charging him but moving ever so slightly. It was as if time was close to a standstill while he was talking to Jack. "I know you are not that person. It was the spell that made you kill those people. It wasn't your fault. Do you understand me? It wasn't your fault, Jack. Not like me. I knew exactly what I was doing when I murdered my brother Josh."

Jack studied the pain and sorrow in Max's face. "Surely...thou accidentally had a hand in thy brother's death."

"No," Max cried. He didn't know what pain was from grief, poison, or injury. "My little brother couldn't swim. We were out on the pier and something inside me...something horrible...wanted to know what it was like to kill someone. So I pushed him in. I pushed him in knowing he would drown. I eventually jumped in after him when I shook the monster off. But it was too late. He drowned. I drowned too. I was in a coma for three months. That's when I first visited the Nexus. I came back. It shouldn't have been me that came back. I wanted him to take over my body like you did so he could live. That was my plan for tonight. It didn't work. What if my brother is drowning over and over again because I murdered him, like the part of you that is being decapitated over and over?"

"I believe that is from the spell in my case."

"Are you sure of that?" Max wasn't convinced.

"Nay, I cannot say for certain. I do not know thy brother's fate."

"My little brother Josh used to sit with my sister under the stars at night searching for UFOs. I want him back so bad. I don't want to be that monster again. I don't want to live!"

"Aye, thou will live!" Jack's voice was strong. "Thou will live for thy brother. It will be painful, thou will not know peace, but it will be thy penance. Thou can't change what thou hast done, but thou can change who thou are. If thou don't want to be the monster, then don't; just like I won't be the monster anymore," Jack finally accepted that he was the Knightmare. "Tell me Max, do thou want to die?"

Max felt the blood pumping out of his body. His

breathing was sparse. Derek was closing in. "Not by him."

Chance had stopped in the distance. He finally found them. He saw Derek charging with murder in his heart. "Max!" He screamed.

A gust blew in. The tree's branches made cracking sounds as they collided together. Max heard his name on the wind. It almost sounded like his dad. There was a whoosh and he was struck in the chest. He picked the object up. It was a bald man's head with a hooked nose. It was Derek's mask. The mask had eyes. Then Derek's head rolled out of the mask. Max looked up and saw Derek's body fall. The Knightmare was there on its blazing horse with its skull adorned sword ready to come down on Max next.

"Arthur Jack Pendragon I release you!" Jonas threw the Elixir of Life at the Knightmare from behind. It struck the dead-head armor and shattered, dowsing it with the liquid.

"No," Glenda screamed with her sisters as they caught up. "You wasted it!"

The red liquid chased through the symbols etched into the armor. The Knightmare's glow blinked out. It dropped the skull sword; the blade pierced the ground. The Death Axe was at its side. The Hellsteed's fire extinguished. For a moment there was a blond haired boy sitting on a white mare and then a whirlwind of flames engulfed them. The cyclone of fire shot up into the sky disappearing with a clap of thunder.

Max looked to Mr. Creeps briefly before his eyes met Jonas' with thanks.

"Max!" Evelyn charged up to him with Lindsey.

Cassandra had told the adults about the phone she gave Max. Agents McCoy and Knight tracked it.

"He needs medical attention, now!" Sam the paramedic was with them.

Dr. Evans looked at Max in horror. "You carved

your brother's name into that horse in Yorick's stable," he flashed the picture to Sheriff Drake. "You were trying to bring him back weren't you?"

"Yes…" the words came out of Max's mouth like sandpaper. It was difficult to speak. *Wait. That wasn't exactly right. Was it? He was in Yorick's stable earlier. He wanted to bring his brother back, but not like he said.*

"You used a satanic symbol with a satanic ritual that required a human sacrifice." He pointed to Derek.

Sheriff Drake saw the decapitated body, Max covered in blood, and the sword next to him. "Maximillian Aiden Dane, you are under arrest for the murder of Derek Reid."

CHAPTER 58

Thunder rolled overhead as Percy stood in front of the silent crowd.

"Tonight we honor our most revered dead," Percy began. "King Uther Pendragon was to many a bold and brash king: '*The Dragon Slayer*.' But all would agree he was a fair king. To me: he was the father I never knew. He took notice of me when others did not. He took me in from the Wild Forest and trained me to become a warrior. Following his virtues allowed me to become a knight. He charged me with training his son and guarding him. King Arthur was only eight-years-old. He was the little brother I never had. His reign was not long, if at all, but he always instilled hope and trust within me. I was fortunate to know him as I did and I value the time I had with him. It is my single most regret I failed in my duty to protect him." Percy struggled to keep his composure. "To the Wicker Man I commit the bodies of our fallen Kings and comrades: Kay, Cador, and Dagonet." Percy raised his sword. "These men I now posthumously Knight in our New Order: Sir Dagonet, Sir Cador, and Sir Kay!" Percy signaled for Lamorak to set the Wicker Man ablaze: a funeral pyre.

Jean-Luc and the other Swiss mercenaries whispered among themselves at this sight. It was strange to see a people burn their dead. "Is it a sacrifice?" Many questioned. They did not understand this ritual. It was against the things that Father Gregory and his fellow priests had taught them. It seemed barbaric. Jean-Luc for one was certain it was some sort of sacrifice to the Wicker Man. He did not understand why Father Gregory aligned himself with these heathens.

Percy instructed his new comrades to kneel down on one knee. He approached Lamorak with the flat of his sword and hesitated. He turned toward Father Gregory.

Father Gregory gave him a reassuring nod.

"We all make an oath to God above any other sovereign to defend his name and his temple against evil in whatever form it may take. We here: his soldiers of virtue, the soldiers of his temple." He slammed the flat of his blade on Lamorak's right and left shoulder. "In the name of the Church and the Almighty God I knight thee! Arise, Sir Lamorak!" He went to the other men and did the same. "Arise, Sir Gwalchmai! Arise Sir Yvain!" He went over to the naked youth and repeated the rite. "Arise, Sir Gareth!" And did the same for the muscular, handsome, one-handed man. "Arise, Sir Bedivere!" Sir Percy shot his arm up toward the thunderous clouds with his sword stretching into the flashing night, "Arise, Knights Templar!"

EPILOGUE

The boy's body bobbed in the lake.

Max Dane was underwater. The boy was there now too. He watched the boy's blond hair sway in the current. His blue eyes were unmoving.

Josh, are you with Jack in Tír na nÓg?

Max's breathing was constricted.

Do you know that I'm the one that killed you? Do you know it was my fault? I know you can never forgive me. I don't expect you to. I won't forgive me.

Not a moment goes by that I don't think of you. I wish you were here now. I tried to bring you back.

Tears spilled from Max's eyes.

I hope you are not in pain. I need you to not be in pain. Please tell me you're not in pain! Can you speak to me? It's Samhain. You're supposed to be able to communicate with me. Please speak to me!

"Josh!" Max screamed aloud.

"That is good," a voice said from behind. "It is Samhain. You should remember the dead."

His arms struggled to move; his breathing strained. Max was no longer underwater. He was sitting on a white hospital bed, but not like the fancy one he had been in before. There were shackles on this one, but he wasn't in them. He was in a straightjacket. The floor was gray concrete and the walls were white with padded squares. It looked like a white waffle.

He jerked his arms trying to move. "Where am I?" He screamed more. "What's happening to me?"

"Trick-or-treat."

Max jerked his body around on the bed to face the voice. He knew that face. It was the wizard with silver hair and a bald dome. He was wearing a cream cloak with white fringe and holding a white oak staff. He looked like some sort of thin Celtic Santa Claus.

"Where's Josh? Why won't he talk to me?" Max figured he had something to do with it.

The wizard reached around his back and then pulled out a flickering Jack-O-Lantern. "You need a lit pumpkin so he can find you."

"That's it? Then he'll speak to me?" Max was skeptical.

"No, there is the distinct possibility that he simply may not *want* to speak to you."

Max felt the tears in his eyes again. He understood why that would be the case and it hurt. "What are you doing here, Ambrosius?"

The wizard squeezed the oak staff and smiled. "You may call me *The Yule King*."

THE END

Coming Soon…

The Nexus:
The Yule King

Follow on Facebook:
www.facebook.com/TheNexusBookSeries.1

Shop for Merchandise:
www.cafepress.com/TheNexusBookSeries

Find out more at:
www.iancadena.com

ABOUT THE AUTHOR

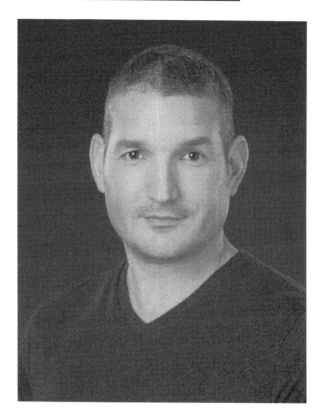

Ian Cadena is an Evil Genius bent on Dominion over the Universe. His first order of business will be to make Halloween a paid holiday throughout the cosmos. He is a Reiki Master and enthralled with all things mystic and paranormal.

He holds a degree in Theater & Writing and works on his novels and nefariously plots from his secret lair. He possesses numerous tarot decks and has had at least one out-of-body experience…maybe two. When not travelling outside of his body, he is either living in Austin, Texas or star-gazing off-grid from their property in Terlingua, TX.

44531066R00257

Made in the USA
Lexington, KY
01 September 2015